Praise for Sandra Hill's previous novels

"Another wonderful story that includes action, adventure, passion, romance, comedy, and even a little time travel."
—*Romance Junkies*

"A perfect ten! *Wet and Wild* is a must-read for everyone who loves great romance with heartfelt emotion. If you buy only one book . . . make it *Wet and Wild*."
—*Romance Reviews Today*

"Only the mind of Sandra Hill could dream up this hilarious and wacky scenario. The Vikings are on the loose once again, and they're wreaking sexy and sensual fun."
—*Romantic Times*

"Feeling down? Need a laugh? This one could be just what the 'dock whore' ordered." —*All About Romance*

Rough and Ready

Sandra Hill

BERKLEY SENSATION, NEW YORK

THE BERKLEY PUBLISHING GROUP
Published by the Penguin Group
Penguin Group (USA) Inc.
375 Hudson Street, New York, New York 10014, USA
Penguin Group (Canada), 90 Eglinton Avenue East, Suite 700, Toronto, Ontario M4P 2Y3, Canada
(a division of Pearson Penguin Canada Inc.)
Penguin Books Ltd., 80 Strand, London WC2R 0RL, England
Penguin Group Ireland, 25 St. Stephen's Green, Dublin 2, Ireland (a division of Penguin Books Ltd.)
Penguin Group (Australia), 250 Camberwell Road, Camberwell, Victoria 3124, Australia
(a division of Pearson Australia Group Pty. Ltd.)
Penguin Books India Pvt. Ltd., 11 Community Centre, Panchsheel Park, New Delhi—110 017, India
Penguin Group (NZ), Cnr. Airborne and Rosedale Roads, Albany, Auckland 1310, New Zealand
(a division of Pearson New Zealand Ltd.)
Penguin Books (South Africa) (Pty.) Ltd., 24 Sturdee Avenue, Rosebank, Johannesburg 2196,
South Africa

Penguin Books Ltd., Registered Offices: 80 Strand, London WC2R 0RL, England

This is a work of fiction. Names, characters, places, and incidents either are the product of the author's imagination or are used fictitiously, and any resemblance to actual persons, living or dead, business establishments, events, or locales is entirely coincidental. The publisher does not have any control over and does not assume any responsibility for author or third-party websites or their content.

ROUGH AND READY

A Berkley Sensation Book / published by arrangement with the author

PRINTING HISTORY
Berkley Sensation mass-market edition / December 2006

Copyright © 2006 by Sandra Hill.
Cover illustration by Jon Paul.
Cover design by Richard Hasselberger.
Interior text design by Stacy Irwin.

ISBN: 0-425-21302-1

BERKLEY SENSATION®
Berkley Sensation Books are published by The Berkley Publishing Group,
a division of Penguin Group (USA) Inc.,
375 Hudson Street, New York, New York 10014.
BERKLEY SENSATION is a registered trademark of Penguin Group (USA) Inc.
The "B" design is a trademark belonging to Penguin Group (USA) Inc.

PRINTED IN THE UNITED STATES OF AMERICA

10   9   8   7   6   5   4   3   2   1

This book is dedicated with much appreciation to all those fans who have told me over these past ten years how much you appreciate my unique . . . okay, warped . . . sense of humor. You know who you are. You are teachers, pilots, therapists, ministers, housewives, Norwegian sailors, college students, nurses, men and women from all walks of life. I have been particularly touched by those of you who say my books have helped you through some life struggle . . . and by those readers who are nobly serving in the military in harm's way.

When I first started writing romance, I had no idea that humor could touch readers so strongly. I thought only books with serious messages helped people. The most extreme example I can offer is the precious fan of mine who died of cancer and asked to have one of my Viking books placed in her coffin so that, at the viewing, people would look and then smile. Yep, humor to the end. But I am equally touched by the working mothers who need a little humor in their lives at the end of the day.

Let's face it, in these often depressing times post 9/11, humor can make anyone's life better.

To show my appreciation, please visit my website, where I have something FREE to offer you:

www.sandrahill.net

If I see a maid with whom
it would please me to play,
I can turn her thoughts.

Yea, I can touch the heart
Of any white armed woman.

HÁVAMÁL, circa 11th century

This maid with ash-smooth arms
is already getting used to
my bad ways.

EGIL'S SAGA, circa 13th century

At the loves of man
To laugh is not meet
for anyone ever.

The wise oft fall
When fools yield not
To the lure of a lovely maid.

HÁVAMÁL, circa 11th century

Prologue

"What would you do if you could change history?"

"Huh? I drove all the way from Coronado for you to ask me *that*!" Torolf Magnusson was not amused.

The question had been posed by his sister Kirstin, a Ph.D. scholar of ancient studies who taught at UCLA. Her Mensa brain was always pondering crap like this.

"If you could go back and eliminate a Hitler before the Holocaust or prevent the Black Death, would you do it?" she persisted.

"Whaaat? This is why you dragged me into these dusty stacks? To ask some dumb-ass hypothetical questions?" Torolf sneezed for about the twentieth time.

"I'm serious. Would you?"

Torolf shrugged. He had only a weekend liberty from his Navy SEAL duties, and he was wasting time playing what-if games with his sister. He'd rather be back at the Wet and Wild having a beer with his buddies and a little female companionship, not of the sisterly persuasion.

"Don't be such a grouch." Kirstin pulled a thick tome with a crumbling leather cover off a high shelf and placed it carefully on a table. "Look at this."

He exhaled with a weary sigh of surrender and sat down in a chair next to hers. The sooner he got this over with the better.

"I think I might have discovered some of the lost pages from *The Old Norse Chronicles*. Look at this."

1020. In this year, Steinolf proclaims himself king of all the Norselands, following a ten-year reign of terror. Thousands upon thousands of Vikings from Norway, Denmark, and Sweden fall to his sword. Torture and rape abound. The heads of babes are carried on his soldiers' pikes. Goblets of sword dew are drunk by his chieftains. God save us from this heathen beast.

A chill ran up Torolf's spine. His family had suffered much at the hands of this monster. Here was proof that his bloody path had gone way beyond what any of them imagined.

"What does this mean? Why do you show it to me?"

Kirstin got that earnest—some might say rabid—look on her face, the one that meant she wouldn't give up till she got her say. "I know that history can't be changed, that a Hitler and the Holocaust can't be erased. But this history . . ." she tapped the ancient book, ". . . no one knows of it but us. Maybe this kind of history *can* be changed."

"Why me? Our family is safe and happy in America. I thought we decided long ago that revenge wasn't worth the danger." He knew how selfish his words sounded once they left his mouth. This went way beyond his family and vengeance.

"This changes everything."

"How?"

Kirstin just stared at him.

"You're right," he said after several long moments of thought. "Someone has to stop the madness."

Chapter 1

Wanna take a little road trip, buddy? . . .

Navy Lieutenant Torolf Magnusson put his face in his hands and counted silently to ten. Only then did he look up at four of his teammates from Force Squad, Eighth Platoon, SEAL Team Thirteen and say, "Get lost!"

"Not a chance!" his best friend, Petty Officer Justin "Cage" LeBlanc, said with a laugh. LeBlanc was a Cajun from southern Louisiana and the biggest thorn in this sailor's ass when he wanted to be. Like now.

Torolf, who was known as Max to his friends, resumed packing. His sea bag sat on the bed in his apartment in Coronado, California, home of the U.S. Naval Amphibious Base, as well as BUD/S training ground for the Navy's elite special forces unit. He would soon hitch a ride on a military transport to Germany and from there take a commercial flight to Norway.

His buddies surrounded him in his bedroom, trying to change his mind about leaving. Not just Cage, but also

Lieutenant (J.G.) Zach "Pretty Boy" Floyd, an ex–race car driver. And Lieutenant (J.G.) Jacob Mendoza, JAM, ex-Jesuit priest. There was also Ensign Merrill "Geek" Good, a young computer prodigy. Geek was the only ring knocker among them, being a Naval Academy grad.

Cage shoved the duffel bag to the side and lay down on the bed, arms crossed under his head, smiling up at Torolf with exaggerated innocence. Hah! Cage hadn't been innocent since he'd fast-roped down his mother's umbilical cord and out of the womb thirty years ago. Right now, Cage was playing self-appointed spokesman for this buttinsky bunch who nodded . . . or grinned . . . at every blinkin' thing he said. Even simple stuff, like, "Where you goin', Max? Really?"

"Norway. I've told you that a dozen times."

"Why?"

"Family honor."

"When will ya come back?"

"Don't know."

"Will ya come back?"

"Don't know."

"Any danger?"

"Oh, yeah!"

"The odds?"

"Against me? I don't know. Hundred to one, maybe."

"The perps?"

"Greedy, vicious invaders."

"*Mon Dieu*, that defines any terrorist cell in the Third World."

"One in particular who would make Osama and Saddam seem like kindergartners."

Cage frowned. "Who the hell would wanta invade Norway?"

Torolf refused to answer and continued packing.

There was a communal rolling of eyes at his evasiveness.

"Well, that settles it." It was Pretty Boy speaking now. "We'll all go with you." While he spoke, Pretty Boy flipped through Torolf's little black book, which sat next to his wallet on the bureau. Torolf grabbed it from him with a snort of disgust. Pretty Boy—who was . . . well, pretty, according to women from two hemispheres—got enough action already. Then Pretty Boy's words sank in.

Oh, great! That's just what I need. A herd of Navy SEALs riding my tail. "I don't need four oversize babysitters."

"That's debatable," JAM interjected. The Hispanic guy was checking out Torolf's books on a nearby shelf. Torolf read everything from Clive Cussler to his sister Kirstin's romance novels. JAM probably had a dozen versions of the Bible.

"Not babysitters, precisely," Cage elaborated. "Ya cain't serve the gumbo 'less ever'one's at the table." He loved to quote his Cajun grandmother's hokey bayou sayings.

"What the hell does that mean?"

"All fer one and one fer all." Cage grinned. "Hey, you guys were there for me and my maw maw during Katrina and Rita." *Maw maw* was Cajun for grandmother. "Me, how could I do any less . . . even if ya've lost yer friggin' mind, *cher*?"

"Norway?" Pretty Boy said, frowning. "It's cold there, isn't it?"

"Damn cold. Norway is where I come from."

"For chrissake, he's gonna start the Viking bullshit again." JAM might have trained for the priesthood at one time, but he used the language of a sinner. In fact, after 9/11 he vowed to kill "every motherfucker terrorist in the world." His exact words, repeated often.

"Guess I'll have to pack my long johns," Pretty Boy said with a loud sigh of resignation.

"You guys are not going with me," Torolf insisted.

No one listened.

"Those Scandinavian women are supposed to be hot." This from Pretty Boy, of course. "Whoo-hoo! What do I see here?" He waved a long accordion strip of condoms that he'd picked out of Torolf's duffel bag. "Planning a marathon, are you, good buddy? You plannin' to keep all those hot Norse mamas to yourself?"

Torolf grabbed for the condoms and stuffed them back in his bag. "Listen, this is serious business for me. It's something I've got to do. By myself."

"Do tell," Cage said, serious himself now.

Torolf inhaled and exhaled, then decided to tell them the truth. Not that they would believe him. "I need to travel back to the eleventh-century Norselands to put an end to Steinolf, the worst tango in the world." *Tango* was a SEAL word for terrorist or bad guy. "He stole my family lands and tortured my sister Madrene. Think Hitler on a longship."

His friends couldn't have regarded him more incredulously if he'd grown propellers and called himself a Black Hawk.

"You're gonna time-travel? Cool!" It was Geek speaking for the first time. He'd been sitting at the desk fiddling with Torolf's laptop, updating some virus software.

Cool? Does he accept time travel? I must be dreaming.

The other SEALs turned to look at Geek, shocked. The message was clear: Geek had an IQ of about a gazillion, and if he could accept time travel, well, holy shit, maybe the rest of them could accept it, too. Scary thought, that.

"You believe in time travel?" Cage asked Geek.

Tell them no. Please, tell them no.

"Not really."

Whew!

"Well, not today, but I think it might be possible in the future."

That is just great!

Geek then went on to spout some crap about time

wrinkles in the stratosphere and research going on at some half-baked interterrestrial institute in D.C. Apparently time travelers and aliens were put in the same category.

"Have you been to see Dr. Goldstein this rotation?" Pretty Boy asked Torolf.

"Yes."

Dr. Goldstein was the base psychiatrist. All SEALs were required to get psychiatric counseling after every live op in which kills were involved. There was a fear that they would go off the deep end over the taking of human life, even if it was the vilest of tangos. After this recent stint in Afghanistan, his platoon—a combined effort of SEALs, Rangers, and other special forces units—had all gotten in their share of killing al-Qaeda suicide bombers and shit-for-brains extremists.

They would start a new rotation next month, this time in Tikrit, where the goal was to make a surgical strike, taking out some of the remaining hard-core Baathists, remnants of Saddam's old regime.

"So, Max, have ya time-traveled before?" Cage was gazing at him with a mixture of pity and concern.

"I have."

That surprised the crap out of all of them, including Geek, who turned to give him his full attention. "How?"

"You guys can't repeat any of this," Torolf said.

"Yeah, yeah, yeah," they agreed, but he could tell that they all thought he was fast turning into a fruitcake.

"When I was sixteen years old, in the year 1000 AD, my father, myself, and eight of my brothers and sisters boarded a longship. We left behind at Norstead, my family's estates, my brother Ragnor and my sister Madrene, both of whom you've met. While in Iceland, or Greenland, or wherever the hell we ended up, a strange storm overtook us, and we saw a vision where this elderly woman was praying. When we woke up, we were still in our longship, but we had landed in modern-day California. Ragnor and Madrene came here later, at different times."

A stunned silence met his words.

Well, he might as well finish off this lunatic tale. "If it was only that Steinolf stole our property . . . if it was only that he'd been vicious in the invasion . . . my family could probably let it go. But that bastard did some things to Madrene that can't be forgiven or forgotten. Even today, her body is covered with scars from the bastard's whip."

"Yeah, but you and your family are safe now," JAM pointed out. "Assuming what you say is true, why put yourself in danger just for the sake of revenge?"

"There's more," he said with a long sigh. "I found this obscure ancient journal that says Steinolf's reign of terror went on for decades, that he ruled all of Scandinavia at one point. His atrocities were unspeakable."

"I still don't understand," Cage said.

"Look, suppose you were able to go back and eliminate Hitler before the death camps. Wouldn't you try? Yeah, it's rewriting history, but if there's even a remote chance that I can stop him . . ." He paused with a shrug. "How can I not try?"

More silence.

Finally, Cage coughed and said, "So, do ya have a time machine or somethin'?"

He had to laugh at the question and gave Cage a noogie on his long-haired fool head. "No, you dipwad!"

"Do you expect to do it on the high seas . . . in a boat?" Geek asked. "Like before? And reverse the time travel?"

"Logical conclusion, but no. I've tried that. Lots of time in a boat off the California coast. I even tried it in Iceland when we were there last year to train the IDF in Keflavik. But nothing happened. Now I'm going back to Norway. I'll stand on the same spot where Norstead was once located. Hopefully, something will happen."

"Ya know you've gone bonkers, don't ya?" Cage regarded him with amusement.

He probably expected him to say something like, "Gotcha!" And admit he'd been joking. *I wish!* "Maybe. But I've gotta try."

"You honest-to-God believe in time travel?" Pretty Boy wanted to know.

"Well, no. But I do believe in miracles. I figure God, or one of the gods . . . probably Loki, the jester . . . destined this for my family."

"Aaah, miracles! That I can understand." JAM was nodding his head in acceptance, which was remarkable to Torolf. He didn't think anyone would believe him.

"This sounds really interesting. I'm in," Geek said. "When do we leave for Norway?"

"Me, too," each of the others said.

"No, no, no!" Torolf said as emphatically as he could.

"All fer one and one fer all," Cage reminded him. And he wasn't teasing, either.

"You can't do this," he tried one last time. "I know you have liberty for a couple weeks. We all do before we go OUTCONUS again. But, man, what if we can't come back? What if we get stuck in the past? Do you want to have a UA on your record?"

"Shiiit! If we're lost in the eleventh century, I don't think an unauthorized absence is gonna matter all that much," Pretty Boy pointed out.

Torolf decided to try a different argument. "Do you have any idea how primitive it was then? No electricity. No running water or flush toilets. No cars or planes. No computers. No condoms."

His four teammates looked at each other, then at him. They didn't believe him. Still, Cage spoke for them all when he said, "We're willing to risk that . . . for you. Do y'all agree?"

The response was a resounding, "Hoo-yah!" And Pretty Boy added, "Make sure we buy a shitload of rubbers to take with us. Make mine supersize."

"The only supersize on you is yer big head," Cage told Pretty Boy.

So it was that a team of five Navy SEALs decided to go back in time to the eleventh-century Norselands. They would never be the same.

You could say she was a Dark Ages feminist . . .

Brunhilda Berdottir was the last living child of Styrr Hardhead and Bera the Weeper, a deceased high jarl of Hordaland and his lady wife. Though she would never be recognized as such in her present condition.

She had a broken arm, a blackened eye, and bruises from head to toe. Still she trudged on, wearing only a rough gown under an over-tunic and thin, deerskin ankle boots, fur side inward, these two days and more along a remote, snow-covered mountain trail, hoping to find her great-grandsire's hunting lodge.

But then she slipped, her feet went out from under her, and her rump hit the ground with a resounding thump. Her stop caused those following behind her to fall as well in a rippling effect.

At first, they all stared at each other. Then one of them giggled. Soon they were all laughing. Not that there was any humor to their predicament, but the old sages were right when they said that betimes 'twas better to laugh than cry.

With her were five other females, ranging in age from twelve to thirty, all of them equally battered, some having been raped as well, repeatedly. The one thing they all had in common was the brutal, maggot-hearted Steinolf, who had invaded farmsteads and estates across the northwestern Norselands in a wave of bloody attacks these past three years. Her family's own Amberstead—named for her father's trading in the prized stones from the Baltic—had suffered the latest of his raids. Hilda could not bear to think of her last image of her father lying in a pool of blood outside the bailey, his body having been dealt the horrible Blood Eagle, a Viking punishment that involved hacking all the ribs away from the backbone down to loins, then pulling out the lungs as an offering to Odin.

In truth, there had been so much sword dew from him and his loyal retainers that it ran like a stream down to the fjord. Thank the gods, her mother and older brothers, Arnsten and Ketil, had passed to the otherworld many years ago.

Actually, there were more than the five of them traveling this remote trail. There was also Bjorn, Dotta, Edla, and Stigandr. Bjorn was a huge ram; Dotta and Edla, his favorite ewes . . . all three brought along for this journey at the insistence of her maid, Inge. Hilda and the women had all cuddled up against the animals for warmth as they slept yestereve.

Stig was, of course, her father's hunting dog. A more contrary, lustsome beast there never was. He would obey no one, not even Hilda, now that her father was gone.

Fortunately, once Stig understood that sheep would not stand still for his carnal efforts, all four animals had behaved well. And Inge—*Bless her soul*—had trailed behind with the animals, picking up their droppings with a wood paddle and sack so that their enemy would not be able to trace their path. Hilda had drawn the line when Frida, her cook, wanted to bring squawky chickens, but Hilda suspected the stubborn woman had breeding eggs nestled in the swath of wool wrapped around her waist.

Over the years, her father had traveled to the far-flung trading towns of Birka, Hedeby, and Novgorod, bringing her finger and arm rings, gold and silver linked belts, silk samite fabrics from Byzantium, a polished brass looking mirror, and a red cloak lined with gray fox fur. All left behind.

"Are we almost there, milady?" Inge asked as Hilda stood and dusted snowflakes off her gunna and wool mantle. They were near a bend in Freyjafjord that they had been following since midday. The others began to rise as well. Meanwhile, the sheep foraged in the snow to nibble at the undergrowth, and Stig licked her hands, seeking some morsel of food or bone.

She ignored Stig, having nothing to offer, and pressed her lips together to stop their shivering. "I've not been here for a dozen years . . . since my eleventh winter . . . but my grandsire always said Deer Haven was only a half day's journey from Freyja's Elbow, a bend in the fjord near the ancient lintel tree."

Inge's weary eyes followed Hilda's gaze to the gnarled tree as wide as three mead barrels with bare branches resembling beastly arms.

"Let us rest here a moment," Hilda suggested.

"A fire?" Inge inquired hopefully.

Hilda shook her head. "Steinolf's men may follow us . . . if not now, eventually. I doubt me there is any imminent danger, but we must be within the safety of Deer Haven's walls, drawbridge up, when . . . if . . . they discover our whereabouts."

"What could they do to us that they have not already done?" Inge remarked with a shudder.

"Skin us alive." It was something Steinolf was rumored to practice on his captured enemies when they did not cooperate.

"For the love of Thor! We can ill afford to linger then," Inge said, and the others nodded in agreement, even twelve-year-old Dagne, whose bloody thighs had borne the seed of a dozen or more men afore they had rescued her that first night. She had not spoken since. Dagne carried a favorite lute clutched close to her chest. Hilda wondered if she would ever sing again.

But they had all suffered.

Steinolf ordered the tip of Astrid's tongue to be sliced off for refusing to take one warrior's manpart into her mouth.

Elise, only seventeen, and a thrall, had watched help-lessly as her young mother had been dragged to one of the three longboats headed for the market stalls at Hedeby where she and twenty others would be sold as slaves. Their fate could be no worse than those left behind. Of course, Hilda would now release Elise from her thralldom, and she would no longer have to keep her hair close-cropped as a sign of servitude.

Frida, the oldest of them at thirty, had lain nude and spread-legged on the high table of Amberstead's great hall for a day and a half.

They were a perverted, cruel bunch, Steinolf's men were, slaking their lust like savage animals. Although Hilda had been beaten, she had not been raped or mutilated . . . yet. Steinolf had been saving her, as the highborn daughter of the estate, for last in hopes of drawing fleeing troops and cotters back to Amberstead. She could not imagine what atrocity he had planned for her, in light of what he'd done to lesser females in the household. There had been mention of a randy stallion out in the stable. That had been when she'd planned her escape.

Hilda looked at each of them in turn. "Heed me well. Keep heart a short while longer. This I vow: Steinolf will pay for his sins . . . someday. But for now, we must find safe harbor, restore our bodies and spirits, and grow strong."

The next morning they arrived at Deer Haven. Hilda sur-veyed it with an eye toward their defense against invaders.

It was a motte and bailey–style structure built in the longhouse style of the Vikings. It sat on an immense, raised, flat hilltop, steep-sloped on three sides and set against an almost vertical mountain background. The rustic castle—and, yea, it was a castle to the Norsemen—was surrounded by a wide moat. The palisade of strong hewn logs was half rotted away. Many hides of land went with this estate, but most of it was untillable. That's why her great-grandsire had abandoned it decades ago.

Much work would be required to restore it to its former impregnable state. The only entrance was through the fjord, which could be made impassable by damming the stream a short distance back . . . something her great-grandsire had once done in the old days when this had been his first home, long before the establishment of Amberstead and the use of Deer Haven as a hunting lodge. The drawbridge was rusted into a permanent open position. The moat was filled with mud and fallen trees. The massive, timber-and-earthworks main longhouse with its wood shake roof was in disrepair but still intact, though the wattle-and-daub huts and outbuildings that surrounded it had long ago lost their thatched roofs.

Despite the condition, Deer Haven was a welcome sight. "This will do as our new home," Hilda pronounced. Astrid, Elise, and Frida dropped to their knees and said prayers of thanks. Dagne wept with relief. But Inge, ever the one to have a sense of humor, chuckled. "By your leave, milady," she said, but without waiting for a response, picked up a sharp rock, which she used to carve runic symbols onto a short plank, which she propped against the edge of the drawbridge.

It read: "Any man who dares enter here uninvited will leave with a shriveled manpart."

"Well said!" Hilda clapped her hands in appreciation.

They all laughed then, even Dagne.

We will be all right now, Hilda decided. *If we can see mirth in the midst of our tragedy, we have the mettle to survive. This will be our sanctuary.* In fact, she stepped forth and took the stone from Inge, adding two words. Later, the same plaque would be nailed into the restored fortress, and it would read:

THE SANCTUARY
Any man who dares enter here uninvited
will leave with a shriveled manpart.

Chapter 2

Tsk, tsk, tsk! You couldn't take them anywhere! . . .

"A-Viking we will go, a-Viking we will go, heigh-ho the dairy-o, a-Viking we will go."

"I for one am in the mood for a little pillaging."

"Where are all those buxom, blonde-haired Scandinavian women we were promised? With names like Ingrid or Ursula?"

"I want a battle-axe. Forget an AK-47, I want a big-ass, friggin' battle-axe."

"Hot damn, it's cold. Pass me my fur mantle. Ha, ha, ha!"

"Where the hell's my plunder? Did you take my plunder?"

"I think I'll do my hair in war braids today."

"Who says Vikings didn't wear horned helmets? I really, really want a horned helmet."

"What's the name of your sword?"

"Johnson."

"What's yours?"

"Mr. Big."

All this ribbing was being delivered to Torolf by his four teammates as they stood on a reproduction of a Viking dragonship on a godforsaken fjord in Norway. A tourist trap, to be sure.

"No kidding, Max, let's go get a mug of beer . . . uh, mead . . . and forget this time-travel crap."

I wish I could.

"Yeah. You need to get your ashes hauled, if you ask me."

Nobody asked you. "Getting laid isn't the answer to everything."

Four sets of eyes turned to look at him.

He grinned and shook his head at the hopelessness of arguing with the blockheads. There were close to two hundred members of SEAL Team Thirteen, but these guys had gone through BUD/S training with him. When down range, these were the guys he wanted watching his six. But when they were inactive—as they were now after five days in western Norway—all that energy had to be directed somewhere. Unfortunately, he was the chosen target.

They were pissing him off big-time, and they knew it. So, he saluted them with his middle finger.

They just laughed. No surprise there.

The wind had died down about a half hour ago, and the longboat had pretty much stopped moving. So, the red and white striped sails had been lowered.

"Out oars!" Svein Olafsson, the pretend captain of this tourist longship, yelled out. Picking up their oars, twelve sets of pretend Viking sailors came to attention. They looked like idiots, probably college students, in their pseudo-Viking duds, designed by some dingbat Calvin Klinesson, no doubt. Sitting on sea chests, they began to row in unison. They may have been dressed like no Vikings he'd ever known, with belt buckles that would rival a rodeo rider's and tunics and braies made of ultrasuede, but the rhythmic sound of oars creaking in oarlocks was not unfamiliar to Torolf.

As the longship plied easily through Freyjafjord, Torolf looked for familiar landmarks, to no avail, even though he'd traveled here with his father and brother Ragnor when they were youthlings. Everything looked different now. Even worse, two days past, Torolf had stood on the very spot where Norstead, his family estates, had once been located. There was a shopping mall there now. Even so, Torolf had dropped to his knees in the parking lot, praying for deliverance back to the past, much to the amusement of passersby. JAM had helped by sprinkling some holy water on the concrete. *Who knew that JAM carried holy water around, just in case there was an emergency!*

"Pssst," Cage whispered, elbowing him to draw his attention back to the present. "The good captain, he is throwin' eye daggers our way."

Hah! *Everyone* was looking at them funny, Cage most of all, with his shoulder-length hair, little gold loop earring, and stupid cowboy hat and cowboy boots. You'd think he was from Texas . . . or Forty-second Street . . . not Louisiana. On the other hand, maybe it was JAM in cammies and an olive-drab T-shirt with the logo "Navy SEAL" on it who was drawing all the looks; that logo was always a chick magnet, not that the good captain would care about that. Pretty Boy wore his NASCAR jacket, also a chick magnet. He and Geek were dressed normally in jeans.

Captain Svein, as he'd told them to call him, even though his real job was a professor at an Oslo university, frowned at him and his SEAL buddies for standing apart from the rest of the tourist group. "The Norsemen were masters of the seas during the Viking age. With good cause, they were called sea wolves."

Pretty Boy made a wolf howling noise.

A mug of mead was beginning to sound good to Torolf, too.

"With fair winds on the open seas, the high-riding long-ships could travel at incredible speeds with sails, called 'cloaks of the wind,' unfurled. But, when the wind went down, as it has now, the Viking sailors needed to start rowing the vessels, which were so light they were able to travel easily on shallow fjords."

On and on Olafsson droned, and Torolf scanned the passing fjord shoreline, searching for clues. The landscape and geographical boundaries had been different long ago. In fact, ancient Norway had been twice as large as it was today. And, yet, they were the same. His heart and his memory told him so.

"Norway is a land of snow-capped mountains and great, barren plateaus," the tour guide pointed out. "Its coastline is broken by hundreds of fjords, each with its own personality. They were carved out by glaciers in prehistoric times. Despite its bleakness, there are picturesque bays and moorlands. Some contend the most beauty is in the forbidding terrain."

Torolf nodded in agreement.

"Although the Scandinavians all spoke different dialects, they could apparently understand each other," Olafsson explained, after a question from one of the visitors. "And, actually, Old Norse, which in no way resembles modern Norwegian, was very similar to the English of that time."

Blah, blah, blah. Let's go back to port. I might as well accept that reverse time travel just isn't going to happen.

"Were they really vicious rapers and pillagers?" one elderly gentleman asked.

"The early histories were written by clerics who had a prejudiced view of the non-Christian invaders. In fact, Vikings were adventurers, settlers, artisans, and traders.

Their law codes were the basis for our modern judicial system. Their sagas bespoke a great love of storytelling and humor."

"I heard they were hunks," one young woman commented, probably a girlfriend of one of the college boy rowers. She wasn't blonde or buxom, but she wasn't unattractive, despite the tongue piercing. He noticed Pretty Boy watching her, too. He would probably be hitting on her before they were back on land.

The professor/captain smiled at her question. "Actually, the Viking men *were* taller and better looking than the average men of that time."

Torolf smirked at his friends.

"Plus, they bathed more often than other folks. No wonder so many women of so many different lands welcomed them into their beds! There's no doubt that they enriched the races of the countries where they settled."

"Did you bathe a lot?" Cage asked.

"How many races did *you* enrich?" Pretty Boy wanted to know.

"This is really interesting," Geek said. He was soaking up the touristy lecture like a sailor at his first strip show.

What a . . . geek!

"Ya know, we Cajuns are a lot like Vikings," Cage said.

"I'll bite," Torolf said. "How are Cajuns like Vikings?"

"They're both drop-dead gorgeous, sexy as sin, have a great sense of humor, and women love 'em."

His remark was met with snickers.

"Besides, like my maw maw always says, 'The truth is in the roux.' "

"What the hell does roux have to do with Vikings and Cajuns?" Torolf would undoubtedly regret asking the question.

"Roux is the heart of most Cajun dishes. At heart, Vikings and Cajuns are good lovers, husbands, fathers, sons."

"That is the most half-assed logic I've ever heard." JAM liked there to be an explanation for everything. It was probably why he was no longer a Jesuit wannabe.

Just then, Torolf noticed something. "Oh, my God!" He shoved his friends aside so he could see better over the side of the longboat. Like a well-oiled machine, his teammates went on immediate alert, joining him in a search for danger, scanning the ship and the quickly passing landscape. They knew what to do in a crisis and how to work together without words. In a situation like this, explanations took precious time away from action.

Torolf shouted to the tour guide, "Hey! Watch yourselves. We're entering shallow waters, and there's a bend or obstruction up ahead." He rushed to the helmsman manning the rudder, and the idiot wouldn't let go. Quickly, he clipped him on the chin, knocking him out, and tried desperately to turn the rudder in the other direction.

Cage and Geek grabbed oars from some stunned "Vikings" and attempted to reach the front of the ship to forestall a crash.

JAM and Pretty Boy were perched on a gunwale, about to dive overboard and secure the anchor.

But it was too late.

There was a loud crashing noise, and everyone standing was thrown off their feet by the impact.

He glanced up from his prone position, and as if in slow motion, he felt the longboat teeter from side to side in its now dry-docked state and then tip over. Before he could react to that catastrophe, something even worse happened. The heavy yardarm and mast came crashing down over them. Under the massive, heavy sails, he heard screams, cracking wood, cursing, more screams, piercing pain in his head and shoulders . . .

And then silence.

So, this is how it ends, he thought. *In death.*

Men . . . can't live with them, can't live without them . . .

"We need men!" shouted Britta the Big, chief archer of The Sanctuary and head of its guard.

Truth to tell, they had only ten axes, one broadsword, which hardly anyone could lift, fifteen shepherd's crooks converted into lances, long-handled cooking ladles, pokers, wooden clubs, slingshots, and bows and arrows. Every woman practiced weaponry regularly, in case of an attack, under Britta's supervision.

"Not for me," Britta explained in an aside to Hilda. "I speak for the others."

Britta's chant was taken up by the sixty other women in the inner courtyard of The Sanctuary. "We need men! We need men!"

Hilda put her face in her hands, counted to ten silently, then said with forced patience, "Men are scurvy curs . . ." Stig and his new bitch growled at her feet with doggie consternation. "We have flourished these past five years *without men*."

"It matters not. *Now* they need men," Britta asserted.

Hilda flung her hands out with disbelief. "Truly, Britta? Must needs we cower under a man's shield for protection?"

Britta, who was as tall as a man, with wide shoulders and muscled arms, stiffened. "Nay, not for our defenses."

All of the women sat on the ground in a five-deep circle under the warm autumn sun. The law speaker, Kelda Sigundottir, had already recited the Thing law codes of their female community, calling on Forseti, god of justice, for guidance. A Thing was held to discuss problems and settle disputes. Minor quarrels had already been resolved today by the debating of both sides of the issues. Two women fighting over a fox fur pelt. A girl negligent in her kitchen duties. An argument over which was the best recipe for curing cheese curds for *skyr*. A game of *hnefatafl* that went badly, resulting in one black eye and a bloody shin. Weevils in a sack of flour. A smelly garderobe.

It had been five years since Hilda arrived at Deer Haven, now The Sanctuary. The first year had been brutal. Often they had feared either freezing to death in the cold fortress or starving to death or being discovered by Steinolf and his comrades-in-cruelty. More escapees had made their way to safety, increasing their numbers. Only occasionally did they have to fend off invaders, small bands of errant knaves. Steinolf was busy grabbing lands in surrounding countries.

Hilda acted as head of this community, much like an abbess in a nunnery or a chief crone in a witches' coven, which was the word they had spread to keep men away. But, really, everyone was equal here, all assigned duties for which they were best suited.

Now, after all this healing and prosperity, they want men here? Hah! I will become a Valkyrie afore that happens! "Frida, do our hunters not bring you enough woodcock, grouse, geese, hares, foxes, reindeer, duck, plover, and the occasional boar? Do the fisherwomen not catch you enough pike, roach, rudd, sea bream, perch, eel, herring, cod, haddock, ling, mackerel, smelt, and lampreys?"

A blush crept over the cook's face. And speaking of bounty, Frida was now the size of a small warhorse due to that bounty.

"Inge, will the goats produce more milk or the rams swive more sheep to increase our flocks if a man were tending them?"

"You know they will not," Inge replied with a touch of affront. Inge, who was the same age as Hilda at twenty and eight, was in charge of all the animals, her original flock of one ram and two ewes having multiplied into four rams, twenty ewes, and twenty-five lambs, not to mention the ten goats they kept for milk.

"Dost envision Viking men tending your gardens, Dagne? Or playing your lute on a long winter's eve?"

Dagne, still folk-shy, lowered her eyes and shook her head sharply. She was seventeen now and had just begun to speak again this past winter. Her recovery had taken longer than most.

Astrid, a bitter woman who spoke with a slight slur due to her mutilated tongue, gave Hilda no chance to question her. "And, nay, I do not need a man to gather honey and meddle in the making of mead and candles."

Elise, now twenty-three, giggled when Hilda's eyes lit on her. Never in all her life had Hilda encountered such a cheerful person. No longer a thrall, Elise organized all the spinning of wool and weaving of cloth. A sizable enterprise for sixty women. "'Tis laughable picturing men with their big, dirty hands working a spindle or weaving cloth."

Still others in the community were cleaning maids, laundresses, gardeners, woodworkers, carpenters, and various other occupations. Each had an opinion on the man situation.

Bemused, Hilda was only half attending as the women continued to chatter among themselves. Finally, she put her hands on her hips and said, loud enough to override the voices, *"Krrr!"* Then, she repeated, "Quiet!" When everyone gave their full attention, she asked, "What is amiss here?"

Inge spoke for the rest. "We need men."

"Bld Hel! All of us have suffered in one way or another from the misdeeds of men. You would allow men with their brutish urges to slake their lust on us?"

"Yea and nay," Inge answered.

Hilda arched her eyebrows. "Is the springtime sap rising in you women? You may not have dangly parts, but have you become lustsome, like nature's animals . . . the ram, the bull, the rooster, and . . . and men? By Odin! That is it, is it not?"

Inge's face reddened, as did others. "Not precisely."

"If not a craving for a good tup, then what?" Hilda could be frank of manner when the occasion warranted.

As one, all the women answered, "Children."

"Aaaah!" Hilda sighed. The maternal instinct. "But you must know, bringing men into this community would change things."

"You say us wrong, milady," Inge said. "We need them for the breeding only. Not for a lifetime."

Hilda laughed. "You expect to bring men here for the mating and then dismiss them when they are no longer useful?"

"Men do it all the time," one voice shouted.

"That I own, but 'twould bode ill for us if Steinolf's men learned the exact whereabouts of our refuge from those discards."

"There might be a way," Britta said. "We could kidnap them and bind their eyes with cloth."

Hilda's jaw dropped. "They would be outraged. They would never accept us on those terms."

"Hah! They would have no choice if they were chained to a bedchamber wall." It was young Dagne who spoke, to Hilda's surprise. Others found great amusement in that prospect.

Hilda had to raise a hand to quell the laughter and ribald remarks. "We must not make a hasty decision. Let us think on the matter and discuss it again at next month's Thing. Mayhap the Norns of fate will guide us."

Everyone nodded and went off, a betwittered mass of laughter and giggles. They had not yet convinced her. Far from it.

Two sennights later, it appeared as if the Norns had indeed intervened. They were in the midst of clipping thorns out of dumb sheep who had waded unkowingly into a briar patch. 'Twas a sweaty, stinksome, greasy job, which could not wait till spring shearing. But then the call to arms came.

"Danger! Get your weapons! Come quickly!" one of Britta's sentries yelled, running up the motte, lance in hand. "A longship has wrecked, and there are men."

Instantly, the community of women gathered weapons. Their demeanor bespoke a mixture of shock and exhilaration.

"Are they armed? How many are there? Best I bring ropes to tie them up."

"The gods have answered our prayers."

"I hope there is a flaxen-haired one. I do so want a flaxen-haired bairn."

"Not me! Black-haired men are more virile."

"Who told you that?"

"Makes no difference, as long as there are seeds in the pods."

Seeds in the pods? Oh, good gods!

"Are any of them comely? Not that it matters. In the dark, all manparts look the same."

"I heard my brother make that selfsame remark about women."

Much giggling and huffing and puffing followed.

I have landed in the middle of mayhem with a flock of randy, lackwit woman warriors, and none of them are considering the fact that it might be Steinolf and his men. Raising her hand, Hilda signaled for them to stop behind a ridge of trees . . . the very place where they had spent many a day building a dam in the fjord, stone by stone. There had indeed been a shipwreck. The longboat lay on its side, splintered, but even more disastrous to those aboard, the collision must have caused the mast and yardarm to fall, crushing those beneath.

"The vessel had to be traveling fast to have hit the low water and then the dam itself," Inge noted.

"The captain of the dragon ship must have been incompetent to have failed to see the obstruction up ahead," Britta commented. "Or else he was *drukkinn*."

They approached the longboat cautiously, many of them grim-faced with disappointment at the severity of the wreckage.

"Be careful," she cautioned. But what she really thought was, *They are probably all dead*.

And, oddly, she was disappointed.

Chapter 3

Is this the ultimate male fantasy, or what? . . .

Torolf came groggily back to his senses and noticed a number of alarming things in a gradually lessening haze, like the slow flicking of a deck of picture cards.

Alarming thing number one: The sails, mast, and yardarm had been lifted off them. *Who did it? And how?*

Alarming thing number two: He had the mother of all headaches. *That's probably blood seeping down my forehead.*

Alarming thing number three: His four buddies were in the same state he was. Geek's right leg was stretched out at an odd angle. Pretty Boy had an ugly slash on his bicep that would need stitches. JAM was bleeding from a superficial head wound, same as him. Cage was the only one seemingly unscathed; even his goofy cowboy hat was still in place.

Alarming thing number four: Everyone else on the longship was gone. That included the captain, the rowers, and the tourists. *Huh? How could that be?* He shook his head to clear it and had to grit his teeth at the pain. Yep, it was just the five of them and—*Omigod! How could I not have noticed right away?*—their arms were restrained in front with ropes.

Alarming thing number five, and it was the most alarming thing of all: A group of wild, screeching women surrounded them, brandishing an odd assortment of weapons. If he didn't already have a headache, he would now from their shrill voices. And their appearance . . . unbelievable! Some wore the traditional attire for a Norsewoman: an ankle-length gunna covered with an open-sided, over-the-head, calf-length apron, held together at the shoulders with brooches. But most of them wore slim pants and over-tunics that went to the hip and were belted at the waist. Their clothing didn't come from Frederick's of the Fjord, that was for sure. They looked like Amazons in a bad B movie.

And, phew, they smelled to high heaven. Sort of like wet wool, dung, and—*Oh, yeah! As a farm boy from way back, I'd recognize that smell anywhere*—sheep. That would explain the shepherds' crooks that doubled as lances in some of their hands.

"Call me crazy, but are we really surrounded by a couple dozen women brandishing cooking ladles?" Pretty Boy stared at the women surrounding them . . . women absurdly trying to appear ferocious. But then Pretty Boy's gaze latched onto one big mama of a woman who was holding a broadsword with two hands. Even big men sometimes had trouble managing a broadsword. This Xena babe had to be six feet tall with the shoulders of a linebacker and the waist of quarterback, although her breasts and long legs under the brown tunic and slim pants spelled W-O-M-A-N. Pretty Boy sighed and said, "I think I'm in love."

Whaaat?

"Is this a joke? Oh, now I get it. Yer playing a joke on

us, aren't ya, Max?" Cage was laughing and would have probably jabbed him in the arm if his arms were free. "First the time-travel crap, now this. Whoo-boy, ya really punked us this time."

"Don't be an idiot. How would I be able to pull this off . . . a freakin' shipwreck, then these loony bird women? I'm not that good."

"You've done dumber stuff," JAM pointed out. "Like the time you talked Ensign Nixon into pretending to be a hooker and luring Cage into a surprise birthday party at the Wet and Wild." The Wet and Wild was a bar near Coronado that catered to Navy guys.

"It didn't take much talking. Celia Nixon has had the hots for Cage for years."

The whole time they were chitchatting like a bunch of imbeciles, the women were talking among themselves, also like imbeciles, "weapons" still raised. The fine hairs stood out on the back of Torolf's neck when he realized something important. The women were speaking in Old Norse. Quickly, he surveyed the area, as best he could from his sitting position. An alarming idea came to him, and he didn't know whether to be happy or scared shitless. Probably both. The enormity of his realization stunned him for a moment.

"I hate to break the news to you guys," he said, "but I think we time-traveled. I'd bet my left nut we are now in the eleventh century."

"Ha, ha, ha! And I'd bet my right nut you're pulling our legs," Pretty Boy said, never taking his eyes off Big Mama. "Hey, sweet thing, how about untying me?" he called out to Big Mama. "Or . . . happy days . . . are you into bondage?"

Big Mama glared at him as if he were an insect under her size-ten boots.

Torolf blinked repeatedly, trying to get his bearings.

Cage glanced at him with concern. "Man, yer weirding me out."

Torolf was where he wanted to be . . . well, where he had tried to be for a long time, but now he was worried. It was one thing to be responsible for himself and the possibility he might be locked in the past. But what about his buddies? Even though they had pushed their way into accompanying him to Norway, they hadn't really expected this.

Okay, time to get this show on the road.

Torolf stood clumsily in front of another woman who had a pair of sheep-shearing scissors in one hand and a short-bladed knife in the other; she seemed to be the leader. Her long, very light blonde hair—platinum blonde, like his sister Kirstin's—had escaped a single braid that hung down to the middle of her back, and there were bits of fleece in the unruly, flaxen strands. Clear blue eyes were framed by thick, light brown eyebrows and lashes. She was tall, though not as tall as Big Mama . . . maybe five eight or so. Barefoot and grimy, she wore a long beige gown belted at the waist with a thin rope. And he could swear those spots on her forearms and gown were sheep shit.

"Who . . . what are you?" he asked.

"A witch," she said.

"A nun," Big Mama said at the same time.

"Oh, no! Please don't tell me you're a nun!" Pretty Boy pleaded with Big Mama.

"Lackwit!" Big Mama turned her back on Pretty Boy, but Torolf was pretty sure her lips were twitching with laughter.

Back to the leader. Torolf flashed her one of his most engaging smiles. "So, Ms. Witch-Nun, what's your name? My name is Torolf Magnusson, but you can call me Max."

The woman frowned as if confused.

He spoke English, but she should be able to understand the gist of what he said, Old Norse and English having so many similarities. Even so, he repeated himself in Old Norse.

"I understood you the first time," she snapped. But then she leaned forward, studying his face. "Do my eyes play me false? Nay, 'tis impossible. You cannot be Torolf Magnusson. That dunderhead is dead."

He shrugged. *Guess what, baby? The dunderhead is definitely alive.*

"Why do you call yourself Torolf the Axe? As I recall, Torolf's weapon of choice was a pattern-welded sword."

"Not axe. Max. And how would you know . . ." His words trailed off as he peered closer. "Is that you, Hildy-Tildy?"

"Ooooh, do not dare to call me that silly youthling name. Have you forgotten what I did last time you did?"

"No. What?"

"I bloodied your nose, that is what."

"I'm already bloody." In fact, the stream of blood was trickling over his nose and down the side of his mouth. He turned his head and wiped the blood on his sleeve. Then he grinned. "So, what're you gonna do about it, *Hildy-Tildy*?"

Her response was to punch him in the stomach. It didn't hurt much, but still it was a rotten thing to do to a man with his hands tied. Oh, well! Before she could react, he raised his arms over her head and down to the back of her waist, yanking her flush against him. Her scissors and knife clattered to the deck.

All her witch/nun comrades-in-lunacy closed ranks around him with soup ladles and shepherd's crooks ready to give him another knock on the head. There were a few deadly knives, as well, he noticed, and tugged Hilda even closer. The women were back to screeching again.

"Unhand me, you mangy weasel," Hilda hollered. Being face-to-face, as they were, that holler about made his ears ring.

"Shall we kill the maggot, milady?" Big Mama inquired. Somehow she had managed to raise the broadsword above her head. He hoped she didn't drop it . . . like on his head.

Hilda hesitated.

"Lady, be careful. I could throttle you, even with my hands tied."

"Not yet," she replied to Big Mama.

"Good girl!" Into her ear, he said, "Call off your fellow witches and untie me." *Pee-you! She stinks.*

"Nay!"

Just like a woman. Makes everything difficult. "Why not?"

"We are a community of women."

Big deal! "No men allowed?"

"No men allowed."

No wonder, the way they smell.

"Dost think the gods sent these men in answer to our prayers?" one young woman asked Hilda.

"Shhhh! 'Tis unseemly to talk about . . . you know . . . in front of these men," Hilda cautioned the girl.

Five sets of male eyes went on full alert at the prospect of their being the answer to some not-so-fair maidens' prayers.

He chuckled. "So, Hildy, you been prayin' for me?"

"Hell and Valhalla! May the gods spare me from half-brained men with smooth-as-cream tongues." Hilda ducked under the circle of his arms, which he had loosened.

He didn't attempt to stop her, even when she reached down to retrieve her weapons. *She thinks I'm smooth? And I haven't even tried yet.* "You think I'm smooth?" He pressed his lips together to keep from laughing.

"What prayers?" Geek asked.

"We need men to mate with," another woman, a teenager, really, said. She was eyeing Geek like she was a Weight Watchers dropout and he was a chocolate sundae . . . with whipped cream. "And then we shall send them on their way," she added airily.

All his buddies looked at each other and grinned.

"I like the one in the strange hat."

"I like the pretty one."

"I like the one with the gold cross around his neck. Must be he is a monk." The woman seemed distressed at that prospect, but then added, "Monk or not, it matters not, as long as he has a dangly part."

"Which one do *you* like?" Torolf winked at Hilda.

"Not you! So save your winks for some feckless maid who would appreciate your dubious charms."

He had no interest in her, either, but her words rankled anyway. "Why not!" *I can't believe I asked that.*

She exhaled with exasperation. "By the runes, you have always been a jesting sort. Never serious."

"I'm a fighting man now. That's damn serious, if you ask me." *Yep. My tongue runneth over.*

"You are a warrior?" That got her attention for some reason.

"This is one practical joke of yers that I like," Cage interrupted.

"Yeah, you can line up multiple sex partners for us any day," Pretty Boy chimed in, "especially if we get to pick from the litter."

"Multiple sex partners . . . Do you mean all at once?" Geek's ears turned red. He might be twenty-six, but he was sexually inexperienced in comparison to the rest of them.

"I hope they're gonna bathe first . . . and use a little deodorant. Eau de Goat doesn't do it for me." JAM crinkled his nose in distaste.

"I told you, blockheads, this is not a joke. We must have time-traveled."

No one listened to him.

Hilda put the back of her hand to her forehead and groaned.

He knew just how she felt. "Let me get this straight. You

women live here alone, but you want men to have sex with, and then you'll boot them out the door?"

"They do. Not me."

"Why not you?" *Like I care!*

"Whoa, whoa, whoa!" Cage said. "They want to get laid? With no commitment? Man, this has gotta be Penthouse Fantasy Number One."

Pretty Boy smiled at Big Mama and said, "I get first dibs on you, baby."

"Pfff! You are too small for me."

"I'm not small . . . where it counts." Pretty Boy waggled his eyebrows at her. "Besides, I'm as tall as you are."

Torolf felt the need to take control. "Listen, Hildy, this is amusing as hell, but you need to release us. Some of us have head wounds that need to be tended."

"I cannot release you."

"Why not?"

"You might be Steinolf's men."

Torolf stiffened with outrage. "If you were a man, I would kill you."

She arched her eyebrows. "You have no love for Steinolf?"

"Hardly. Haven't you heard what he did to Norstead . . . and my sister, Madrene?"

She nodded. "I have." The compassion on her face lasted only a second. "And where were you during that happenstance? If you did not die when everyone thought you did, why were you not here to protect your family estates . . . to protect Madrene?"

She is really pissing me off, especially when her criticism hits so close to home. "Enough of this chitchat! We can discuss all this later." He pulled his hands from the ropes, which he had been working at the whole time, and grabbed for Hilda, putting her in front of him in a choke hold, with his one arm around her neck from behind and the other around her waist. The other guys did the same with different women, except for Geek, who was unable to get to his feet fast enough. It happened so quickly that the women had no chance to react at first.

"How did you get loose?" Hilda squealed.

"Knot Tying 101, baby. Or, rather, Knot Untying 101."

"You *are* Steinolf's men then."

The word "Steinolf" kept being repeated among the women. Some began to weep, even some who held weapons at the ready.

"Take me and let my women go. Or be merciful, and kill us all. We would rather that than be in that beast's hands again."

He cursed, that they would think he was like Steinolf, then said against her ear, "We are not Steinolf's men. I told you that before. I have as much reason to hate him as you do."

"I doubt that."

By now the other women had closed ranks around them again.

"Tell your . . . uh, followers . . . to drop their weapons and back off. Tell them to head back with my men to that fort . . . or whatever it is up there on the hill. We'll follow. No one will be harmed if you do as I say."

Reluctantly, she did as ordered. "Go back to the keep!"

JAM and Cage half carried Geek by supporting him between their two shoulders. Pretty Boy picked up the broadsword and was herding the women up the hill, but not before he'd restrained Big Mama with her hands behind her back. He grinned like an ape while the woman tossed graphic Old Norse curses at him.

"You know what's really odd," JAM called back to him, "I know that she . . . they . . . are speaking some other language, but I can understand it."

"Yeah, yer right," Cage said, and the others agreed, too.

Torolf figured that if time travel could take place, then language barriers should be no problem, either. God and his miracles and all that.

Soon the others were gone, and he remained on the wrecked ship with Hilda. "Now, Hildy," he said, "I am going to release you. Then you and I are going to sit down on those sea chests over there and talk. Agreed?"

At first, she remained stiff and unyielding, but then she nodded.

"I mean it. If you don't calm down, I'm going to truss you like a chicken and hang you from that tree over there."

She made a growling sound. "I said I would listen, you lack-brained, insolent, cod-sucking son of a cur."

"Why don't you tell me how you really feel?"

"I am loath to believe you are who you say you are."

"Well, stop loathing. You already said you recognize me, and you know for damn sure that the Ericsson and Magnusson clans have long been friends with your family." He eased his hold on her slowly, then took her by the forearm and pushed her down to sit on a sea chest.

"You shame your family by doing this." She raised her chin like a bloody princess in her rags.

"No, I don't. I haven't hurt you, and I don't intend to, unless you do something foolish."

She bared her teeth at him.

He pulled a sea chest over so that he could sit opposite her, knee to knee. "Let's start over, shall we?"

She tilted her head suspiciously.

"Well, hello there, Hilda! How are you? Haven't seen you in ages. Then you say, 'Torolf! Welcome to Deer Haven.' That is where we are, isn't it?"

"'Tis called The Sanctuary now."

"Whatever. You say, 'Welcome to The Sanctuary, Torolf. Come share our food and have a cup of mead. I will tell you all the news that's been happening while you were gone, and I'm dying to know where you've been.'" He waited.

"Tell me true, Torolf. Are you here with ill intent?"

"I am not."

"You have no bond with Steinolf . . . or any other villains?"

"I do not."

Her shoulders relaxed, and she smiled.

His heart actually skipped a beat. It was a very nice smile, even if she did have that space between her front teeth . . . perhaps *because* of that enticing space. It made a guy want to . . . well, whatever. In any case, she was almost attractive, despite her wild hair, awful clothes, and the smell.

"*Gan dag,* Torolf. I wish you good tidings. Welcome to The Sanctuary. Do you plan a long stay?"

"No. At least I hope I won't be here long. A week or two . . . three at the most."

She stood then and extended her hand. "Come. We have a bathhouse where you can refresh yourself. And I will have Inge put mutton on to roast. I know which stubborn sheep it will be, too." She stared pointedly at the spots on her gown.

He laughed. Taking her firmly by the elbow, he began to escort her back toward the hill fort when a big, furry animal—a dog—came barreling down the hill toward them, barking like crazy. When the animal got to the bottom, it skidded to a stop at their feet. Then the animal glanced up at Torolf, sniffed his leg, and began to hump it. The mutt probably smelled his dog, Slut, on his jeans leg, and, yes, he had named his dog Slut because, frankly, she was a slut. Even after being spayed, she wagged her tail at every hound dog in the neighborhood.

"Stig! Stop it!" Hilda said, trying to pull the animal away by the scruff of the neck. Her face was red with embarrassment. "My apologies. I do not know what has gotten into him. He has never done that afore . . . to a person." While Hilda was shooing the animal away, it kept glancing at Torolf's leg as if it was a tasty bone . . . or a doggie hooker.

With him grinning and Hilda frowning, they continued up the hill where he noticed a wooden sign at the base of the motte which read:

THE SANCTUARY
Any man who dares enter here uninvited
will leave with a shriveled manpart.

He laughed and yelled out to the guys who were already at the top of the motte, "Guess what this sign says." And he read it to them.

Cage glanced down his body and yelled back at him, "No shriveling here."

"None here either," each of the other guys yelled, all of them laughing.

"Enter at your own peril," Hilda said with a sniff of disgust.

"Does anyone . . . any man . . . believe that shriveling business?"

"Some do, as well they should."

"And the witch stuff. Does anyone believe that?"

"Some do. And best you beware, I know spells aplenty."

"And a nun, too. Tsk, tsk, tsk."

"Always the jester, are you not?"

"Who's jesting? So, tell me about these prayers for sex."

She rolled her eyes at him. "You will not believe it."

"Try me."

When she was done—and he suspected she told him only part of the story—they were almost to the top of the motte. Wiping tears of laughter from his eyes, he said as somberly as he could, "I don't think my men will need any coaxing."

"And you?" she inquired.

"I'm saving myself."

"For whom?"

He looked at her for a long moment, then said, "You." Why he'd said that, he had no idea. The thousand-year-old air must have affected his brain.

But she appeared as poleaxed by the prospect as he. Finally she scoffed. "Never."

Never, he mimicked her in his mind. She was probably right . . . no, she was definitely right . . . but he couldn't let her derisive answer stand. "Never say never to a Navy SEAL."

"I thought it was, 'Never say never to a Viking.'"

"Correction then. Never say never to a Viking Navy SEAL."

Chapter 4

And then she made him an offer he couldn't refuse . . .

Hilda surveyed the great hall of The Sanctuary that night and moaned her dismay. *How did I lose control so quickly?*

Before she had even come into the hall, she had been forced to lock Stig in the woodshed because he kept following Torolf around, hanging onto his blue braies, attempting to fornicate with his leg. It must be something about Torolf 's male scent that was attracting the dog, because he did it to no one else, except every female dog he could catch.

Along the massively long tables, there were three open-sided hearths running down the center of the great hall on raised platforms; they were for heating more than cooking. Unlike many Norse keeps, there were no rushes on the floor, just swept, hard-packed dirt . . . straw being a prized commodity in these parts. Along the walls were sleeping closets, one bedchamber, and compartments for storing linens and other household items. Cooking implements and dried herbs hung from the ceiling. Every bit of space in a Viking home was utilized.

The fare offered tonight was plain but more plentiful and varied than their usual evening meal. Roast mutton was supplemented with smoked eels, fresh pike, and *hrút-spungur*, that Norse delicacy of ram's testicles pickled in whey and pressed into a cake, usually saved for special occasions. There were vegetables aplenty, too. Turnips, small white carrots, edible seaweeds stewed with garlic, and tiny onions in goat cream sauce. For sweets, there were honey cakes studded with walnuts and dried bilberries. Goat milk or mead quenched their thirsts.

On either side of the tables, sitting on benches, which would be later used for pallets, were a handful of grinning men and dozens of eyelash-batting, riband-wearing, teeth-baring, twittering females, who also happened to be so clean they nigh sparkled. Their gunnas and tunics were plain, but they'd chosen ones with color and embroidery: woad blue, madder red, lichen purple, broom yellow. When the lines at the bathing house had been too long, many had dunked themselves in the frigid waters of the fjord. *All for the sake of* . . . she shuddered . . . *MEN*.

Not her, though. Nay, she'd washed the sheep dung off her arms and soaped her face, but she'd chosen apurpose not to change her gown or comb her hair, lest she be viewed as one of the pathetic mass, looking for a bedmate.

Oh, she knew she was being harsh. She did understand their yearning for children and male companionship. But did it have to be so obvious?

"Did you say something, Hildy?"

Hilda gritted her teeth at his use of that childish name. "Dost get joy of pricking me, lout?"

Torolf began to cough, as if something was stuck in his throat.

She clapped him on his back a few times.

"If I had ever *pricked* you, I'm sure I would have enjoyed it," he said finally and smiled.

That innocent smile . . . she would like to wipe it off with . . . with . . . She looked at the table in front of her and at the bowl of small onions swimming in goat cream. Then she grinned, picturing the lout next to her at the high table with his pretty dark blond hair and godly features covered with the side dish which had accompanied the roasted lamb.

"First, you talk to yourself. Now, you grin to yourself. Tsk, tsk, tsk. How about sharing the joke, sweetie?"

She misliked the endearment "sweetie" almost as much as she objected to "Hildy," and the lout did it deliberately. "I was picturing you with a bowl of creamed onions on your head, upside down." She gave him a sugary smile.

"Isn't that a coincidence? I was picturing you, too. Without that dirty gown . . ."

She gasped.

"Get your mind out of the moat. I meant, in a clean gown of silk and fine wool, as I recall seeing you before."

She misdoubted that was what he'd meant.

"And I was picturing you without that sheep shit in your hair."

For the love of Frigg! She put a hand to her head. "Oh, you! I do not have . . . *that* in my hair."

He leaned closer to her, so close she could smell Effa's pine-scented soap on his skin. Peering closer, he said, "Ah, I must have been mistaken. It's just bits of wool and leaves and . . . What is this?" He picked something from her hair and laid it in front of her. It was a cream-coated onion.

"Oh, you!" She jabbed him in the arm. "I should have remembered your knack for sleight of hand games. But last time, 'twas a dead mouse you put in my hair."

"Me?" He slapped a hand on his chest with mock affront. "You have a long memory. But then, all women do."

"Your memory appears to be long, as well."

"Longer than you could imagine."

The last time Hilda had seen Torolf, she had been only eleven and he an almost adult at fourteen. He and his father and his brother Ragnor had come to visit her father at Deer Haven. A grand hunting party had been planned, but Torolf had stayed back at the lodge due to an injured ankle. That had given him the opportunity to pull one prank after another on Hilda.

"Dost recall the time you took me fishing, whilst the men went boar hunting?" She cast him a sideways glance while she idly picked apart a piece of manchet bread.

"And we both landed in the fjord, dripping wet." He laughed, and when he laughed his eyes, warm brown like clover honey, crinkled at the edges. "I built us a fire, though, handy fellow that I was . . . am."

"And then, rascal that you were, and no doubt still are, you talked me into removing my wet gunna whilst you took off your own wet garments. You promised not to look."

He was laughing out loud now.

How nice that she could still be the source of his amusement!

"And what makes you think that I did . . . look?"

"Because your brother Ragnor told me later that you said my breasts were so small they looked like bee stings."

"He didn't!" Reflexively, his gaze flitted over her bosom, as if he could see her breasts through the thick fabric . . . breasts that were still small, though bigger than bee stings now. "My apologies if I embarrassed you . . . then."

"Liar! You enjoy teasing me."

"Yep," he said without apology.

"Are you never serious?"

"You asked me that before. Yes, I am. But life is too short and full of so much pain." He shrugged.

"And that is why you take every opportunity to make merry?"

"I suppose. It's not a bad philosophy of life. Besides, in my opinion, God must have a sense of humor to have created men and women the way they are, with all our foibles."

"You speak the same language I do, and yet I fail to understand what you say by half."

"Okay, here's a good example of what I'm talking about. Consider Adam and Eve in the Garden of Eden. You've heard that biblical tale, right? Well, what's not to laugh about with good ol' stud muffin Adam being tempted by sexpot Eve? Toss in the apple and the snake, and it's damn funny." He was picking fleece out of her hair as he spoke, making a small pile on the table.

"The One-God of the Christians? That is who you are saying has a sense of humor?" she asked, disconcerted by his touching her, even if it was only her hair. She swatted at his hand, but he just moved to another part of her head.

"Uh-huh! Where I come from . . . the country where I now live . . . doesn't worship the Norse gods."

"Stop your wandering fingers!" She took his wrist and placed his hand on the table.

He just grinned. The lout!

"And what country is that?"

"America."

"Where is it?"

"Far away?"

"Too far for you to come back and help your countrymen . . . to help Madrene. And, by the by, where is Madrene now? Last I heard, she was in the Arab lands."

"Yes, America is too far away. Madrene is safe now with our father in America."

She nodded. "That is good." His explanation raised as many questions as answers, but they could wait. "How many wives have you in Ah-mare-eek-ah, Torolf?"

He laughed. "None."

"Have they all died? Or left you? Or did you cast them

aside?" *It was probably the latter. He is too comely by half and no doubt dipped his wick hither and yon, as his father had.*

"None of the above. I've never been married."

"Really? A man your age?"

"I'm not that old. I'm only thirty-one."

She arched her eyebrows. That was old enough to have had several wives. "And children?"

"Not that I know of."

"Is there something wrong with you?"

"Not that I know of."

"One of my husbands, Gudrod, had a problem getting his dangly part to do anything but . . . dangle."

Torolf choked on the mead he had been sipping from a wooden cup. "Hildy! No, I have no problem getting it up. I must say, I'm surprised at your bluntness."

"Well, 'tis the truth about Gudrod."

"So, you've been married?"

"Three times. After all, I am twenty and eight years old."

"That old, huh? Can I assume, since you're living like a nun here with your . . . uh, coven . . . that you're no longer wed?"

She nodded. "All dead. They were short-lived marriages."

"How short?"

Hilda could feel her face heat. How did they get on this subject? "Very short." She exhaled with a whooshy breath. "One died on the wedding night. The second died on the fifth night of our marriage. And Kugge lasted six months afore he also died . . . at night. Alas, all were straw deaths."

Straw deaths were abhorred by Viking men, who preferred to die in battle, guaranteeing a sure welcome to Valhalla.

But then he frowned with confusion. "They all died at night? Why is that relevant? And one of them on your wedding night . . ." His words trailed off as understanding seeped into his thick skull. "They died in bed with you?"

"I would rather not discuss this any further."

"It must have been awful for you, but I can't help but wonder. Hell, you must be something else in the bedsheets if you could knock off three husbands in the act. I'm impressed."

"Oh, please! They were old men. They could as easily have died of excessive snoring or breaking wind in bed."

He choked on his mead again. "How old?"

"Why do you care?"

"How old?"

"Fifty, sixty, and seventy, if you must know."

"And how old were you?"

"Aaarrgh! You are like a dog with a bone. Fourteen, sixteen, and twenty. And that is the end of it."

"Hildy, Hildy, Hildy." He sighed. "You deserved better."

"Yea, I did, but my lot was no different than many others. Better than some."

"I can't imagine you being so compliant. Agreeing to marry men you didn't choose."

"I was different then. A good daughter."

"And now?"

"Now, I do as I choose."

"And that choice is . . . no man?"

"Exactly. I have a roof over my head, food to eat, and blessed safety. There is much to be said for a peaceful life."

"What about passion? Doesn't sound like there's much passion in your life."

"I have passion for the land, for my ladies, for a self-sufficient living."

"That isn't the kind of passion I meant." He rubbed his chin with a forefinger thoughtfully. "Wait a minute. You said Kugge. Surely not Kugge Big Wart."

"Yea, the selfsame."

"Holy hell, Hildy. How could you stand to kiss him when that big wart was sticking out from the tip of his nose like a giant booger?"

She was fairly sure she knew what a booger was, and it would be an accurate description. "Kugge wasn't much for kissing." *Thank the gods!*

"That's a shame. Not a shame that you didn't have to kiss Kugge, but that you have been deprived of good kissing for such a long time. By the way, have I told you I am a very good kisser?"

"You are incorrigible."

"It's one of my best qualities."

"And the others?"

He grinned. "I don't know you well enough to tell you . . . yet."

Their conversation was cut short then by a bustle of activity just below them in the cleared area between the high table and long tables. To her amazement, Dagne was taking out her lute, something she had not done these past five years. Encouraging her was the young man named Geek. What an odd name! Sounded more like what a person said when stepping in sheep droppings. Geek had his leg in a splint, even though his knee was just sprained, not broken.

Dagne adjusted the strings and leaned her head down, checking the tones. Then she began to strum softly. Once the room was totally silent, except for the sizzling of the fires, the clack-clack-clacking of the hand loom being worked by one industrious weaver, and Frida clanging some pots in the scullery, she began to sing one of the old saga songs. It was the tale of two twins, Toste and Vagn Ivarsson. She told how inseparable these two twins were from birth, even when they went to war together, where they presumably died together. But each had been rescued and began different life journeys, each thinking his other half had long gone to Valhalla. In the end, the two brothers found each other again. It was a love story, of course, which held the women in thrall, even though most of them had heard it many times before, but it was also a poignant story of the love two brothers had for each other.

Hilda glanced at Torolf to see his reaction to the music. He appeared stunned, but then he stood and began clapping. His men did the same, and soon the women followed suit, realizing that the clapping showed their appreciation.

When Torolf sat back down and Dagne began another song, Hilda glanced at him, noting the serious expression on his face.

Sensing her scrutiny, he said, "I feel the same connection with my brother Ragnor who, you know, is the same age as I am, though we had different mothers. I suffered the same loss as those twins when we were separated for more than ten years."

Hilda decided that mayhap there was another side to Torolf. She wasn't altogether happy with that prospect. It would not do for her to be attracted to the rogue. As one of the old proverbs said, "If a rogue woos you, count your teeth." *Not that Torolf would ever woo me.*

"Your lips are moving. Are you talking to yourself again?"

She made a face at him. "Why are you here?"

"Steinolf."

She raised her eyebrows at him.

"I've come back to avenge my family honor and to rid our land of this heinous villain."

"How?"

"By killing the bastard and returning Norstead to its rightful people."

"And who would rule there? You?"

"Not if I can help it. I'll find someone to take my place. I intend to go back to America, if I can."

"Perhaps you are not aware of how powerful Steinolf is.

He has not only overtaken Norstead and Amberstead, but many other estates in the northwest."

Torolf was not pleased with that news, but then he shrugged. "Whatever. Steinolf is a dead man, that I promise."

Hilda's heart lightened at his words. "You cannot fight Steinolf with a mere five men . . . unless you have an army following you. Do you?" she asked hopefully.

"No, but we're Navy SEALs. I know it'll sound like bragging to you, but five of us can do what fifty men can, in the right circumstances." Seeing the confusion on her face, he added, "SEALs are elite forces with specialized talents for fighting."

"Like Jomsvikings or Varangians?"

"Sort of."

"How are your methods different?"

"Many ways. The weapons are different, we use strike and retreat guerrilla tactics. In essence, we use our heads as much as our brawn."

"Can you teach us those skills?"

"Huh? Who?"

"Us women. There are sixty of us here. Despite our poor performance earlier today, we train regularly and thus far have defended ourselves against invaders, though, truth to tell, our defenses have not been tested yet in any serious way."

"You want us to train a bunch of women how to use cooking ladles and shepherd's crooks as military weapons?"

"Do not patronize me. We have no men to defend us and do not want them for that purpose," she added quickly. "We must needs learn to defend ourselves better. Are there no women fighters in your new land?"

"Not in the SEALs, but, yeah, there are women soldiers."

She raised her hands, palms upward. "So why can you not help us?"

"I don't know. We really don't have much time. Maybe." He seemed to be considering the possibility, but then a mischievous twinkle came into his brown eyes . . . eyes that she had already decided were too pretty for a man. "What's in it for me?"

She stiffened. "You would want payment?"

He shrugged. "That's usually the way, isn't it?"

"We do not have much coin."

"I don't want or need money. And don't you dare offer me sheep or a goat." He was outright laughing at her now.

She studied the lout for a few minutes, and he studied her back. "You do not mean . . . oh, surely, you would not want me to share your bed furs?"

He was clearly shocked by her question. "Would you?"

She thought a moment. "Yea, but 'twould be an unfair bargain on your part. A few minutes of tupping in the bed furs in return for days and days of military training for us women."

"A few . . . a few minutes?" he sputtered.

"Yea," she said slowly, suspecting that she had stepped into some hole of his making.

"Number one, making love with a man should take more than a few minutes. Number two, I am rarely satisfied with one bout of *tupping*. Number three, you've been missing out on a whole lot in your life, sweetheart."

Her face felt hot as if she had been standing near a hearth fire. "Number one, do not call me sweetling. I am not your sweetling. Number two, how many bouts? Number three, how long each time?"

Torolf was shaking his head and laughing. She did not care. This was important business to her. They may never again get such an opportunity to learn military skills.

"Probably three or four times each night, and, oh, let's say an hour or two each time."

Her jaw dropped. "You cannot be serious."

"Hey, I'm virile."

"Your self-love is impressive."

On the other side of Torolf, the dark-haired man wearing a strange hat and gold ring in one ear, with the odd name of Cage, was blatantly listening in on their conversation, laughing so hard tears were brimming over in his eyes.

"You have my consent," Hilda said with disgust.

"Huh?" It was Torolf's turn to have his jaw drop.

"You may swive me for one night, dusk to dawn."

Torolf's jaw dropped farther, and the laughing rogue beside him said something that sounded like, "Way to go, dude!"

As she got up to go to the scullery and advise Frida on the meal to be served when the men broke fast in the morning, she heard Torolf murmur, "Oh . . . my . . . God!"

Praying . . . the lout is praying at a time like this. Truly, I do not understand men.

Chapter 5

MTV it was not . . .

Torolf watched Hilda walk away, head held high, hips swishing from side to side. If she only knew that he was watching her heart-shaped ass, she would have a fit . . . probably clomp him over the head with a cooking ladle.

"What a woman!" he murmured. She surprised him at every turn, especially the way she'd taken all the disasters that had come her way and risen above them. Steinolf hadn't defeated her and these other women . . . not totally. And Torolf couldn't help but admire that.

But offering to sleep with me? Holy shit! I was teasing, and she took me seriously. She's gonna kill me when she finds out.

In the distance outside, he could hear the dog, Stig, howling his opposition to being locked up. The animal had developed an unnatural attraction to his leg, much to the embarrassment of the women and the amusement of his buddies.

Hilda was talking now with another woman standing in the circle of people surrounding the lute player. He could tell by the way the other women deferred to Hilda that she held a place of great respect in this community.

"Hilda hoisted you on your own petard, my friend." Sitting beside him, Cage passed him another full cup of mead.

Torolf raised his mug to his friend. *"Skál!"*

"Ditto," Cage replied with a grin. "This stuff is great, by the way. Better than beer."

"Be careful. It's more potent. Its wallop can hit you like a grenade in a Taliban cave."

"Hey, after the day we've had, I deserve a wallop or two."

The guys still didn't believe that time travel had taken place. They honest-to-God thought this was some kind of loony reenactment place, like that pioneer village that Oprah went to one time. They probably hadn't thought it through yet; otherwise, they would've questioned the shipwreck and the missing people who'd been traveling with them and the unsettled terrain. He would have to set them straight soon.

"So, you gonna do the dirty with the nun-witch?" Cage asked with a big Cajun grin.

"Hell, no! I was just kidding. Threw me for a loop when she offered *that*. And I guarantee that these women are not witches. Definitely not nuns, either, by the way they're making moves on us."

"Yeah, isn't that great? Kinda nice to have the tables turned. Not that women don't hit on me all the time."

Something is fishy in paradise. Sex on a platter, no strings? Nope, I'm not buyin' it.

"Did ya know that some of these women have been here fer five years . . . without men?" Cage waggled his eyebrows at him. "And not even a vibrator available."

Torolf laughed. "Since when do you know women with vibrators?"

"You'd be surprised, big boy!" Cage took another drink

of mead. Like my maw maw allus says, 'Fer every old slipper there's another old slipper.' I think you and Hildy make a great pair."

Just great! Now I'm an old slipper. And Cage is back to the matchmaking crap again. "Why? Because she smells like sheep shit?"

Cage laughed. "You could hold your nose while she's holding your—"

"Enough! I'm not going to sleep with Hilda. I don't need to 'pay' to get laid."

"Does that mean we're not gonna teach these babes to fight?"

"I don't know." He rubbed his forehead with his hand. His head still ached, despite the good ministering and the "megrim powder" given to him by the resident healer, a woman missing her two front teeth. The whole time she'd been stitching the cut on his scalp, she'd been rubbing her voluminous breasts against his shoulder. Apparently, she eyed him as a potential bed partner.

Just then, he noticed Pretty Boy making his way through the crowd. All day he'd been bird-dogging Britta the Big, who didn't want anything to do with him. Probably playing hard to get, which would be a switch for Pretty Boy. Pretty Boy was talking to the lute player. Then the lute player stood, and he sat down.

"What? Does he think a lute is the same as a guitar?" Torolf asked.

"I guess so. They're both string instruments that ya pluck with the fingers. But I cain't imagine they'd sound the same," Cage said.

Pretty Boy played the guitar as a hobby. When he was blitzed, he sometimes went up on the stage at the Wet and Wild and joined the band in a few numbers.

"Sit down, everyone," Pretty Boy ordered. When many of them were sitting on the hard-packed dirt floor, he began to strum, experimenting with different strings. It didn't sound at all like a guitar, but it wasn't bad.

"I don't recognize that song. Do you?" Cage was into all kinds of music, especially Cajun. And dancing. Lordy, the boy could dance!

"Shiiit! That Pretty Boy is so freakin' smooth. How does he do it?" It was Geek speaking now as he came up and plopped down on a big chair on Torolf's other side.

Torolf and Cage gazed at Geek with frowns of confusion as Pretty Boy began to sing. Now they understood. He was singing Van Morrison's "Brown-Eyed Girl," and he was staring at Britta standing on the other side of the room. Slowly, everyone began to grasp that Pretty Boy was singing a love song to his girl—or who he hoped would be his girl—and they alternately swooned over his singing or craned their necks to see Britta's reaction. Pretty Boy would wear her down eventually. He always did.

"Yep. That boy is smoother'n gator spit." Cage grinned with admiration. "I thought I had smooth down to an art form, but he's got me beat by a bayou mile."

Torolf had to agree.

After that, Pretty Boy played a few country songs. "Your Cheatin' Heart" went over big with the ladies, who kept nodding their heads in agreement. Apparently, they'd met a few wandering boys in their day. Then he tried Ray Charles's "Hit the Road, Jack," which also rang a few memory bells in these babes. Willie Nelson's "Always on My Mind" had them swooning again. When he sang "Sixty Minute Man," the women didn't understand, but they liked the ballad nonetheless.

After a while, Cage stood, put his hands to his mouth, and yelled, "Hey, guitar man, how 'bout some dancin' music?" Then he turned to Torolf and Geek. "C'mon. We cain't let Pretty Boy take over this party."

Torolf declined, but Geek limped off with Cage. JAM was at the far end of the hall talking earnestly with some woman. Knowing him, they were probably discussing religion rather than her preference for bottom or top. JAM had been pretty serious with a schoolteacher a year or so ago. Torolf had no idea what happened, just that JAM told them it was over.

The party really took off then, as Cage and a limping Geek taught the women how to twist to that old Chubby Checker song, "Let's Twist Again." Then, "Shake It Up Baby." The women were shocked at first, especially when the guys encouraged them to "shake it on out," but then they gave it the old college try, and soon, after a number of lively songs, many of them mastered the moves of the twist.

Torolf wished his brother Ragnor were here to witness these Dark Ages ladies lifting the hems of their gunnas to do the twist. Not to mention shaking their bonbons like modern women did.

After they all made fools of themselves for a couple more songs, laughing like hyenas, Pretty Boy called out, "This is the last song, folks." Then he played a few chords, starting with the lyrics, "People say I'm the life of the party . . ."

Torolf laughed. That was a cue, if there ever was one, in light of Hilda's criticism of him earlier. He saw Hilda standing in the doorway that led to the kitchen and walked over to her. "Wanna dance?"

"Nay!" She looked at him as if he'd asked her to strip naked and do the hula.

Cage and Geek, even JAM now, were attempting to teach some women how to slow dance.

"C'mon, Hildy." He held his arms out to her.

"I do not dance."

"Are you afraid if you get close to me, you won't be able to resist my charms?"

Her damn-the-torpedoes blue eyes practically shot sparks at him, and she stepped forward into his arms, taking hold of his hands, instead of letting him hold her in a dance position. She must think they were going to slow dance a yard apart.

With a chuckle, he pulled her flush against his body and locked his hands behind her waist before she could shove him away, which she tried hard to do, muttering such endearments as "Big oaf!" "Loathsome lout!" "Arrogant son of a maggoty flea!"

"Hold still. I'm trying to teach you how to dance."

They swayed from side to side.

"This is not dancing. 'Tis nigh fornicating."

I know. That's the only reason most men dance. Foreplay. "That's how they dance in my country."

"I can hardly credit that. 'Tis scandalous."

Only when you struggle and rub your breasts against my chest.

Eventually, she relaxed. She even let him put her hands on his shoulders.

"I see you changed your clothes."

Hilda had combed her pale blonde hair and rebraided it into a single plait down her back. Her gown was plain drab brown, but clean. She was tall, slim, with a narrow waist and small breasts. In a pair of tight jeans and a tank top, she wouldn't look half bad, despite the lack of cleavage. She wasn't beautiful by any means. Her lips were too large for her face, and there was that slight space between her two front teeth.

He sniffed her neck. "You smell good." She had bathed. He recognized the same pine-scented soap he'd used earlier.

"I didn't do it for you," she said defensively. "Stop holding me so close."

You ain't seen nothin' yet, toots. "Stop complaining."

"Stop smelling my neck."

He laughed and licked the curve of her neck, which was exposed by the collarless gown. And surprised himself at how good it felt. Okay, not just good. He'd felt an erotic shock shoot from his tongue on her neck down to his most favorite body part. Amazing! He was getting turned on by good ol' Hildy.

She gasped with shock.

In Torolf's experience, it was always good to make a woman gasp once in a while. "I can feel your heart beating."

"No wonder. You're squashing me."

Liar! You're probably getting horny, too. Okay, maybe not horny, but slightly aroused. Okay, maybe not aroused. But not disgusted. That's something. "Are you listening to the lyrics of this song, Hildy? It's about a guy who's a clown on the outside, but inside he's crying."

She stopped struggling. "Are you crying inside?"

Hell, no! "Maybe."

"Are you going to start teaching us women how to fight on the morrow?"

He shrugged. "What would you do if I kissed you?"

"Do not dare. I agreed to let you tup me for a night. I ne'er agreed to any kissing."

Hilda, Hilda, Hilda! You do have a knack for stepping into my traps. "Didn't you know that kissing is part of . . . tupping?"

"Always?"

"Oh, yeah!"

"Is that another custom in your new land?"

"Yep!

"I never know when you are teasing and when you are telling the truth."

Thank God!

"Exactly where is this new land where you live?"

"I told you. America. Far, far away." *Like five thousand miles and a thousand years.*

She narrowed her eyes with suspicion. "Have you been hiding out in the Arab lands? Perchance with a harem of your own? Swiving everything in sight?"

Sonoma, California, is a long way from the Arab lands, although I have been in Iraq and Afghanistan lately. "I'm wounded that you have such a low opinion of me." *Actually, I'm more amused than anything.*

"'Tis not you precisely that I view in that manner, but all men who think with their dangly parts instead of their heads."

He just smiled. Hilda just blathered on, never realizing how some of the things she said came off.

"If not the Arab lands, then where is this Ah-mare-eek-ah?"

He hesitated, then leaned his head back so he could look at her. Pretty Boy had stopped playing, anyhow. "Do you want the truth?"

"Of course."

"I live a thousand years into the future now."

She made a snorting sound of disgust, obviously thinking that he teased again.

"I time-traveled."

She snorted again.

"Cross my heart and hope to die." He made the sign of the cross on his chest. "A dozen years ago, my family and I traveled into the future a thousand years. And now I have come back."

She shoved herself out of his arms. "You must consider me half-brained if you think I would believe such folly."

Torolf caught himself grinning as she stomped away. And that was really surprising to him, because he had thought he would be miserable if he came back to this primitive time.

I like Hilda. I really like her, he realized. Then almost immediately thought, *Uh-oh!*

How to Seduce a Man, Part I ...

Despite the late and unusual events of the night before, Hilda and her women were up before dawn starting their daily chores. The days were short this time of year in the Norselands, and they had to take advantage of the lessening daylight hours.

The debris left from the sheep work had to be cleaned up, and the groomed sheep driven up into the hills. Goats and chickens were fed, and the goats were milked. The cook was making porridge and the day's manchet bread; everyone would break fast after the initial chores were done. Elise went into the weaving shed and set her helpers to carding wool, spinning and weaving cloth. A half-dozen women were hauling deadfall limbs down from the mountain; a vast amount had to be cut into firewood for the hearths before the winter snows came. The sisters, Dissa and Dotta, were drying fish that had been caught two days before and strips of venison. Astrid was bringing in the last of the honey and the combs to be used later not just for a sweetening but also for mead and candles. Dagne and her helpers picked root vegetables ... onions, carrots, and turnips.

The men were up already, too. They were in the storeroom where Sigrun was attempting to find braies and tunics and belts that would fit them, along with ankle boots. Some of the women here were as tall of stature and bigfooted as men.

Hilda was hoping that the men would begin training them this afternoon, but she did not want to ask Torolf about it again, lest he bring up the bedding. Holy Thor! Why had she agreed to such a deal? *Because I had to, if we are ever to be able to defend ourselves once Steinolf comes.*

But first the women had requested that a Thing be held. Hilda had no doubt what the subject of discussion would be: the men. That's all the women had been chattering about all morning. She had no idea if any of them had actually mated with them yet, and she was not about to ask. She especially did not want to know if any had been with Torolf.

After everyone was seated in a circle, they dispensed with the reading of the laws by the law speaker, since they'd held a Thing such a short time ago.

"Who wants to speak first?"

Grima, the healer, stood. "There are nigh on sixty of us and only five of them. How are we going to divide them fairly?" One of Steinolf's men had knocked out her front teeth two years past when she'd failed to cure one of his warriors of the devil's disease of the manparts.

Hilda put her face in her hands. *Blessed Frigg! They think they can divide men up, as if they were apples.*

"We could take turns. Five at a time. If the men are still here after twelve days, and pray to the gods that they will be, then we can start the rotation over again. By the time they depart The Sanctuary, hopefully some of us will be increasing." This was the ever-logical Gunnvor speaking.

Five men swiving twelve women each? It sounds ridiculous, and yet I have known men who would do it in a trice.

"Where will the mating take place? Some men do it out in the open, like pigs rutting, but I for one want privacy." Hilda was shocked to hear Inge make this observation.

The others voiced their agreement.

"We could set aside places," fifteen-year-old Tofa suggested. "Like a corner of the weaving shed. A section of the storeroom. The goat byre. The guardhouse. That extra large sleeping closet. The scullery, if it is late at night."

Hilda's eyes widened with surprise. Where had those ideas come from in such a young girl?

"Yea, and we could put soft wool blankets and candles in those places," Elise suggested.

Son of a troll! How obvious can they be?

Hilda held up her arms for silence. "Slow down, ladies. You are making many assumptions here. For example, are there any of you who are not interested in coupling or breeding?"

A dozen women raised their hands, including herself and Britta.

"That is all well and good, but just because you all want to mate, that does not mean the men do. Men are a lust-some lot, to be sure. But dost not think the men should do the choosing?"

Some women were disgruntled, mainly those who were not very comely, but in the end, they all agreed that it was only fair that the men make the choice.

"But we can help them make that choice." It was Rakel speaking now. Rakel carried a mix of Viking and Saxon blood. Rumors said she had been a woman of easy virtue at one time, mayhap even concubine of a nobleman.

"How?" a number of women asked, believing that Rakel must know some secrets in the bedsport.

"Seduction," Rakel said bluntly.

The unskilled women looked at each other with dismay.

"I never knew how to flirt," Britta said, "and do not wish to learn now." In Hilda's opinion, Britta did not need to learn. The pretty man followed her around like a newborn pup. But then, Britta was among those who had decided not to have children.

"I have been too long away from society to remember how to flirt," Inge remarked. "Exactly how does one se-duce a man?"

"There are ways," Rakel said with confidence.

Oh, my gods and goddesses!

"There are ways to dress that would entice a man." Rakel ripped her gown at the neck, parting the material so the tops of her generous breasts were exposed.

The women listened to her intently, no doubt planning to alter their apparel once they left the Thing.

Hilda looked down at her almost flat chest and grimaced. She would never be able to entice a man.

"And you should walk a certain way to entice a man." Rakel demonstrated by arching her shoulders back and swishing her hips from side to side as she strutted across the clearing.

Hilda put a hand to her mouth to stifle a giggle. The men would think all her women had gone barmy if they walked thus.

"Bend over in front of them betimes. Some men like a shapely arse." Rakel bent over at the waist and aimed her backside at the group.

Never, ever would Hilda do that. Not purposely.

"Bat your eyelashes, like this. And give them sultry glances with your lids half-shuttered."

How absurd! Half of them are looking cross-eyed.

"Most of all, there is the art of good bedsport. How many of you have tried tongue kissing?"

Chapter 6

Where was Juan Valdez when you needed him? . . .

"Can y'all believe it? There isn't a drop of coffee in this whole damn place," Cage griped early that morning. "Honest to God, a Cajun cannot live without his chicory fix."

Little do you know, my friend. There is a whole lot more missing than meets the eye.

"My back is killing me. Men were not designed to sleep on hard wood benches." It was Pretty Boy complaining now.

"Did any of you notice that there isn't one single book here, not even a Bible?" That was JAM, of course.

Stop complaining. You have that miniature Bible that you always carry in your back pocket.

"And the head is outside. Shiiit! I do not like freezing my ass when I take a whizz. But you know, something isn't quite right here." Geek was studying the interior of the great hall where they were sitting like it was a specimen under glass.

Wait till he goes into computer shock. I can't imagine our resident genius laptop-deprived.

"I kind of like it here," Pretty Boy said.

They all snickered at that remark.

"Forget conveniences. I told Britta that she doesn't need to use a shredded twig for a toothbrush. Everyone knows that kissing keeps the teeth white and healthy. Yep, tonsil hockey encourages saliva to wash food from the teeth. It even lowers the level of acid that causes teeth to decay and get plaque."

"Fuckin A!" Cage saluted Pretty Boy. "Here's to saliva!"

"Unbelievable," JAM commented. "Where do you come up with this shit?"

"What did Britta say to that baloney?" Geek wanted to know.

"Oh, well, she told me to go kiss the backside of a sheep."

Pretty Boy joked a lot about Big Mama, but Torolf saw something more. He'd fallen hard for her. In fact, they could be in a cave, and Pretty Boy wouldn't object, as long as his personal Amazon was there.

They sat down on two sides of a long table, at the far end of the hall, waiting for breakfast. A huge fire blazed in the hearth, providing welcoming heat on this cool autumn day and some light. Even in daytime, the hall was dark and dreary.

If they're expecting hotcakes, ham, eggs, and buttered toast, they are sure gonna be surprised. More like unsweetened gruel, except maybe for honey, and dry manchet bread, if they're lucky.

"Let's cut the crap here, *cher*," Cage said, patting him on the shoulder, "Joke's over. I fer one have had enough playacting, as if we're freakin' Vikings. When do we go home?"

"Yeah, this is taking reenactment to a new level," JAM agreed, wiping his fingers with distaste over the tabletop to remove some of the ash from the fire. You could say JAM was a bit anal about cleanliness. In fact, he had a cleaning lady come to his Coronado apartment twice a week, and he lived alone. *How much dirt could one man make?*

"My family went to one of those time capsule kind of villages when I was a kid," Pretty Boy said, "except it was Colonial, like Williamsburg, and people stayed there for vacations and pretended they were really back in time. Some vacation! My brother Danny and I got the only spanking of our lives for putting a bag of salt in the communal kettle of porridge."

"My dad took me on one of those trail rides when I was ten. You know, like *City Slickers*. My mom had just died, and he wanted to cheer me up." Now this was something. JAM rarely talked about his childhood. "I never ate so many baked beans in all my life . . . on tin plates. I always wondered . . . Did cowboys have permanent gas with all those beans they ate? I mean, really, do you think Roy Rogers farted in front of Dale Evans?"

They all grinned at that image.

"I'm confused about one thing. The language," Cage said. "I can tell that these ladies are speaking a different language, but I can understand them perfectly."

Torolf nodded. "One reason might be that Old Norse is similar to modern Icelandic, and we all took the short course in Icelandic before we went there last year. Old Norse isn't at all like Norwegian today. Even a thousand years ago, though, there were enough similarities between the Viking and Saxon languages that people could speak to one another."

"How do you explain the women being able to understand us?" Pretty Boy asked.

Torolf shrugged. "A miracle?"

"Seriously, Max, you've made yer point," Cage said.

"All that Viking crap yer always spoutin' . . . we get it now. Life was hard, yada, yada, yada. Now, let's go home."

They are not going to believe me about the time travel. Not yet. "I want you to help me get rid of Steinolf first."

"For real?" Pretty Boy asked.

"For real. He's as bad a motherfucker as those crazies who took down the twin towers. He's terrorized most of the people in this region. If someone doesn't stop him, he's going to take over all the Scandanavian countries. I'm not going home till he's dead meat, along with his sadistic followers."

"Okay, we stay till Steinolf is gone. Right, guys?" Cage looked at each guy in the group, individually. They all nodded.

"What do we use for weapons?" JAM asked. They were all sharpshooters, to some extent.

"Necessity is the mother of invention and all that. Yeah, we have no night vision goggles, or thermal imaging, or a boatload of weapons, but we'll improvise." He pulled the KA-BAR knife out of his boot. "This is all I have."

The other guys had knives, too, and JAM had a ninja throwing star.

"Any of you good at archery?"

Cage and Geek raised a hand.

"I doubt if any of you have used a broadsword, but all you really need to know is how to swing it in an arc to lop off a head or slice off a limb. Aim for the neck."

They all gave him a look of wonder.

"I can use a slingshot really well," Cage offered. When Pretty Boy elbowed him with a chuckle, he added. "Hey, don't knock it. I can down a rabbit at fifty feet with a slingshot. I even downed a bear one time, but then I had to finish it off with a bowie knife."

"You are so full of shit," Pretty Boy said with a laugh. "You had me till that bear bit."

"Okay, so I knocked off rabbits, not bears. Same thing."

"In what world?" Pretty Boy countered.

"Enough, guys! We can make some other weapons," Torolf concluded. Besides, he didn't need to tell these experienced SEALs that in the best battle no shots were fired. He doubted they would be able to claim that for Steinolf's gang when all was done. In fact, he wasn't leaving till the bastard was lying in his own blood. Suddenly, Torolf went stiff and wide-eyed.

"What?" everyone asked as one. SEALs were alert to the least change in one of their teammates. They even knew each other's scent.

"Sonofabitch! It's the damn dog again." He swung his right leg out from under the table and over the bench. Stig was clinging to his leg like a SEAL trainee hugging the greased pole on the grinder in BUD/S. He limped to the door with the stupid dog hanging on, then he pushed it outside.

When he got back and the guys were done laughing their asses off at his expense, the pragmatic Geek asked, "How far are we going to have to travel? And is that longship salvageable?"

"Feet on the ground all the way," he replied. "As for distance, I'm not sure. As little as ten miles, up to twenty."

They all nodded. Traveling by foot was no problem for a SEAL. They often ran thirty miles a day, just for exercise.

"As for the longship, I'll check it out, but I'm not so sure we want to use it. Too visible."

They nodded at this, too. SEALs preferred to travel under cover, usually at night. But then they had night goggles.

"Okay, then, we're good to go. If all goes well, we should be back home within two weeks, sipping suds at the Wet and Wild."

"Hoo-yah!" they all chanted.

Geek, who sat on Torolf's other side, looked at him

strangely when the others began to talk about some of the women here who had been hitting on them and counting how many condoms they had among them. "This isn't make-believe, is it?"

Torolf hesitated. "No, this is the real thing."

Geek made a clucking sound of acceptance.

"You believe me?"

"I don't know. I need to investigate more. All I know is . . . this is too authentic. Most of all, the thing that boggles my mind and convinces me something is askew is the language situation. I know they are speaking Old Norse, and we all understand them. I know *we* are speaking English, and they understand us. Either we have died, we have landed in some futuristic society where people have implanted translators, or we really have time-traveled to the past by some miracle of God or scientific method I'm unaware of."

"And how do you feel about that? The time travel?"

A slow grin spread over Geek's face. "Cooool!"

Who were these men . . . warriors or lackbrains? . . .

Hilda left the courtyard finally, as the women continued with their seduction lessons and the divvying up of the men.

This was an absolutely ridiculous and pathetic effort on their part. But she could not blame them. Their goal was an admirable one . . . to have children. And she had to admire them as well for being receptive to bedplay after most had all been ill-used in that regard in the past.

She ran into Torolf in the corridor leading from the great hall to the scullery. Her head had been down, and she'd been muttering, when she hit his hard chest.

"Whoa!" he said, taking her by the upper arms so she would not fall. "What's your hurry, sweetie? And what are you muttering about?"

"You do not want to know."

He cocked his head in question. "Does it have anything to do with the meeting you women have been conducting outside?"

"You do not want to know."

"Does it have anything to do with me, or the other guys?"

"Yea, unfortunately."

"Tell me."

She shook her head. "You'll find out soon enough."

He took her hand, linking her fingers with his, and tugged her forward. "C'mon. My men and I need some intel from you about Steinolf so we can plan our attack."

"Attack? You are going to attack? Have you taken leave of your senses? There are only five of you. I thought you were going to work on defensive methods of fighting."

"It's what we SEALs do best in covert operations. Hit the ground running and shooting. Swoop in. Strike. Then leave. Guerilla warfare to the max."

"I have ne'er heard of such."

"Better to fight than sit on your ass. Not your ass precisely, I meant asses in general." He grinned.

What a lout! "If we are going to discuss battle tactics, Britta should join us."

"I agree." They were in the hall now, and Torolf yelled out to the men, who were sitting at a far table before one of the hearths, "Yo, Pretty Boy! Can you bring Britta to join us?"

Pretty Boy grinned as if Torolf had asked him to hunt a boar, or swive a maid.

Men! Hilda sat down at the table, and Torolf plopped himself next to her, way too close with his thigh and hip pressing against hers. With a glower, she moved a bit. He just moved after her. *Always teasing!*

"You know Geek, Cage, and JAM," he said.

Each of the men inclined his head to her.

On the tabletop, something had been scrawled with a stick of charred wood. "This is a rough map, showing our present location, where Norstead and Amberstead are located, and some of the other estates in northwest Norway, including the Vestfold," Torolf explained.

She studied it with a frown.

"I know that some of it may be wrong. I haven't been here for a long time. We're hoping you . . . and Britta . . . can make corrections and additions."

She nodded.

Just then there was a loud commotion coming from the courtyard. A man laughing. A woman squealing.

It was Pretty Boy, carrying Britta across his shoulder like a sack of wheat, her legs kicking at his chest and her hands pounding at his back. "Behave, Britta," he said with a laugh and placed a palm directly over her bottom. That brought sudden silence and stillness from Britta.

Hilda was shocked. Pretty Boy was tall and slim, though muscled well enough, but Britta was a big woman. She doubted Britta had been picked up by anyone since she was a babe.

"Good Lord, Pretty Boy, what're you doing?" Torolf exclaimed.

The other men were chuckling, not at all surprised by Pretty Boy's actions.

"You asked me to bring my sweetheart, and I did." He set Britta down on the bench across from Hilda and Torolf, right up against Cage, then quickly set himself down on her other side so that she was bracketed by the two men.

"I didn't tell you to carry her here to discuss battle plans," Torolf said.

"She resisted."

"You . . . you did not tell me why you wanted me to come here, you horse's arse," Britta sputtered. "And I am no more your sweetling than . . . than some horse's arse.

By the by, you are not pretty to me. Nay, you are homely as a warthog. Homely as a pudding face. Homely as—"

"Whatever you say, sweetheart. You are so cute when you're pissed off at me," Pretty Boy replied. "And by the way, my real name is Zach, if you get tired of calling me Pretty Boy."

"Cute? A newborn cat is cute. A chick is cute. You must be blind. Not me. And stop looking at me like that."

"Like what?"

"Like I am cream and you are the cat."

Hilda put her face in her hands. Yestereve she had bemoaned her spiraling loss of control here at The Sanctuary. Now it appeared she had not only lost control but was in the midst of a maelstrom of chaos.

"Don't worry, Hildy," Torolf whispered into her ear. "Everything will work out."

She gave him a sideways glance of disbelief and just then realized that he was still holding her hand. With an exhalation of disgust, she pulled her hand away.

He just grinned.

"Are we agreed that I'll be the OIC?" Torolf asked. At her and Britta's obvious confusion, he elaborated, "Officer in charge. Leader."

Torolf, a leader? How . . . surprising!

After that, Britta and Hilda worked to perfect the map on the table.

"Wouldn't it be a lot easier to just use paper?" Cage asked.

She and Britta both raised their eyes from the table.

"He means parchment," Geek explained. "And I suspect you have none here." Geek and Torolf exchanged glances that seemed to have some significance.

"How many men do you figure that Steinolf has at each of those locations?" JAM asked.

"Perhaps two hundred at Norstead, a hundred at Amberstead, and fifty or so at each of these other smaller estates. He also has a fleet of at least ten longships raiding along the coastlines, and those have fifty men each," Britta said. "He winters at Norstead."

Geek appeared to be calculating the numbers in his head.

"You do not appear daunted by those numbers," Hilda observed to Torolf.

"That isn't a huge force, considering how many estates he's invaded. Plus, it's splintered. Isn't he absorbing the vanquished soldiers into his ranks?"

"Nay. He either kills them on the spot, tortures and then kills them, or a fortunate few flee into the hills."

"Hmmmm." Cage tapped his chin thoughtfully. "I wonder if there are friendlies . . . people who would join our cause?"

"Yep. Force multiplication," Torolf agreed. Special forces did it all the time in Third World countries that the U.S. wanted to help maintain a democracy, like Afghanistan, Iraq, Bosnia. They taught the indigenous people to protect themselves.

"Possibly," Britta said, "but we have been reluctant to seek them ourselves for fear of capture. In truth, how would we know the friend from foe?"

"We've got to set up a mission plan," Torolf said.

"What kind of plan?" Britta was still skeptical.

"Mission analysis. Development of alternative courses of action. Intelligence. Specific course-of-action and tasking of personnel. Planning and more planning. Briefings. Rehearsals."

"Methinks you all think too much," Britta observed. "All wind and no sails."

"I've got wind . . . and sails," Pretty Boy told her.

"Blow the other way then," Britta replied.

To the group, Pretty Boy said, "I think she likes me."

These men, especially Torolf, were forever making jests.

"Timing is everything," Torolf told Britta. "A good beginning is half the work."

"But there are so many of them and so few of us," Hilda pointed out.

"An army of sheep led by a lion could defeat an army of lions led by a sheep."

"After handling dozens of smelly, dirty, dumb sheep yestermorn, I hope you are not likening us women to sheep," Hilda said with a surprising stab at humor.

"Never underestimate a Navy SEAL," Torolf told her, as if that made any sense to her. "Cunning is always better than strength. But cunning with strength, ah, that's the best."

"Will you be helping me train the women here?" Britta addressed Torolf.

"We can start this afternoon and continue every afternoon. By the time we go active, we should have had at least a dozen training sessions. Not enough, but it'll have to do."

"This is gonna be only the most basic training," Pretty Boy told Britta with more seriousness than he'd previously used around her before. "Navy SEALs come into training with very buff bodies and a fair amount of skills. It takes three years of training to make them what they are today, and even then we need to continue training on a regular basis."

Britta's mouth was agape at first, but then she clicked it shut and asked, "Am I supposed to be impressed by that?"

"Hopefully," Pretty Boy replied with a laugh, and then pinched her backside for good measure, which caused Britta to pinch his backside back.

"Oh, baby, I love it when you touch my ass."

Several serving maids carried food to their table then so they could break their fast. The other women were streaming into the hall, as well, to eat their first meal of the day. They all stared down at their group with interest but knew not to approach unless given permission by Hilda.

On their table was day-old manchet bread, porridge, cheese, and chunks of leftover lamb, with goat's milk for washing it down. Even a bowl of creamed onions, which Torolf looked at, then turned and winked at Hilda, recalling her comment of the night before.

The men began to eat with gusto, helping themselves to liberal amounts of the various dishes.

"What is this?" JAM asked, sniffing at the cheese. "God! It smells worse than Limburger."

"Gammelost," Torolf said with a laugh. "Legend says that gammelost contributed to King Harald Fair-Hair's victory at the battle of Hafrsfjord more than a hundred years ago. He supposedly fed his warriors gammelost for lunch prior to battle, thus turning them into berserkers."

"It smells like it could walk by itself," JAM said, his nose turned up with distaste. "And I prefer to go berserk on my own, thank you very much."

They all laughed, and no one protested when the dish was shoved down the table, away from them.

After the meal, Torolf took Hilda's hand again and urged, "Come, walk with me. I have some questions that need answers."

"Ask me here?"

"No."

"Why?"

"I want to be alone with you . . . when I ask."

Chapter 7

When testosterone has a mind of its own . . .

Torolf and Hilda walked hand in hand—he had a death grip on their linked fingers—down the motte and toward the fjord where the longship had wrecked.

Her blasted dog, Stig, nipped at his heels the whole time, till the beast spotted a squirrel in the distance and practically did somersaults trying to catch it. At least it kept his doggie mind off Torolf's leg.

Torolf liked holding hands with Hilda. He wasn't sure why. Because he enjoyed irritating her? Yeah, that was part of it. But he also had this melting sort of sensation in the region of his heart as his callused palm pressed against her callused palm. He fancied that the pulse beats at their wrists blended into one rhythm. All this was new to Torolf. And scary.

Sex was usually tops on his agenda with women. He didn't have female friends, just work acquaintances. There were no female SEALs, but they did work with military personnel from other units, including women. In his personal life, he usually gravitated toward women who liked a good time. Mutual enjoyment. No strings. He wasn't a love 'em and leave 'em kind of guy. He just never stuck around that long. But Hilda? *Dangerous thinking, man! Very dangerous.*

She would probably hit him upside the head if she knew what he was thinking. Actually, most women would whack most men if they knew what they were really thinking when they asked, "What are you thinking, honey?" *Hah!* "About nailing your sweet ass to the wall, that's what I'm thinking, *honey.*" *Aliens must have stolen my brains—or else my brains got lost in the time warp—for me to be having these kinds of thoughts in the presence of good ol' Hilda.*

The cold autumn breeze picked up, causing them both to shiver momentarily. She wore a long wool cape. Drab brown, as usual. He wore a Navy SEAL lined windbreaker over his Viking-style tunic and jeans. *Perhaps I'll set a new trend here in the Norselands. Change fashion history and all that.*

"You're smiling again."

He squeezed her fingers. "I'm happy. Is there anything wrong with that?"

"Yea, there is, when there is naught to be happy about."

"I don't know about that. I'm alive. I'm young. Oh, don't look at me as if I'm ancient. Thirty-one isn't old in my country."

"Why do you keep saying that? *This* is your country."

"It *was*, but you're right. I may not be able to leave here again, and if that happens, I've got to get used to thinking of this as my homeland again. God forbid! I've become used to bodily comforts."

"You speak in riddles."

"That's because you're not ready to hear the truth."

Without releasing her hand, he sank down to the ground,

taking her with him. The remains of the longship still sat in the shallow water up against a crude stone-and-tree dam, but many of the loose pieces had already floated down the fjord toward the North Sea. The dam was a primitive engineering marvel, really, with a large wood door in the center that could be opened and shut with a rope pulley system to regulate the flow of water.

"Who built the dam?" he asked.

"We did. One stone and one limb at a time. It took us two years and many cuts and bruises, but we finally managed to obstruct the flow of waters from the mountain. There is still a thin stream, of course, but it only results in an ankle-high depth now. Of course, we must continually work to maintain it."

He could see that this was a bare-bones defensive tactic, which would have to be continually kept up. It wouldn't stop committed invaders, but it would certainly slow them down. "Where does the mountain runoff go now?"

"We diverted it so that it runs through that wooded area over there and emerges farther down the fjord."

"I can't imagine how you women managed that hard labor."

She raised her eyebrows at him.

"Don't get your tail in a twist. I would've said the same thing to a man." Actually, he wouldn't have, but that was beside the point. "Tell me about yourself and the other women here."

"What? All sixty of us?"

"I want to know the history of each of you so I can best judge how to use your talents in fighting Steinolf. There may be weak links here that even you are not aware of."

Little by little, she discussed the women who had come to her. Not all of them, but many.

"You should be proud of yourself for giving sanctuary to so many."

She shook her head vehemently. "Each of us builds on the strength of the others. I may have provided the initial keep, but I could not have done this on my own."

"You do know that Steinolf could take this place with little effort if he really tried, don't you?"

At first, she bristled. Then her shoulders slumped. "Mayhap we are not as safe as we would hope."

"What precisely do you want? If you could defeat Steinolf, what then?"

She pondered for several moments. "Each of the battered estates to be restored and returned to its people. An Althing held to establish laws—fair laws—to be administered to all the people in those regions, as a whole, not separately. A return to peaceful ways. Farming, trading, everyday living without the threat of constant war."

He smiled. "And would there be no adventuring in this perfect world? The men . . . would they go a-Viking no more?"

She smiled back at him.

That melty sensation in the region of his chest turned hot and moved lower.

"Men will be men," she conceded.

Oh, yeah! Even me! He leaned forward so Hilda wouldn't look at his lap. *Holy shit! What a time to get turned on!*

"I doubt anyone could prevent a Norseman from going a-Viking when the season comes."

With more calm than he felt, he asked, "How about you? Would you go back to Amberstead? Marry again?"

"Pfff! I will never wed again. Three times is enough. If I can find a good man to take over there, I will not return. There is naught for me there anymore."

"What would you do?"

"Stay here. I find that I like helping other women."

"Hmmm. It would be like running a women's shelter in my time . . . uh, country."

"Yea, that is what The Sanctuary is. A shelter for women."

"Commendable . . . but lonely."

"How can I be lonely when I am never alone here?"

"Come on, Hildy. You know what I mean."

A pink bloom filled her cheeks, and she glanced away. "Men always think that women have this great need for them."

"Some . . . most women do," he said gently, using the forefinger of his free hand to tip her chin toward him.

"I am not most women. Dost think I am unnatural because I do not crave the mating . . . because I do not crave *you*?" She was angry now, as well as embarrassed.

Wow! Talk about a loaded question! "No, not unnatural. Just . . . untested."

"Oh, you are such an arrogant lout. Let me guess. You are the one who would test my resolve. I do not think so."

"Hildy, shut up."

"What?"

"Shut up," he repeated, yanking her closer to him. She was too surprised at first to protest. "I'm going to kiss you."

"Nay, you are not," she said, but she had stopped struggling. Probably curious.

Curiosity killed the cat . . . and apparently the SEAL, too, he thought with irreverent, self-deprecating humor.

The blasted dog came back and sniffed at his lap, but he shooed him away with a wave. Luckily, this time the stubborn animal did as he was told. *God must be on my side. No, not God. He would not condone what I'm contemplating. Would he?*

Still holding her left hand with his right, he used his left hand to cup her nape and tug her even closer. She smelled like pine soap and cold skin, and he was so hot for her his body trembled. He had gone from mildly interested to horny as hell in record time, even for him. As he prepared to settle his lips on hers, he noticed that her blue eyes, now the color of a Norse fjord on a summer day, were wide open and staring at him with incredulity. He laughed against her lips and said, "Shut your eyes, sweetheart."

She did, her brown eyelashes fluttering closed like fans against her pale cheeks.

And then he kissed her.

His downfall.

They came to a meeting of the minds . . . uh, lips . . .

The lout was about to kiss her.

Just before he touched his mouth to hers, he licked her bottom lip. The shock of that small gesture curled like wildfire and shot through her whole body, which caused her to part her lips with surprise. Thus, when he kissed her, her mouth was open, as was his.

For the love of Frigg, people did not kiss with their mouths open. Did they? Oh, they must . . . *they must . . .* because it felt so bloody good.

He moaned.

She whimpered.

The kiss deepened as he shaped her mouth with his, and then, she could not believe it, but he slipped his tongue inside her mouth, then out again, then in again. *Ah! So, this is the tongue kissing Rakel alluded to.* Every part of her body went on alert. Her heart raced. Her nipples pearled. Her lower belly thrummed. There was a sensual pooling between her legs. She felt as if she was being sucked into warm quicksand. She had to struggle to the surface, but she could not.

She was about to tell him nay, to stop this nonsense when she realized two important, alarming facts. She was lying flat on her back with the lout leaning over her, and her tongue was in the lout's mouth. How did that happen?

"Nay," she murmured, jerking her face to the side.

"Shhh," he said, blowing in her ear.

She jerked upward at the intense pleasure his breath brought to her ear, of all places.

The lout used that opportunity to slip his arms under her and arrange himself on top of her, resting on his elbows.

"Have you lost your mind?"

"Yes, I think I have." His mouth was wet from kissing her, and his eyes, now the color of the darkest amber, were slumberous with desire. He renewed his kissing then, but now it was with a wild hunger that frightened and thrilled her at the same time. He undulated his hips so that his hardness hit her woman's center. In a haze of passion unlike any she'd ever experienced before, she heard Torolf swear, "Go away. Dammit! Go away."

Opening her eyes, she saw that Stig was straddling Torolf's leg, humping the back of his thigh.

She wanted to laugh and cry at the same time. Laugh at the idiocy of the dog and cry that she had put herself in this ignominious position.

Realizing that the moment was lost—*thank the gods!*— Torolf raised himself, swore at the dog, and sat down beside her, his face resting on arms crossed over his upraised knees. He was panting like a warhorse.

Once she stood and straightened her clothing, she looked down at him, speechless for the moment. *How could he? How could I?* "You must think I am a wanton."

He raised his head and looked at her. "Hardly." After he stood and glowered at the dog, who sat at his feet, tongue lolling in adoration, he turned to her. "I'm sorry. I shouldn't have done that."

She turned her back on him and walked as proudly as she could under the circumstances back to the keep.

From several paces back, he yelled, "I take that back. I'm not sorry. I liked kissing you. A lot."

She refused to look back at him to see if he was teasing

or not. To Hilda's way of thinking, this was the worst thing she had done since she'd put saltpeter in her third husband's mead, which may or may not have contributed to his death.

"But don't think that because I like to kiss you that you're going to trap me," he said, coming up closer behind her.

She stopped and turned slowly. "And why would I want to trap you?"

"To stay here. No offense, honey, but I'm outta here once Steinolf bites the dust." In a lower voice, he added, "If I'm able to leave."

"Let me understand. You think that I am so charmed by your bloody kisses that I will be begging you to stay with me."

He had the grace to blush at her words. "Well, you did kiss me back."

She bared her teeth and fisted her hands till the nails bit into the flesh. *Do not rise to the lout's bait. Do not claw his eyes out. Do not scream.* With the most restraint she'd ever garnered, she turned again and proceeded to walk away from him briskly.

He caught up with her again. This time he was beside her before he spoke. "I said that all wrong."

"I should say so."

"It's just that . . . well, a lot of women get ideas, and—"

"And you thought I was like all your other women? For a certainty, you are not inclined to meekness."

"Dammit, Hilda, I didn't say you were like other women. And I don't have any women in my life currently."

She laughed at his thickheadedness. "Currently?"

"I haven't had a lot of women. That's what I meant."

"Oh? Define 'a lot'?"

He blushed again.

She rather liked making the lout blush.

"What I don't need in my life right now is a high-maintenance woman."

"And I am high maintenance? Well, who asked you to maintain me? Dost think I cannot maintain myself?"

"Stop twisting my words. Bottom line, babe, we aren't going to kiss again . . . or anything else. That way there will be no misunderstandings or hard feelings."

Ooooh, he makes me so angry. She stopped again, put her hands on her hips, and gave him her most cynical smile. "Do you not think you should wait till you are asked afore setting these restrictions? Furthermore, if I decide there will be kissing, there bloody damn hell will be kissing." With that, she raised herself on her tiptoes, pressed herself closer to his body, and . . . licked his lips.

It was with the greatest of pleasure that she heard him swearing under his breath as she stomped away.

GI Janes they were not . . .

Torolf surveyed the exercise area, a hard-packed dirt space in the bailey the size of a football field, where he and his men were trying to teach the women how to fight. They were aiming for a primitive replica of the O-course on the grinder back at Coronado. Instead, it was like a bad Monty Python parody of military training.

The women were divided into six groups with different Close Quarter Defense exercises taught by each of the SEALs. By the end of the day, each group should have gone through the different evolutions at least twice. Archery; knife and lance throwing; slingshotting; karate; free climbing; silent kills, like garroting; and regular PT.

One of the CQD exercises, which Pretty Boy had just finished, taught the women how to roll with the blows, which was a joy to watch. Not! Lots of people didn't realize that soldiers—good soldiers, like SEALs—needed to learn to bounce well when hit. It was called "taking the beat." If a soldier allowed himself to be slammed to the ground, a leg or other body part could be broken. Plus, it placed them in a vulnerable position.

Geek was teaching archery at the far end of the field. Some of the women weren't too bad, but there were arrows sticking out of the palisade wall, the eave of the keep's roof, a wooden wheelbarrow, and various other places. An enraged Elise, a weaver, had even got an arrow in the butt, which ended her exercises for the day. And Stig and his latest girlfriend, a mangy black dog with fleas, had run off, whimpering, when one of the arrows had barely missed them rutting near the drawbridge.

Behind him, Pretty Boy was starting another evolution of PT. First, he had them doing push-ups in sets of ten. "Drop! Down one, down two, down three. Recover. Now drop again. Down one. Down two. Come on, ladies. Push 'em out!" They were the most miserable push-ups Torolf had ever seen, even from women.

"It's better to sweat in training than bleed in war," Pretty Boy told them.

One woman, about five feet tall with a butt the size of an artillery target, retorted huffily, "Methinks ye are getting too much joy from our woman-sweat. Methinks it turns you lustsome seeing us wimmen bendin' and stretchin' our female parts."

Pretty Boy, not missing a beat, replied, "Oh, yeah, honey, that churns my butter, all right." Then Pretty Boy changed to a simple toe touching exercise in rotations of twenty. At that point, a disgusted Frida, the cook, who had to weigh two hundred pounds, swore in Norse and told Pretty Boy, "If the gods wanted me ta touch me toes, they would have put them on me knees." With that, she stomped off to her kitchen.

Pretty Boy laughed at Frida's abrupt departure and said,

"Hey, ladies, remember: the only easy day was yesterday."

To which, one woman yelled, "Yesterday I was wrestling sheep to ground. Naught is harder than that. You want to wrestle?"

"Not right now, sweetheart. Maybe later."

Cage had set up a target on a tall evergreen tree outside near the forest. He was instructing a group of women in knife-throwing, telling them how to aim for the fat line on a man: that area between the neck and the groin, where all the vital organs were located. Plus, they had constructed homemade slingshots and were practicing with those, too. He was having more success than some of the others with his lessons.

Earlier, Torolf had hacked the narrow side limbs off of the straight trunk of a pine tree and taught a group of women in braies how to free-climb so that hopefully they would be able to gain quick access to the upper ramparts of Norstead and Amberstead. They were all going to have cuts and splinters in their hands by nightfall and black-and-blue butts from their numerous falls.

JAM was doing defensive moves: karate, Tae Bo, that kind of thing, including the throwing star. "Come on, Max. Let's show them how to react when danger comes on you suddenly, and you don't have a weapon handy."

A dozen sets of eyes watched closely as he approached.

JAM said, "Pretend I'm approaching Steinolf's keep, turning left and right, surveying the area carefully, but this creep comes up behind me."

"What is a creep?" one woman asked.

"Bad guy," JAM answered.

JAM pretended to be walking forward, glancing right and left, when Torolf came up behind him and wrapped an arm around his neck, pressing a knife into his back. JAM twisted and had him flying over his head, landing on his back. The women gasped in surprise, but it was no big deal. This was a maneuver they practiced over and over in PT.

"Now, let's suppose we are approaching each other directly, both of us armed . . . in this case, with knives," JAM said.

He and JAM walked warily toward each other. In a blink, Torolf had lifted a leg and karate-kicked JAM in the gut. When JAM bent slightly to get his breath, Torolf used his foot to hook him behind the knees and bring him to the ground. In less than a second, he had JAM on his back, with his hands held over his head with one fist, and a knife to his neck.

" 'Tis unfair fighting that way," one woman said.

"Lady, there's nothing fair about war," JAM replied.

"We could never learn to do that," one woman complained.

"Yes, you could. These maneuvers are taught in women's self-defense classes all the time. Let's partner up and practice a few exercises."

Torolf's eyes connected with Hilda's at the edge of the group, just as she swiveled and began to leave. When she glanced over her shoulder and saw him following, she began to run. But he ran faster and with a flying leap, he tackled her, rolling at the last minute so that he took the brunt of the fall.

While he lay on his back with Hilda on top of him, her back to him, he deliberately placed one hand flat over her belly and the other arm across her chest, holding her in place.

He was laughing as JAM was telling everyone, "That's another move that can be used, even by a woman on a man. Roll with the blow. Hey, Max, how about doing that again?"

"Later," he said.

Hilda began to struggle, but he was still laughing, holding her even tighter. Into her ear, he whispered, "So, who's calling the shots now, Hildy?" And he made great ado about pulling her hair to the side and kissing her loudly on the neck.

Chapter 8

When a hardheaded woman meets a hardheaded man . . .

"I'm leaving tomorrow."

"What?" Hilda turned to Torolf as he came up and sat down at the high table beside her. She had been avoiding him all day since he'd embarrassed her by taking her to ground, then kissing her neck in front of one and all. But her blood turned cold at the prospect of his leaving already. "Where do you go?"

"Norstead. I need to see for myself what's going on."

"I have told you all there is to know."

"Intelligence is perishable. What was true last year . . . last month . . . may not be true today."

"I can see the wisdom of your words. Still, 'tis insanity for you to go into their midst. You will be recognized."

"I know how to disguise myself, to blend in."

"Will you go alone?"

He nodded. "Best that way."

"How long will you be gone?"

"Two days . . . maybe three."

"I have a bad feeling about this." She wrung her hands in her lap, wanting to tell him to forget about Steinolf. They had survived here these five years. Mayhap the brute would never bother them. Almost immediately, she recognized her foolishness. Steinolf would come eventually, no doubt about it. "What about Amberstead?"

He tapped his fingertips on the table. "I'll try to go there, as well. If I have time . . . if I'm able."

She thought a second before declaring, "I will go with you."

"You . . . will . . . not!"

"Yea, I will."

"You would only slow me down."

"I can be fast."

"I move silently . . . like a shadow."

"I can move softly."

"I would be worrying about protecting you all the time."

"Well, do not. My fate is my own, not your responsibility."

"Aaarrgh!" he said, pulling at his hair.

"Does that mean I can come?"

"Hell, no!"

"Be reasonable. It behooves you to accept my help."

"How?" he scoffed.

"I know secret tunnels leading into Amberstead. And I might be able to show you some of the hiding places in the hills for both of our peoples."

That got his attention. "You didn't tell me that you knew where some of them were hiding. And you never mentioned any tunnels when we were tasking our mission this morning."

She shrugged. "Some secrets are meant to be kept till trust is assured."

"You don't trust me?"

She declined to answer.

"Sonofabitch!"

"No need to curse!"

"Oh, I think there is. You're blackmailing me."

She smiled sweetly, not entirely sure what blackmailing meant. "What time shall we leave?"

He let out a whooshy exhale of surrender. "First light."

"Heed me well, knave. If you leave without me, I will just follow. In fact, I will bring Stig with me, and he can tup your leg the whole time."

He swore again. "I'll probably kiss you again."

What a pathetic attempt to put her off! "You could try."

He grinned. "Is that a challenge, Hildy?"

She decided the wisest course was not to answer. "Shall I dress as a man?"

"Yes."

"Should I cut off my hair?"

"Please don't."

"Huh?"

"There's no need to cut your hair. Just braid it tight and tuck it in a head covering of some kind."

"I know. I have a leather helmet here somewhere."

"Good. And wear pants . . . braies."

She nodded.

"Make sure they're not too tight. I don't want to be drooling over your sweet ass all day."

He thinks my arse is sweet? How . . . disgusting! "You are revolting."

"You can always stay here."

"It will take more than you ogling my backside to deter me."

"Dirty your face and teeth. Then go hug a goat or something so you smell like you did when I first got here. Then I won't want to kiss you again."

She bared her teeth at him.

He smiled at her.

Fool me once, shame on you; fool me twice . . .

It was pitch-black outside when Hilda awakened.

In truth, she had slept only fitfully in the only separate bedchamber at The Sanctuary. This small amount of privacy was her only indulgence these past five years. The room had been used by her grandmother on the rare occasion when she'd traveled to Deer Haven with her grandsire.

She dressed in the man's clothing she'd laid out on a low chest and tucked her tight braid into a leather battle helmet that hugged her head. She also used a small pottery container of ashes mixed with mud to darken her face.

The hall was quiet except for the occasional snore and popping of embers in the hearth as she crept along to the scullery, where she filled a cloth bag with manchet bread and hard cheese. Only then did she go looking for Torolf.

He was not yet up. So, first she sat near the door, waiting. When he still did not get up, she went looking for him. He was not among those who slept on benches along the wall, though she did find two of his men holding two of her women in their arms. Pretty Boy lay alone; apparently Britta had not succumbed to his charms . . . yet. At least, these two couples had had the decency to remove themselves to the far end of the hall where their wanton acts would not be viewed by others. In the end, she found a sleepy-eyed Geek and shook him awake. "Where is Torolf?"

He jerked quickly to a sitting position, pulling out a deadly looking knife. Luckily, he hesitated, then blinked several times. "JesusMaryandJoseph!" he prayed with a shake of his head. Apparently he had not recognized her in her helmet and darkened face.

"Didst think I was an enemy warrior?"

"No, I thought you were Freddy Krueger on Halloween."

"Huh?"

"Never mind."

"Where is Torolf?"

He frowned, combing his fingers through his unruly red hair. "I don't know. Maybe he went to the head . . . the outhouse."

"Oh." Suspicious, she stormed out of the keep and up to the privy, yanking the door open. There was no one on any of the five holes. "Aaarrgh!" she screamed.

The lout had left without her.

And it took her hours to find Stig tied up in the forest with his favorite bitch. He had made sure that Hilda would not follow him with Stig. *The lout!* He must be laughing at how gullible she had been.

The first day Hilda complained to everyone till none of her women would come near her for fear of being subjected to another of her tirades. The men just laughed.

The second day, when Hilda launched into one of her tirades again, Cage snapped, "Stop the bitchin'. Max did what was best for you and everyone here. Have the friggin' sense to trust that the man knows better than you about some bloody things."

Chastened, Hilda held her tongue, but she still boiled inside at the injustice of being left behind.

The four men—*seals*, they called themselves, of all things—worked intensively with the women in small groups. From early morning till late afternoon, they kept rotating the groups so that they all got training in archery, knife throwing, hand-to-hand combat, defensive tactics, even the way to move silently when doing surveillance, which meant spying and not being caught. They all ached by the end of the day but had to admit they had accomplished much. For that, Hilda had to be thankful.

That night, with Torolf still absent, Hilda lay in her bed, unable to sleep again. But now, instead of anger, worry began to fill her head. Was he dead . . . or worse yet, captured? Was he at this moment being tortured? She prayed to the gods that he was not. If he was not back by the morrow, there was a good chance he would not come back. To her surprise, the possibility of his death saddened her greatly, not just because of its effect on The Sanctuary, but because . . . well, just because . . .

Would she go out then to attempt to find him? For a certainty, his men would. They were ever quoting something about "no man left behind."

The next morning, Hilda continued to participate in the military exercises. That afternoon the men brought many dead limbs down off the mountain and chopped them into firewood. Amazing how much easier it was for them! Hilda helped Astrid drain honey from the last of the combs and wash the combs for wintertime candle making. Still others in the scullery were churning goat milk into butter, baking crab apple tarts, and putting vegetables and a few bones into the cauldron that was always simmering in the hearth. By midafternoon, Pretty Boy and Cage had gone out with two of the women skilled in hunting, coming back soon after with a reindeer and a small boar.

That evening, Hilda wasn't the only one who was solemn as she ate her meal. Without a doubt, everyone was worried about Torolf.

Before Hilda crawled into bed that night, she slipped down to her knees and put her hands together. Many Vikings practiced both the Norse and Christian religions, mainly to please the Saxons after some battle or other. So, it was not surprising that, after Hilda exhorted Odin with his wisdom and Thor with his mighty hammer Mjollnir to protect Torolf, she added: "Dear God, please send the lout back to me."

In the still of the night . . .

It had to be well past midnight when Torolf made his way back to The Sanctuary. And he was not alone.

He waved away the sentries he met outside the keep, including one who told him, "The mistress has been worried sick over you." *Nice to know!* Then he crept quietly inside.

Leading a woman with him by the hand, he motioned for her to take an empty space on one of the sleeping benches and tossed a wool blanket to her. Into her ear, he whispered, "Rest here for the night, Brynhil. You're safe now."

She nodded, grateful tears welling in her eyes.

Most everyone was asleep. The few who were not raised their heads and nodded with a smile of greeting. He tapped Cage on the shoulder and quickly grabbed his wrist before he put a knife to his heart. With hand signals, he indicated that he was safe and was going to find some place to crash. Before he left, his good friend took his hand and squeezed, an indication of how happy he was that he was back and safe. Torolf barely noticed the woman who was cuddled next to Cage.

Taking off his windbreaker, he set the broadsword he'd taken with him on the table. Then, ever so quietly, he opened, then closed the door to Hilda's bedchamber.

If she was worried about me, she probably won't mind, one side of his brain said.

Ha, ha, ha! the other side said.

Oh, well!

It was a small room, hardly bigger than a jail cell, with only two small slits for windows, which let in the full moon. A candle still burned in a steatite holder . . . an extravagance for Hilda. (The candle, not steatite—better known as soapstone—which was a natural outcropping in Norway.) She must have fallen asleep before snuffing the candle. By that dim light, he could see her lying on her back, arms flung over her head. Her pale blonde hair was loose and strewn about her like a mantle. Under the bed fur, she was naked, or he assumed she was since it was the custom in this land and this time. Something jolted inside Torolf. Arousal or something more dangerous.

With a sigh of exhaustion, he set his knife on the bed where it would be within easy reach. Then he removed his own clothes, sniffing with disgust at his body odor, not having bathed in days, but he was too tired to do anything about that now. Instead, he slid under the bed fur beside Hilda, chuckling at what she would think about that, and almost immediately fell asleep, warmed by her delicious body heat. At any other time, he would have been more aware of her nudity. Aware, hell! More like bone-hard and ready to party. But not now. Maybe later. No, not later. Never. Not with Hilda.

It was still dark, but the sky was graying outside, presaging dawn, when Torolf's eyes shot open and his body went on high alert. He was lying on his back, and Hilda's head was on his shoulder, her hair spread over his chest and her hand on his cock. She was fast asleep.

This is what SEALs, and men throughout history, called the "Oh, no!" second.

Good Lord! What do I do now? If I wake her up, she'll kill me. If I don't wake her, she'll kill me. I better do something pretty quick before my rocket decides to launch . . . or I do something really stupid, like roll over and fuck her brains out.

As gently as he could, he lifted her hand off his dick, which of course had a mind of its own and tried to follow, jerking upward. Torolf was pretty sure his eyes rolled back in his head at the utter ecstasy.

He placed her hand on his waist, and what did the wench do? With a soft moan, still asleep, she swung one leg halfway over his so that she was sort of straddling his thigh from the side. And she moved her face up into the curve of his neck so that her right breast was now resting on his chest. He looked down and stifled a moan himself.

Her breast was small, as he'd imagined, but nice. Very nice. All pink areola and rosy nipple. He couldn't help himself, his forefinger, like his cock, had a mind of its own and touched her nipple. Just a whisper of a touch. But the nipple pearled and grew bigger.

He closed his eyes and tried to think of something far removed from sex and breasts and raging erections. How about the devastation he'd seen at Norstead and Amberstead? How about the oat fields gone fallow and the cotters' huts burned to the ground? How about the woman he'd rescued from several now-dead hirdsmen of Steinolf's, who had been about to gang rape her after kicking her black and blue? How about how difficult the task would be up ahead to unseat Steinolf and his horde of barbarians?

He drifted back to sleep.

"EEEEK!"

A scream caused Torolf to jackknife up in bed, or half jackknife, since Hilda lay half-sprawled over him. Her hands were beating his chest, and she was yelling for him to release her.

"Release you? How about you release me?"

"You're lying on my hair, you oaf! EEEEEEKKKKK!"

"Hey," he said, "you're taking all the bed fur."

She was covered now, up to the neck, but he was bare-ass naked. Not that he cared all that much, but she probably did. "Is this about our agreement?"

"What agreement?"

"I agreed to let you swive me for a night in return for your ridding the world of Steinolf."

"What . . . no . . . it's not about that. I meant to explain—"

"Do not think to get payment in advance. You must give me fair warning afore I submit to your skin-crawling advances."

Torolf started to laugh.

"Get . . . out . . . of . . . my . . . bedchamber," she said through gritted teeth. The whole time she was staring at his cock sporting its hearty morning erection.

Jeesh! I can't take the thing anywhere!

"EEEEK!" she screamed again when he didn't move quickly enough.

The door slammed open as people drawn by her screams came crowding into the small room, including his buddies with weapons at the ready. For one split second, he and Hilda just stared up at the gawking crowd. Then Hilda realized that they were both naked; her scream could probably be heard across the English Channel. This time a long line of obscenities directed at him accompanied the scream.

Cage studied the situation and observed, "Sweet!" flashing him the victory sign. JAM and the other guys, laughing like hyenas, began herding everyone out of the bedchamber.

"I will never hear the end of this," she moaned.

"Hah! Neither will I." That statement didn't draw any sympathy from her.

"Why were you in my bed?"

"It was late. I was exhausted. There was no more space on the sleeping benches. And the thought of a soft mattress was too tempting."

"Can you not cover that . . . thing?"

He looked down. "Yeah, I can. But, man, what a welcome home! I thought you'd be glad to see me back. I thought you were worried about me. I thought you'd want to know what I found." *It's always good to play the guilt card.*

She closed her eyes and appeared to be counting. "Of course I want to know those things," she said once she was calmer and her eyes were open, "but I did not expect to get a report from a nude man with a flagpole sticking out from his body."

"You do have a way with words, Hildy. My flagpole and I offer our apologies." He drew on his braies and pulled the tunic over his head. Sitting back on the edge of the bed, he was putting on his boots when there was a scratching at the door. If it was that horny Stig, they were going to be having dog stew for lunch. But no, when the door opened a crack, he saw it was not the dog.

"Hilda, this is Brynhil. I brought her back with me." He beckoned with his fingers that Brynhil should come into the room. "Brynhil, this is Hilda. She runs The Sanctuary."

He glanced at Hilda, then did a double take. She was looking at him with such hurt in her eyes.

Huh? Why would Hilda be hurt? Unless she cares about me . . . and thinks Brynhil and I are . . . *Oh, no! No, no, no!*

Before he had a chance to explain, Hilda stood with the bed fur wrapped around her from breasts to ankles. She looked like a hot-damn sex goddess of some kind. *Penthouse* would love her, tiny breasts or not . . . perhaps because of her tiny breasts. Chin pointed northward, she extended her arm with a forefinger pointing to the door. "Out! Both of you!"

Brynhil began to cry.

Stig made an appearance then, nudging the door open wider with his nose. Then he leapt on Torolf's chest, knocking him backward onto the bed.

Hilda was screaming again.

Outside there was male laughter.

And Torolf tried to remember a time when his life had been simpler.

Women!

Chapter 9

The best laid plans . . .

Early that morn, after the first meal, they sat down for a "briefing," which Geek explained was a telling of what Torolf had learned on "reek-on-a-sands" and what to do with that information.

Hilda sat with Britta and several of the women who had become adept at SEAL fighting skills, or at least not abysmal at SEAL fighting skills. All the men were there, too.

Torolf spoke first. She'd avoided him like a stinksome midden after he'd been in her bed and seen her naked . . . *The bloody arse!* "I went to Norstead, then Amberstead and a few of the smaller estates between the two. Conditions were as bad or worse than I expected." He then went into detail about the number of men, their weaponry, how many guards, the vanquished people who were still there, everything that he saw.

"Any friendlies?" Geek asked.

"A few. I didn't want to push too hard around Norstead

for fear I'd be recognized by my family's old retainers. Then, near Amberstead, those I encountered were distrustful of me. They've been burned before by Steinolf's men pretending to be on their side." Torolf looked directly at Hilda and added, "Some said that I would have been more believable if Hilda were with me."

"I told you so," she said, but he spoke over her. "I did find a man who'd been a soldier under my uncle Jorund at one time. Hervor. I asked him to go into the mountains and tell people who're willing to fight to come here where we'll be gathering forces."

"You did *what*? You told them where we are located?" Britta questioned.

"You had no right." Hilda stood, so angry her voice wavered.

"Cut me some slack, you two. I wouldn't have entrusted that information to just anyone. This man can be trusted."

"I do not doubt the loyalty of this one man, but you do not know how Steinolf tortures information out of people. This man may not be able to help himself." Hilda was shaking her head at Torolf with dismay.

"Actually, I do know. There are things I saw that defy humanity. Talk to Brynhil. After I rescued her, she told me what she's seen and experienced the past year."

He rescued her? She is not his bedmate? And that poor woman . . . I treated her unfairly and gave her no offer of sanctuary!

"Sometimes you have to take a chance," he insisted. "One more thing. Hervor told me that two of my cousins, Thorfinn and Steven, have been looking for any of my family left from Norstead. They came two years ago, and have been seen in the vicinity a month back."

"How is that significant?" Britta wanted to know.

"Well, my aunt Katla married some noble Viking from

Norsemandy before I was born. If any of her sons have come here, it would be to help. And hopefully bring warriors with them. In any case, let's plan our mission for one week from today. In the meantime, we continue to train and come up with specific task training and simulated tactical situations."

JAM said, "That forested area down below this fortress would work well."

"Yeah, and during that time, hopefully more men will arrive here to help," Pretty Boy added.

Hilda's blood chilled at the thought. Everything was changing here at The Sanctuary, spiraling out of control. Even if these men . . . these SEALs . . . were the only ones to ever come here, The Sanctuary was never going to be the same.

"I'll make a computer-like grid of the various sites and terrains allocating our resources where best needed," Geek said. "JAM gave me a couple of blank flyleaf pages from his Bible."

"I can work with you on that," Britta offered.

"Me, too," Pretty Boy added, to no one's surprise.

"We've got to be careful of collateral damage," Torolf emphasized. "Many of the people inside Norstead and Amberstead are there against their will."

Hilda did not understand half of what they said, but she noticed how efficiently the men worked together, almost finishing each other's thoughts. Even if she had not been told so, it was obvious they had worked together in the past. And she had to be impressed the way each man and woman was being assigned a specific role in this mission. She could not help to be impressed with Torolf's leadership, as well. How different from his usual jesting self!

In the end, the group broke apart, chattering among themselves. Britta was slapping Pretty Boy's hands away as he attempted to put an arm over her shoulders. They made an attractive pair.

"You're smiling," Torolf said. "Does that mean you're not still mad at me?"

They were the only ones left. "I am still angry with you. What were you thinking . . . to crawl into my bed furs?"

"I wasn't thinking."

That is no doubt the first honest thing he has said to me. "Do not do it again."

"I won't . . . unless you ask me to."

"Hmpfh! Do not flatter yourself. Oh, I see. You are teasing me again."

"That wasn't teasing."

"Yea, 'twas. You have no interest in me . . . that way."

"I don't know about that. After all, I've seen you naked."

She rolled her eyes at him. "I am not enamored of my own scrawny body. Nor are you. So give up this nonsense."

"Scrawny?" He pretended to be studying her body and pondering. "Nah. Slim, would be my description."

"Let us put an end to this unsavory discussion. I have no breasts to speak of, and everyone knows that men crave big udders."

He choked at her crudity, then grinned. "Haven't you ever heard that the best gifts come in small packages?"

"Enough!" she said, red-faced and mortified that she'd let him draw her into such a bawdy conversation.

He waggled his eyebrows at her before walking away.

Fool that she was, she refused to let him have the last word. To his back, she said, "There are parts on you that are smaller than normal, too." Immediately, she regretted her coarse jest.

He turned slowly. "Tsk, tsk, tsk! Now I will have to prove to you how wrong you are. You should have stopped while you were ahead, Hildy. You definitely should have stopped."

"I am not afeared of you, you . . . lout."

"You should be."

Hilda stared after him in shock and was even more shocked when he spun on his heel and came back to her.

"I am so sorry, Hilda. That was uncalled for. I shouldn't bait you like that. I shouldn't be so crude. I shouldn't have made intimate observations about your body. I shouldn't have crawled into bed with you. I honest-to-God don't know what comes over me when I'm around you." He put his hands on both of her upper arms and squeezed. "Forgive me?"

She stared at his face, no longer twitching with humor, and recognized his sincere effort to correct his mistakes with her. Numbly, she nodded.

This time, as he walked away again, he muttered the oddest thing. "I am in serious shit here."

Welcome all you roosters to the henhouse . . .

The next day, the select group of thirty women and five men drilled from dawn till dusk preparing for a mission that might very well kill them all.

Right now, they were jogging from the keep to the fjord and back again, over and over . . . an exercise that was as natural as breathing to the SEALs, but that the women considered ridiculous.

Inge said breathily, "I do not care how many muscles my thighs get. My breasts are bouncing like a ship in a storm."

"Good thing I am not nursing," Helwig joked. "Otherwise I might be churning butter here."

The guys looked at each other and rolled their eyes, knowing any words they said would be taken the wrong way.

Hilda's eyes connected with Torolf's, and he knew she was thinking about her small breasts and what he must think about their lack of jiggling.

Lord, how did I get myself in this mess? He decided the

best course was to not remark at all . . . and to definitely not look in the region of her chest. He would never tell her, but he thought her breasts were nice just the way they were . . . and, yes, dammit, he had been thinking about them way too much.

Several of the sentries came running through the woods, downstream from the fjord. "Men coming, men coming!"

Everyone immediately took their prearranged positions, weapons at the ready, most of them hidden from sight. Torolf and JAM, Hilda, and Britta waited in the open, though, figuring no men would be coming in such an exposed way unless they were friends . . . or pretending to be friends. First came Hervor, raising a hand in greeting. Following Hervor were ten men . . . no, fifteen . . . no, twenty. As they watched, more and more of them came streaming into view. They were a scruffy bunch, almost emaciated, and filthy.

He saw the panic on Hilda's face. "Oh, my gods! What will we do with all these men? How will we feed them? And find sleeping space . . . and clothing?"

"Don't worry. A hunting party will go out in the morning and get game. And Cage'll catch a pig load of fish."

"I cannot have them inside the keep . . . I just cannot."

He saw the wild fear in her eyes. Men had been the root of these women's problems. In her mind, the walls of her refuge were beginning to crumble. "These men have probably been living outdoors these past few years, anyhow. A few more weeks won't matter. You don't have to have them inside the keep."

She looked at him and back to the scrawny group, the most nonthreatening bunch he'd ever seen. She moaned and looked at him again. "How can I deny them? These are my . . . our people." There were tears in her eyes as she stepped forth. "Good tidings, Hervor. I see you have brought us good men to aid in our cause. Welcome."

Hervor straightened his body, raising his chin with a

dignity he probably hadn't felt in years. "Good tidings, mi-lady," he said in a choked voice. The men behind him, many of them sick and crippled from torture and malnutrition, did likewise.

Hilda walked among them, touching a shoulder here, a hand there, asking soft questions, uncaring that they reeked of long-unbathed bodies and oozing sores. Some she even recognized with small cries, and they her.

Torolf was so proud of her that he could barely speak.

They do WHAT to increase their virility? . . .

Hilda heard some women giggling in the scullery as they helped to prepare the largest meal The Sanctuary had seen in the five years since it had been established.

She had just come from the weaving shed, which had been cleared to be used as a hospitium of sorts for the injured men. Still others were in her own bedchamber, which she had gladly given up for their comort. For the most part, what they needed was good food and rest before they prepared to go forth and unseat Steinolf.

"What are you twittering about?" Hilda asked, coming into the scullery.

"We are talking about bedsport, of course," Inge said, grinning.

"Of course." *After five years manless, you would think that the subject of these women's conversation would have changed. 'Twas an ageless subject, though. In truth, that biblical Eve had no doubt been discussing sex when she gathered with her women friends after being sent forth from the Garden of Eden.*

"These men . . . these SEALs . . . have the most unusual custom when making love." Dagne put a hand over her mouth as she tittered.

Hilda cocked her head in question, surprised not just by the subject but that it was sweet Dagne who mentioned it. "Unusual? Methought there was only so much a man could do with that dangly part of his."

"They put these things over their manparts," Dissa explained and burst out laughing.

"Things?"

"Yea, cone-dumbs. They looks like sausage casings," Dissa's sister Dotta said with a snort of laughter.

Well, that is certainly . . . dumb. "They put sausage casings over their manparts? Why?"

Several of the women shrugged.

"I know men are vain about their manly staffs, but really, dressing one up—in a sausage casing, of all things— that does press the bounds between sensible and laughable. 'Twould be like putting a tunic on a dog or a gunna on a chicken."

"Methinks it is to increase their virility," Inge said, and the others nodded.

"'Tis unbelievable! The things a man will do in the name of his prowess!"

"I knew a man once who used to slather lard on his cock so it would glisten," Rakel said. "And another who claimed eating onions increased a man's virility. Little did he know that he reeked so bad, it mattered not a whit how large his lance was."

"There was a Viking man my sister knew who combed and trimmed his man hairs," Elise told them.

Several jaws dropped at that news, followed by more giggles.

"I have noticed that men are sensitive about the size of *it*." Inge rolled her eyes for emphasis. "Women worry about clean bed linens, lice in the hair, whether there will be enough boar for the morrow, while men worry about how impressed their bedmates will be when they pull *it* out of their braies."

"And does it—this sausage casing—increase virility?" Hilda asked.

They all started giggling again, which presumably meant that it did. Hilda wanted to ask if Torolf had lain with any of them, but she could not. They already thought she had opened her legs for the lout. Why else would he have been in her bed furs?

"Dost your man not use the cone-dumbs?"

"He is not my man."

"'Tis the oddest thing," Astrid began, speaking with the slight lisp caused by her imperfect tongue. "That evil thing that Steinolf's men made me do—putting their horrid manparts in my mouth—well, I did not know that normal men did the same thing. Cunning-ling-us, they call it." Her young face flamed with embarrassment, as several of the others nodded.

Hilda frowned her confusion. "I do not understand. Men can suck on their own man parts?"

The women burst out laughing, even Frida who was stirring a sweet-smelling custard of eggs, goat milk, honey, and dried bilberries over the fire. "Believe me, they would if they could."

"Noooo! I meant with women . . . men using their mouth on women's female parts." Astrid's face flushed with embarrassment at Hilda's misunderstanding.

Hilda's face bloomed with heat, too. "I have ne'er heard of such, and I have been wed three times."

"Mayhap your husbands did not care about your pleasure in the bedsport," Inge remarked, not unkindly. Inge had been with Hilda a long time and knew of the sad state of her various marriages.

"Hilda!" *Speaking of the devil!* There came Torolf into the kitchen, calling her name. "Hilda! I need to talk to you about . . ." His words trailed off as he noticed all the women gawking at him. "What? What did I do now?"

Laughter erupted all around him, even from Hilda.

After that, she and Torolf helped the women carry tray after tray of food into the hall, where Dagne was already playing her lute. She was being accompanied on the flute by a young man who had arrived that day. Everywhere people, including some of the recent arrivals, were talking and smiling, as if none of the horrors of the past five years had taken place. If the mead kept flowing as it was now, they would soon run out of a supply that would normally last them through the winter. And there were always lines at the privy, which was not intended for such a large number of mead-drinking people.

"What did you need to discuss with me?" she asked after they set the trays down.

"Let's walk back here," he suggested, pointing to one of the storerooms behind the high table. "More privacy."

She followed him, both of them carrying torches, which they'd picked from the wall. She watched as he examined the various wares on the shelves. Of a sudden, she noticed the sparkle of something on the front of his blue braies, reflected from the torch in his hands.

"What is that?" she asked, pointing.

He looked down, then up at her with surprise. "Uh, my genitals."

"Genny-tails?"

"My cock."

"Dolt! I meant that shiny thing. What manner of country do you come from that you wear an ornament against your belly?"

"Oh, that! It's a zipper . . . a type of fastening used in my, uh, country . . . and this here is a button." He demonstrated.

She gasped with wonder. "Let me." Kneeling, she proceeded to open and close the button, then run the zipper up and down and up and down. She leaned in very close to study the workings.

"Whoa, Hildy. That will be enough of that. Unless you've developed this sudden attraction to me."

"What?" she said, glancing up at him, then at the zipper again. Only then did she notice the bulge behind the zipper, which had not been there before. Red-faced, she stood.

"Maybe our talking in private isn't such a good idea," he said and led her out of the storage room and back to the high table.

While he ate, Torolf grew serious. "You need to understand where I come from."

"You have told me afore. Ah-mare-eek-ah."

"Yeah, but I've also told you that America is a thousand and more years in the future. Really. I know you think I'm the world's biggest clown, but this is no joke. Really." He put up a hand to halt her when she was about to voice an opinion. "Let me get it all out. You have heard of Leif Eriksson, haven't you? Well, he discovered a country he called Vinland that eventually would be called America . . . beyond Iceland and Greenland. When my father took his longship there with me and eight of my brothers and sisters, it was the year 1000. Somehow, in the middle of some storm or weird event out on the seas, we ended up in Hollywood, a city in America, and it was the year 2003."

Hilda put her hand on his arm. "I believe you may have landed in some other land, like the old legends, but the future? Nay, it has to be impossible."

"I thought so, too. But let me tell you what it's like there. They have cars, which people drive down roads . . . horseless carriages is the only way to describe them. Then there are airplanes, which transport people in the skies.

Electricity that provides instant lighting and heat in homes. Stoves and microwaves that cook food without flames. Ships and boats that require no rowers to move. Telephones that allow a person to talk to someone in another land. Hot and cold running water inside the house. And that's just a few modern inventions."

With each of Torolf's revelations, Hilda shook her head. She could see that he believed all that he said, and who was she to say him nay? "Mayhap it is a land of magic, and not the future after all."

"No. It's the future, all right."

"And people can travel back and forth in time on a whim."

"As far as I know, my family members are the only ones who've time-traveled into the future, and I'm the only one who came back. For sure, this is the first time a group of men have traveled back in time. Maybe there are others. Who knows?"

"How do you time-travel?"

"Each person has been different. Some have been involved in shipwrecks and thought they died. Uncle Jorund encountered a whale with a sense of humor. Madrene was caught in a strange lightning storm. In all cases, though, one second the person was in one time and then in another."

"'Tis hard for me to credit what you say, but I accept that you believe it to be so, that you are not teasing me *this time*."

"My men don't believe it either."

"And still they would agree to fight Steinolf in this make-believe world."

"SEALs are a brotherhood of sorts. They do it for me. Besides, there are terrorists in any time, Hilda. Ones as bad or worse than Steinolf, believe it or not. For example,

Hitler was . . . well, suffice it to say that evil men never die out."

"I know Steinolf did great harm to your family, but why risk danger when your family has found safe haven and prosperity elsewhere? I live here in the Norselands, so Steinolf's reign of terror continues to be a threat. But you . . . ?"

He shrugged. "*Someone* has to stop him."

"Why is it important to you that I accept your story?"

"Because I want you to know why I *must* leave here eventually. Norstead is my heritage, but it isn't relevant to me anymore. I've made a new life."

She nodded, feeling oddly hurt that he could put aside so easily this time and people . . . her. "So, you want me to understand that you come from the future and you are not going to stay behind once Steinolf is dead."

"Bingo!"

"I told you afore, and I will repeat it again: What makes you think I would want you to stay?"

"C'mon, Hildy, be honest. You and I have so much chemistry going on between us we practically make sparks."

"Huh?"

"Sexual attraction."

She gasped. "You think I want you as a bed partner? Oh, you are by far the most arrogant man I have ever met."

The look he gave her called her liar, but what he said was, "Okay, let's say it's one-sided then. I want you so bad my teeth hurt, and my toes curl just looking at you."

"Why do you say such things to me?"

"On the chance you might want to fool around a little, I guess." He winked at her.

That wink went right down to her toes which, surprisingly, felt as if they'd curled. And the way he was studying her body so intently, well . . . "You are thinking to cunning-tingle me, are you not? Well, forget that notion right now."

He repeated the word several times in confusion, "Cunning-tingle, cunning-tingle, cunning-tingle? Oh, my God! You mean cunnilingus." He pronounced it as kunna-ling-us. "Where did you hear that word?"

Her face was no doubt bright red.

"My guys have been busy beavers."

"Let us change the subject."

"Does that mean we're not going to hit the sack together?"

"Not till our agreement night."

"Even if I *can* make you tingle?"

"Dost think I want to tingle, you idiot?"

"There's a lot to be said for tingling," he said with a laugh. "About that deal, Hildy, I was just kidding."

"Make up your mind, you loathsome lout. Either you want me or you do not."

"I want you, but I don't want you if you don't want me."

"Oh, that makes as much sense as . . . as cunning-tingles."

He grinned. "I could show you how much sense it makes . . . and tingles."

"I could show you how it feels to have a horn of mead dumped over your head."

"You know, Hildy, I just discovered something. You and I bickering together has become a sort of foreplay with us. Turns me on. How about you?"

She was about to tell him what she thought of that notion but held her tongue lest he think she was engaging in foresport with him. Besides, her nipples had hardened into aching buds. It was a sad state of affairs when a lady could no longer argue for fear of appearing wanton. And the way he continued to grin, he knew it, too.

Well, two could play at this game. She knew how to shut the lout up. Yea, she did.

"I have decided, Torolf, that tonight shall be the night I fulfill my end of our bargain. Swiving. Best you practice up on your cunning-tingles."

Torolf was stunned speechless.

Chapter 10

It's the truth, the whole truth, and nothing but the almost-truth . . .

Torolf's buddies surrounded him at the high table a short time later. You could say it was a sort of intervention.

"This Viking reenactment crap has gone far enough," JAM started them out. "I mean, I was willing to help you wipe out some terrorists. I still am. But all these victims arriving here today? That's not reenactment. That's reality."

"That's what I've been trying to tell you guys."

"I jogged about twenty-five miles downstream this morning, and there's nothing there. *Nada.* None of the small towns or farms we saw on our way here." JAM's brow furrowed. "I mean, how could all signs of civilization just disappear?"

"I can explain. Well, you might not consider it an explanation, but it's the truth."

"What the hell is going on here, Max? These women have never even heard of Victoria's Secret . . . or panties, for that matter," Cage pointed out.

"I know you don't want to hear this, but you guys have

time-traveled. I swear this on my Budweiser. Thirteen members of my family have time-traveled to the future. My uncles Rolf and Jorund, my father, myself, and ten of my brothers and sisters. Call it magic, call it scientific wrinkles in time, call it a freakin' miracle, but it damn well happened."

They all looked at each other, still unconvinced, except for Geek who said, "I believe you."

"Ask anyone here what year it is. Do you think each of them will have been prompted to lie? Do you think I'm lying?"

The four guys stared at him, then at each other. JAM summed it up for all of them. "Welcome to the twilight zone."

"Think about the possibilities here, y'all," Cage told them. "We could write a book, get on *Oprah*, have chicks by the zillions wanting to get boinked by us. I mean, really, being a SEAL is chick magnet enough, but add time-traveling SEAL, and we've got a real hook here. Talk about!"

"I've always wanted to meet Oprah," Pretty Boy said.

"Forget Oprah, betcha I could get a date with Katie Couric." Geek sighed loudly at the prospect.

"Katie Couric!" they all exclaimed.

"She's old enough to be your mother. Haven't I taught you to home in on the young, hot ones, son?" Pretty Boy patted Geek on the shoulder in a fatherly fashion, which was ridiculous, Pretty Boy being thirty-one and Geek twenty-six!

"No, no, no! You can't go blabbing about this when . . . if . . . we go back. You'd find yourself living in a bubble in some scientist's lab for the rest of your life, being poked and prodded, sliced and diced, examined inside and out." Torolf and his family had discussed this numerous times in the past. It was a secret best kept to themselves.

They all looked suitably horrified.

"Okay, let's say we wipe out Steinolf and the other tangos. Then what?" JAM asked.

"I find someone to take over at Norstead and Amberstead . . . maybe Hilda . . . maybe those cousins. Then we try to go back."

"Whoaaaaa! What do you mean, *try* to go back?" JAM's mouth tightened with anger. "You better not have gotten us lost in some time warp or something. I have tickets for an Aerosmith concert next month."

"I told you guys not to come. I warned you."

"And I have a date with Cindy on the nineteenth . . . that's Cindy the gymnast," Pretty Boy said, waggling his eyebrows.

"I thought you were all hot for Britta," Torolf said.

"I am, but that doesn't mean I'm singing any wedding marches. Besides, Britta hasn't given in yet."

"What? A woman who resists The Man?" Cage teased.

"Shove it, birdbrain. She will . . . eventually." Pretty Boy's face turned all pink with embarrassment. Torolf couldn't recall Pretty Boy ever having trouble getting a woman he'd targeted, except maybe for his sister Madrene, who'd had eyes only for Master Chief Ian MacLean.

"Back to my question," JAM said. "*How* do we go back?"

"I'm not sure."

Four sets of teeth gnashed at that news.

"I promise, I'll do my best to get us back."

They all nodded, though not too happy with the vagueness of that promise.

"Y'all wanna go put some giddyap in this party?" Cage asked then, taking a long draw on his mug of mead.

"I'm thinking a knee-walking bender might be just the thing," JAM replied.

They all agreed.

Pretty Boy put two fingers in his mouth and whistled

loudly, causing everyone in the place to jerk with surprise. "Yo, Britta, where you hidin', babe?" he yelled at the top of his lungs. "Here I come, ready or not."

A shocked Britta at the end of the great hall raised her head, saw him moving purposefully toward her, then turned to scoot out the door.

Britta was one dead duck.

Speaking of dead ducks, where's Hilda? No way could she offer herself on the half shell, then walk away. No way could she bring up oral sex and expect him to forget about it. No way could he have seen her nude body and then wipe it from his horny mind. Yep, he was about to teach Brunhilda Berdottir a thing or two about teasing a man, especially a Viking man.

Whoo-boy! I can't wait.

Of course, I'm just going to tease her a little.

Ha, ha, ha!

Really. No going all the way. Just partway. Maybe, halfway. Okay, three-quarters of the way, tops.

I am waist deep and sinking fast.

Where's the mead? No, where's Hilda?

Come out, come out, wherever you are, honey. Here comes the big bad wolf . . . and he's huuuuungry.

Never tease a teaser . . .

It was hours later that Torolf found Hilda and gave himself a mental *Gotcha!*

There was Hilda in the bathhouse, reclining on one of the wide, high platform benches in the steam room, eyes closed, wearing nothing but a thin chemise and a layer of perspiration.

The bathhouse was just a small building with a stone-flagged floor. Red-hot stones nestled in the open hearth's peat fire. Water was poured over the stones to create steam.

Usually, people sat nude in here, but she probably exercised caution because of all the strangers about.

Softly, he closed the door to the outer chamber and propped a bar against it, locking them in. After that, with a mischievous grin, he removed all his clothing, except for his low-riding braies.

Softly, he crept barefooted to the bottom of the bench and whispered, "Hildy."

She tried to jackknife to a sitting position, but he was on her like a bear on honey. He settled himself over her body, pressing her down.

Flailing against his bare shoulders, she shrieked, "What are you doing here?"

"You invited me . . . for a night of swiving."

"I was teasing."

"It worked."

She stopped slapping and lay perfectly still. "Go ahead then. Do it and be done. I have chores yet to do tonight."

He laughed against her ear and noticed how she shivered. She was obviously one of those women whose ears were highly erotic zones of sensitivity. He blew softly, and her hips jerked up against his. A mistake, that. A part of his body he had difficulty controlling liked that jerking of hers very much. So, masochist that he was, he pressed the tip of his wet tongue into her ear, in and out a few times, and she began to whimper.

Whimpering is good, baby.

He braced himself on his elbows and looked down. Her eyes were wide, aquamarine colored. Her mouth was big and full, with the lower lip slightly more puffy. A very kissable mouth. The kind of mouth men fantasized about.

"Let's just kiss and pet a little."

"I am not an animal to be petted."

"We'll see," he said against her mouth. And then he kissed her. And kissed her. And kissed her. Her mouth opened under his persuasion as he slanted and shaped her. And then he tongue-kissed her. Moist. Slippery. Hot. In and out. He couldn't tell who kissed who, he couldn't tell where his body ended and hers began. And he didn't care.

As his tongue thrust and parried with hers, his lower body did the same, and Hilda, bless her soul, met him thrust for thrust. *And, holy shit, how did I manage to get between her legs, and when did her knees bend and bracket my hips?*

Slow down, cowboy. This is just a little fooling around. Not the whole nine yards. But first . . . but hot-damn first . . . "Let me look at you, Hildy," he said, his voice raw with arousal. He rolled to his side on the wide bench and began to inch her chemise off her shoulders.

She put up her hands. Her eyes were luminous with arousal and her lips heart-stoppingly wet and bruised from his kisses, but he knew she was self-conscious about her small breasts.

"Please, honey, I need to . . . oh, man, oh, man . . ." Her breasts were small, with nipples like small marbles. He rolled her to her back again, her chemise nestled on her hips. Kneeling between her legs, he put his hands to both breasts, kneading them. The nipples felt like bullets pressing in his palms. Still kneading, he used his thumbs to strum the nipples into even harder peaks.

At first, her eyes went wide, then she closed them with a shudder, but she didn't fight him anymore. Instead, her fists clenched the sides of the bench, and her chest arched up for more.

And then, and then—*Yeeeees!*—then he did what he'd wanted to do since he'd first seen her again this week. He lay over her and put his mouth to her breast, sucking her, hard. Then he did the same to the other breast. He couldn't get enough. Over and over he alternated. Sucking. Flicking her with his tongue. Rasping her with his teeth. Then sucking again.

He looked down at her wet breasts. "You are so fucking beautiful," he murmured.

She either didn't hear or ignored him. Instead, she was keening now and bucking against him, and he realized that he could make her come just by playing with her magnificent, small breasts. *Note to Torolf: ears and breasts, highly erogenous zones on Hilda.* "Don't fight it. Let it go, that's the way."

"Oh, oh, oh, oh . . . shhhhh, shhhhh, shhhhh . . . oh, my gods . . . oh, sweet mother of Thor!" she wailed, her hips raised so strongly she lifted him up. And then she crumpled flat with a long sigh.

And he was so hard he could have probably drilled concrete with his dick. *Note to Torolf: take care of your own business while you're doing Hilda.*

Now would be a good time for Hilda to zap him with one of her witchy, cock-shriveling curses. Instead of shriveling, he felt himself grow even harder. *I sense a world-class blue steeler coming on.*

Okay, there was an exercise called hooking, which military men were taught when flying jets or race car drivers were going faster than fast. It involved tensing and untensing the abdominal muscles to brace against fierce gravitational pulls, called g-forces, that occurred at high rates of speed. Well, man, he was hooking like crazy now, for fear he was going to embarrass himself. He inhaled sharply, bracing himself, trying to focus, focus, focus. *Shit! I might as well give it up. They can put on my grave marker, Died of Hilda's Gravitational Pull.*

He levered himself off Hilda and sat on the bench, his elbows on his knees, face in hands, taking long breaths in and out.

"Well, that was interesting," Hilda said. He heard her behind him, adjusting herself.

"Interesting?" he choked out.

"Yea. Interesting. So that is what cunning-tingles are all about? Interesting."

He started to laugh then, and laugh, and laugh. At least he was no longer horn-dog hard.

Hilda sat beside him on the bench, staring at him as if he'd lost his mind. Maybe he had . . . and frankly he didn't give a rat's ass . . . because he was about to do something . . . well, crazy.

"No, Hildy, there may have been tingling involved, but that was not cunnilingus. But I'd be glad to demonstrate."

Before she could say, "Demonstrate what?" he lifted her up and over him, straddling his lap. Then, while she looked at him with surprise, he spread his legs wide, taking hers with him. She didn't have to be a modern woman to understand she was totally exposed to him now. She inhaled sharply.

Lifting the hem of her chemise, he raised it over her head and tossed it to the side. She moved to put her hands over herself, and he brushed them away. "Uh-uh-uh! Modesty is not welcome at this party, sweetheart."

Trailing his fingers along the insides of her thighs, he whispered, "Welcome to my world, baby."

There are tingles, and then there are TINGLES . . .

Hilda was sitting on the lout's lap, naked as the day she was born, with her legs spread like the worst wanton.

"I must be losing my mind," she muttered. *Touch me.*

"Me, too."

"I should smack you." *Touch me.*

"Or jump off my lap and run for your life."

"For a certainty. But I can't move." *Touch me.*

"Why?"

"I am still recovering from that amazing thing you just did to me." *Touch me.*

He smiled a slow, lazy smile that caused her nipples to

tighten even more than they already were. She glanced downward. From this angle her breasts did not look quite so pathetically small. *Touch me.*

"You shouldn't say things like that to me, Hildy."

"Why?" *Touch me.*

"It encourages me."

"To do what?" *Touch me.*

He smiled some more. "Everything in my repertoire."

"Ah, a bedsport repertoire. And is it vast, this repertoire of yours?" *Touch me.*

"Very vast."

"Show me," she said, then slapped a hand over her mouth, shocked that she would say such a thing. "Never mind. Forget I said that."

"No, no, no! That is not the kind of thing that can be taken back."

For way too long, even before Steinolf's invasion, Hilda had been living her life for others. To please her mother, she had been a good girl growing up, never running wild as her brothers had. To please her father, she'd married three men who were far from favorable to her. To please her people, she had learned everything there was to know about running an estate. To please all the victims of Steinolf's abuse, she had established The Sanctuary. None of these things did she regret, but she could not recall the last time she'd done something strictly for herself. Perchance now, just one time, she would allow herself to think only of her own pleasure.

She smiled at the rogue, teasingly. "Show me," she repeated, this time in a husky voice of seduction.

She felt his thighs spasm under her. "Put your hands behind your back and lock your fingers together." Without hesitation, she did as ordered. And felt deliciously wicked. *Mayhap now he will touch me.*

He fluttered the tips of his fingers against her nether hair and murmured, "Blonde, too," then asked, "How does that feel?"

At last, at last, at last! "Like butterfly wings, inside and out."

"Good. And this?" He used the back of his middle finger up and down through her woman folds.

Feelings Hilda had never experienced before flooded her body, from that place where he touched, to her breasts, to her loins, to her belly. It was like before, but different.

"Don't close your eyes, Hildy. I want to see you come . . . again."

"Come where?" *Why must the dolt keep talking? Just keep on touching me, you fool.*

He laughed, then slid a finger inside her body, then back out, in again with two fingers, out, then three. She gasped at the fullness inside her and the tremors that rippled out from there. Plus, there was a part of her body down below that seemed to ache in an odd way.

"Now, Hildy, listen carefully. Are you listening?"

I am too busy concentrating on your touching.

"Put your hands on my shoulders and ride me. Slow at first."

"Huh?" *Why can he not just keep touching me?*

"Like a horse."

At first, she didn't understand, and then she did. Holy Thor, she did! "I am not sure I can." But she did, awkwardly at first, but then with more ease. Every time she came back down on his fingers, a part of her hit his thumb, and she nigh saw stars.

He put his free hand to her nape and drew her face down to his. He wet her mouth with his tongue, then inserted his tongue into her mouth, catching the same in-and-out rhythm as her riding him. She slapped his hand away from her neck. "Nay, I cannot concentrate on both places. 'Tis too much. Toooo much!" She dug her fingernails into his shoulders, pressing her lower body hard against him, rubbing that special space against the bulge in his braies. She was exploding with sparks of the most incredible pleasure . . . so powerful, they were almost painful. From far away, she heard his groan and her long, unending whimper.

She must have fainted then, and Hilda never fainted, because she found herself lying on his cloak on the bench, and he was leaning over her.

When she opened her eyes, he said, "Wow! Are you ready for me to go down on you?"

She frowned her confusion.

"Cunnilingus."

"That was not . . . *it*?"

"No, honey, it was not. This is." With those words, he parted her legs, shimmied himself downward so that his face was *there* and began to lick her. *Licking? There? Oh, good gods!* Mortified, she tried to shove him away, but he would not budge. "Be still, Hilda, I want to eat you."

Eat me? Eeeeek! "Nay, stop it at once."

But he would not stop, and soon she did not care. In fact, her fingers were in his hair, encouraging his talented tongue. In the end, when he sucked on her there, she screamed. Low and long. Until there was silence and she lay limp as a soppy rag.

When she was finally able to sit up, she noticed that Torolf had doused himself in the cold waters of the rinsing pool, and even as she watched he slid under the waters totally, coming back up with a splash, then raking his blond hair off his face with his fingers. He raised his head, and his eyes made contact with her. They were hot and hungry. Glancing lower, she saw that he had removed his braies, and his manpart was long and hard, even in the cold water. She realized then that while he had given her pleasure three times, he had taken none for himself.

Do I have the nerve? Yea, I must. 'Tis only fair. She opened her arms to beckon him forth. "'Tis your turn now."

He stood and shook his head, even though his staff jerked at her words. "No, I was only teasing when I made that deal with you. I never intended to follow through."

She pondered his words as she joined him in the pool and splashed the sweat from her body, sweat brought on by the steam but also by his ministering to her needs.

He was already out of the pool, drying himself with his tunic and then pulling on his braies. *Nay, nay, nay! It cannot be done with.*

She walked out of the pool, strangely uninhibited in her nakedness as he watched her. Slowly, she dried herself with a linen, aware of a strange sensation between her legs . . . not soreness, more like awareness. After she pulled her gunna over her head, she looked at him. *Two can play at this teasing game. I only hope I am talented enough.* "If you had told me yestereve that you were teasing, or even this morn . . . bloody Asgard! . . . if you had told me this an hour ago, I would have cursed you to hell. But now . . ." She shrugged.

"Now?"

"Now, I would welcome you . . . for this *one* night." She dried her hair, plaited the wet strands into a long braid as he watched her like a feral cat and she the tasty mouse. *Does the lout take the bait? He looks interested. But he is stubborn.* "Tonight I sleep in the stable. There are no horses there anymore, of course, but there are bed furs. Come, if you want. Or not."

With those words, she walked past him, swaying her hips the way Rakel had taught them.

Follow me, Torolf. Follow me.

But he did not.

Chapter 11

Surrender is sweet . . .

Hilda made a bed for herself in one of the former horse stalls. The stable had been unused for that purpose for fifteen or more years, but the scent of animal and hay still lingered.

She put a large candle resting in a soapstone candle holder up on a shelf so that there would be no risk of fire. Then she settled one red fox bed fur onto the straw, fur side up, and lay another on top of it, fur side down. It was chilly in here, but not so cold as outside, since the timber sides buffeted the frosty winds. Any sennight now the snows would come.

She dropped her gunna and was about to blow out the candle when she heard a rustle behind her.

"Don't." Torolf stood there, pulling his tunic over his head, staring at her hotly. "Don't blow out the candle." He toed his unlaced boots off, then shrugged out of his braies, leaving him nude. And aroused.

He came! Oh, my! Now what? Hilda was still shy about her body, despite what she'd let Torolf do to her, but she restrained herself from covering her intimate parts with her hands. "I thought you were not coming."

"I didn't want to."

Dost hope to seduce me with insults, knave? "You told me afore that you did not want me if I did not want you. Well, mayhap the opposite is true, too."

"I don't mean that I don't *want* you. Hell, the genie's out of the bottle now." He waved a hand downward and smiled ruefully. "I just know it's not a smart idea."

"Then go." *Do not dare!*

"I don't think so. There's not much fun in smart."

"Fun?" she squeaked. *Hmmmm.*

"Oh, yeah!"

"I must needs remind you that I am not a virgin. My virtue cannot be forfeit any longer. Some men are repelled by that notion."

"I'm not some men. Besides, you know what they say. Virginity is like a bubble. One prick, and it's all gone."

"Huh? Is that another of your jests?"

"I'm not a virgin either, Hildy. Does it matter to you?"

"Of course not."

"There you go." He knelt down and flipped the top fur over and slid in between. Holding a hand out, he invited her to join him. "Come on, sweetie. I'll show you how the big boys play."

And he did.

Torolf felt the same adrenaline rush he did when jumping out of a Black Hawk over bloody Iraq. He was soaring through the air, his chute not yet open, but he still hadn't pulled the cord. He glanced downward at his . . . cord. *Hold on, boy. Your time is coming.*

With a self-deprecating chuckle, he adjusted Hilda

under him, then rubbed himself back and forth over her. His cord was real happy about that. "You feel so good."

"So do you." She had to be feeling the soft fur under her and hard body on top. *Penthouse Fantasy #2 . . . sex on a fur rug in front of a roaring fire. The only thing missing is the fire.* He decided to make one himself . . . figuratively speaking. "I want to make this first time long and special for you, but I'll never make it. This first time has to be short and sweet, to take the edge off. Okay?"

She nodded hesitantly.

He reached over and got a condom from his pocket. She watched intently as he peeled it on. Then, reaching down, he touched her. Satisfied with the slickness he found there, he spread her legs, pressed her ankles back practically to her ass, and entered her with one long thrust. She was tight and hot and wet and spasming, and he thought he might just die. Gritting his teeth, he arched his neck back and scrunched his eyes shut. Once he'd regained a modicum of control, he looked down at her.

If ever a woman was poleaxed, here she lay.

"What are you doing to me?" she whispered.

Turning you on. I hope. "Making love."

She reached her hands up to touch him, but he pushed them back down. "Just be still and let me do the work. This time." *Unless you want this heat-seeking missile to fizzle out.*

He was braced on both hands in sort of a push-up position, but his thoughts right now were far from PT. Leaning down, he placed his lips over hers, and then he began the long strokes against the abrading muscles of her inner walls. She sucked at him *there*, then let him slide. *Merciful heavens!* He'd thought to be the one running the show, but she was the one unconsciously calling the shots. He heard himself making woofing sounds and chanting, "Yes, yes, yes, yes, yes, yes . . ."

She had begun to match his thrusts, now hard and short, with her own undulating hips. *Either I'm a good teacher, or she's a good student, or I'm nuts for trying to figure anything out when I'm in this condition.* Then she spread her legs wider so he could go in farther, and his eyes about rolled back in his head from the sheer ecstasy.

He was out of control.

She was out of control.

He ground out his mind-blowing release.

She arched her belly up against his and refused to let his cock go as she convulsed around him, pumping every drop from him.

He was in dick heaven.

There was going to be hell to pay for doing this. He knew it, sure as SEALs loved sexy women, but he couldn't stop himself. Not now. Not when he planned to take her again. And again.

And then he did it again . . .

Hilda was stunned speechless, probably for the first time in her life.

So this is why men rut so much. This ecstasy, which is hidden from women, is what drives them.

"You're smiling . . . again," Torolf said, gazing down at her face. He was lying on his back, her head on his shoulder.

"So are you."

"You have no idea."

"So, is it this way for you all the time . . . every time you rut?" *Please do not say this was nothing special.*

"No! *Making love* has never been like this before."

Thank you, even if it is a lie, thank you. She tilted her head to the side, unconvinced.

"That's not a line, Hildy. You're incredible. Together we're more than incredible."

"Really?"

"Oh, yeah!"

"Can we do it again?"

"I thought you'd never ask." He nuzzled his face into her neck. "But we'll have to wait a little while till I . . . um, regroup."

"Hmmm." She placed her hand over his limp manpart, and immediately he grew against her palm. She smiled. *I love the way I can make his body do things, just as he can make mine do things, too.*

"Witch!" he said, rolling over on top of her. "This time we're going to take it slow. Very slow. And I'm going to learn all your secrets."

"I have no secrets." *That you need to know.*

"Wanna bet?" he said. "First, I think we need to find your G-spot."

"My what?"

"G-spot," he repeated, putting a hand over her nether hair. "It's right about here . . . on the inside."

"And what does this spot do?"

"It will make you come . . . like a man."

Hilda furrowed her brows, unable to figure out what he meant.

"And after that, I think we should find your Viking S-spot."

"You jest."

"No, I do not, babe."

"I have ne'er heard of it. How can you call it Viking?"

"Well, maybe only the Vikings in my family know of it."

"And where is that S-spot located?"

"Uh, uh, uh! It's a secret, but I'll give you a clue. It can only be found with the male tongue."

"You are teasing me."

"You'll find out."

And she did. Praise Valhalla, she certainly did.

Oops, she did it again . . .

"Hilda? Are you in there?"

Hilda was hiding in the storeroom late the next morning, trying to gather extra garments for the men who had come yesterday.

"I've been looking for you everywhere," Torolf said, coming into the room. "Are you all right?"

"Yea, I am all right." *Nay, I am not all right. I have lost my bloody mind.* "I am just . . . oh, my gods . . . your mouth looks all bruised and—"

"As if I'd been kissed . . . a lot?" He grinned. "You have a hickey on your neck."

She had a fair idea what he meant by hickey and slapped a hand to her neck.

He came closer.

She backed up. "We decided, Torolf. No more bedplay."

He nodded and still came closer.

She hit the wall.

"Just a kiss." He rubbed a thumb across her bottom lip.

She moaned. "We cannot."

He settled his lips on hers and coaxed her with little licks and nibbles to open for him. Then, somehow, his tongue was in her mouth, her gunna hiked to her waist, his braies pooled at his ankles, her legs wrapped around his naked hips, and his manpart stoking the still burning fires within her. A short time later, they lay sated on a pile of wool blankets.

"That was the last time," Hilda said.

"Absolutely," he agreed.

"Why were you looking for me?"

"Oh, my God! I can't believe I forgot." He sat up quickly, but not quickly enough.

The door to the storeroom swung open, and there stood two tall, black-haired men in magnificent Viking garb.

Behind them stood Torolf's fellow SEALs, grinning, of course . . . all of them.

"Yoo-hoo!" Pretty Boy said.

"Sweet!" Cage said.

"Way to go, dude!" Geek said.

"Dum de dum dum," JAM said.

"Oooops!" Torolf said.

"Forget oooops. I am going to kill you," Hilda said.

Torolf stood quickly and pulled on his braies. Meanwhile, Hilda wrapped herself in a blanket.

The two black-haired strangers just stared, one of them with mirth, the other with grimness. The one with dancing eyes said, "Do my eyes play me false, brother? Is that our cousin Torolf? Yea, I would recognize his arse anywhere."

Torolf grinned at the teasing man. "This is what I came to tell you, Hilda, before you distracted me."

All the men guffawed, and Cage remarked, "That's a new word for it . . . distracted. More like, way-*laid*."

"I would like you to meet my cousins, Thorfinn and Steven," the idiot said, as if she were not standing there bare-arse naked under a blanket and everyone else fully clothed. One of the men wore a black cloak of the softest wool, embroidered along the edge with red and gold thread in a writhing animal design, and lined with fleece. The other's wide shoulders were covered with a skin coat that reached nigh to his ankles, and upon his head was a gray fox fur cap.

But their finery matters not. More important, how could the lout forget his cousins had arrived? How could he forget that there were probably a shipload of men entering The Sanctuary, as we tupped away like Stig and his latest bitch? How could he forget—

"And this is Hilda Berdottir, the chatelaine of this sanctuary," he said with a wink at her. "And that's not a hickey on her neck, in case anyone's interested. It's just a bruise she got from bumping into a wall. And my mouth is bruised from hitting the same wall. So, don't anyone—"

She smacked the lout upside the head, wrapped the blanket more tightly around her, picked up her gunna, turned her chin to the ceiling, and left the stunned men behind her. Through the great hall, through the kitchen, through the back courtyard, she passed her suddenly quiet women as they worked at their normal chores. Only when she got to the stable did she drop the blanket, dress quickly, then put her hands to her hot face.

"What have I done?"

Betimes, naught will do but to kill a lackwit . . .

Hours later, Hilda sat on a stump high on the hill behind The Sanctuary. She was contemplating the bleating sheep before her and the sad state of her life when she heard Britta calling to her from a distance.

Esme, the shepherdess, looked up, as did Hilda, when Britta came running into the clearing, holding her side and panting for breath. "Milady . . . mistress . . . you must . . . pff, pff, pff . . . come quickly. They . . . pff, pff, pff . . . chop down . . . the dam."

"Whaaat? Who?"

"Torolf, his kin, the bloody SEALs and more men than you can count. With axes and battering rams and shovels, they are making quick work of demolishing the dam it took us so long to build."

Hilda was already rushing down the hill, Britta and Esme at her side, when she asked, "Why? Why would they do such a thing?"

"The cousins brought with them twelve longships, which are anchored many hides away down the fjord. They break the dam to raise the level of water so they can bring the vessels closer."

"Twelve . . . twelve longships!" Hilda sputtered. Then another thought occurred to her. "That must mean hundreds of men. Oh my gods! The Sanctuary will be filled with men."

When they neared the back courtyard, Hilda directed Britta, "Get me the broadsword. Gather those proficient with slingshots and lances, and follow me."

Soon they were rushing down the incline, over the large grassy sward, then the boggy swale, toward the fjord. The area was indeed flooded with men. Well-armed men. They carried halberds, scramasaxes, long-bladed single-edged knives, spiked maces, broadaxes, and shields.

She directed Britta and six of her women soldiers to aim for the men standing atop the dam, supervising the demolition. She motioned for the others, with lances, two dozen in all, to follow her. "Leave the lout for me. I will take great pleasure in lopping off his traitorous head."

"To the death!" they all shrieked then as they launched their assault. The two cousins and the pretty SEAL went down with small stones slung at their heads. Other men were ducking here and there to avoid the barrage of thrown lances, some of which were actually hitting their mark.

"Holy Thor! 'Tis a herd of witches flying at us," one Norseman exclaimed, throwing himself to the ground, hands over his head.

"If my manpart starts shriveling, someone is going to pay," another Norseman said, also throwing himself to the ground, but this time covering his precious organ with a shield.

It seemed then as if the crowd parted and Torolf, the bloody miscreant, stood spread-legged, hands on hips, wide-eyed and slack-jawed, especially when she raised the broadsword high and prepared to swing it in an arc, hopefully hitting his neck.

"Son of a bitch!" At the last second, Torolf ducked to

the side, and Hilda was propelled forward with her weighty sword, which flew from her hands as she landed flat on her face with an ignominious "Ooomph!" For a second, she saw stars.

When she raised her eyes, she saw Torolf's tanned leather boots in front of her. Coming clumsily to her feet, she met his angry gaze with an angry gaze of her own.

She and her women were surrounded by dozens of men wielding fierce-looking swords and battle-axes. Several of the men nursed bloody cuts from the slingshots and lances.

Torolf raised a hand for the men to stand back and hold arms. Then he addressed her in a steely voice, "Is this how you treat all your lovers, Hilda? Tsk-tsk-tsk! No wonder they are all dead."

"Is this how you treat all your lovers, Torolf? Tsk-tsk-tsk! No wonder you have never wed."

"What the hell is wrong with you?"

"I will tell you what is wrong, you filthy, untrustworthy, uncaring maggot of a man! How dare you destroy my dam? How bloody dare you?"

"Huh?"

"Lackwit, lackwit, lackwit! My dam!"

"That's what you're going ballistic over? Dammit! I thought it was something important. Sweetheart, that freakin' dam is hindering our mission."

"*Our* mission? By your leave, *sweetling*, ne'er did I approve the destruction of that . . . what did you name it . . . *free-can* dam, which, by the by, has been the one visible thing we women have been able to do to protect ourselves these past five years whilst you, your cousins, and every other able-bodied man in the Norselands was off somewhere else, doing only the gods know what . . . rutting their cocks off, no doubt."

Silence greeted her long, insulting lecture. But then, a loud, ominous noise filled the area, and water from the mountain runoff, which had been in a holding pond, and water that had been diverted and no longer was, rushed forth like a noisy waterfall. Hilda just stared, heartbroken, at all this breach represented. She blinked, willing herself not to cry, as some of her women already were.

"Be reasonable, Hilda. It's just a dam."

"Just a dam? You are a bloody idiot."

"We make a good pair, then. Because you're the one acting like an idiot, going postal over a bunch of rocks and twigs."

"You and I are no pair . . . in any way. Do not think that because I spread my thighs for you that it makes us a pair of anything. Not then, and for a certainty not now."

His brown eyes flashed, as if about to challenge her assertion. But then he visibly tamped down his temper. "Dams can be rebuilt. We'll help you . . . later. The demolition was best for our mission to defeat Steinolf."

"And if you do not defeat Steinolf? What then? If no men return to The Sanctuary, what then? Dost realize how helpless we would be here if longships were able to come so close?"

His silence and gritted teeth spoke much.

Understanding Women 101 . . . rather, Misunderstanding Women 101 . . .

Torolf watched with a mixture of anger and distress as Hilda and her women walked up the hill toward the keep, silent, as if they'd sustained some great loss.

Women! Even when you do them a favor, they get their noses out of joint. No appreciation!

"You ambushed her, Max. It really was a mistake to tear the damn thing down without even asking her," Geek pointed out.

"Guess you won't be getting any tonight, big boy." JAM

grinned at him. Sometimes JAM wasn't as saintly as he appeared.

Cage put a hand on his shoulder. "As my maw maw allus says, 'Ya cain't cook the crawfish lessen ya gots a flame.' And I'm seein' a big freeze in your future, Casanova."

"Not to worry, good buddy." Pretty Boy patted him on the shoulder. "Some days you're the dog, some days you're the hydrant."

"Cut the crap, all of you."

Thorfinn and Steven came up to him, swearing a blue streak in Old Norse.

That's all I need. Pain-in-the-ass, full-of-themselves Vikings, on top of pain-in-the-ass SEALs, not to mention a pain-in-the-ass female.

Just then, Stig came strolling by, carrying a stick the size of a baseball bat in his mouth. He didn't even give Torolf a second glance. Thank God!

"Hey, dude, is that your tighty whities I see wrapped around the stick that horn dog is carrying?" Pretty Boy pretended to be shocked. Who was he kidding? Torolf could have wrapped a condom and Pamela Anderson's phone number around the blasted thing and Pretty Boy wouldn't be shocked.

"It was the only piece of clothing I was willing to give up," he explained. "And it worked. So don't give me any grief."

"Should I tell the men to resume dismantling that dam?" Thorfinn asked him, his voice ringing with surliness. "Surely we will not cower beneath the scorn of that witch's fury."

Somebody is achin' for a breakin' here, and it's not me. "That witch owns this place."

"And that signifies how?" Thorfinn shot back. "Since when do the men in our family lie still for a maid's boot on their necks?"

"I think yer cuz might be sayin' yer pussy-whipped," Cage said.

"I don't need a freakin' translator." *Nor do I need cousins with an attitude.*

"Me, I'm jist tryin' to help," Cage said, grinning.

"We do not understand by half the way you talk now, Torolf," Steven said, staring at him with a puzzled expression on his face. "For example, you are a seal? Ha, ha, ha!"

"SEAL is just a name for the military group I'm with." Torolf noticed his SEAL buddies listening to him with as much attention as his cousins. It was still hard for them to accept that they'd time-traveled.

In fact, that was proven when Geek asked his cousins, "By the way, what year is this?"

Thorfinn and Steven gawked at Geek.

When Thorfinn answered, Geek exchanged looks with the rest of them . . . a mixture of surprise, horror, and excitement.

"Most of our men won't go up to the keep because of that bloody sign. Witches, nuns, shriveling cocks . . . enough to turn any full-blooded man away," Steven told Torolf. "I suggest we let them set up tents here in this clearing."

Pretty Boy whispered in an undertone to Cage, "Did you get a gander at some of those Vikings? They look like the barbarians on that Capital One TV ad . . . the one where Genghis Khan is riding the kiddie train at the mall and another brute is a flight attendant with a mace swinging from his shoulder."

"I know what you mean," Cage whispered back. "Y'all doan wanna meet any of 'em on a dark night on the bayou, thass fer sure. Even the gators would run away."

"Here's a news flash, Steve-o," Torolf told his cousin. "Those women don't want you or your men in their hall anyhow."

"That signifies how?" Thorfinn repeated, folding his arms across his chest and glaring at Torolf. *No family warmth here!* "Really, Torolf, you have been too long gone from the Norselands. Women must needs bow to a man's greater intelligence."

"Whoo-boy! You better not ever meet up with Gloria Steinem," Geek said.

"Glory sty-in-ham? What have glorified pig stys and hams to do with aught?"

"Never mind," Geek said, a grin splitting his freckled face.

I never thought I'd call another man a male chauvinist pig, but this cousin of mine is earning the title. Torolf pinched the bridge of his nose before looking at Thorfinn and matching him glower for glower. "The Sanctuary belongs to Brunhilda Berdottir by odal right. And it *signifies* that she has the right to expect courtesy from you, not insults or aggressive behavior."

Thorfinn's odd, grayish blue eyes narrowed at him. "What is she to you? Are you wed? Betrothed? Do you have claims on The Sanctuary and Amberstead?"

Torolf laughed. "None of the above. But our families . . . yours *and* mine, through your mother, my aunt Lady Katla . . . have been friends to Amberstead for many years. Hilda still has the right to answer to the name *lady*, even though she doesn't exercise that right at the moment. Treat her with respect, or . . ." He let his words trail off, deliberately.

"Or?" Thorfinn put his fists at his hips and glared at him some more. His cousin, who gave new meaning to dark and brooding, was aching for a fight, and everyone around them recognized that fact.

Steven stepped between the two of them. "The wench . . . uh, lady . . . is not married?"

Torolf shook his head slowly.

"Well, that is good news." Steven thumped his brother on the back. They were both tall, well-muscled fighting men, with black hair and those odd blue eyes, but where Thorfinn was grim and surly, Steven was smiling and friendly. "Finn and I are the youngest in our family. Landless knights."

"I think landless means poor as a Harlem church mouse," Geek explained to Pretty Boy.

"I know what landless means, dickhead," Pretty Boy shot back.

"Why would Hilda's marital status be good news?" Torolf asked.

"We seek wealthy wives with estates," Steven explained.

"Speak for yourself, lackwit," Thorfinn said. "I will not wed again. You may have Hilda and her estates if you wish."

So, Thorfinn had been married before. But what was this? They spoke of Hilda as if she had no choice in the matter. And, even worse, Torolf's heart sank at the prospect of Hilda marrying either of them. Which was ridiculous . . . because Thorfinn and Steven might be landless, but they had many hirds of soldiers who could help her recover and then hold Amberstead. *I'm a classic case of dog in the manger! Pathetic! Beyond pitiful!* "See, there you go again," he told Thorfinn. "Making assumptions about Hilda. Giving her no say in the matter. Just like the dam. You've gotta ask for her permission."

"You're the one who told us to go ahead with the dam destruction," Thorfinn pointed out. "Dost expect us to stop now and wait on the lady's whim to proceed?"

Torolf's face heated. He'd forgotten that he'd given final orders to demolish the dam. *Wait till Hilda finds out about that. She'll have my head in a basket.* "No, go ahead and finish the job. I'll take care of Hilda."

His buddies laughed at the idea of him "taking care" of Hilda. He trudged back up the hill to the keep, clearly dragging his feet. Thorfinn and Steven snickered.

"Chin up, little buckaroo," Pretty Boy advised.

Chin up, or chin down, Torolf dreaded the confrontation to come with Hilda. A lot.

Where's a suit of armor when a guy needs it?

Chapter 12

Making up is hard to do . . .

"You're mad at me."

Hilda flashed him a killing glance as he sat down, un-invited, beside her on a bench in the small milkhouse with its cold underground spring for cooling the goat milk, butter, and cheeses. "How can you tell, you clueless idiot?"

"Okay, *really* mad."

"Begone, lout. I am in no humor to deal with you now."

Hey, I'm in no hurry to deal with you either. Except maybe on your back or against the wall or straddling . . . oh, good grief! "When, then?"

She laughed. "A year or two."

"Let's clear the air here. Hindsight is great, but what good are woulda-coulda-shoulda's? Bottom line, I should have consulted you first about the dam."

"And you did not. Why?"

She is going to draw every drop of blood from me.

"I assumed you would want us to take every step leading to Steinolf's downfall."

"Not when any of those steps mean breaking down The Sanctuary's defenses."

"That's not being reasonable." *Like women are ever reasonable!* "Oh, don't go apeshit again. It's true. A troop of four hundred fighting men are better than just five military men and a handful of untrained women."

"You said it could work."

Since when do you listen to anything I say? "It might have, but now we don't have to take the gamble."

" 'Tis still a gamble."

"Yeah, but the odds are more in our favor now."

"How dare you gamble with our lives?"

"Life's a gamble, babe." *Man, I could use a beer.*

"Gods save me from your lackwit proverbs!"

"I promise, I'll rebuild the dam . . . when the battle is over." *Maybe two beers.*

"And if you die?"

Oh, nice! "Act as if you care, darling, why don't you?"

"Sarcasm ill suits you."

"I can't believe we just spent the night fucking each other's brains out, this morning, too. And now we're arguing."

"Must you be so crude?"

Sometimes the only thing that will do is a good F word. "Must you be so stubborn?"

"I prefer to forget the event ever happened."

"Events, honey, events! As in four friggin' times."

"Aaarrgh!"

Torolf figured he was making some progress if he provoked a growl out of her. It meant he was wearing her down. Still, he paced back and forth in the small dairy. He was tamping his temper down by taking long breaths in and out. "I'm sorry." *Wanna have sex?*

"For what?"

"Everything." *I said I'm sorry. That's usually the cue to have makeup sex.*

"Convenient apology. Covering thus and all."

"Yeah. Listen, what's done is done. What do you want us to do now? I'm not going to send my cousins and their soldiers away. Looking a gift horse in the mouth and all that."

"What horses? Thor's Teeth! Do not tell me they have brought horses with them. How will we ever feed all those men . . . and horses, too? Not only have you destroyed our biggest means of defense, but you will wipe out our food supply as well."

I've always wanted to have sex on a horse. But there are no horses here. Hmmm. Sex on a goat? Not quite the same. "There are no horses that I know of. That was just an expression. As for food and drink, tons of both are being carried from the longships as we speak. You'll have enough food left over to last you two winters. Besides, I'll send men out to hunt for game and to fish."

She nodded. "I have conditions."

"For what?"

"For allowing you and those other men to stay here."

Talk about backhanded hospitality! "And what're those conditions?" *There better be sex in there somewhere.*

"One, I do not want those men raping my women."

"Whaaat?"

"There are sixty women here, and hundreds of lustsome men out there . . . men who are wont to take what they want without asking. I insist they be warned of the consequences if even one woman is breached against her will. And I mean death for rape."

"Agreed. But I can't stop them from having consensual sex. So, if you want to avoid trouble, tell your women to keep their legs crossed. Some of your so-called nuns are hot to trot." *How about you, honey? Don't you feel even a little hot to trot?*

She didn't bother to ask what he meant by hot to trot. The curl of her upper lip indicated she understood. "I'll talk to them."

"You should know that Steven and Thorfinn have their eyes on you." *Dammit!*

"For the love of Frigg, why?"

"Marriage." *Dammit!*

"Are they barmy? Are you barmy?"

Yes and yes. "They're younger sons, looking for landed estates. You have odal rights to Amberstead. Marrying you would be the smart thing to do . . . for either of them. You could do worse. Steven is particularly interested."

"Pffff! He's younger than me. And too merry of heart. Even if I were in the market for a husband, which I am not, it would not be someone like him."

Yay! Torolf felt inordinately pleased at her outright rejection of Steven.

"The grim one is more to my taste."

Boo! Torolf felt inordinately displeased now.

She waved a hand dismissively. "I want those two no more than I want you."

"I could make you want me." *Holy shit! Why did I say that? I must have a screw loose.*

"Talking with you is like nailing gruel to the wall," she remarked with a shake of her head. "You say these things just to bait me. Well, I will not react to such folly."

He had to bite his tongue from saying something even more baiting. Like, "You have the most kissable mouth. It's big and pouty and fits mine just right. I especially liked the way you used it to—"

"Now, condition two. Britta and I and the other women you have been training must be a part of this mission . . . both in the planning and the execution."

"It won't be necessary now."

"Do not say me nay on this. We were good enough to play a role afore. Besides, I have a personal reason for going."

He quirked a brow at her.

"Steinolf put a Blood Eagle on my father's back. I plan to do the same to him."

"Personally?"

"Personally."

"You've got to be kidding. I doubt whether you've ever killed anyone, let alone butchered a body in that way. Not that he doesn't deserve it, but you won't be the one to do it."

"Have a caution, Torolf, you are not my master. I *will* come on this mission."

"We'll see." *Not in this lifetime.*

"And I expect that Britta and I will be involved in all the planning sessions."

"We'll see." *This ought to make Thorfinn thrilly-thrill-thrilled.* "Sure. Why not?"

"Condition three. No more bedplay betwixt us."

She's probably right. Nope, she is definitely right. But he couldn't resist saying, "We'll see."

"Hear me well: you will not take your ease on me again. So, stifle your brutish urges."

My brutish urges weren't so bad last night. "How about you taking your ease on me?" *What a ridiculous way to say "having sex"!* "You can be as brutish as you want."

"Why must you gainsay me at every turn? Will you agree to keep your lewd fingers to yourself?"

Lewd fingers, huh? She must be hot for me. "I'll try."

"Condition four. I will welcome you and your SEALs, your two cousins, and only a dozen of the hesirs into my hall for dinner tonight. After the meal, those chieftains will all bed down with their troops outside the keep."

"And what if your women invite them to stay?"

"I will speak with them first. None of my women will be allowed in the hall if they do not agree aforehand."

"Good luck outlawing sex." *Especially with me.* He grinned.

" 'Tis not a subject for mirth. Not to me."

"Okay, I'll tell them, but you'll probably hear the laughter all the way up here from the tent city down below."

"Assuming that you are able to unseat Steinolf and his vicious wolves, and that is not a certainty, how long will you remain here in the Norselands?"

"After I rebuild the dam?" he joked.

Her mouth didn't even twitch with a smidgen of laughter.

"As soon as we're able to leave to return to the future, we will. Don't you have any desire to see all the modern marvels?"

"Is that an invitation?" He must have blanched, because she laughed. "Do not worry, Torolf. I have no inclination to leave the Norselands, despite your hugely self-touted charms, not even to time-travel to the future . . . not that I believe that is possible. 'Tis just another of your jests."

I wish!

The wheels of the mission go round and round, round and round . . .

Hilda listened carefully as Torolf led the meeting with his SEAL friends, Thorfinn, Steven, several chieftains, and fifteen of the women. She was impressed, despite her best intentions.

On the outside, Torolf portrayed himself as a no-care rogue, more intent on bedeviling than serious undertakings. Apparently, it was a facade.

The meeting, held in the lower end of the hall, started with Thorfinn protesting the presence of her and the other women. "What need have we of twittering females doing men's work?"

Before Hilda had a chance to leap forth and slice off the haughty knight's tongue, Torolf raised a halting hand. "The women stay. Their stake in this mission is as great or greater than our own. You seek riches. I seek revenge. The women seek a return to peaceable times."

"You take responsibility then," Thorfinn said.

"I will. My men and I can do a tight package on Hilda."

"A tight package?" Hilda and Thorfinn asked at the same time.

"We surround the person as we are going into the kill zone," he explained.

"You will not package me in any way," Hilda ordered. "We women carry our own weight in this mission. Yea, we are not as strong as men, but we can be used in other ways."

"I agree," Steven said at her side, putting an arm over her shoulders. The man had become like a gnat on her backside.

She shrugged out of his arm and noticed Torolf glaring at Steven, who smirked back at him.

"Okay, we'll use Rakel and two of the other women if it becomes necessary to lure the guards out."

"I can lure, too," Hilda insisted. *He better not hint that I am not lure-worthy; he will get more than goat milk on his head.*

Torolf hesitated, but then he said, "If you want."

He wasn't fooling her, though. He would still resist.

"I view this as a three-pronged attack," Torolf said then. "By surf penetration to Norstead, by land to Norstead, and by land to Amberstead. The other estates can be taken care of later. Two SEALs assigned to each prong. Thorfinn, you can lead the sea insertion, if that's okay with you?"

Thorfinn nodded. "I can take two hundred men in four

longships and leave the other men for land entry. I know the sea area well. A rock portage to the north side would be best."

"Steven, you can lead a hundred men—and, yes, Hilda, some women—to Amberstead. I'll take Norstead. Each of us will have a hundred or so men with us. Hilda, will you go to Amberstead with Steven since you know those secret tunnels?"

She shook her head. "'Tis Norstead for me. That is where Steinolf is reputed to be."

Torolf was about to argue with her, knowing her intent, but then he relented and went on to other subjects. "I suggest that we put off our D-day for one week so that we can all work together on plans and exercises. Agreed?" He looked at each person individually, but there was no disagreement.

"It's important that we engage the enemy in all places at once," Geek said. "Inserting into the kill zone has got to be synchronized for optimum surprise."

"We SEALs prefer to operate at night. I'm thinking ten o'clock, when Steinolf's men will be less alert, ready for sleep, probably drunk." Torolf walked back and forth in front of the rest of them, who were seated. "Usually we SEALs hit the ground running. Arrive fast, engage, then leave fast, but in this case, I assume we'll be sticking around to clean up and establish order and new leadership."

"How will we all know it is ten at night?" Thorfinn scoffed. That cousin seemed to have some grudge with Torolf, or mayhap he was just a surly sort.

"Watches," Torolf said, pointing to a piece of jewelry on his wrist made of leather and glass. At a motion of his head, Geek and JAM took off their watches, showing them to Steven and Thorfinn, who were seemingly amazed. When Torolf showed Hilda his watch and explained its working, she was amazed, too. Truly this land where Torolf had come from must be a wondrous place if it had these kinds of marvels.

Much time was spent oohing and aahing over the watches, before Steven and Thorfinn were given one each for the mission.

"The logistics of all this can be worked out among us over the next week. We all use different weapons and have different styles of fighting, but I think we can complement each other's talents. For now, I say, let's eat, suck a little foam, and start working hard early tomorrow morning."

Thorfinn glanced at him and then at Hilda, questioning. Torolf had already told the man of her rules, which must have offended him, that she would imply they were rapists, but she could take no chances.

Hilda stood and addressed them all. "Everyone is welcome to stay for the evening meal. Mayhap the SEALs will even entertain you with their music. We have no sleeping quarters for you, being a small keep and a women's sanctuary, but you may take turns using our bathhouse."

"We have been long at sea," Thorfinn said, standing to stretch. He was a fine-looking man, though lacking in good sense, for he blathered on, "We need our clothing washed. And send some women to tend us in the bathhouse with fresh linens."

Hilda bristled.

Britta snorted.

Several of the SEALs snickered, and Cage said, "In the bayou, we call this an uh-oh second."

Thorfinn, the lackwit, looked about him, unaware of his blunder. It was true that many households provided hospitality to their guests, including help with bathing and washing their clothes. But these were uninvited, could hardly be classified as guests, and there were bloody four hundred of them.

"Behave, Hilda," Torolf whispered in her ear.

"Hah!" she whispered back. "On second thought, methinks you men should bathe in the fjord . . . both your clothing and your bodies. My bathhouse will be in use by my women, who have much *other* work to do."

A silence descended, broken only by the crackling of the fire in the nearby hearth and by the noises at the other end of the hall, where casks of food and ale and Frankish wine were being carried in.

The men shuffled outside then. Steven stayed behind, much to Torolf's apparent displeasure. "I just wanted to tell you . . . my brother means no disrespect. He has suffered much at the hands of a woman and is betimes unable to repress his hostilities."

She tilted her head in question.

"His wife left him two years ago, ran away with an outlawed Viking, and took Thorfinn's infant son with her. Pirates attacked their longship, killing everyone on board except his son, whom they carried off to only the gods know where . . . possibly the Arab lands. It is believed the child is dead, too, since no trace has been found of him, and, believe you me, Thorfinn has tried."

"How terrible!"

Torolf came back in then and yelled from the doorway. "If you're done sucking up, Steven, maybe you could come out here and tell your brother to stop pissing off everyone in sight with his sweet personality."

Steven laughed and went out the door.

Torolf stomped up to her, kissed her hard, and shoved her out the door in front of him with a familiar hand on her bottom.

The lout! she thought, but she was smiling.

I'm not thinkin' about you, baby, except when I walk and talk and eat and sleep and . . .

Torolf felt like he was in the eye of a tornado, totally at the mercy of forces beyond his control. It didn't help that he was half-blitzed from his cousins' stash of French wine.

No wonder he was disoriented, though. Time travel. Landing in a sort of nunnery. Training female soldiers. Now helping to plan a combined mission of know-it-all Vikings, women, and SEALs. It gave new meaning to the term *special forces*. And then there was Hilda. Lordy, Lordy, he was in deep and drowning fast.

He could only imagine what his buddies must think of this bizarre scene surrounding them. Hell, he'd been here before—in the past—and he found it beyond belief.

Pretty Boy was enjoying himself, though. Right now, he had Britta trapped between a bench and a hearth, giving her the full-throttle assault with his accumulated store of seduction techniques. Britta looked a bit shell-shocked.

Thorfinn was in a serious discussion with JAM, something about the similarities between Viking and Christian religions.

Cage had Hilda's good friend Inge sitting on his lap wearing his cowboy hat. This, despite Hilda having given her women orders not to have men in their bed furs while the Norsemandy Vikings were in the area.

Dagne was playing the lute, and a young man on another lute accompanied her to some soft medieval-style songs. They could hardly be heard over the volume of noise. There were only a dozen or so of the Norsemandy Viking men here, but add to that the five SEALs, about three dozen women, and the Norstead and Amberstead men who had come to The Sanctuary the day before . . . talking, laughing, playing dice or the board game, *hnefatafl*, and drinking . . . lots of drinking.

Hilda flitted in and out of the hall as she supervised the meal and cleanup. His eyes followed her everywhere, and he was not happy to see Steven at her side, helping her, making her laugh, touching her arm or shoulder.

He was becoming obsessed with the woman. Why, he had no idea. *Ha, ha, ha!* Sure, there had been the mind-blowing sex. But so what? Sex was sex. Some of it mind-blowing. Some of it so-so. *Note to Torolf: you are full of shit.* And he was worried about her. *If Steinolf ever got ahold of her . . .* And she annoyed the hell out of him. *Big time.* And he wanted to nail her so long and so hard that her blasted hot blue eyes rolled around in her head like the cherries on a slot machine. *You gotta love the male imagination.* Yep, he was losin' his mind. Testosterone: God's way of reminding men that, cut to the bone, they are only dumb men.

"Why are you muttering to yourself?" Hilda asked, pouring more wine into his goblet. He hadn't realized she'd come back into the hall. Her hair hung down her back in a single braid, but many tendrils had escaped due to the heat in the hall from the fires and body heat from so many people.

I am not picturing it as it looked loose and spread out like a silver blanket, the dark red of the fox pelts beneath her, and me above her. And that lurch of pleasure between my legs is just an alcohol buzz. Oh, this is just great! Half-blitzed and now half-hard, too!

She wore a finer gunna tonight than she had previously . . . a dark blue wool. Nothing like the silks she'd no doubt owned in the past, but pretty nonetheless.

Is she dressing to please Steven or Thorfinn?

He bit his bottom lip to keep from growling.

Steven came up then and smiled at Torolf as if they were good friends. "Hilda, come rest a bit, and we can discuss those hidden tunnels of yours at Amberstead."

Hah! I know which hidden tunnels you're interested in, Steve-o-lech, and they aren't at Amberstead.

Hilda set the urn of wine on the head table beside him, then wiped her hands on her apron before removing it. She was about to walk off with Steven when she glanced his way, then did a double take. "What ails you, Torolf? Your face looks fierce, as if in some pain."

Oh, yeah, I've got a pain all right. "Gas," he said, and stood, waving a hand for them to take the empty seats at the head table, while he walked off to join his buddies. *Time to take this half blitz to a full-tilt boogie, knee-walking, mind-numbing drunk.*

A short time later, he and his buddies, to the accompaniment of Pretty Boy on his lute-guitar, were belting out drinking songs. First, Garth Brooks's old favorite, "I've Got Friends in Low Places," which the Viking men loved and asked them to repeat three times. Then, The Animals' "We Gotta Get Out of This Place," a particularly apt song for him and the other SEALs. They sang that one three times, too. By the time they got to "Crazy," a mix of Patsy Cline and Aerosmith, they were all schnockered and more than a little bit . . . yep, crazy.

He awakened the next morning with a big head. A big head that was resting on the hall's trestle table where it had fallen the night before. His head felt the size of a pumpkin, and he could swear an AK-47 was ripping out ammo inside. His fuzzy tongue tasted like gammelost. And he suspected he was drooling.

Can life get any better than this? Or worse?

Turns out, it could. Try teaching four hundred Vikings with the ale head how to jog.

Chapter 13

Men will be boys . . . even Viking men . . .

Hilda stood at the top of the motte, surveying the incredible scene down below, across the wide sward that led two hectares toward the fjord.

Dozens of tents and small fires dotted the landscape where hundreds of Viking warriors stood about, eating, sharpening weapons, and practicing warfare skills. And here, in the section closest to the motte, a large group watched Torolf and his two cousins entertain the crowds.

"What are the fools doing?" Hilda muttered to herself.

"It's a trick Max and all of his family members can perform," Cage told her, coming up behind her on the drawbridge. "They claim they can do this in the middle of a battle, but, me, I doan know 'bout that."

Torolf stood at one end, about twenty paces from Steven, who stood twenty paces from both him and Thorfinn. Each held deadly lances in their hands. Torolf threw his lance with accuracy toward Thorfinn, who caught the spear, and, in one deft movement, twirled it about his fingers and threw the lance back at Torolf. Torolf, in turn, caught the lance, flicked it betwixt his fingers and sent it to Steven, who also caught it. Over and over, they performed this exercise, laughing like youthlings over silly games. Even the dour Thorfinn was mirthful today.

Stig was tied to a tree off to the side, sitting and watching Torolf with an adoring expression on his dog face.

"Torolf told me once that he has a great uncle, King Olaf, who perfected this talent, and all the rest of his family have learned to do it, too."

" 'Tis a dubious talent."

Cage wore that ridiculous cowboy hat and boots. *Who ever heard of a boy who was a cow?* But he was a wickedly handsome man, ever jestful, just like Torolf. "I doan know 'bout that, *chère*. It sure impresses the ladies back home." He waggled his eyebrows at her in a lackwit manner.

"Speaking of your home . . . this Ah-mare-eek-ah, do you share Torolf's assertions that it is a land far away *in the future*?"

Cage's mischievous expression turned serious. "Hard to believe, but it sure seems so. Either that, or we're all in the middle of some fantastic dream. It's gone on too long for it to be a joke, and, me, I've never had a dream with such detail."

Hilda still thought there had to be some other explanation. "Are you anxious to get home?"

"Yeah, I am."

"Do you have family there?"

"Just my maw maw . . . that's Cajun for grandmother."

"No wife or promised one?"

"Nope, I like to play the field. Spread myself around."

She had to laugh at the rascal's merry words. "And Torolf?"

"Why not ask him?"

"I have, but 'tis hard to know when he teases and when he tells the truth. The man does joke overmuch."

"Don't judge a book by the cover."

"Huh?"

"Max gives the impression of allus bein' cheerful, but he's deep, like all of us. I think he feels guilty fer havin' a more privileged life . . . fer not bein' here to help Norstead and his sister, Madrene. And he works damn hard to defend his country. Mostly, he's a good friend to me, and good friends are rare."

"I did not mean to give offense."

His eyes were dancing merrily again. "I know that, but Max and I are very close. We finish each other's sentences . . . can sometimes read each other's thoughts. So, hurt him, and you hurt me, too."

"What makes you think that I could hurt Torolf?"

"He cares about you, Hilda."

"Hah! He cares about what I have betwixt my legs."

Cage laughed and hugged her about her shoulders. "That, too, babe. But, seriously, my maw maw, she allus says, 'The apple, she gotta fall from the tree sometime.'"

She was afraid to ask, sensing a trap. "What does that mean?"

"It means that every man and every woman gots to bite the love bullet sometime."

"Love? I do not understand you by half, but one thing I do know, there is naught of love betwixt me and the lout."

"If you say so," Cage replied with a grin. "Another thing my maw maw allus says, 'Everyone gotta have a little joie de vivre in their life.'"

"Jwah duh vee?"

"Yeah, love of life. So, bit of advice here, *bébé*, let some of Max's joie de vivre rub off on you. It's a good thing."

Torolf saw them coming and set his spears aside. "Hey,

Hildy, I have something to show you." His eyes danced just as merrily as his friend Cage's.

She looked down below his belt to his zip-per and said, with a sauciness that was new to her, "I have seen all you have to show, knave."

Cage squeezed her shoulder and said, "Way to go, honey!"

But Torolf got the last word in when he replied, with equal sauciness, "Wanna bet?"

Just a little male bonding . . .

Torolf and his buddies sat around a campfire with Thorfinn and Steven, sipping fine ale, following a day of hard military exercise.

The two Norsemen had no knowledge of modern weapons or military maneuvers, but they were excellent warriors, just the same. All of the SEALs, himself included, had been impressed at how well they had kept up with a hard routine today. And, actually, the two men had taught them a thing or two about fighting, as well.

"I know we believe in different types of fighting," Torolf started off with his cousins, "but there are some basic tenets we all have to follow on this mission . . . or all bets are off."

"What tenets?" Thorfinn asked suspiciously.

"First of all, we—the five of us—are U.S. Navy SEALs."

Steven grinned and made a barklike sound mimicking seals: "Ork, ork, ork!"

"Not that kind of seal, lamebrain," he remarked to Steven, not unkindly. It was hard not to like Steven. Hilda would say it was because they were cut from the same "jestsome" cloth. "SEALs is the name of an elite military group that stands for sea, air, and land."

Thorfinn studied him closely. "Why did you not just say so, instead of taking on that silly name?"

Aaarrgh! "One of our integral exercises is based on CQD, or Close Quarter Defense. That's what we insist be followed in taking Steinolf down."

"Insist? What gives you the right to insist?" Thorfinn again. *The jerk!*

"Norstead is mine, and Amberstead belongs to Hilda. That gives me the right."

"You cannot win without our help," Thorfinn pointed out.

Torolf shrugged. *Asshole!*

"Tell us what you have in mind," Steven intervened, "and then we will *all* decide what is best."

"Your brother could take personality lessons from you," Torolf told Steven.

"Dost really think I care what you think of me?" Thorfinn gave him a superior, snoot-up-in-the-air glance of disdain.

"That chip on your shoulder must really weigh you down."

"You do not even speak like a Viking anymore."

"Please!" JAM stood and raised his hands in the air like a referee or a priest. "Let's calm down and work together."

Torolf and Thorfinn both grinned at each other. They'd enjoyed the verbal sparring.

"CQD is a combination of martial arts, commando-style fighting, and spiritual focusing. It's based on the idea of an inner warrior." Torolf was having a hard time explaining modern military terms in eleventh-century language.

"Speak clearly, cousin. Your words are clear as mud," Thorfinn told him.

"There's one part of CQD that is important to us, and we think it has to be followed here. CQD can be explosively violent in one situation and mild in another. It's called earned treatment. In other words, not all of the enemy deserve to be killed, and that decision has to be made on the spot. There may be people, even soldiers, in Norstead and Amberstead who do not deserve death."

Thorfinn drew his lips in thoughtfully. "It has always been my policy to spare women and bairns."

"That's not what I mean."

"How do you tell the good enemy from the bad?" Steven asked.

At least Steven was allowing that there might be both.

"If a man is coming at you with a weapon, of course, you kill him," Geek interjected. "But what if some dumb fuck is shivering in a corner, wetting his pants? What if some men surrender, hands up? What if there are just too damn many of them to kill them on the spot?"

"There has to be a difference. There has to be humanity," JAM added.

Thorfinn looked at JAM as if he'd sprouted two heads. "That is the most demented thing I have ever heard. Are you a priest or a warrior?"

"Actually, JAM was a priest at one time, but that's beside the point," Torolf said.

"Almost a priest," JAM corrected.

"As my maw maw allus says—" Cage began.

And four SEALs groaned.

Cage flashed them a fake glower. "As my maw maw allus says, 'Ya cain't tell the chipmunk from the squirrel till you got 'em in your crosshairs.' "

"What in bloody hell did he just say?" Steven asked Torolf.

"The same thing I just said. On-the-spot decisions need to be made about who deserves to be killed and who doesn't."

"I am not going to put my men in danger," Thorfinn insisted.

"I'm not asking you to. Just be careful, and let us teach you how to make that split-second decision."

"Why should we do what you ask?" Thorfinn asked him.

"In return, I give you Norstead."

"Whaaat?" Thorfinn was poleaxed by that generous offer. "Why would you do that?"

"Because I intend to leave here after the battle. If possible, me and my buddies are going back to America. It
would be a favor to me, actually, if I knew Norstead was in
good hands . . . in family hands."

"And Amberstead?" Steven asked.

"I'm pretty sure Hilda would rather stay here, but that
can be decided later."

Steven waved a hand in the air dismissively. "I will have
Amberstead, one way or another. Either by gift or wedlock."

You overconfident dickhead! "You're awfully sure of
yourself."

"I have wordfame with women," Steven bragged. "Seduction is one of the gifts the gods have favored me with.
In truth, there are ways to turn a woman lustsome for a
man's touch."

No kidding!

Torolf heard his buddies snicker, but he barely restrained himself from belting his cousin.

"If you are worried about Hilda, do not be," Steven continued. "I would treat her well. And if she chooses to stay
here at The Sanctuary, that is all well and good. I intend to
bring my mistress from Norsemandy anyhow."

Torolf clenched his fists.

"I need to visit the bathhouse," JAM said, and the other
guys stood up with him. Torolf remained sitting.

As they were walking off, he heard Pretty Boy ask the
others, "Do you think Britta would take a bath with me?"

Laughter was his answer.

Once his buddies were gone, Torolf took a deep breath.
"There is something important I have to tell you. It's about

where I've been all these years . . . where my entire family has been. They are not dead."

Thorfinn and Steven gave him their full attention.

"I have time-traveled to the twenty-first century to a land called America . . ." When he was done, a long silence followed as Thorfinn and Steven stared at him with a mixture of pity and disbelief.

"Is this a jest, or have you gone barmy?" Steven inquired as he took a long, final draw on his horn of ale.

As Torolf walked off then, he heard Steven say to Thorfinn, "Methinks we arrived just in time. Our cousin is destined for the barmy farm."

All bad things must come to an end . . .

This was the day.

Hilda could hardly contain her excitement as they approached Norstead with only the light of a half moon. Norstead was designed over many years in the hill fort style: concentric rings of walls and ditches around a central enclosure, all surrounded at the edges by moat and drawbridge. In front, there was a grassy sward used for military exercises.

She, Torolf, Cage, a dozen women, and one hundred men moved silently through the forest in a series of trains. That was where a person carried a weapon in their right hand and kept the left hand on the shoulder in front of them, snaking their way forward. Torolf was the point man in front of her train and Cage the tail man in back. Cage had made jokes, which she did not understand, when first told he would be the tail man. They all watched for hand signals, which they had learned this past week to indicate silence, man up ahead, number of men up ahead, stop, spread out, ready weapons, those kinds of things.

With silent signals to Torolf, Cage made his way, like a black shadow along the edges of the forest, then ran in a crouch to the moat on the side of the keep, which he crossed. Then he climbed up the timber sides with the agility of a cat. When he was at the top, he waved to Torolf, then disappeared. Another and another and another followed suit on both sides of the keep, moving stealthily. Dozens of the cousins' hirdsmen had trained over and over for this part of the battle.

The rest of them hid at the edge of the sward, following Torolf's signal to spread out two strides apart all around the semicircle of forest. A perimeter, it was called. Torolf looked at the ornament on his wrist and indicated it was not yet time. He then held up ten fingers, to show that it would be ten minutes till Thorfinn and his hird were at their appointed place near the rock wall, behind the keep. Steven would be at the ready, as well, at Amberstead.

Their initial assault would be a combination of SEAL and Viking military methods. The leapfrog maneuver of Torolf's special forces would get them in position of the Norse *svinfylkja*, or swine wedge, with its triangular tactical assault formation, its point facing the enemy.

The drawbridge was already down . . . thank the gods . . . due to Steinolf's overconfidence. They needed to draw the sentries forward, away from their shields and guard wall. That would be her and Rakel's job, along with a small band of Torolf's hird, which would pretend to be the assault soldiers, leading Norstead's invaders in the wrong direction.

They hoped.

All of the men and the other women, except for her and Rakel, had their faces cammied up with mud and dirt to blend in with the forest. Blond hair was covered with hoods or scarves on male and female.

Torolf raised a hand for her and Rakel to come forth. He was still angry with her for insisting on participation in this part of the battle. Well, there was naught new in that. He was ever fuming over one thing or another. She and Rakel dropped their fur mantles. Their hair lay loose over bare shoulders of deliberately indecent gowns. Torolf's eyes took in her appearance, and despite the danger of their situation and the coldness betwixt them, she could see appreciation there. Or mayhap he was appreciating her suddenly buxom chest, which she had stuffed with two balls of yarn. Yea, he noticed, all right. His lips were twitching with a grin.

She and Rakel began to stagger drunkenly across the clearing, up to the moat, laughing and singing a bawdy song, with their arms over each other's shoulders as if for support. The night air was cold, and they shivered with the chill, or more likely they shivered because they were frightened to the bone.

"Who goes there?" a guard leaning over the parapet asked.

Rakel looked up, pretended to sway, then fell on her rump, pulling Hilda with her. "Two merry maids," she called up, ending with a very believable and loud hiccup. "Be there any merry men up there?"

There was laughter and several more men joined the first, leaning over the parapet. "Are ye *drukkinn*?" one asked.

"Nay, jist a bit tipsy from me uncle's ale," Hilda slurred.

"Can we come in?" Rakel asked, also slurring her words.

"Well, that depends," the first guard said. "There are four of us and only two of you."

Rakel said something so vulgar that Hilda could scarce comprehend its meaning, something about what she could do with three men at one time.

Much hooting laughter greeted her words.

Rakel must have sensed her stare, because she turned to wink at her. "Men! They will believe anything when it comes to their precious manparts."

"Come in then, lassies. We have somethin' fer you in here. Somethin' big and hard. Ha, ha, ha!"

"How disgusting!" Hilda muttered.

Rakel pretended to try to stand, then fell back down. "Methinks I might need a bit of help here. First one here, gets me specialty."

Five sets of feet could be heard scuffling away, then pounding down some steps.

"What exactly is your specialty?" Hilda asked.

"Shhh. Later," Rakel said.

The men were rushing across the drawbridge, pushing at each other to be first. Just then, Hilda and Rakel heard a short bird whistle, the signal for the diversionary hird to come forth on the far side of the field. When they became visible, shooting arrows at first, then lances, she and Rakel rushed back away from the fighting, running toward Torolf and his hird.

Behind them, they could hear a bell being rung, alerting the rest of the keep to some danger. Men came rushing out, most having been awakened, since they were still pulling on their clothes. Despite their state of unreadiness, they had swords and lances and battle-axes at the ready.

"You did good," Torolf said to Rakel. He squeezed Hilda's shoulder and whispered against her ear, "You, too, sweetie."

His praise should not matter to Hilda, but it did. She did not even resist as she stepped back to the end of the formation as planned. Torolf had promised that she would get her revenge against Steinolf in the end.

Now that many of Steinolf's men were outside the keep, running after the thirty or so men who were to lead them into the open, Torolf kept muttering, "Double back, double back," as if the men on the far side could hear him. The moment he saw them do just that, he let loose with a wild war whoop, and he and his men went rushing forth, yelling out battle cries. "Go, go, go!" "To the death!" "Luck in battle!" "Mark them with your spears!" "Smite the bastards!" "Be crows, not carrion!" "Save Steinolf for me!" Those first and last came from Torolf.

In essence, Steinolf's troop was pinned in by their forces on two sides. There would be those inside, of course, but this would be a good start.

Presumably, Thorfinn and his hird of one hundred would be assaulting the keep from the back at the same time.

For almost an hour, Rakel and Hilda stood watching, the sounds of swords clanging, the ringing of arrows, the slap of leather, the crack of axe hitting bone, and over it all groans, and shrieks, and screams of hurt and dying men. Sword dew aplenty flowed, and many broke the raven's fast, even as they watched. One of Torolf's SEAL friends, JAM, cleft a man to the teeth with an axe, then moved on without looking back. There were berserkers on both sides, those gone mad with the bloodlust. She could not be sorry for the lifeless bodies, because many of the dead would be those who had invaded both this land and hers during the past five years. Vicious, vicious men with no souls. The other four women with them were up in trees near them, picking off stray soldiers who came in their direction with sharp arrows. They were able to differentiate their brothers-in-arms from the foemen because at the last moment theirs had tied a strip of white linen on their left upper arms.

The men under Torolf and Thorfinn fought with great wrath, in some cases backing the enemy up against a wall before spearing them through the heart or garroting them with a thin rope. Thorfinn and Steven had gifted Torolf with a finely crafted sword, which he'd immediately named Avenger. Hilda noted that he was weapon skillful with the broadsword, as were his cousins, hewing down men even larger than themselves.

Though the battle appeared to be over, she and Rakel still waited. And still no Torolf. Geek came over to her at one point and said, "We've found the package," which she interpreted to mean they'd found Steinolf. "Stay put. Max's orders."

Orders or not, she could wait no longer. What if Torolf were injured? What if he had died of the sword drink, like so many others? Her heart beat wildly as she ran toward the keep, crossed the drawbridge, and headed for the great hall.

She found Torolf near the stable, fighting hand-to-hand with Steinolf. His men stood back, probably at Torolf's direction. The beast had not aged well. Never handsome to begin with, his hair and beard were mostly gray now, tangled and unkempt.

Torolf's tunic and braies were covered with blood, as were Steinolf's. Torolf had a mean slice across his cheek that would need stitching, and another on his thigh. But most worrisome, Steinolf, yellow teeth bared with savage fury, had a lock secured on Torolf's neck from behind with an arm, pinning his right wrist with the other to prevent him using his sword. But Torolf managed to escape Steinolf's slippery hold on him and sprang around and back on his feet. They were both panting for breath.

It was then that Hilda noticed the mortal stab wound in Steinolf's chest, but that was not all she noticed. From his burly neck hung an amber medallion encased in gold, suspended on a thick chain. Her father's.

Hilda went berserk then. All the destruction and pain caused by this man hit her like a mace to the head. She saw him through a red haze as she ran, dagger drawn. Without thinking, she lunged forward, reflexively aiming the sharp knife in the manner the SEALs had taught her . . . no direct stab, but arcing upward from his fat belly where the vital organs were located.

Everyone was stunned speechless, watching her.

Steinolf's eyes went wide with horror, and his last words were, "Bloody bitch!" afore he fell backward to the ground, blood gushing forth in pools.

The red haze began to clear, and the buzzing noise in her ears subsided as she began to register the scene before and around her. Torolf was coming toward her, a worried look on his face. *Why? I am fine. Steinolf is dead. The Norselands will be at peace again.*

Torolf picked her up.

She wanted to tell the lout to put her down.

He kept whispering nonsensical soothing things in her ear, as if she would be shattered over killing the beast. She tried to tell him to put her down, that she was glad of mood, ecstatic over the killing, but no words would come from her mouth. She glanced in front of her, saw the bloody knife still in her hand, and screamed. It was Steinolf's blood, and it almost totally covered the white skin of her hand.

She dropped the knife with a whimper. Then she lost consciousness.

Chapter 14

You can't go home again . . .

"Find a clean place for me to lay the lady down," Torolf yelled to the cowering housecarls and maids in the hall.

"Yea, milord."

"'Tis fair good to see ye back, milord," a toothless old man told him, his rheumy eyes tear-filled with joy at his presumed return.

"May the gods bless ye for comin' to save us from the beast," one maid said.

Over and over, his people—that's how they regarded themselves, considering him jarl of this estate—touched him in passing or called out their thanks. Little did they know, he was not staying. Still, he was touched by their sentiments and heartsick over what they must have suffered.

The maids led him to a large master bedchamber off the great hall, which had its own fireplace for heat, a novelty in the Norselands at this time. Torolf knew this because his own grandsire had designed it for his wife, Lady Asgar. One maid was pulling soiled linens and bed furs off the bed, and two others were already putting on clean sheets and a wool blanket. Tears streaked their faces, no doubt tears of joy.

He placed Hilda down gently and kissed her forehead. Then he motioned for the women to clean up the rest of the filthy chamber. He also whispered to one woman to bring a tub and hot water here for a bath, if one were available. Hilda would want to wash off the blood as soon as she awakened.

While the women did their work, he went out to find Thorfinn, who was already lording it over everyone. Torolf had told him days ago that Norstead was his for the taking as long as he paid Hilda for her lifetime ten mancuses of gold each year, or sent to The Sanctuary its equivalent in game, oats, produce, and trade goods for a period of no less than twenty years. He'd also advised Steven to do the same with Amberstead, in the event Hilda would not wed with him, which she had sworn she would not, preferring to continue her work at The Sanctuary.

"How many dead and wounded?" he asked Thorfinn.

"A hundred of Steinolf's men dead, including himself and three of his chieftains. Thirty-seven wounded, some gravely.

"Our side?"

"Ten dead, ten wounded. I have heard naught from Steven. There may be more on their way to Valhalla or to the healer."

"And captives secured?"

Thorfinn rolled his eyes. "More than I care to mention. Each will have to be dealt with separately. I will hold a Thing on the morrow, and some of your old retainers here can help me identify those who can be trusted to join with us and those guilty of such cruelty that we would not want them in our midst."

"What will you do with those?"

Thorfinn looked surprised at his question. "Send them to burn in the fires of Muspell, of course."

Torolf nodded. "You said you have no intention of marrying again. You'll have to marry if you're to rule here. There must be heirs to carry on."

"I suppose, though not anytime soon." He shrugged. "If Hilda does not take my brother, mayhap I will offer for her one day. She is not very comely, nor built to please a man's hunger, but then my wife was comely, with breasts to turn a monk to sin. She turned out to be a harlot. Yea, methinks I will seek a homely wife this time."

"Are you blind? Hilda is not homely," he snapped. "And if you measure a woman's sexiness by the size of her boobs, then you are a world-class . . . boob."

Thorfinn grinned, or what passed for a grin with him. "Smitten, are you?"

"I am not smitten. It's just that I admire Hilda tremendously. You have no idea what tortures she and her women experienced under Steinolf, and how hard Hilda worked to build a refuge for them at The Sanctuary."

"A saint, she is, then?" Thorfinn arched his eyebrows at him in the infuriatingly condescending way he had. "'Tis not much joy in bedding a saint, if you ask me."

Torolf fisted his hands and willed himself not to argue with the jerk anymore. He hated to think of Hilda giving herself to such a cold man. It wouldn't be much of a marriage. Hardly better than her other three husbands, though Thorfinn was younger. Would he give her pleasure, or care only about making a child and his own needs? *I should not care. I do not care. It is not my problem.* "I'll help you here at Norstead as much as I can. Then I'm going back to The Sanctuary with any of the women who care to return. From there, my friends and I are going home." *If we can.*

"What should we do with Steinolf's body? He is a

nithing, and I am loath to give him any respect, even in death. Better that his body be left for the wolves to savor."

"I agree."

"The others we will put on a funeral pyre away from the keep. The stink will be unbearable. We could toss them off the rock cliff and into the sea, but I fear they would just wash back with the waves."

"Fire is best, but no funeral rites for these villains. And let me talk to Hilda about Steinolf first. She had some . . . um, plans for Steinolf's body. I'm not sure she would really go through with it, but I have to ask."

Thorfinn tilted his head in question.

"The Blood Eagle."

Getting to know you . . . me . . .

Hilda awakened, disoriented, in a strange bedchamber, to find Torolf washing her face and hands with a damp cloth. The wooden basin on the floor was red with the blood he'd wiped off her . . . Steinolf's blood.

It was an oddly intimate thing for him to be doing, ministering to her personal care. Tears welled in her eyes and began to leak out, both at his tender gesture and at all that had happened that day, including her fainting. Overwhelmed, that is how she felt.

"The bodies are going to be burned soon, Hilda, away from the keep. But I need to know what to do about Steinolf. You don't really want to put a Blood Eagle on him, do you?"

She thought for a long moment, then shook her head no. "I thought I needed to do to him the same as he did to my father, but 'tis enough that he is dead." A soft sob escaped her lips.

"Oh, baby, don't cry. It's all over now." He tossed the cloth aside and took both of her hands in his, kissing the knuckles of one hand, then the other.

When the tears continued to flow, he lay down on the bed beside her, boots and all, and took her into his arms, making soothing sounds as he rubbed a hand from her shoulders to her waist, over and over. Unbidden, Hilda recalled something she had heard one time when she was a child, whispered betwixt her mother and friends.

"No more tears? Good. What are you smiling about?"

Without thinking, she told him, "There was a famous lady who once said to her lady friends, 'My lord came home from the wars today, and he made love to me with his boots on.'" She was immediately embarrassed to have revealed her thoughts.

Torolf stilled his hand, glanced down at his boots, then looked her in the eyes. "Hilda?"

"Torolf?"

"You want a victory . . . celebration?"

Yes. No. "Mayhap."

"You said you didn't want to do it again."

"Can a woman not change her mind?"

"Oh, yeah." He was already peeling off her belt and loose-necked gunna, grinning at the balls-of-yarn breasts. "Thank God women change their minds. Thank God you've changed your mind."

"It would only be this time." *'Tis embarrassing how many times I have said that and then yielded.*

"Definitely."

She impatiently untied his belt and tugged his bloodstained tunic over his head. Moving to the end of the bed, she helped him unlace his boots. Soon they were both naked, kneeling, looking at each other. He had a beautiful, muscle-sculpted body. He had beautiful, thick, dark blond hair. He had beautiful, warm honey-brown eyes fringed with dark lashes. His manpart jutted out, thick and long, and it was beautiful, too.

If she was not careful, she could grow to love this rascal. *Good thing I am a careful woman.*

"Your cut needs stitching," she remarked, touching the deep cut still oozing blood that ran from cheekbone to chin. "Your thigh, as well."

"Later." He ran the fingertips of one hand across her lips, over her chin, then a straight line from her neck to her groin, creating a path of fire and pleasure. "Hilda, have you ever masturbated?" At her obvious confusion, he explained, "Self-pleasure."

She shook her head slowly, having no idea one could do to oneself what he had done to her. Well, yea, she knew men sometimes touched themselves, but not women, surely. "Dost mean a woman could make herself peak?"

"Definitely. Men have been doing it through the ages. There's even a line in the Bible about some guy spilling his seed upon the ground. The sin of Onan, that's what they call it. And, honey, there's only one way a guy spills his seed on the ground. Jacking off. Or leaving before the Gospel."

"But Onan was a man." *What a lackwit thing to say! A woman wouldn't be spilling her seed.*

"Okay, sweetie, here's my gift to you. I'm going to teach you how to do yourself."

"Why?"

"Believe me, I'll get as much pleasure from watching. More important, though, I don't want you to ever feel you need to marry someone just to have sex."

"As if I ever would!" *Is he thinking of someone specific, like Steven or Thorfinn?*

He grinned. "Well, you might now that you know what sex *can* be. In any case, if you can climax yourself, you don't have to be all hot for a man to do you."

Do me? "Oh, I am not sure I could—"

"Will you do it for me?"

She nodded hesitantly.

"Keep on kneeling, but spread your legs, honey." He shimmied himself into a prone position with his legs straight between hers, his manpart close to her nether parts. "Wider."

She did, and while she should have been embarrassed, she was surprisingly not.

"Close your eyes and touch your face, like a lover would. Learn your contours, pretend it is a man's fingers tracing you."

She did as he instructed, and then some. When the tracing of her lips with a forefinger brought her a slight tingling, she put the finger in her mouth and sucked. It felt so good, her nipples pearled, and her nether parts swelled. It must have felt good to Torolf, too, because he groaned.

"Caress your body now, everywhere. Keep your eyes closed. You're still picturing a lover's hands on you . . . *my* hands on you."

She was tentative and shy in her self-caressing but found herself getting aroused.

"Your breasts now, Hildy. I love your breasts . . . yes, I do. They're like no other breasts in the world. Perfect for you. Raise them up from underneath. Like that. Oh, baby! Play with the nipples. Find out what feels good."

She experimented. Hard and soft. Rubbing and flicking. "I cannot do to my breasts the best thing," she confessed and opened her eyes.

His eyes were hazy brown, half-lidded, his mouth parted. "What is that?"

"Suckling. I love when you suckle me."

His manpart lurched at her words, and she smiled that she could affect him that way. "Witch!" he said, not unkindly. "Wet your fingertips in your mouth and pretend it is my mouth."

She did. It was nice, but not as nice as his wet lips and tongue.

"Lower now, honey. Lower. Real slow. No, don't close your eyes. I want to see if your eyes change when you come."

Hilda figured "come" must mean the same as peaking. She tried to recall the way in which Torolf had caressed her lower body. Her waist and belly, her buttocks, then a whispery pass over her woman's fleece. She whimpered at the almost too intense pleasure that brought.

"Keep going," he encouraged.

She did an unspeakable thing then. She touched herself betwixt her legs, and she was wet. She whimpered, and her suddenly weak legs gave way so she now sat on her haunches.

"Do you know what a clit is, Hildy . . . a clitoris?"

She shook her head. It felt as if her blood had thickened and grown warm. All over her body, she felt more sensitive, as if even the fine hairs that covered her were standing at attention, waiting for some monumental event.

"Every woman has a sort of bud between her legs, the center of all her sexual pleasure. A woman can climax without her clit ever being touched, but usually it makes it more intense, better. Can you find it yourself? Do you want me to show you?"

She dipped her middle finger, testing. It felt incredibly good exploring her folds, but then—*Oh, my gods and goddesses*—she found the nub to which Torolf referred. "Oh," was all she said at first. "Is this it?"

He smiled knowingly. "Jackpot!"

She tested that spot, around its side, over its hood, feeling it grow bigger, more sensitive, almost too sensitive.

"Now, inside your body."

She put a finger inside herself, then two. All over, down

below, she was throbbing and hot and slippery wet and buildingbuildingbuilding toward something she needed so bad she was keening her need. He directed her other hand back to the nub, even as the fingers of her other hand were still inside herself. As she played the nub now, she began to stiffen, to brace herself, to resist some powerful waves rippling over her.

"No! Relax. Don't fight it."

And then it happened. Wave after wave of pleasure seemed to come from inside her woman parts, out, over her pleasure nub, to her breasts, her skin, everywhere.

In the end, her chin went to her chest and she breathed in and out, trying to calm her fast-beating heart.

"How was that?" he asked in a husky voice.

She looked up. "Wonderful and not wonderful. Yea, I peaked, but, in truth, I like it better when you are inside me."

"That's what I like to hear." He chuckled and lifted her up and over him so that he impaled her.

To her embarrassment, her inner muscle began to ripple around his staff, and her pleasure nub swelled and throbbed. She came again.

"JesusMaryandJoseph!" he prayed, gritting his teeth.

"I'm sorry. I didn't mean to do that. Did I hurt you?"

He choked out a laugh. "Don't apologize. That felt so damn good I almost exploded." At her questioning look, he added, "Too soon."

"I do not understand. Oh, you did not peak yet."

"Okay, baby, let's see how you can ride this cowboy." He lifted her off of him, then reached over the side of the bed to his braies and pulled out one of those animal intestine things, which he quickly slipped over his manpart. She wanted to tell him he had no need to increase his virility with her, but words failed her when he put his hands on her hips and placed her back on top of him. Soon she was performing a delicious exercise akin to riding astride a horse.

And soon she was coming again, and he joined her in the frenzy, calling out her name at the end.

When she was nestled in his arms, when their breathing was close to normal, she said, "That was amazing."

"Adrenaline sex." He kissed the top of her head.

"Hmmmm?" She had just discovered that she liked the feel of his chest hairs on her hardened nipples.

He inhaled sharply. "Adrenaline sex is when people have sex after battle or some catastrophe or a supercharged event."

She thought this was more than that but did not tell him so. It would scare him, she sensed, just as her growing conviction that she loved him would drive him away in a trice. He was leaving soon. He'd told her that more than once. He could scarce wait to be gone.

But in the meantime, she let him make gentle love to her. Only later did she allow her fears to surface, not fears of Steinolf or some new invader, not fears that she would be unable to feed and clothe her women, not fears that her life at The Sanctuary would be different now. Nay, it was a new fear.

What will I do when my heart is broken?

Slip-sliding away . . .

For the past two weeks, Torolf and his fellow SEALs had done everything in the world to reverse the time travel.

They'd used one of the longships Thorfinn and Steven had left behind and gone out to sea, hoping that might trigger them back. Nothing happened, except they'd all about frozen in the cold ocean air.

They'd tried standing on the exact spot where the modern-day longship had crashed. Nothing. Except Hilda had figured that while they were there they may as well clear up the rest of the remnants of the dam. They'd been aching and bone-weary at the end of the day. And still in the past.

They'd even tried praying under JAM's directions. Nothing.

His guys were frustrated and anxious to get home, even Pretty Boy, who was still trying to boink Britta on every surface inside and outside the keep, to no avail. He suspected Pretty Boy had fallen in a big way for Big Mama, and Pretty Boy wanted to be a thousand miles away, or a thousand years away, to escape a fate worse than death for him: commitment.

As for Torolf and Hilda, she'd sutured his two wounds and fussed over him incessantly. They were in the midst of a tentative peace. She never said so, but he could tell she was hurt every time he and the guys left the keep, conceivably not to return. She'd given up trying to convince him he had an obligation to stay and help his people . . . help her people, too. She'd probably been praying that their time travel would fail.

And Stig . . . holy cow, the dog was whining all the time and following him around, even more than usual. It was as if the dog sensed he was leaving.

All of Torolf's loose ends were tied up here. Thorfinn and Steven were in place at Norstead and Amberstead. Steven had brought Hilda a bundle of items he'd found at her former home: jewelry, several silk gowns, some soft leather slippers, and a leather pouch filled to the top with rare pieces of amber from her father's trading. She'd refused Steven's offers of marriage, and he'd gone away smiling, promising to offer again . . . and again . . . till she relented.

And The Sanctuary, now housing only fifteen women—the others choosing to live in the outside world—was flourishing. Food and wood had been stored for the upcoming winter. Hilda spoke of possibly taking on her father's trading profession, going to the market towns of Birka and Hedeby come spring. Torolf wanted to discourage her from doing that. These were dangerous times for women to travel alone, but he didn't dare mention his reservations. She wouldn't appreciate his advice on that subject.

So it was that he was escaping from his guilt today as he made his way to the far side of the mountain where Hilda and her women had dug a diversionary channel when the dam was still in existence. These past few days, the weather had turned unseasonably warm. Torolf couldn't recall it had ever been this balmy, nor could Hilda. And rainy. They'd had so much rain they all felt as if they should be growing feathers and webbed feet.

He sloshed through the mud and pounding rain, making his way to his companions, who were trying to block the muddy channel so that the mountain water would go its normal route instead of being half diverted here. The guys were cursing up a storm, pun intended, when he reached them. Leaning on shovels, they glared at the mess the rain was making of all the work they'd done so far. Instead of filling the channel, they were just creating a muddy mess.

"God, I wish I were in the Wet and Wild, nice and dry, sipping on a longneck," Pretty Boy said.

"Ditto that," JAM said. "These women have half talked me into becoming a priest again. A priest who fornicates." His grin was the only white spot in his muddy face.

"I miss my computer." Geek sighed.

They all looked at him. Of all the things the rest of them missed, lowest on the totem pole would be an electronic device.

"If I don't get out of here soon, I'm going to find myself wedlocked . . . and I mean *locked*," Pretty Boy complained. "Can you imagine me monogamous?"

None of them could.

"Me, if I ever get home, I'm gonna quit the Navy and live the rest of my life out on the bayou." Cage's statement surprised them all. Cage had always planned to be a lifer.

"We're gonna get out of here; I know we are," Torolf told them, taking the shovel JAM shoved into his hands.

"That's what you said last week and the week before that," Pretty Boy pointed out.

"If y'all ask me, this is what we in bayou land call a one hundred proof, finger-up-the-ass snafu," Cage said. "Situation normal all fucked up."

"Yep," the rest of them agreed.

"Uh-oh! You better brace yerself, *cher*. Here comes yer woman, yes, and she's practically got smoke comin' outta her ears."

Torolf turned, about to protest that Hilda was not "his woman," but man oh man, she had a bug up her behind for sure. The rain was pelting down now, a biting rain. Her hair was plastered to her head, and her gunna was wrapped around her slim body like a big ol' roll of dark Saran Wrap. It was no surprise that thunder clapped and lightning flashed when she reached him. If he didn't know better, he would think she was the witch she'd professed to be when they first arrived here.

He was leaning on his shovel, grinning.

Hilda shoved him with a palm to his chest.

He slipped and almost fell into the muddy ditch.

"You bloody cod-sucking son of a toad!"

His buddies all laughed.

And she turned on them. "All of you!"

That shut them up quick.

"What's the problem, honey?"

"Do not bother with those false sweet words. I will tell you what the problem is. Those sausage casings you all put on your dangly parts. Cock coats, we women call them."

Snickering rippled among the guys. There was nothing more amusing than watching another guy getting reamed by a woman in public. Not that she wasn't blasting all of them.

"Sausage casings? Cock coats? For chrissake, do you

mean condoms?" *I'm standing in the frickin' rain. Hilda is about to drown standing up. And we're talking about birth control. Unbelievable!*

"Yea, cone-dumbs. Their purpose . . . is it to increase male virility?"

"Huh?"

"Do not 'huh' me. You led us women to believe you wore those ridiculous sheaths to improve your virility."

"Hey, my virility is just fine, thank you very much," Pretty Boy said, and the others agreed.

Torolf's brow furrowed. "Condoms are birth control. They have nothing to do with virility." *Uh-oh. I sense a failure to communicate here.*

"Aaarrgh! That is what Rakel told me this morn. You lied to us."

"You are so busted," Pretty Boy hooted.

"You all lied," Hilda said pointedly to Pretty Boy.

"Hilda, don't you think we should take this talk to a private place? I mean, I had no idea you wanted a baby. Not that I would give you one and leave it behind, but, hell, if you want a baby, maybe you should marry Steven . . . or Thorfinn."

"Do not dare to suggest what I should do with my life." She shoved him in the chest again.

He stood, immovable. *Okay, now I'm getting mad.*

Did she have any idea how awful she looked, screaming at him in the middle of a thunderstorm, resembling a wet homeless person in rags? The only thing missing was the shopping cart.

"I do not want your babe, you arrogant lout. But all the other women do want children. Why else do you think they welcomed you men to their bed furs from the beginning?"

Torolf hitched one hip, then the other, trying to appear unaffected by her flipping her lid over a simple misunderstanding. "Because they were horny?" Torolf blustered.

She gave him a glare that put him in the same class as, oh, let's say, Howard Stern . . . a Dark Ages version of Howard Stern, timeless male chauvinist pig.

"Hey, wait a minute. Are you saying that all these women were so willing because they wanted kids, not because they were hot to trot?" JAM asked.

"And they thought we'd leave our kids behind?" Geek was so naive. He thought women were pure of heart. Hah!

"You made fools of us all," Hilda charged.

"It sounds more like you women made fools of us," JAM said.

"Hey, I never said anything about increasing virility. Did you?" Torolf turned to his buddies, who all denied having made that claim, too. "It must have been an assumption on your part."

Just then, lightning cracked again up the mountain, very loud. The hard rain turned to torrents. And before anyone could run, the roar of what turned out to be an avalanche of mud and stone and limbs rushed down the mountainside. They all turned in slow motion but too late. Within seconds, they were buried.

As Torolf drifted into unconsciousness, his last thought was, *Here we go again.*

Immediately followed by, *Good-bye, Hilda.*

Chapter 15

You could say they did the dirty . . .

"Here we go again," Torolf said with a wide grin as he crawled out from the mud and debris and saw his buddies doing the same thing. An ambulance could be heard in the distance, and a bubble-top car over near the road said Malibu Police Department.

Malibu, California? Well, why not? The time travel is reversed. Hallelujah!

The guys were using a fireman's hose at low pressure to wash the mud off themselves. When Cage was done, he hosed Torolf off as well. "I've gone on some wild rides with you before, *cher*, but this one? Talk about!"

"So, we're back?" Pretty Boy asked, incredulously. "From Norway to Norseland, from Norseland to Malibu, all in a flash?"

"Looks like it," he replied.

"Cool!" Geek said. "I can't wait to get on the Internet and investigate time travel."

"This was the most incredible experience of my life. I'm gonna have to rethink my religious beliefs. It had to come from God." JAM frowned, trying to understand the unexplainable.

"Be careful who you tell about this experience," Torolf advised. "I wasn't kidding when I said you'll find yourself living in a bubble in some lab."

"Y'all think this really happened . . . that it wasn't a dream?" Cage was shaking his head as if to clear it.

"Five people having the same dream? Any idea what the probabilities on that are?" Geek asked.

"It wasn't a dream. More like a nightmare. But it's over now." To himself, he thought, *Not all parts of it were a nightmare. Ah, Hilda, I WILL miss you.*

"I'm gonna miss Britta," Pretty Boy said, then grinned, "but not too much."

They all agreed to talk about this later, once they were done answering the police questions and letting the EMTs give them a once-over before releasing them to return to Coronado.

The police began talking to Pretty Boy and JAM about the mudslide, a phenomenon not uncommon in this part of California. JAM had already called Slick, another Navy SEAL, asking him to come pick them up. Slick had a place near Malibu, though he was pretty much a loner and no one had ever been there. Luckily, he was at home and soon arrived on the scene, wide-eyed at the spectacle they made.

Just as they were about to leave the scene, Torolf thought he heard Hilda calling to him. It was his conscience tugging at him. In some ways, he felt as if he'd abandoned her, even though he had helped rid the Norselands of that scumbag, Steinolf. True, the guys hadn't left the women with buns in their ovens, as they'd unbelievably expected, but that was a good thing, not bad. Now that there was peace, the women would find husbands. All would be well.

Then, why am I so troubled?

"Where is he? Where is the lout? Toroooolf!"

Torolf and his buddies turned as one to see a fireman pulling something out of the mudslide. *Creature from the Mud Lagoon*, he joked to himself. But this was no joke. It was tall and slim and covered with mud from head to toes and *small breasts* in between.

"Oh . . . my . . . God!" He rushed forward and took her hand. "Hilda, is that you?"

"Who do you think it is, you bloody maggot?"

"Britta better not be hiding under that mud pile," Pretty Boy said, his face white with worry. They soon found out she wasn't there, which caused Pretty Boy to let loose with a loud exhale of relief.

Torolf grabbed the hose from Cage and began to wash the mud off of her. She screamed and squealed and cursed at him as he did her that favor. The whole time, his stunned brain kept repeating, *Hilda is here. What am I gonna do with her? Hilda is here. What am I gonna do with her?*

When he was done hosing her down, she kept rubbing her eyes. "Give me something to wipe the mud from my eyes. I can't see."

An EMT came up and handed Torolf a linen cloth. He wiped, but Hilda continued to complain that she couldn't see.

"Let me," the EMT said. Lifting her eyelids, one at a time, he stepped back and nodded some hidden message to his partner. To Torolf, he mouthed, "Blind." To Hilda, he said, "We've got to get you to a hospital, miss."

Hilda is here. And she's freakin' blind. What am I gonna do with her? What am I gonna do with her?

Over her protests that she wasn't going to any bloody "hospitium" and have monk healers prodding her body and bleeding her with leeches, he and two EMTs managed to get her into the ambulance and strap her down. One of the paramedics was on the phone, talking with a doctor, who advised him to sedate her before bringing her to the emergency room. Soon she was dead to the world, so to speak.

Hilda is here. And she's freakin' blind. What am I gonna do with her? What am I gonna do with her? "Blind? Hilda is blind?" he said to no one in particular. "No, it must be some temporary thing from the shock. She'll get better. She has to. Then what? Talk about the need for an exit strategy! Oh, my God! We are in serious shit here."

"No, *mon coeur*," Cage said, patting him on the shoulder. "*You* are in serious shit here. *We* are free at last, free at last, thank God, thank God, we can go home at last."

The other guys laughed. Not him, though.

Hilda is here. And she's freakin' blind. And she's sure as shit gonna blame me. What am I gonna do with her? What am I gonna do with her?

He gave the police and ambulance driver all the vitals and told Slick, "I've got to go to the hospital first. Hilda will be a madwoman."

"We'll all go with you." Cage squeezed his shoulder.

Once the ambulance took off and they completed their reports, barely avoiding a TV crew and newspapermen who'd just arrived, the five of them got into Slick's SUV.

"XO Gilman is ready to put you all in the brig for not answering your beepers. Where the hell have you guys been?"

They all looked at each other, then began laughing hysterically.

"You wouldn't believe us if we told you," Torolf said.

"Try me."

"We were fighting a battle."

"Well, shiiiit, why didn't you invite me to come along? My ex-wife was in town, and I would have taken any excuse to kick butt somewhere else."

" 'Somewhere else' about says it all."

Hilda is here. And she's freakin' blind. And she's sure as shit gonna blame me. And now I'm responsible for her, and I feel so damn bad. What am I gonna do with her? "What if Hilda never regains her sight?" he murmured aloud. "What if she's locked here in the future?"

Pretty Boy summed it up well. "One thing is clear in this whole damn mess. You are a classic case of FUBAR."

Yep! Fucked up beyond all recognition.

When they got to the emergency room, Torolf was the only one permitted to enter and then only because he claimed to be Hilda's fiancé. He felt like a vise was squeezing his heart when he saw her lying on a gurney. Straps restrained her across the forearms and chest, belly, and thighs. There was mud in her silvery hair. Her skin was ghostly white.

"Is she unconscious?" he asked a guy whose name tag ID'd him as John Flanigan, RN.

"We had to sedate her. She was screaming and flailing to beat the band, could have hurt herself or one of the orderlies. She claimed she was going to kill the lout if he didn't show up and take her out of here." Flanigan gave him a knowing look. "Don't suppose you're the lout?"

"In person. Has she been examined yet?"

"Yes. Dr. Hendershott over there can give you the lowdown."

He walked over to the nurse's station, where the middle-aged doctor was writing on a clipboard. Torolf introduced himself and again repeated—*shudder, shudder*—the fiancé story. After filling out some admission forms as best he could—How does one explain that a thousand-year-old woman doesn't have medical insurance?—the doctor took him into a small office.

"Ms. Berdottir has sustained a blow to the head. We need to hold her overnight . . . maybe longer . . . to make sure her vital signs continue to be okay."

That sounded like good news. "So, she's not blind anymore?"

The doctor shook his head. "She still has vision problems, but that should be temporary. Of course, we'll have her checked out by a neurologist and ophthalmologist, if necessary. Don't worry, son. She should be back to normal in a day or two." The doctor paused and took in his mud-splattered clothing. "Why don't you go home and shower? Get a good sleep. Hopefully, I'll have good news for you when I make my rounds tomorrow morning about eleven."

Torolf shook his head vigorously. "Hilda is a stranger here. She'll be frantic if I'm not there when she awakens."

The doctor shrugged. "We're going to keep her sedated, give her body and brain a chance to rest. She won't even know you're there."

"When do you think the tranquilizers will wear off?"

Another shrug from the doctor. "Eight a.m. or so. When the nurses change shifts would be my guess."

Torolf glanced at his watch. It was four p.m. "Nah, I think I better stick around."

When he went out to the waiting room, he told the guys to head back, that he was going to stay. They agreed reluctantly.

By eleven, Hilda still hadn't awakened. Once again, he was told, this time by the night nurse, that Hilda would not be awakening till morning because of the orders for sedation every three hours.

Torolf thought about the necessity of reporting in to the base, a two-hour drive. *I could go to Coronado, take care of business, and be back in plenty of time*, he convinced himself.

So Torolf left.

Big, big mistake.

She was in an alien place . . .

Hilda was frantic.

She was blind. She was strapped to some kind of mattress. There was an odd, unfamiliar scent in the air. Every time she awakened, screaming for answers, there were soothing voices and a prick in her arm, immediately followed by deep sleep.

Where is the lout?

What did he do to me?

Oh, gods, what if I am really blind? I would fain be dead than blind.

The next time she emerged from the strange sleep, she forced herself to remain calm lest they give her the magic jab her in the arm again. Pretending to still be asleep, she listened to the voices. There appeared to be two, a male and a female.

"No change, dock-whore. Mzzz Berdottir gets frantic and flailing every time she awakens."

"Has her fee-ant-say returned yet? Someone's got to give an explanation for these blood results. I've never seen anything like it before in my entire career."

"We're running another series right now. There must be a mistake."

"Absolutely." The woman giggled then. "You won't believe what Dick Phillips down in the lab believes. He thinks we've got an ale-yen on our hands."

"God! Is he the loony who came from the National Center for Alien Research?"

"Yeah. He's a good tack-nit-shun, though, except when he goes off on one of these ale-yen tan-gents."

Hilda's brain was hurting, and not just from the blow suffered in the mudslide. She was confused. Where was this hospitium she was in? The closest hospitium to The

Sanctuary that she knew of was days distant at Oslofjord. These people in her room . . . they spoke an English unlike the Saxon English she was familiar with. She could understand much of it, except for the occasional word, like ale-yen, dock-whore and fee-ant-say.

She moaned and opened her eyes. All she saw was a gray haze, but that was an improvement over the blackness she'd seen before. Her arms were strapped down, which caused her to panic, but she tamped that down, merely clenching her fists. "Where am I?"

"You're awake?" the man said. "That's good, that's good. How do you feel?"

"The sedative shouldn't have worn off yet," the woman said, probably to the dock-whore.

"Terrible. I cannot see."

"That will probably pass. Nurse, get her bee-pee and temp."

More words I do not understand. "Where am I?" she repeated.

"Holy Cross Hospital. You've had an accident, but we're taking good care of you. I'm Dock-whore Hendershott, and your nurse is Miss Wilson. Don't worry. You're in good hands."

Good hands? Since when are a whore's hands good hands? And since when are there male whores? Well, I am learning new things every day. If a woman can pleasure herself, why can there not be male whores? "Holy Cross Hospitium? I have ne'er heard of such a place here in the Norselands."

The dock-whore's voice sounded worried, and she thought she heard him whisper to his nurse in a worried voice, "Hall-loose-nation." He patted Hilda's hand and asked, "Norselands? Do you mean Norway?"

"Yea, Norway." *The idiot. An idiot whore.*

"You're not in Norway. You're in Ah-mare-eek-ha."

"Whaaat?" *The land that Torolf spoke of . . . a land far away.* "How can that be?"

"Now, relax, dear. Would you like a drink of water?"

"Yea, I would." *Or a cup of mead. A big cup.*

"Nurse," he said.

Something was stuck into her mouth. She gagged. When it was pulled out, she snapped, "What was that? I asked for water."

"It's just a straw, honey," the woman said, placing the object into her mouth again. "Just suck."

She did and surprisingly, water came up. Why they couldn't have just put a cup to her mouth was beyond her comprehension.

"How long will it be afore my sight comes back?"

There was a pause. Then, "No telling right now. We need to run more tests. It might come right back in an instant. Or it might . . . uh, take months."

"Months?" she screeched, bucking against the straps. "Where is Torolf? I want Torolf. Get the lout so I may kill him."

Hilda felt another jab in her arm, and she drifted back to sleep. Not surprisingly, she dreamed of putting her hands around the neck of the lout, but then the dream turned on itself, and it was his hands on her neck . . . and everywhere else on her body. How could she dislike a man so much who made her feel so good?

It was a nightmare, not a dream.

And, in the midst of that nightmare, she heard two men talking in whispers over her . . . neither of them the dock-whore who had been there before.

"I don't know, Dick, she looks pretty normal to me."

"Yeah, but you haven't seen her blood tests. There's no blood type in existence like hers. It's like the dean-nay you get from ancient artifacts, thousands of years old. Of course, they think it's just a mistake here, and they'll be retesting in the morning. The dock-whores don't see any urgency yet, because apparently this oddball type is compatible with type B, and besides she hasn't had an open wound yet."

"And you think she's an ale-yen?"

"Could be. Must be. It's worth investigating. But we've gotta find a way to get her to the lab in Dee See. I've already alerted the board."

"The hospital will never release her to us, and I doubt she'd come on her own."

An evil laugh. "Who could blame her? Willingly submitting to dice-section? I . . . don't . . . think . . . so."

"We'll wait for the right chance and slip her out. Late tonight. Can you get a van ready that quick?"

"Yep."

"This could be our greatest discovery . . . the one thing that convinces the world there really are ale-yens."

The voices drifted away.

Hilda was left with the disquieting sense that danger lurked. They wanted to take her somewhere and perform some tests, apparently without her permission.

Where is Torolf?

And then the lout came strolling in . . . ELEVEN hours later . . .

Torolf arrived at the hospital at ten a.m. the next day.

The reaming he and his teammates had gotten from their commanding officer at the Special Warfare Center took longer than he'd expected. Where the hell had they been the past few weeks, out of beeper range? Their explanation that they'd been in Norway hadn't cut any ice. Punishment would be in the future; Gig Squad had been mentioned more than once. They had one week to get ready to muster out again on a new deployment. One week! He sure as hell hoped he had Hilda back in eleventh-century Norway by then, or settled God only knows where.

He'd left Coronado, stopped at his apartment to shower and change clothes, and called his sister-in-law, asking her to take care of Slut a few days more. Luckily, Alison hadn't been at home, and he'd been able to leave a message on her answering machine.

He had inquired by phone about Hilda's condition several times, and he'd been assured that she still slept. The doctor on duty, not Dr. Hendershott, had told him that Hilda was moved to another floor, no longer needing critical care. A good sign, in Torolf's opinion.

He went directly to the desk in front of the elevator. "Can you give me Brunhilda Berdottir's room number?"

The nurse, a skinny, no-nonsense woman whose skin was as white as her uniform, asked, "Dare I hope that you're the lout?"

He laughed. "That would be me."

"Visiting hours aren't till one. Only family members are allowed now." She peered at him over the top of her granny glasses. "Are you family?"

If I say no, they probably won't let me in. He took a deep breath and blew out. "Her fiancé." He kept his fingers crossed behind his back for fear God would hear him lie *again* and make it come true.

"Room 317."

Torolf walked down the hall, feeling apprehensive at what he would find, feeling worried about Hilda's physical condition, feeling guilty for getting her here in the future. *Will she be happy to see me? Or angry? Maybe I should have brought flowers. Damn, I never thought about flowers.*

He got to Hilda's private room and walked in softly, closing the door behind him. He didn't want anything they said to be overheard. Hilda was lying flat on the bed, her platinum hair spread out on the pillow, her arms and legs strapped to the bed, an intravenous tube leading into her arm, a sheet covering her up to her waist. Wearing a hospital gown, she looked so white and helpless.

He leaned over her and whispered, "Hilda? Wake up. Hilda?"

Her eyes shot open. "Is that you, Torolf?"

Oh, shit! She must still be blind. He put his hand over one of hers. "Yeah, it's me. How you doing?"

"How do you think I'm doing?" Her voice was sweet . . . too sweet.

Uh-oh! "Can you see at all?"

She shook her head. " 'Tis better than it was, though. The black has turned to gray, and I can make out some shapes, such as your big loutish body."

Uh-oh! "You're upset."

"Dost think so?" Still, that sweetness in her voice.

"What can I do for you?"

"Take this thing off my arm. It feels like a needle."

"It is a needle."

"This is how they torture people in your country? Pfff! Take it out."

"That's not a good idea. I should ask the doctor if—"

"Take the bloody thing out, or I will lean over and take it out with my teeth."

"Okaaay. It's probably just for fluids anyway." Carefully, he removed the tape and slipped the needle out.

"Now, take the restraints off of me."

"Oh, no! I'm going to call the doctor and see—"

"They have only restrained me because I was being wild and demented. I am no longer wild . . . just demented." Her sense of humor was misplaced and suspicious.

"You won't do anything foolish?"

"Would you like to hear my new talent . . . screaming?"

I must have done something really bad for God to pun-

ish me this way. "Hold your horses." He unbuckled the restraints.

"Torolf," she said so softly he barely heard her. "Come closer. I would tell you a secret."

When he leaned forward over the bed, she jackknifed upright, grabbed him around the neck, twisted, using one of the karate moves he'd taught her, rolled them both, so that he lay half on and half off the bed, with her on top of him, beating his chest, saying over and over, "Lout, lout, lout, lout!"

"What the hell's the matter with you? I thought you were blind."

"I am blind, but I'm not a lackwit." She continued to beat at his chest, sometimes missing and hitting his head or his shoulder. "What have you done to me? Why did you take me to your country? *How* did you take me to your country?"

"*What* is going on in here?" It was the white-faced shrew nurse he'd met on his way in. "Oooh, I know what you were doing. Have you no shame? This patient is blind, and you cannot wait till she is better to put your hands on her?"

Hilda was grinning down at him.

"Here's a news flash, Nurse Ratched. Hilda is the one pinning me to the bed."

"He made me do it," Hilda said. "See how his hands hold me down.

His hands were loosely grasping her waist. He pinched her butt.

She pinched his belly . . . down real low. She must have been aiming higher and missed. Or maybe not.

"And you pulled out her IV," the nurse accused him. "Tsk, tsk, tsk! Wait till I report this to Dr. Hendershott. I've always heard you SEALs are crazy, but this pushes the bounds of decency. Having sex with a blind woman in a hospital bed!"

"I was not having sex . . . or thinking about having sex."

But now that you mention it.

"Hah!" Hilda and the nurse said at the same time. Hilda was squinting her eyes at the nurse, and he suspected she was beginning to make out her shape.

"Hilda pulled out the IV herself," he lied. "I was just trying to make her more comfortable in the bed when you came in, and I slipped, and then I rolled so that Hilda wouldn't be hurt."

"That doesn't pass the giggle test, mister."

Torolf lifted Hilda off of him and back onto the bed. Into her ear, he whispered, "Behave yourself, or you'll get me kicked out of here."

"I've got to check her vitals. She needs rest. You can go home now."

"No!" she and Torolf said at the same time.

Shocked, the nurse glared at him, as if he had some nerve refusing to leave. She also gave Hilda a disapproving look.

"I do not want him to leave," Hilda said in a whiny voice, accented with sniffles. "I am afraid here in the dark."

Hah! Hilda had killed one of the most vicious beasts in all the Norselands. The dark wouldn't frighten her. On the other hand, being blind would.

"Well, I suppose you could stay since you're her fiancé. Just put a lid on your sex drive."

Hilda turned her face on the pillow, facing him. "What is a fee-ant-say?"

He hesitated. "Betrothed."

Hilda's eyes went wide. But she must have realized that he had a good reason for the lie, because she remained silent.

While the nurse wrapped the blood pressure gauge on Hilda's arm and took her temperature, he kept reassuring Hilda that what the nurse was doing was harmless.

When the door clicked shut again, he asked, "Why are you so damned mad?"

"Aside from being upset that you have taken me from my homeland and from The Sanctuary, that you caused me to fall in a mudslide, that you turned me blind, and that you caused me to time-travel?"

"Oh. Well, I'm sorry."

"I need to relieve myself. Where is the privy?"

He stood and helped Hilda stand.

"What . . . Holy Thor! What kind of garment is this I am wearing?" Her hands examined the back of the hospital gown. "My arse is bare." She held the back section of her gown together while he led her, muttering Norse curses, into the bathroom.

He parted her gown for her and showed her how to sit on the toilet, which she said felt strange for a privy hole. Before he had a chance to leave her for her privacy, he heard the sound of her piss hitting the water. He put his face in his hands. He didn't think he'd ever been in a bathroom when a woman was taking care of her bodily needs. It was an oddly intimate thing for him to witness, but it was too late now. He took some toilet paper off the roll and handed it to her. "What is this?"

"It's for wiping. I'm turning around now. Tell me when you're done."

When she stood, he flushed the toilet.

She jumped at the noise. "Son of a troll! What was that?"

"The toilet flushing. I'll explain all this when you can see."

After he helped her wash her hands and settled her back in the bed, her muttering once again over the indecent hospital gown, she asked, "Did you look at my arse?"

"Who? Me?" *Just a little.*

"You are smiling. I can hear it in your voice."

"I can't help it, Hildy. You have a pretty ass."

"Nobody has a pretty arse."

"I beg to differ. Want me to tell you what I like about yours?"

"No!" she all but shouted.

He propped his butt on the edge of the bed and watched as she craned her neck this way and that, trying to see the room.

"Are you a little calmer?"

"Nay, I am not calmer. Didst know they prick my arm every time I raise my voice? Didst know there is something odd about my blood? Didst know they intend to take more of my blood to test? Didst know they want to dice-section my body?"

"Dice-section? What is . . . omigod! . . . do you mean dissection?"

"Is that not what I said?"

"Someone said they want to dissect your body? Who? No, you must have heard wrong."

"I may be half-blind, but I am not deaf."

His heart was racing with alarm. She must have misunderstood. Still . . . "A doctor here said he wanted to dissect you?"

"A dock-whore? The first man here was a dock-whore, but how would I know if the men who came later were dock-whores? All I know is one of them thinks I am an ale-yen who has peculiar blood. He and the other man—"

"What other man?"

"If you would stop interrupting, I would tell you. Two men were in the room near my bed when I awakened the third time . . . or was it the fourth? They plan to get a van—dost know what a van is?—and take me away in the night to some hidden place where they will dice-sect me."

"Sonofabitch! I was afraid of this. My blood type was different when I first got here, too. We think it was the same with my entire family. Don't ask me to explain why, or how it changed, but gradually our blood types became type B. Maybe it was the food or the climate or another of those frickin' miracles, like time travel." He pulled out his cell phone.

She must have heard the rustle of his pulling it out because she asked, "What are you doing?"

"Calling Cage."

"Cage is here? Where?"

"Not here. He's in Coronado . . . the town where we live."

"Then how are you calling him?"

"Never mind. I'll explain later."

"LeBlanc here," Cage answered his cell phone. Torolf could hear music in the background.

"Max here. Where are you?"

"The Wet and Wild. Yeah, I know it's barely noon. Why dontcha come over, *cher*. That CIA babe you were dating last year is here. You know, the backbend goddess. She asked about you."

Gina, he thought. He'd spent a long, very interesting weekend with her in her D.C. apartment last spring. And, yes, she could do backbends. "Can't make it today. I'm in Hilda's hospital room."

"How is she?"

"Still having vision problems."

"Whatcha gonna do with her?"

"Hell if I know, but that's not why I called. Big trouble here, buddy, and it could affect all of us." Quickly, he explained the situation. "So, you can see why none of you can discuss this trip, except among yourselves. In the meantime, I've got to get Hilda out of here before those bozos come back."

"You takin' her to your apartment?"

"Nah, that's not a good idea. I gave my name and address to the EMT as a contact in case of emergency. The hospital probably has it on file."

"So, you gotta find someplace to hide her for a while?"

"Yeah, any ideas?"

"You could take her down on the bayou. My maw maw would take her in. In fact, she'd get a kick outta hearin' Hilda talk about Vikings and the eleventh century. Prob'ly have her speakin' Southern in no time. Fix her up with some Cajun dude."

A picture of Hilda lounging on some bayou stream with a Cajun dude leaning over her flashed into his mind, with her drawling out, "Frankly, darlin', ah doan give a damn. Y'all kin taste mah biscuits any ol' time y'all want." Oddly, he was the Rhett Butler in that mind blip. "Thanks for the offer, but that's too far away."

"How about your dad's place up in Sonoma?"

"No way!" *My family would have me married to Hilda before I could blink.* "They would be in as much trouble as Hilda if those screwballs caught up. I can't risk that danger for them."

"Hey, I know . . . How about that place you hid out last year after your accident?"

Torolf grinned. "Hog Heaven?"

"That's the place."

Hog Heaven was a biker RV/trailer park in a remote area north of Coronado, and it was within driving distance. Hilda would fit right in with the other crazies there. "Thanks for the suggestion."

"Sure you don't want us guys to come up there and wipe out the alien dodo birds?"

Torolf could just envision the scene. A bunch of drunk Navy SEALs fighting with some skinny scientist types. "No. I'll let you know how it works out. And I'll be there on the grinder next Monday. Don't want to raise any red flags there."

"Max," Cage said just before he hung up.

"What?"

"Doan go gettin' married or nothin' . . . not unless I'm there ta be yer bes' man."

"Ha, ha, ha!"

After he clicked the phone shut, he looked up to find Hilda standing at the window. "What are those things with wheels out there?"

At first, Torolf couldn't answer. Hilda had forgotten about the hospital gown. *Be still my heart! Yes, Virginia, there is such a thing as a pretty ass.* "They're cars. It's a parking lot."

She turned.

Damn!

"What did you discuss with Cage?"

"I know a place I can take you where you can recuperate."

"Ray-coop-raid? You would take me to a chicken coop?"

He laughed. "Recuperate means get better."

"Why did you not say that?"

Nag, nag, nag! "Do you want to know where I'll be taking you or not?"

Just then, he heard voices outside the door . . . a man and Nurse Ratched. It must be the doctor coming to check on Hilda. Quickly, he picked her up in his arms so he could lay her in the bed, but when he picked her up, his bare hand landed on her bare ass. She screeched and tried to squirm out of his hold.

"Be still, Hilda. Someone's coming, and I've got to put you back in—"

The door opened. Slick stood there dressed in one of those green doctor outfits. He even had an ID tag clipped to his pocket and a stethoscope around his neck. And Nurse Ratched was smiling as if George Clooney had just arrived from *ER*.

"Well, well, well," Slick said, taking in Hilda in Torolf's arms and his hand on her ass. "Just what the doctor ordered."

Chapter 16

Lady in the red dress, red dress . . . uh, red suit . . . oh, my! . . .

Hilda was in another land . . . a land of magic.

Could it really be the future? Or was it just one of those fanciful places that the Norse legends spoke of where trolls and dragons and such resided. Not that she'd seen any dragons here . . . yet, though the lout did qualify as a troll.

Said troll was off somewhere getting his hog so that they could ride on it to a place called Hog Heaven. She did not even want to think about how they were going to ride a hog and live in a hog shed, but she'd already asked so many questions. And, after riding in that horseless carriage during the night, at an ungodly speed, she supposed anything was possible here.

Torolf and Slick were tired of answering all her questions about every little wonder in this bloody world during the past day and a half. They'd escaped the barmy sign-tiss at the hospitium, and Torolf had taken her to Slick's keep on the ocean.

Right now, she sat on the beach, watching the ocean and Slick as he ran up and down the beach, over and over. A barmy exercise, if you asked her, but no one did, of course. And, yes, her vision had returned gradually so she could see fine now.

Slick walked up and sank down to the sand beside her. He wiped the sweat off his bare chest with a towel, wearing only short braies that had been cut off at the upper thighs, appropriately called shorts, and special shoes made for running. He was a good-looking man with dark hair and eyes and a well-muscled body, which seemed to be a requirement for all the SEALs, but he rarely smiled and was grim, much like Thorfinn had been. She wondered what tragedy he had in his past.

Then he checked a small black box lying on the blanket. "There's a text message from Max. He's on his way. Should be here in less than an hour."

"How did you . . . ?" She started to ask how he had gotten the message from Torolf, but decided her brain was filled with too many new ideas already. " 'Tis a beautiful spot where you have your keep . . . uh, cottage . . . but why are the cottages so close together?"

"Hey, this is Malibu. This place would be beyond my means if I hadn't inherited it from my great aunt."

She nodded. "I did not mean offense."

"I know you didn't." He tugged her lone braid, which hung over one shoulder. "Wanna go for a swim?"

"Why would I swim . . . unless I had to? Like to escape from a sinking longship or to bathe."

"For pleasure?"

"You must be barmy. Besides, ne'er will I expose myself in that bathing garment you gave me. 'Tis wanton."

"That suit belonged to my ex-wife, and, believe me, it's tame compared to what she usually wore. It's not even a bikini. Like that bikini there." He pointed to a woman running along the shoreline, wearing two small scraps of bright yellow cloth, one across her breasts and the other barely covering her nether hair and buttocks. Her breasts bounced as she trotted.

"Do not tell me that is not scandalous."

"Not at all. I like it."

"And why not? You are a man, and men like to see a woman flaunting her bare udders." She looked down at the white tea-ing *shert* she wore over the bathing garment. "Except for me, who has no udders to speak of."

He laughed. "Big breasts are highly overrated."

"That is what Torolf said."

"Is that so?" Slick's mouth twitched with humor.

They stared ahead for a while. The sun beat down on them, hotter than any sun she'd felt before. Some children were feeding the seagulls. An elderly couple wearing matching long-sleeved *sherts* and braies walked by.

More people in brief bathing garments walked by, and there was even a young man riding the waves on a board. Amazing how he could stand on water using the board! Like the Christian Jesus.

Finally, Hilda had had enough of the blistering sun. "Mayhap I will swim a bit after all. 'Tis hotter than the pits of Muspell." She forced herself not to flinch under Slick's scrutiny as she shrugged off the *shert*, uncovering the red bathing suit.

"I'll join you."

Soon they were swimming in the cool waves. Well, she was attempting to swim. He was laughing at her as she kept getting washed ashore in the surf.

They were still laughing as they emerged from the water, walking up the sand to the blanket that she had been sitting on . . . until they noticed Torolf walking toward them, a frown on his face. The frown he directed at Slick. To her, he gave a hot once-over from her wet head to her bare toes, and lots of time in between. She raised her chin high, refusing to cower under his regard. Slick just chuckled.

"You two having fun frolicking out there while I'm running from the mad sign-tiss?"

"I do not frolic," Slick said with a laugh.

"The sign-tiss chased you?"

"Did you lose him?" Slick asked, no longer laughing.

"Damn straight I did. Two dingbats in a van marked National Center for Alien Research followed me all the way down I-5. I lost them before I got off the Escondido exit. Good thing I left my car in Coronado, though. Now that they've got my license number, they'll be able to track where I live."

"I'm gonna go in and fix us some lunch," Slick said.

They waited till Slick was some distance away. Torolf took her hand, starting to walk along the beach. She should have pulled her hand out of his grasp, but she rather liked the feel of his palm against hers. He wore the blue braies many men in this country seemed to favor and a green teaing *shert* which said, U.S. Navy. She knew what it said because he'd told her earlier. She was self-conscious about walking about in the scant bathing garment but did not want to call attention to herself by protesting her almost nudity.

"We need to talk," he repeated.

"Every time you say that you want to talk to me, I end up in trouble . . . either on my back with you betwixt my legs . . . or in another bloody country."

He grinned at her. That is all. He just grinned.

The lout.

It's a vibrator, no matter what you say . . .

As long as he lived, Torolf would never forget the image of Hilda walking out of the surf wearing a wet, red, one-piece swimsuit molded to her body.

He knew that Hilda had issues about her body and her sexuality, but, good God, if she could only see herself the way he saw her. Being close to five nine, she had very long legs. The suit wasn't overtly suggestive, more like the tank suits that Olympic swimmers wore, but it clearly outlined her narrow waist and the flare of her hips. And her small breasts with their jutting nipples . . . He had to stop looking there, or no telling what he would do.

"When can I go home . . . to The Sanctuary?"

"I don't know."

"I do not like the sound of that. Explain yourself."

"Hilda, you're in the future. I swear to God you are. Don't ask me how it happened. I haven't a clue, except to say that miracles happen sometimes."

"So, call up another miracle and send me back."

"I'm not sure I can. Each of our time travels has happened in a different way, and never on demand. As far as I know, it's only happened in my family, until this latest incident with my buddies and you."

"Perchance, if you take me back to the Norselands, the miracle will happen for me there, as it did for you."

"I will . . . eventually."

She stopped and narrowed her eyes at him.

"Norway is far away, Hildy. I would need to get plane reservations and—"

"What is a plane?"

"Uh . . ." He looked up at the sky and pointed. "That up there is an airplane. It probably has two hundred people in it and is headed to an airport in L.A."

She gasped. "Are you saying we would have to travel up in the sky?"

He nodded.

"Oh, that is just wonderful! What have you done to my life? I swear, I have had naught but trouble since you came back."

That goes both ways, cupcake. "I got rid of Steinolf."

"Yea, you did. I should not be so ungracious. Still, you have nigh ruined my life by bringing me here."

"I didn't do it deliberately. It was an accident."

"An accident is falling and breaking a leg. An accident is spilling a pail of goat's milk. An accident is a longship sinking. Sending a person through time and across lands is not an accident. It is a disaster."

No kidding. "I'm sorry."

"Do not be sorry. Do something about it."

Nag, nag, nag. "I'm trying. First, we have to get you in hiding. Don't get excited. It's just for a short time till these kooks are out of the picture. You have to know that they think you're an alien, a person who lives up in the sky on one of the planets . . . um, other worlds up there."

"Hah! 'Tis no worse than being from a thousand years ago."

"In any case, they would like to take you to a place where they can study you . . . really study you. Like cut you open and see how you are different. They would never let you be free again."

Horror overcame Hilda, and she sank down to the sand, putting her face in her hands.

He sank down beside her and put an arm around her shoulders. "Don't worry, honey, I won't let that happen. You'll go into hiding . . . hopefully just for a few weeks. I'll go back to the base, go on assignment as if nothing is out of the ordinary. Then, when the coast is clear, I'll try my best to get you back to The Sanctuary. In the meantime, enjoy yourself."

By nightfall, they were on their way, riding his Harley up I-5. It was a balmy night, the stars were out, and Hilda sat behind him, wearing jeans and a sweatshirt and sneakers that had belonged to Slick's ex. She held on for dear life, and he kinda liked her being up close and personal to him like that, unable to talk over the roar of the engine.

When he pulled into the parking lot of a diner two hours later, he helped her off the bike and had to hold her up for a second to steady her legs.

They sat down in a booth and placed their orders. Hilda looked really cute sitting there, staring at everything in wonder. Even the menu amazed her.

And when their food came, two Italian hoagies with a side of fries and two chocolate milkshakes, she just stared at everything and watched as he took a bite of the hoagie, then dunked a fry in catsup and popped it into his mouth. "Now what?"

"My mouth is big, but not that big," she protested, gazing at the huge sandwich.

I know exactly how big your mouth is, and what it can do.

"And what is it with you and hogs? We ride a hog, we will be staying at a hog haven, and now we eat hog-ees."

He laughed and told her to open wide. When she did, he pressed the edge of the hoagie against her lips and said, "Bite." She did, messily, but at least she understood.

And he barely restrained himself from leaning over the table and licking the oil off her lips . . . maybe even her tongue, too.

She liked the fries better, never having heard of potatoes before, and the milkshake . . . well, it thrilled her. Of course, she had never experienced ice cream, either, but when he explained that it would be like adding snow to sweet cream and adding flavoring, like strawberries, or his favorite, chocolate, she understood perfectly.

Torolf found that he enjoyed showing off all these things to her, recalling how he'd felt when he'd come here more than ten years ago.

"How did you like the ride?" he asked as she continued to sip on her straw.

"I thought we would be riding a real hog."

"I know."

"You did not warn me that it was a self-pleasuring hog."

Torolf's jaw dropped. "What . . . did . . . you . . . say?"

"What? Why are you gawking at me like that? Do not try to say that spreading your legs over a vibrating object did not pleasure you?"

"Hildy, Hildy, Hildy." He put his elbow on the table and rested his chin in his palm, staring. This woman had a knack for pulling the rug out from under him all the time. "And did you climax, there behind me?"

"Nay, but I tingle."

Tingling his life away . . .

By the time they arrived at Hog Heaven, it was one a.m., and Torolf had been sporting a hard-on since they'd left the diner.

How could the witch tell him she tingled and then expect him to not think about that tingling . . . a lot? He was a man. When a lady tingled, a guy got turned on. Eve probably tingled a lot, just to tease Adam.

Despite the lateness of the hour and the mostly dark trailers and RVs, Spike and Serenity were waiting for him. The eccentric biker couple, married for well over thirty years, had sort of adopted him for a short time a few years back when he'd suffered a head concussion and memory loss following a bike accident. Spike was a former Microsoft engineer who sold Harley parts on the Internet and did body piercings on the side. Serenity was a tattoo artist, with blonde hair accented by black roots hanging down to her leather-clad butt, eight rings in each ear, two gold studs in her nose, and tattoos up one arm and down the other. A match made in heaven.

"Max." Spike shook his hand. "Good to see you again."

"Maxie," Serenity squealed and ran down the steps of

their trailer to give him a huge hug. Then she leaned back and looked him over.

He took Hilda's hand and pulled her forward. "Hilda, this is a good friend of mine, George Morgan."

"You can call me Spike, honey."

"And this is his wife, Serenity Morgan."

Hilda was gaping at Serenity's earrings and tattoos, not to mention her short-sleeved, red-lip-imprinted white nightshirt.

Grabbing her in a big bear hug, Serenity hugged her warmly, saying, "Aren't you the prettiest little thing, sugar? I've been waiting a long time for this boy to bring his lady here."

"Uh, she's not really my lady," Torolf started to explain.

But Hilda jumped right in. "We are betrothed."

Oooh, I knew she'd get back at me for sayin' that.

"That is wonderful!" Serenity was practically jumping up and down, her big breasts bouncing. "We can celebrate your engagement at Spike's big fiftieth birthday bash on Saturday night at the Stump Hollow fire hall. All the old gang is coming in. You two got here just in time."

Hilda glanced at him, waiting for his cue . . . for once.

This nightmare just gets worse . . .

"Your friend Cage called tonight, to see if you got here yet. I invited him and your other buddies to come, too."

. . . and worse.

Hilda waited for him to respond, but a teeny, tiny smirk began to draw the edges of her lips up. *Did I think her lips were nice? No, her lips are definitely not nice. Her Angelina Jolie lips are turning into Mick Jagger lips, right before my eyes.*

"Cage said to tell you he might bring along Gina, the CIA babe. I never met a CIA babe before. Have you, Hilda?"

The teeny, tiny smirk became a full-blown smirk. Definitely good ol' Mick.

Then he put her in a box . . .

They had settled into a small keep known as a trail-her at the end of the Hog Heaven estate.

Hilda looked around her with dismay. It was so cramped she could scarce move. There was a small solar, an even smaller scullery, a bathing room, and two bedchambers that could hold little more than a bedstead in them.

Hilda tried not to complain. Torolf had done his best to find a safe place for her till they rid themselves of the mad sign-tiss and she returned to The Sanctuary. Also, Spike and Serenity had gone to great bother preparing this dwelling.

Now Torolf was in the bathing chamber showering his body. For the second time today! Viking men were cleaner than the average man, but even they usually bathed no more than once a sennight.

She still had trouble comprehending a culture that had indoor privies and hot and cold running water. And rolls of paper just for wiping one's arse. And mirrors in every household. There was even one in the bathing chamber that was so tall an entire body could be seen. What luxuries! Especially for such a small keep as this trail-her.

Sitting in a soft chair, she stared at a black box with pictures flickering on it. It was a tea-vee. What she saw was so beyond Hilda's comprehension that tears smarted in her eyes. How could she exist, even for a short while, in a country that put small people in boxes just to entertain other people?

Just then, a loud ringing noise caused her to jump. It was Torolf's talking box. Another marvel she failed to understand, and did not want to. Sad to say, there was not another person anywhere in the world, not even the eleventh century, that she wanted to talk to. 'Twas the third time the phone had been ringing while Torolf bathed himself.

Frigg's foot, the man must be scouring his skin off, he'd

been there so long. In truth, he was probably avoiding her. Ne'er had she been as waspish as she was around the lout. With cause, of course.

"Oh, good, a *Saturday Night Live* rerun," Torolf said, coming out of the bathing chamber where steam could be seen emerging. He was looking at the tea-vee where a man with hair combed to a ridiculous point and braies hiked up to his chest was dancing about like an idiot. Mayhap he was having a fit.

But Hilda was not looking at the tea-vee. She was looking . . . rather gawking . . . at Torolf as he walked into the too-small room wearing naught but shorts.

Hilda had grown up in a household of men, and she'd been wed three times, but ne'er had the male body held such appeal for her, not till now, knowing what pleasure such a body could give a woman. Or was it just Torolf's body? She prayed not.

I am sinking fast. Please, gods, send me a rope here. "Can you not put some garments on?"

"Why? I'm just going to bed."

Because I like it too much. "Because it is not decent."

He grinned. "Hilda, you've seen all I've got. It's a bit late for modesty, don't you think?"

"Well, do not expect me to flaunt my body like that."

"We're stuck here for a few days. Enjoy the moment."

Is he suggesting . . . ? She threw her hands up with disgust. "Pfff! How like a man! Do not touch me again. I am warning you. Do not touch me again."

"I've heard that song before, babe, before you jumped my bones . . . again. By the way, any chance you're still tingling?"

She stood, outraged and embarrassed that he would throw her wanton behavior back in her face . . . not the tingling remark, but the reference to her newfound enthusiasm for bedsport with him.

He must have sensed her offense, because he reached out a hand to her, which she slapped away. "I'm sorry, Hildy. I was just teasing. I'm the one who's always hot for you. I'm the one who's always thinking about jumping *your* bones."

Her jaw dropped. Every time the lout said something like that, her defenses melted. In truth, he made *her* melt.

Walking in front of her, he pressed a spot on the tea-vee that caused it to go black. The little folks had disappeared somewhere inside. Did they sleep now?

"I'm going to bed. The bathroom's all yours. You can have the other bedroom. Good night." He picked up his weapon . . . a gun . . . and took it with him. Did he sleep with the thing?

"Ga ntt," she replied, but what she thought as he walked away from her was, "What a nice arse! 'Tis so hard it could probably be used as a whetstone." She giggled then, and Hilda almost never giggled.

Torolf turned at his bedchamber door and arched his eyebrows. "What?"

"Nothing. I was thinking about stones."

This is how scientists go mad . . .

"I'm this close to nabbing her. You'll have her within the week."

Dick Phillips made this promise to Dylan Atkins, chairman of the National Center for Alien Research in its Washington, D.C., headquarters.

"I don't know, Dick. Maybe we should hire some professionals."

"No, no, no! I got a two-week leave from the hospital lab. I traced that guy listed as her contact for the hospital. Torolf Magnusson, a Navy SEAL. He's at some biker trailer park in California, presumably with the target."

"Whaaat? We don't want to be messing with any military, especially a Navy SEAL."

"I don't intend to go one-on-one with the guy. I'll get the specimen alone, drug her, and bring her back here for study."

"You can't hurt her in any way. I don't want any cuts on her or any signs of physical injury."

"I understand. I'll be real careful. And, really, Mr. Atkins, this is going to be the biggest breakthrough for our cause. People won't be laughing anymore when we mention aliens."

Mr. Atkins smiled and tented his fingers in front of his face. "I've already prepared some press releases, but we won't issue them for several weeks, not till we've had time to dissect . . . I mean, study the specimen."

Dick frowned as a thought came to him. "What if she dies?"

"Oh, she'll undoubtedly die after all our . . . um, observations. First we'll get our answers and documentation."

"Won't the public be upset?"

"No, because an alien isn't a real person. It will be sort of like studying Bigfoot."

Dick was glad he'd said that. As excited as he was about finally catching an alien, he'd been a little wary about the dissection. This relieved him of any guilt. "Uh, I was wondering, dontcha think it would be kinda neat to know if alien women can have human sex?"

"Undoubtedly," Mr. Atkins answered with a little smile. "Under controlled circumstances, of course."

Dick felt a rush of blood to his cock at the possibility that he might be the one doing the experimentation.

"Okay, you've got the chloroform, you've got restraints, you have the new van downstairs, all gassed up and ready to go. When can I expect to hear from you?"

"Well, I went to this guy Magnusson's apartment building in Coronado. Talked to a few people. I know he's got to be back by next Monday for an assignment. I'm thinkin' he'll be leavin' the alien at the trailer park while he's gone."

"You've done a good job. We're proud of you here at NCAR."

Dick beamed at the high praise.

"Are you sure you don't need any help?"

"No, it's better if I do it alone. Attract less attention."

Atkins nodded.

They shook hands then.

"The next time we meet, I promise I'll be delivering an alien to you." *Or die trying.*

Chapter 17

The best kind of wake-up call . . .

Torolf awakened in the middle of the night, unsure what
had disturbed his sleep. He glanced at the bedside clock. It
was three a.m. He'd only been asleep for an hour.

He got up to go to the bathroom and saw a light under
the closed door. He went outside, barefooted, and walked
to the edge of the woods where he pissed against a tree.

When he came back in and washed his hands at the
kitchen sink, he noticed the bathroom door was still closed
and the light still on. But no sound of water or other activity. He checked Hilda's bedroom, but her bed hadn't been
slept in yet.

He tapped lightly on the bathroom door. "You in there,
Hildy?"

No answer. He opened the door a crack . . . and almost
had a heart attack . . . or a dick attack.

Her long hair, still wet from a shower, had been combed
down her back in a wet swath. Hilda was sitting on the floor

in front of the full-length mirror. Her legs were bent at the knees and spread wide. And she was hot-damn buck naked.

Be still my heart! "What the hell are you doing, babe?"

"Looking. Go away."

Not a chance! "At what?"

"My nether parts. Go away."

When SEALs take a vow of chastity! "Why?"

"You told me I should know my own body. Go away."

"Why are you frowning?"

"Because I can't find it."

I am almost afraid to ask. "Find what?"

"My clete, you dolt."

Clete? Clete? Oh, my God! She means her clit. His you-know-what stood up and practically waved yoo-hoo. "I could help you find it."

"Go away. I told you not to touch me again."

"I could show you, without touching you." *Unless you ask me to, which is the plan, of course.*

She met his eyes in the mirror. Hers were dubious. His were hopeful.

Before she had a chance to say, "Get real!" he sank down to the floor behind her, his thighs straddling hers. He felt her wet hair against his chest. He felt his erection touch her ass. "Okay, what's the problem?" *Other than my world-class boner.*

"I already told you. I can't find it."

"That's because you're not aroused. Until you get your juices going, it'll hide under a hood."

"You are not serious."

"Yeah, I am. But I can't touch you. I promised. So, you have to do it yourself." *This has got to go down in history as man's greatest fantasy.*

"Do what?"

Oh, baby, come into my web, thought he, the spider. "Excite yourself."

"You mean self-pleasuring?"

I may just have a heart attack and orgasm at the same time.

Without asking for any further direction, she put both hands under her small breasts and lifted them. They were the size of orange halves with pink areolas and darker pink nipples.

"Have I told you how much I like your breasts?"

"Many times. Do not distract me. I cannot concentrate when you interrupt." She was rubbing her palms over her breasts, then pulling at the even more turgid nipples. "Oh, I can feel that down below, and my heart is racing."

Mine, too.

She caressed herself then, a dreamy expression on her face. She caressed her abdomen. Her belly. Her calves and thighs.

He held his breath, waiting.

And then she caressed her hair, which was golden and curly. "I think I can see it now," she said in a whisper. And she sure as hell saw more of it as she began to stroke herself, creating a visible slickness.

In an attempt to control his arousal, Torolf bit his bottom lip and thought about okra, a vegetable that made him gag. It helped a little.

As Hilda began to touch her sweet spot, her thighs twitched, and she stiffened. She closed her eyes and arched her head back.

He could actually see her orgasm coming. *Mercy!*

"Oh . . . oh . . . oh," she whimpered, canting her pelvis forward. Then, "Ohmygods! Ohmybloodygods!"

Her eyes were still closed, and she was whoofing out loud exhales, as her body tried to come back to normal.

Enough of this shit! Now it's my turn, babe. While her eyes were still closed, he reached into the pocket of his jeans, lying on the floor where he'd left them before his shower. Always good to have condoms handy. Torolf had found that if a guy had to get up and go look for condoms, it gave a woman that window of opportunity to change her mind. He wasn't taking any chances here, not that Hilda had agreed. Yet.

He shimmied back a little, shrugged out of his shorts, put the condom on, and took Hilda by the waist, lifting her so she was on all fours, him behind her, both of them facing the mirror.

"What are you doing?" she asked, her voice rather dazed from what she'd just done. "You promised not to touch me."

I lied. "This is for your own education, honey. For future reference." *Ha, ha, ha!* "It's women's number-one favorite sexual position. Doggie style." *God, don't strike me dead for the lie.* Before she had a chance to challenge his contention, he pressed her elbows to the floor and entered her from behind, almost losing it when her tight muscles clenched and unclenched him in a second orgasm. Now he was the one grinding out, "Oh . . . oh . . . oh!" before he got himself under control.

"I have ne'er heard of such a position. Is it a perversion?"

"A good perversion."

"Are there good and bad perversions?"

"Shut up, Hildy. Let me show you why women love this position. See, it allows the male to touch the woman's breasts while he's buried in her. And I can touch you here, too."

The sound Hilda made as he fluttered her and fucked her at the same time was a cross between a moan and a scream. He liked it. You know who liked it, too. A lot. His cock twitched. *It's probably giving me a high five.*

In too short a time, he was moaning, too, with a mind-blowing, toe-curling explosion of a climax. Hilda was probably climaxing, but who could tell with all that was going on down there? He collapsed on top of Hilda, who looked poleaxed as she stared at the two of them in the mirror, her a sandwich between him and the tile floor.

He took her to his bed and crawled into the sheets with her. Within seconds, they were both asleep.

Life is good.

You dog, you! . . .

Hilda felt so warm and all-over peaceful when she heard a loud knocking noise and opened her eyes to see herself cuddled up with her back against the lout. He was snoring into her ear, with his hairy leg sprawled over her thighs and one hand resting familiarly on her breast.

"Aaaaccck!" she screeched.

He shot to a sitting position and reached reflexively for his gun. "What? What?"

She jumped out of the bed and put her hands on her hips, trying her best to ignore that achy pleasure *down there*. "You promised not to touch me."

Placing the gun back on the bedside table, he said, "Well, hell, Hildy. If you didn't want me to touch you, you shouldn't have sat in front of a mirror, buck naked, with your legs spread, searching for gold."

"You are the one who said I should learn my own body. You are the one who showed me how to master-bait."

"Don't blame me for having red blood in my veins."

"You should not have touched me."

"You weren't protesting then."

"And that is an excuse? Turn my bones to butter and that makes everything all right?"

He grinned. He actually had the nerve to grin.

She threw a pillow at him. "I suspect something else, too."

"What would that be, sweetheart?" The whole time he spoke, his eyes were feasting on her nude body.

"That doggie business . . . you said it was a woman's

favorite position . . . well, I suspect it is more like a man's favorite position."

There was a coughing noise in the hallway. They both turned as one to see Cage leaning lazily against the open door, arms folded over his chest, ankles crossed. "Well, this is all very interesting, but don't you think you two should answer your door? You never know who might walk in."

"Eeeeek!" Hilda cringed, covering herself with a big towel. Torolf got up, totally uncaring about his nudity, and stretched.

"What're you doing here?" Torolf asked with concern.

"You've got a problem."

Hilda and Torolf were suddenly alert.

"Your brother made me bring someone here."

"Which brother?"

"Ragnor. He said that if I didn't bring her here, he and Alison would be evicted from their apartment. Apparently, the neighbors are complaining."

"She. A woman?" Hilda shrieked.

"Oh, God, please tell me it's not Gina," Torolf groaned. "Where is she?"

Cage was grinning, as if at some secret jest. "In your kitchen, eating a leftover hoagie on the counter."

"What?" Torolf asked in confusion.

He was not the only one who was confused.

Just then, a huge animal rushed past Cage, lunged at Torolf, with fur flying everywhere, knocked him backward on the bed, and proceeded to lick him all over. "Slut, you old dog, you," Torolf said, laughing as he tried to escape the dog's drool.

Once the dog settled down, after licking them both up and down, Hilda and Torolf put on their clothing, with her glowering at him and him grinning at her, offering her something called wild monkey sex. They prepared to go

out to the scullery, where Cage was preparing them a
break-fast. But first Hilda put a hand on Torolf's arm. She
was still mad at him for tricking her into sex play last night,
but she had a more important issue now.

"Who is Gina?"

When a guy's bad deeds come back to bite him in the butt . . .

Torolf kept stealing glances at Hilda across the small table.
He was falling for her, hard, and she blamed him for every
friggin' problem in her life.

"Do you want more?"

His head jerked up. *Is she reading my mind now?* Cage
grinned at him across the small table as he read the morning newspaper, something he'd been doing ever since he
got here. Grinning, that is.

Turning, he saw that Hilda held the frying pan in one
hand and a turner in the other. Wearing an old red-and-
white-checked apron—the type that slipped over the neck
and tied behind in old movies—she was offering him more
of the mushroom and cheese omelette Cage had made for
them. He shook his head, and she put some on her plate
with another piece of toast. "I really like that apron on you,
but—" *Good Lord, I must be developing a good case of
foot-in-mouth disease.*

"But?" she said, sitting down and tearing the omelette
apart with her fingers. He hadn't taught her about the use
of forks and knives yet. Slut was crowded under the table,
tongue hanging out to catch Hilda's droppings.

Cage smiled and told her, "Torolf meant he would like
you in that apron with nothing under it."

She stopped eating and speared Torolf with one of her
"the lout" looks. "Is that what you were picturing?"

He thought about lying, then shrugged. "Sure. Why not?"

"Do women in this land walk around bare as bairns under their aprons?"

"All the time," he told her.

She looked to Cage for confirmation.

"All the time," good ol' Cage agreed with a wink at him.

"Thanks," he mouthed.

"Anyhow, Max, your brother wanted to know where the hell you were hiding. He suggested there must be a woman involved."

"Gina, no doubt," Hilda said with sugary sarcasm.

"You didn't tell Ragnor, did you?"

"Nope. I'm enjoying your mess too much. Moving on, *mon coeur*. Slut is spayed, but apparently she has attracted every hound dog in Ragnor's neighborhood. Howling dogs are breaking their leashes to get to her."

"Shame on you, Slut," Torolf said, although he was kind of proud of her for being such a hottie.

"Wanna help me decorate for the big bash tomorrow night?" Cage asked Hilda.

"I am not sure how much help I can be, but certainly I would like to be useful."

You could be useful to me, Torolf thought with continuing lack of sense. And, hey, why Cage had asked Hilda and not him raised a few red flags. "By the way, where are you staying?"

"He is staying here with us, of course," Hilda offered. Vikings were known for their hospitality. He should have known.

"I could sleep in the second bedroom."

"That's my bedchamber," Hilda said.

At the questioning tilt of Cage's head, she added, "That was a mistake, my sleeping in Torolf's bed. He cannot keep his hands off me."

Cage was enjoying Torolf's discomfort immensely. "Okay, I guess I can sleep on your couch. As for the rest of the guys, Serenity assured me there will be plenty of single girls to hook up with."

"This is turning into a bloody nightmare," Torolf pronounced. Hilda, on the other hand, smiled as if everything was okeydokey.

"She's gonna give me a tattoo today." At their surprised looks, Cage said, "Just kidding."

"I would not mind getting a tattoo," Hilda said, wiping her mouth with a paper napkin, which she folded neatly to use again.

"Why would you want a tattoo?" he asked.

"To remember this place when I am gone," she answered.

Strangely, his heart sank at that apparent yearning on her part, to be away from this place, which pretty much meant away from him, too.

"Where would you put the tattoo?" Cage asked.

"I do not know. Where do people usually put them?"

"Usually on the butt," Torolf told her.

"They do not!"

"Yeah, they do. Hearts, butterflies, whatever. You never know what you're going to find when you get down to business."

"And you get down to business a lot, do you?"

Well, I stepped right into that one. "On the rare occasion when I have the opportunity to view a bare female behind."

Cage snorted his opinion of that statement. Hilda did, too. She was learning bad things from Cage.

"Body piercings are another jolt to the eyeballs when ya get down and dirty." Cage was on a real roll now. "I met this woman one time. It was in the French Quarter, which shoulda given me a clue. She had herself pierced right here." He pointed to his crotch.

Hilda was shocked. "Why, for the love of Odin?"

Torolf knew what was coming next.

"She had this little ring, down there, and she also had

this thin chain she could attach to it. She wanted me to lead her around on a leash. Talk about!"

Several seconds passed while they all pictured that scene.

"And did you?" she asked finally.

"Nah. I'm not into kinky stuff," Cage said with a straight face. Then he leveled his mischievous gaze on Torolf, batting his eyelashes like a blinkin' neon sign. "How about you, Max? You into perversions?"

He was about to tell him to shut up, but it was too late.

"Just doggie style rutting," she told Cage, "but that is a good perversion. There are good and bad perversions, you know."

"I did not know," Cage said, still with a straight face. "Shame on you, Max, for never sharing that information."

I am never, ever going to live this down.

Sensing that she had disclosed something she should not have, she added to Cage, "But do not tell anyone."

"Like the entire sixteen teams of SEALs on both coasts," Torolf said with a groan.

I am never ever going to live this down.

Chapter 18

One perversion, two perversion, three perversion . . .

Hilda was happy.

And that was a real surprise to her.

Oh, she still wanted—nay, intended—to return to The Sanctuary. But for now, she was enjoying these new people she was meeting here in Ah-mare-eek-ah.

Yesterday, she had helped Serenity and several other women decorate the great hall named Fire. In many ways, women throughout the ages were the same. They talked about men, clothing, men, their monthly flux, men, women's work, jewelry, men. One difference was the amount of time women here spent worrying over their sizes. In this country, or mayhap just in this time, being very, very thin was the ideal. Hard to fathom a starvling woman being considered the comeliest.

This morning, some of the women were taking her to a large shopping mart, called a mall, to buy a special garment for tonight's event. Torolf did not know she was going, though she had taken some parchment from his pocket to pay for her purchases. He was being a grumpy bear over her even leaving the trailer to visit with neighbors in the hog park for fear the sign-tiss would arrive.

Right now, Torolf and Cage were off chasing Slut, who kept evading them as she found every male dog within shouting distance and beyond. Hilda was learning an assortment of new swear words from these two. In many ways, Slut reminded her of Stig, whom she missed. Later, the other SEALs would arrive, and they would be watching some kind of horseless carriage races. Strange country, this Ah-mare-eek-ah!

At the last minute, Serenity decided not to go with them to the mall.

"Is this about Jolene?" Linda asked. Linda was a young woman who had just started call-ledge, a school for adults, and who took off her clothes and danced for money one day a sennight.

Hilda was trying hard not to judge the girl. A woman did what she had to do to survive. She knew that better than most.

"I thought I heard a scream last night," Linda remarked.

Hilda went immediately alert. *A scream?*

Serenity's face betrayed her. She must have heard a scream, too. "I wanna go over and see how she is, once that asshole of a husband is on the road again."

"I swear, we oughta all get together and do an intervention with that girl," Lizzy declared with obvious frustration. She was a teacher of young children who was several years older than Hilda. She spent her summers and some weekends here at Hog Heaven, as did many others, their common interest that they all owned hogs.

"No, I'll tell you what we oughta do. We should pull an Earl on that husband of hers, who just happens to be named Earl. You know, that Dixie Chicks song where the women go off and kill Earl, the bastard that was beating one of their best friends."

Seeing Hilda's confusion, Serenity said, "Jolene is a young woman. Only about twenty. She's married to a trucker. They have no kids, thank God. He hauls freight from coast to coast. He beats the crap out of his wife, occasionally, and we think Jolene ought to either leave the jerk or at least file charges the next time he raises a hand to her."

Hilda felt rage boil up in her. Did men never change through the ages? Were there always those who felt it their right to beat their women, as if they were property or dogs? "I want to stay and go with you. In my country, I have a sanctuary for women. Although I cannot take this young woman there, I can give her advice."

Everyone gazed at her with surprise . . . and admiration.

Hilda was not looking for praise. This was something she could do, and she did it well.

"You run a women's shelter?" Linda asked.

"Yea, I do."

"Good for you," Tissie said, reaching over to squeeze her hand. Tissie was a woman with beautiful reddish brown skin, stemming from her chair-oh-key ancestors.

"No, you go to the mall today, Hilda. It's better if I talk with Jolene alone this time. Maybe later." Then she laughed and tried to change the subject. "While you're out, I want you all to pick up a joke gift that I set aside for Spike at The Horny Toad. Just give them my name."

"Ooh! A sex shop," Lizzy said. "Maybe I'll get a new set of Ben Wa balls."

"What are Ben Wa balls?" Hilda asked.

The others giggled, even Serenity, who kept saying, "I'm too old for this stuff."

"Serenity, I've learned more stuff from you than *Sex and the City*," Linda said.

Serenity beamed.

Lizzy explained what Ben Wa balls were, and Hilda's face got hotter and hotter.

"They're great when you're having sex with a man," Tissie elaborated, "but I enjoy them as much just riding my Harley."

"Yea, those hogs are a wonderful self-pleasuring device, are they not?" Hilda remarked.

There was a stunned silence, then a burst of laughter.

"Sweetie, you are a breath of fresh air." Serenity gave her shoulders a squeeze. "I'm gonna love havin' you around."

Hilda wasn't sure what she'd said to prompt such a reaction, but it was rather nice to be mothered.

Then Linda said, "I might buy a new set of nipple rings. My old ones are getting tarnished."

No one appeared fazed by Linda's comment; so, Hilda bit her tongue. She could scarce imagine how a woman could wear rings on her nipples.

The final shock came from Tissie, who added, just before the four of them rose to leave Serenity's trail-her, "I'm hoping you can touch up my tattoos before I leave this weekend."

"Sure, hon," Serenity said. "Let me see what's happening, and I'll get my tools out while you're gone. I brought some home with me from the shop."

"Oh, dost have a heart or butterfly on your butt?" Hilda asked, trying to appear less naive than she apparently was.

"Hell, no!" Tissie raised her tea-ing *shert*, and showed them both breasts totally covered with tattoos.

Hilda's eyes nigh popped from her head.

Tissie explained that Serenity had tattooed them to look like ice cream cones, whatever that was.

Hilda could not keep her thoughts to herself. "Blessed Thor, I have been married three times, and ne'er have I heard of such things. I thought the things Torolf favored were perverted, but they are not like this."

All eyes turned on her with interest.

"What?"

"C'mon. Spill," Linda said. "You can't say that and not finish."

"Oh, 'tis naught like the things you have all mentioned. Just teaching me how to pleasure myself."

"My, my, my! I always thought Max had some mojo hidden away," Lizzy said. "Don't go lookin' so crushed, though. He turned me down."

"Me, too," the others said.

That was interesting . . . that Torolf had declined sex with these very attractive women. Not that she cared. Much.

"Any other perversions Max has?" Linda asked with casual interest, which might not be so casual.

"Just the woman's favored sexual position."

Silence.

Then Tissie asked, "And that would be?"

"Doggie sex."

Everyone laughed except a puzzled Hilda, who decided that while she was opening her big mouth, she might as well finish. "Of course, he knows the famous Viking S-spot, as all Northmen do, though not my three husbands, the know-nothings. The S-spot is not really a perversion. Leastways, I do not think it is."

When they finally left for the mall, which was a big shopping mart, they were all chattering away. It turned out she had as much to teach them as they were teaching her.

"Tell me again where this S-spot is," Linda said.

"Oh, I cannot explain it. Really. It can only be found with a tongue. A man's tongue."

"Honey," Linda said, looping an arm over Hilda's shoulders, "you are my new best friend."

"Me, too. Me, too," the others said.

It was always good to have new friends.

Doggone it! . . .

Navy SEALs were trained to fight the hardest terrorists in
the world. They took down tangos around the world and
destroyed their caves and safe houses. Lots of U.S. enemies feared them.

Why then did it take five SEALs to catch a friggin' dog?

For more than an hour after the other guys arrived, they
chased, almost caught, slipped down a hill, climbed up a steep
embankment, fell in a pond, and called out the silliest things in
the world, "Here Slut, here Slut!" "Hey, Slut, I got a boner
here for you!" "Look, *101 Dalmatians* is on the tube. Hurry!"
"Is that a hot pit bull I see over there? He's got somethin' for
you, *chère*." "Hey, Slutty mutty!" "Think dog pound here,
Slut!" "Think doghouse here, Slut!" "Even dogs have to give
it a rest sometime! I'm tired. Aren't you tired, Slut? C'mon,
let's go take a nap!" "Uh-oh! Is that a T-bone I spy over
there?" And finally, "Get the fuck over here, you motherfucker, before I stick a bone up your ass and make dog soup!"

They found Slut sitting by the steps of the trailer. Her
tongue was lolling out of her mouth, drool making a pud-
dle at her feet, her tail wagging like crazy.

"She got *some*," Cage concluded, and they all agreed.

"You dog, you!" Torolf said. You couldn't help but admire a dog who knew what she wanted and went after it.

He led the way into the trailer with his buddies.

"Where's Hilda?" Geek was already checking out
Torolf's laptop, making tsking noises about his failure to
defrag regularly.

"She's over at Serenity's trailer."

"You got any beer?" JAM asked.

"Is Slut a slut?" Torolf answered with a laugh.

Cage flicked on the tube. "NASCAR's about to come on."

"Why's Pretty Boy down in the dumps?" he whispered
to JAM.

"I think he's missin' Big Mama. He went home alone last night from the Wet and Wild, and he almost never does that."

Everyone was soon comfortable, sitting around the tiny living room. Torolf was feeling pretty good. He was back in the present. He was drinking beer and watching the races. They were going to a party tonight. Yep, life was good.

Cage zapped him then as he said as blithely as if he was commenting on Junior's latest win, "So, did y'all know what women's favorite sexual position is?"

Even Viking women like to shop . . .

If there was ever anything that would make a woman want to stay here in the future, it was the mall.

Oh, my gods and goddesses! It was every woman's dream come true. Hilda had been to market towns . . . Hedeby, Kauptang, Birka. And they had contained goods from around the world. But this!

First there had been the ride to the mall in Tissie's horseless carriage box, known as a Jeep, colored bright red, of all things. They raced down the road at an ungodly speed. All the while, there had been dozens of other carriage boxes going in either direction, some even faster.

Hilda's brain practically spun at all she saw at the mall. It was so big, with so many people, all of them in a hurry. Such different attire, much of which would have been considered scandalous in her time. Foods ready to be served, without any cooking fires. Bright lights everywhere. And noise: people talking and laughing, music coming from walls, babies crying. Holy Thor, 'twas enough to make a person put her hands over her ears. And so much color . . . almost too much brightness.

They were entering a department store, and a lady stepped up to her and squirted her with some substance.

Accustomed by now to her surprise at every little thing, Linda took her arm and said, "Don't be afraid. She was just squirting you with scent to see if you want to buy some perfume."

"Huh?" Hilda sniffed her hand, and there was indeed a delicious flowery scent. "How wonderful!"

"It's called Joy," the squirting lady said.

"Joy? You name your perfume?"

The squirting lady looked at Hilda as if she was demented.

"Can I buy some?"

Soon she had a bagful of everything from a squirting container of perfume, body lotions, soap, and even bubble bath. Among her purchases were two pairs of braies, blue and black, so tight she could scarce breathe; women wore braies as much as dresses or short gunnas in this country. Then she had also bought colorful *sherts*, two pairs of soft-soled shoes, and one pair of running shoes—although she kept protesting that she had no intention of running unless someone was chasing her—and hose made of a magic transparent material.

They walked down the mall, planning to stop at a restrunt to break their fasts when suddenly Hilda stopped dead in her tracks. "*What* is that?"

Her three companions grinned mischievously.

"We saved the best for last. Victoria's Secret," Linda said. "Come on, ladies. Let's party."

Hilda bought six pairs of different colored, silky undergarments called pant-hees, but disdained the bras, laughing at any suggestion that she might need support. She had also refused to even consider the outrageous item called a thong, even though the other three women purchased them with great glee. She did let them talk her into a tight black top, which the ladies assured her could be worn outside, called a busty-air. She had to admit her breasts did not look quite so small when uplifted like that.

Finally, Hilda made her most extravagant purchase of the day, what they called a baby doll nightie. It was made of red and black lace, exposed her neck and shoulders, and reached only to her upper thighs. To her, it was an extravagance because, really, who needed garments to sleep in?

After she'd eaten a hot dog—and, nay, it was not a real dog—and a cold root beer, which bubbled and tickled her nose, and tasted not at all like beer, they headed toward the sex shop at the far end of the mall, separated from the rest of the marts. The sign outside said, The Horny Toad, and under that, Tasteful Adult Toys.

"You can wait outside, if you want," Lizzy told her.

"Why?"

"It's too raunchy for some women."

Hilda shrugged. She wanted to learn everything she could while in this country.

And learn, she did.

While Lizzy was picking up the gagging gift that Serenity had ordered, and Linda and Tissie made some purchases, she browsed the aisles. First, she noticed the big paper books, called magazines, showing nude women, even ones exposing their female parts, and ones with udders so big and firm that she wondered that the women could walk without falling on their faces. Then there were the men with manparts so big and long they nigh dragged on the floor when they walked. They made her three husbands . . . even Torolf . . . look like boylings in comparison.

She giggled and moved on. The massage oils and herbs, she could understand, but why would anyone want to put clamps on their nipples, and why whips and paddles?

The others were ready to leave, noting the lateness of the hour and the need to prepare for tonight's event.

"I would like to purchase a gift for Torolf first."

All heads turned to her.

"This," she said, holding out a jar of chocolate with a brush attached. "He loves chocolate."

They all laughed, as if at some private jest.

The lout did not deserve gifts, except that he had rid the Norselands of that beastly Steinolf, and that was no small thing.

"Should I be buying a gift for Spike's birthing day celebration?"

"Nah!" Lizzy said, "Just tell him about the gift you bought for Max. That will be gift enough."

What an odd thing to say!

Chapter 19

He was gonna become a chocoholic . . . or die trying . . .

Torolf looked at his wristwatch and wondered where Hilda was. She'd been at Serenity's for several hours.

And, actually, he was getting tired of all these guys crowding his space. His and Hilda's space, to be more precise. Oh, he knew why they came, and it wasn't for some birthday bash. They were worried about him and Hilda and the threat from some nutcase alien hunters, especially after they'd researched the National Center for Alien Research. These pseudoscientists had pulled some deadly stunts in the past, in the name of science.

He picked up his cell phone, leaned against the kitchen counter, and waited for someone to pick up. The guys had watched reruns of *Desperate Housewives* after the races ended, and were standing, about to leave. There was no beer left.

He had his cell phone in one hand and Slut's dog collar clutched in the other. Slut, straining at his hold on her, would love to shoot out the door when the guys opened it to leave. She hadn't been out shaking her bootie since this morning, a dry spell in her doggie dating world.

"Hello, Morgan residence. Serenity, master tattoo artist."

"Hey, Serenity, how about sending Hilda back here? The guys want to say good-bye to her before they leave."

Said guys scoffed at his lie, but he didn't want to sound anxious to have her back with him, which he was, dammit.

"Uh . . ."

Red flags went up in Torolf's brain. *"Uh" is not a good sign.* "Serenity . . . ?"

"Okay, she went to the mall with Linda and Lizzy and Tissie, and you shouldn't worry about her, she'll be all right, she's in good company, and look, I think I heard their car pulling up right now."

"You mean, Linda of the Ben Wa balls, Lizzy the stripper with the nipple rings, and Tissie of the ice cream cone tattooed breasts?"

Each of the guys, big ears tuned on high, turned around and sat down. No way were they going to leave now.

"You don't have to be sarcastic," Serenity told him.

"I'm sorry. It's just that Hilda doesn't know her way around here." *And she's from the bleepin' eleventh century.*

"She's really sweet."

"Who?"

"Hilda, of course."

"Well, I don't know if I'd call her sweet." *Unless I'm eating her. Then she's sweet, for damn sure.*

The doorknob rattled, and he said, "That's her now. Bye."

Hilda came in carrying two shopping bags with mall store imprints on them. One of them was from Victoria's Secret.

Every single male eye in the room took note of that fact.

"Greetings," she said to each of the guys. To Torolf, she just gave a glower. Apparently, she was still in a snit over waking up in his bed. *Why is it that women can engage gung ho in the deed, then blame it on the guy the next day?*

"I thought I told you to stick close, that we have to worry about that alien research wacko." *Big mistake!* He realized it the second the words left his mouth.

"You are not my master. I needed garments for the birthing day celebration, and Serenity asked us to pick up a gift for Spike that was being held for her in a store at the mall."

"So, Max, spill. There are going to be babes at this party tonight who have nipple rings, tattooed breasts, and Ben Wa balls? Is that why you didn't want us to come? Keep the goodies all to yourself, huh?" This was JAM speaking, a smirk on his face.

"Oh, do you speak of Linda and Lizzy and Tissie?" Hilda asked, unaware of the suggestive nature of their questions. "They are my new friends. I will introduce all of you tonight."

"Thank you, *chère,* 'specially since Max failed to tell us about these lovely ladies." Cage was enjoying the hell out of Torolf's squirming.

He glanced at her bags. "Looks like you had a good day."

"Yea, I did. I hope you do not mind that I took some parchment money from your pocket."

"That's all right."

"I bought so many things. Garments, shoes, soap, even Joy."

They all arched their brows at that.

She took out a bottle and squirted it into the air, filling the air with an overpowering scent.

Perfume. She meant perfume.

"We did not realize it was so late, but in the end we had to go get Serenity's gift for Spike."

"What did she get him?" Torolf had brought a box of Cuban cigars with him. Spike did love his cigars, though Serenity made him smoke them outside.

"I don't know. It is from The Horny Toad."

"Oh, my God!" Torolf put his face in his hands, just knowing what was going to come next.

"Uh, isn't The Horny Toad a sex shop?" Geek asked.

"Yea, 'tis," Hilda answered, not at all embarrassed. "Oh, I see you have a gift? Is that for Spike?" She was looking at the ribbon-and-foil-wrapped box on a side table.

He nodded, even as he was giving the guys dirty looks, encouraging them to leave.

Which they ignored, of course.

" 'Tis good you brought a gift for Spike. I did not realize till too late that I had not bought anything for him. But then my new friends told me that if I told Spike about the gift I bought for you, that would be gift enough for him."

I hope it's see-through undies from Victoria's Secret. No, I don't. I'm just kidding. Hah! Who am I kidding?

Every guy in the room was grinning.

"Uh . . . what gift?"

"Do not be thinking that you deserve a gift, not after being such a slimy slyboots, sleeping with me after I distinctly told you not to touch me again, but you did remove Steinolf from this world, and for that I am thankful. 'Tis your favorite."

This oughta be a whopper.

She leaned down and took an object from one of the bags, not the Victoria's Secret one.

Cage, who was closest, took the object from her, looked at it, then laughed out loud. "Yep, it's your favorite, Max." Then he paused in a ta-dum manner. "Chocolate body paint."

Amping up the ammunition . . . uh, temptation . . .

Hilda stomped away from her metal keep toward Lizzy's metal keep.

The lout watched her progress, to ensure her safety, he'd

said. No doubt he did so with that incessant frown on his face . . . or a grin. 'Twas ever one or the other with him.

He was sorely mistaken if he thought she was going to stay there and prepare for the birthday celebration with him watching over her shoulder, making observations on every little thing. The lip gloss, which he'd deemed unnecessary. The white silk pant-hees, which he'd wanted her to model for him. The tight black braies which he'd called slut jeans, even before she'd put them on. Slut had been lying on the bathing chamber floor at the time, splattered out like a rug, and had growled at his master's apparent insult. Hilda was beginning to realize that Slut was not a proper name for a dog . . . or a woman.

She knew he just teased her, and he was just as uneasy as she about this unwanted attraction they both suffered from, and he was genuinely concerned about her safety, though she failed to see the immediate threat. Of a certainty, there was no need for Torolf to give her an irksome list of orders, as if she was a witless child. "Do not talk to any strangers." "Do not tell anyone you have time-traveled." "Do not mention the eleventh century." "Do not discuss the mudslide and your stay in the hospital." There were so many "do nots" she could have screamed. And when he'd said, "Do not flirt," she'd had enough and picked up the parchment sack with her new clothing inside, declaring she would go to dress with the other women.

Lizzy opened the door at Hilda's knock. "I'm so glad you decided to dress with us. I can't wait to get my hands on that hair of yours."

"Torolf was being a horse's arse."

"Enough said!" Linda peeked out of the bathing chamber.

When she got closer to the bathing chamber, she saw that another woman was in there with Tissie. That woman, who had seen no more than twenty winters, if Hilda guessed correctly, was sitting on the closed seat of the privy, with Tissie applying a flesh-colored, hiding lotion to her face. Her one eye was blackened, and there was a cut on her bottom lip.

It must be Jolene, the abused woman they had mentioned earlier. That fact was soon borne out when Lizzy said, "Hilda, this is Jolene. It took a lot of convincing, but she's going to come with us tonight."

Hilda assumed that the brutish husband must have left . . . for now. Otherwise, she misdoubted that he would allow the girl out of his sight.

Jolene looked up at Hilda through green eyes reddened from tears. Her black hair was lank and straight. Her petite body was broom-thin.

"Good tidings!"

"Hi!" the girl responded.

Hilda could not help herself. She knelt down in front of the girl and took her in her arms. "Oh, sweetling, in my country I have a sanctuary for women just like you. I cannot tell you how many times I have welcomed women with pain in their eyes . . . pain usually caused by brutish men. I will help you."

The girl's tears soon soaked her neck as Hilda made soothing noises. This country may be different than hers, this time period might be different than hers, but this one thing Hilda understood: Women needed other women to survive bad men.

Once the tears stopped and warm cloths held over Jolene's eyes to reduce the redness, they all dressed and got ready to go. It took them two hours, but what a picture they made when they all piled into Tissie's red Jeep and drove to Fire Hall.

Jolene's bruises were still visible, but not so much as before. With some face paint and hair ornaments holding her hair off her face, she looked very pretty and younger than her age.

Hilda had also undergone an amazing transformation. Her hair had been curled with hot rollers, and subtle paint had been applied, giving her face a natural glow. And blessed Frigg, her eyelashes were so thick and long now, she could scarce lift her lids. She wore the tight black slut braies that Torolf had commented on, and it had taken her lying down on the floor and sucking in her stomach to get the zipper pulled up. She had no idea how she would manage if she had to relieve herself during the evening. As for her upper attire, the only word that came to mind was *wanton*. She would have never worn the busty-air, which also required her to suck in a deep breath, if not for the sure knowledge that Torolf would disapprove. In the end, she'd lost her courage and would not wear it unless covered with a sheer white blouse studded with gold stars, which she tied at the waist. It was still wanton, in her opinion.

A box inside the horseless carriage box was playing loud music, something about rolling stones and satisfaction.

Tissie, who sat with Hilda in the backseat, glanced at her and smiled. "Sweetie, you look hot!"

"Will Torolf think so, too?" Hilda realized that she was starting to care too much what Torolf thought of her.

"Oh, yeah! Him and every other male in the hall."

"Good," she said, but what she thought was, *Am I pushing the bounds of decency just to make a point with the lout? Am I playing a fool's game here, and me the biggest fool of all?*

Just when you think you've figured women out . . . Bam! . . .

"She's driving me crazy."

Cage didn't even have to ask him who he meant. "Good crazy or bad crazy?"

"Definitely bad." He took a long swig of beer from his

glass. There was a keg behind the bar on which he and
Cage leaned at the local fire hall. The place was all decorated with crepe paper and balloons for Spike's party. He
and Cage had been among the first to arrive, but people
were streaming in steadily, many arriving on motorcycles
if the rev of motors outside was any indication. Serenity,
who was in the kitchen fussing over the food to be served,
had invited more than a hundred guests.

The five-piece band, in cowboy gear, was tuning its instruments as Spike came up to them. "Damn, I need a
beer," he said, waving to the bartender.

"Happy birthday, big boy," Torolf said.

"Thanks, but I don't think there's all that much to celebrate. Lose hair, gain weight, piss more, have sex less.
What's to celebrate? This is all Serenity's goofball idea."

"Hey, I hear she bought you a gift at The Horny Toad,"
Cage mentioned.

"No kidding?" Spike grinned. "Maybe this birthday
business won't be so bad, after all."

JAM and Geek came in then and told them that Pretty
Boy insisted on coming alone. They all had beers in hand,
and the band was playing Hank Williams Jr.'s "All My
Rowdy Friends Are Coming Over Tonight," when Pretty
Boy strolled in.

"You are freakin' unbelievable!" Torolf told Pretty Boy.

"What?"

"Who wears a silk T-shirt and a sport coat over designer
jeans to a fire hall? And where the hell did you get those
creases in your jeans? Don't tell me you iron?"

The others began to razz Pretty Boy, too, with remarks
like, "You're a freakin' Brad Pitt." "Is that mousse in your
hair? Or snot?" "You smell good enough to eat, boy. Oops,
I guess that was your goal, huh?" "You so pretty, y'all
could make a gator sigh, yes."

"Hey, we're talking tattooed and pierced women here.

Gotta pull out all the ammunition if I'm gonna be the first one to strike pay dirt." Good ol' Pretty Boy. Always playing the odds.

"First? Says who?" Cage jabbed Pretty Boy in the arm.

Soon they were all placing bets on the bar as to who got lucky first, and then arguing over what specifically and graphically denoted lucky. Despite the teasing, Torolf opted out. "That's all I need, to go off with some woman and leave Hilda here alone to fend for herself. She'll feel out of place."

"I doan know 'bout that," Cage said with a big grin.

His other buddies looked in the direction Cage was staring, along with other men in the hall. One by one, grins passed over their mouths like the wave in a college football stadium.

"Hot damn!" JAM said.

"Wanna borrow my silk T-shirt and jacket?" Pretty Boy inquired too generously.

Then they all looked at Torolf, just waiting for his reaction. *I have a feeling I am not going to like this.* The band launched into a loud version of Toby Keith's "How Do You Like Me Now?" which was really appropriate, Torolf realized, as he finally turned around.

Hilda came in with her new friends . . . a Hilda so far different than the one he'd known back in the Norselands he hardly recognized her . . . in fact, far different even than the one he'd seen leaving the trailer earlier tonight. *And, oh, yeah, Toby, I like her now. A lot.*

She'd poured herself into a pair of tight black jeans, which showed off her exceptionally long legs. On top, she had some kind of black bustier thing, which was visible through the sheer white blouse she wore over it. The most amazing transformation was her hair and face. Her long blonde hair had been curled and blown so that it looked like one of those fantasy sex kitten spreads in *Playboy* . . .

the kind where the girl said she likes long walks on the beach and giving blow jobs. Her face had been made up to be all eyes and pouty red mouth.

She is so far out of my class now she won't give me a chance. Not that I want a chance, but if I did, she'd blow me off, and I don't mean blow job.

The other guys had already pushed themselves away from the bar and were practically tripping over each other to be the first to introduce themselves to Hilda's friends. Hilda ignored them and strutted up to him, chin raised defiantly, as if she expected him to say or do something offensive.

"You look great."

That took her by surprise. "You do not disapprove?"

"Not at all." *Except it should be only for me . . . and in private.* "Did you think I would?"

"Yea, I did."

And that's why you dolled up like this, isn't it? To annoy me? Well, guess what, cupcake? I'm likin' it.

"I can hardly breathe." She put one hand over her flat tummy and another over her bustier.

His heart began beating so fast he could almost hear it, like it did in the middle of some high-tension live ops. "I can hardly breathe watching you hardly breathing."

She tilted her head in question.

"You turn me on."

"I do?"

"Always."

"What does it mean? That I turn you on?"

"You arouse me."

"Oh."

"I'd say that outfit, especially the bustier, is my second-best rig on you."

"You know what a busty-air is?"

He grinned. "Honey, all red-blooded men know what a

bustier is. Likewise garter belts, fishnet stockings, and stiletto heels."

"Huh?"

"Never mind. Suffice it to say, you are the hottest woman in this room."

"And the best is what?"

It was his turn to say, "Huh?"

"You said this," she waved a hand to indicate her attire, "was your second-best rig on me."

"Nothing, baby. Just bare skin."

He'd expected her to say something shrewish, like "lackwit son of a troll," and storm away. Instead, she said, "You look good, too."

Oh, man, oh, man, oh, man! She is about to reel me in, hook, line, and sinker. And do I care? Hell, no! "Yeah?" He didn't want to examine his elation too closely, or else he'd be forced to run like crazy.

She nodded. "But I still do not want you touching me."

"Did I say anything about touching?"

"Your eyes did."

"Hard to control my eyes, sweetie."

"See? You should not even be calling me sweetling."

"Why?"

"Dangerous."

"Dangerous to whom?"

"Both of us."

"Do you wanna dance?"

"You change subjects like a bird flitting from one tree to another. I can't dance."

"I'll teach you, like I did before."

"You mean that foresport business? Oh, that will tamp the danger down."

He loved the way she could make him smile, even when she was being sarcastic, even when he could swear that smiling was the last thing in the world he wanted to do.

Taking her by the elbow, he steered her out onto the dance floor where the band segued into that old Ray Charles hit, "I Can't Stop Loving You."

Pulling her close, he arranged her arms around his neck, and he put both his arms around her waist. Her face was close to his, and his heart started racing like the repeat on a machine gun. Rat-a-tat-tat-tat-tat! For just a second, he closed his eyes and relished the feel of Hilda's body in his embrace . . . the rightness of the fit. "Do you have any idea how much I want to kiss off that red lip gloss?"

Instead of making a disparaging remark, she confided, "It's strawberry flavored."

"I love strawberries."

He put a hand to her nape, under all that glorious hair, and pushed her face against his shoulder. "Your hair smells nice. Apples?"

"Yea, and the soap I used was peach scented. Is that not amazing? Is this country not amazing?"

"You're a regular fruit salad, honey."

She babbled on then about how she would have to teach Effa how to add fruit and flower scents to her soaps when she returned to The Sanctuary and how they needed sanctuaries in this country, too. Then she moved on to blow dryers, zippers, and transparent hose. He only half listened, too intent on relishing the feel of her body in his embrace. Finally, she noticed his silence. "Is something wrong?" she asked, her breath tickling his ear.

Sweet ripples of pleasure swept over him from his ear to his groin. "Yeah, something's wrong." He inhaled deeply, for courage. He was about to say something he shouldn't, and it was going to take a helluva lot of nerve. "I think I'm falling in love with you."

"You cannot . . . I mean, it is nice to know . . . but I will be leaving here soon."

Nice? My telling her that I might love her is nice? I

think I'll go in the corner and suck my thumb. "I know you're leaving eventually. Just thought you ought to know. A little secret you can take back to the Norselands with you. You can gloat that some dumb schmuck, *the lout*, fell hard for you."

She was silent then as they swayed from side to side to the music. Later, he wouldn't be able to say if they were the only couple on the dance floor or one of dozens. Just when he thought she was going to kill him with her silence, she spoke up, "I would not gloat. In truth, it would be impossible for me to do so, in good conscience."

"Why is that, heartling?" *Holy shit! Did I really say heartling? I must be regressing to my Viking past.*

She kissed his neck and whispered, "Because I think I am falling in love with you, too."

Wham, bam, a shot to his already shaky heart.

That was for sure the final nail in Torolf's coffin.

Chapter 20

The three words that scare all men, even SEALs . . .

Hilda could tell that she stunned Torolf with her revelation. Well, he'd stunned her, too.

Somewhere between being blistering mad and planning to flirt with every male at the party, and seeing Torolf standing on the other side of the room, looking as handsome as all the gods, she realized something important. She loved the lout.

How did it happen? When did it happen? Was it the first time I saw him after all those years, back on the shipwreck? Was it when he first taught me what bedsport could be? Was it when he rid the Norselands of Steinolf? Was it when he rescued me here in this new land?

"Why are there tears in your eyes?" Torolf asked her, tipping her chin up with a forefinger.

"This is an immense revelation to me."

"That I love you?"

She noticed that he no longer said that he "thought" he loved her. Now it was a fact.

"Nay, that I love you."

The band was playing some loud, raucous music about "jam-ball-eye-ah" and people were doing faster dances with hips shaking and arms flailing, except for Cage, who was doing a very fancy dance involving intricate, sexual moves, with Linda, both of them laughing and singing at the same time. She and Torolf were just standing still. She had no idea how long they had been standing thus, arms looped around each other loosely, staring into each other's face.

"You are so unhappy about loving me that you weep?"

"Nay. 'Tis just that I have ne'er been in love afore. And it frightens and exhilarates me at the same time." She shrugged. "I am confused."

"I like the exhilarated part," he said, winking at her. He had a very nice wink, one that made her tingle all over.

Before she knew it, she and Torolf were sitting at a back table near the wall, she with a glass of clear wine, a novelty for her, and he with a glass of mead.

"I still do not want you to touch me," she told him, looking pointedly at his one arm resting casually over her shoulders.

"You've got to be kidding. No, no, no! You can't tell a guy that you love him and then put up a Do Not Touch sign."

"You know this from experience?"

"No. I've never been in love before, Hildy. Let's get that straight from the start. And if you think you're frightened by this, it's nothing compared to how I feel."

She smiled. "I thought Navy SEALs were afraid of nothing."

"You thought wrong," he said. "Fear is our friend."

"Is that another of those lackwit sayings of yours?"

"Yep." He leaned forward and lightly kissed her lips. "Strawberry kisses. Is there anything better?" Then he smiled back at her.

Her heart nigh galloped at that warm smile, and she feared that everyone could look at her and see the effect Torolf had on her.

"Back to that no touching business, I give you fair warning. I intend to touch you a lot tonight. I can't wait to see what it's like to have sex with a woman I love."

"I am trying to be sensible here, Torolf. Are you asking me to stay here in the future with you?"

A red bloom suffused his face and even his ears.

She laughed. "Oh, do not run scared, rogue. I know you were not asking that. But can you not see then why our lovemaking would be a mistake? I must go back to The Sanctuary. I am needed there. It is a time and culture I know."

"Your point being?"

"I do not want to make my departure harder than it will be already. Loving you and leaving will be difficult enough."

He was peeling the paper label off his bottle of mead with the thumb of his free hand as he pondered her words.

"Dost agree with me? You will halt your touching?"

He looked up from his paper peeling and grinned at her. "Hell, no. You're right; we're on a fast track to heartbreak. God, I can't believe I said such a hokey thing. But while you're here, I'll probably do everything to convince you to make love."

She shook her head at his hopelessness. Always a rogue.

"Sometimes you just gotta live in the moment. The work I do—hell, I could die any time I go out on an op, it's an occupational hazard—so I gotta think that we should grab whatever happiness we can when we can. Besides, you can't buy body paint for a guy and then put up a red light."

Her brow furrowed with puzzlement.

"That chocolate body paint you bought for me. And, by the way, that was a great gift. If I didn't say thank you before, I intend to later . . . with my tongue. Yum-yum!"

"You speak in riddles. I bought you paint?"

He explained what body paint was, and with each word, her jaw dropped lower and lower.

"Oh good gods! No wonder your friends were so amused."

"Hey, forget amused. They were jealous."

Said friends came to the table then, along with her new female friends. They were laughing and carrying drinks with them. Apparently, the band was taking a break, and the meal was about to be served.

Geek seemed to have developed an affection for Jolene, which could be dangerous, considering her husband.

She murmured to Torolf, "Geek best be careful. Jolene is married, and her husband beats her."

Torolf's head jerked to attention. "How do you know that . . . about the beatings?"

"Because she told me and because . . . well, look at her. Can't you see the bruises under the face lotion?"

He nodded slowly.

"Dost think you could kill her husband?"

"Whaaat?"

"He is a nasty, vicious man who will not allow her to leave. Whene'er she has tried, he brings her back and beats her more."

"Hilda, you shouldn't be getting involved."

"Why not?"

"Because this type of jerk would come after you, too."

She shrugged. "Mayhap. But someone has to help her. Methinks that whilst you are gone a-Viking or a-fighting or whatever it is you SEALs do, I will form my own sanctuary here for troubled women like Jolene."

He groaned. "Hilda, you are supposed to lay low here, not draw attention to yourself. In fact, I've been thinking about sending you to stay with Ragnor and Alison."

"You said it would be best if your family was not involved, lest the sign-tiss try to dice-section them, too."

"I know, but I'm beginning to think leaving you here alone would be a bad idea, even if I ask Spike to watch out for you, or have you stay in his trailer with him and Serenity."

"Is it because you love me now and you did not afore?"

He smiled. "Maybe."

"Well, I do not want to stay with your brother and his wife unless I must. I like these people here."

"All right. For now. I'll give you Ragnor's telephone number, though, and at the least sign of trouble, you call him."

She nodded.

Looking around the table, she noticed that only Pretty Boy sat alone, brooding into his beer. It had to be by choice, because a number of women kept staring in his direction.

"What's up, Pretty Boy?" Torolf asked his friend.

"I'm thinkin' 'bout goin' back to Coronado tonight."

"Why? Heavy date?"

"Nah. I'm just tired."

Torolf and his buddies exchanged glances, then Torolf told her in an undertone, "We think he's missing Britta."

Over the next hour, they ate their meal and drank their beverages and sang Happy Birthing Day to Spike and watched the dancers once the band played again.

"Do you know what I want to do with you when we leave here?" Torolf asked in a silky-smooth voice.

"Shhh! Behave," she hissed at him.

"First, I'll strip you naked, real slow. Then I'll paint you with chocolate and lick it off from your forehead to your toes."

She gaped at him and wanted to protest his sinful words, but the mind picture robbed her of speech.

"Then I will flip you over and do your back side."

She shouldn't encourage the man, but she wanted to know, "I am a big person. Can you eat that much chocolate?"

"I'm damn sure gonna try."

"It could be messy."

"I hope so."

"Do not think that we would take a shower together to wash it off and then have sex in front of the mirror again."

"Oh, yeah, go ahead. Give me ideas."

"And there will definitely be no cunning-tingles."

Cunnilingus? Chocolate cunnilingus? Have mercy! The ideas you plant in my . . . head! "Hilda, Hilda, Hilda. You are going to be the death of me yet."

"Nay, naught of which you speak will happen, because there will be no touching." That is what she said, but what she thought was, *I wonder if I have a taste for chocolate, too.*

Aliens and chocolate and Victoria's Secret, oh, my! . . .

All of Torolf's grand plans for seducing Hilda came to a screeching halt when they got back to the trailer.

He had just unlocked the door and stepped inside behind Hilda, when his cell phone rang. It was Slick.

At first, his brain didn't comprehend what Slick was saying, because Hilda was on the other side of the small room, which was ungodly hot, having been closed up while they were gone. She was taking off the white shirt, giving him his first full-blown view of the black bustier. He already knew she had pretty breasts. This wisp of male testosterone torture announced it to the world by pushing them up into a real-live cleavage. Who knew? Good thing she hadn't taken off the shirt at the birthday bash. He would have had to beat guys away with a stick.

"Are you listening?" Slick asked with exasperation.

"Huh?"

"Is Hilda there with you? Am I interrupting something? Not that I care a rat's ass. But I can tell your mind is elsewhere."

Yeah, like smack-dab in the middle of bare skin and chocolate paint. "What's the deal? Make it quick."

Slick chuckled. "Turn on your laptop and look at the downloads I'm sending. Do it now while I'm still on the line."

He put his hand over the phone and told Hilda, "Give me a sec, hon. I need to check something out for Slick."

She nodded and turned to go down the hall.

"Don't get naked, though. I want to do that for you."

"No touching," she answered without turning back.

Was she kidding or just teasing? Either way, there was hot-damn sure gonna be touching. He could guarantee that.

Once he had the laptop booted up and Slick's e-mail opened, he downloaded the first of the files. It was a picture of a middle-aged man, probably late forties with red hair and a receding hairline, which he had combed over. "I've got it."

"That's Richard Phillips, a lab technician at Holy Cross Hospital in Malibu. Get this. He's taken a two-week vacation."

Torolf didn't need to be told what that meant. "The jerk is out to get Hilda."

"Yep. Is Hilda an alien?"

"*Good Lord!* No. Do you believe in aliens?"

"Just thought I'd ask. Something is strange about her."

"I'll tell you later. You won't believe it."

"Try me."

"Is Phillips dangerous?"

"He has a license to carry."

"Is he operating alone?"

"So far, I think he is, under the center's direction, I suppose. The PI I hired thinks these people at the National Center for Alien Research are more than wackos. They believe that the world is on the fast track to self-annihilation, and the answer to saving it lies with alien nations. They also claim to have met aliens in the past, some of whom have taken earthlings captive. But this will be the first alien in captivity that they can study. And I mean, study . . . like dissection, autopsy, and a whole lot of other unsavory crap.

"The other files I've sent are in the attachment . . . mostly stuff about the center and its chairman, a real ding-bat . . . except he's a dingbat with a Ph.D. Read them over, then let me know what you want me to do as a follow-up."

"Oh, man! This guy's timing really stinks."

"About to get lucky, are you, Max?" Slick guessed.

"Real lucky."

"I heard about the chocolate body paint."

"Damn! Are there any secrets in this team?"

"Hey, some of us live vicariously."

"Yeah, right. What I meant about timing is our team going rough and ready. We'll be boots down in Iraq the week after next. I figure minimum two weeks for this rotation."

"Yep."

"I'm not sure she's safe here anymore."

"I don't know of another soul in the world who's heard of Hog Heaven." Slick was laughing on the other end of the phone.

"I suppose. But all I've got for protection here is a fifty-year-old biker who does body piercings. Maybe I should hire a few bodyguards."

"You better do it quick. You've only got twenty-four hours or so before you head back here."

"Maybe Spike knows someone. Hey, thanks, Slick. You've been a big help."

"No problem."

Torolf felt a headache starting at the back of his neck. His life was becoming a royal goat fuck. And now he had to give Hilda the bad news. "Hilda," he yelled to her in her bedroom.

"What?" she said, scaring the hell out of him. She was standing only a few feet behind him, frowning as she listened to his half of the phone conversation.

And she was licking a finger that she had just dipped in the chocolate body paint.

Hoo-yah!

How do you feel about bondage, baby? . . .

"What is amiss?"

Torolf was staring at her finger as if it were some miraculous object, but that was not why she asked her question. He was worried about something, something Slick had told him on the talking box.

"I need to go find Spike."

After all his talk of seduction, he was going to leave her. To talk with Spike. Not that she wanted a seduction or that she would have succumbed. But still . . . she was surprised. "Spike? Whatever for? He is no doubt still back at Fire Hall."

"Something has come up. Slick has been checking up on that Phillips character. He's looking for you, all right, and I've gotta see if Spike knows some men who can stay here with you."

"You would have men stay in this metal box with me? I do not think so!"

"I can't go away for two weeks or more and just leave you here. Do this for me, if not for yourself."

"Nay!"

"Don't force me to make you obey."

"Obey? No man forces me to obey, you loathsome lout."

"It was a poor choice of words. Come here, honey." He motioned with the fingers of both hands for her to come to him.

"Dost think you can order me to live with bodyguards and then waggle your fingers, and I will jump into your arms?"

He laughed. The man had the nerve to laugh at her. "The genie is out of the bottle, honey. No putting it back now."

"What does that mean?"

"When you bought that chocolate it was tantamount to rubbing my lamp."

"What lamp? . . . Oh, you are so crude," she said, spinning on her feet, about to walk away from him.

He grabbed her from behind. "Uh-uh, you're not walking away from me."

"Go! You said you had to go find Spike. Do so, now." Hilda was the one doing the ordering now.

"I've decided that I can wait till morning." He was holding her around the waist and nuzzling her bare shoulder, something she could not let him do, lest she fall under his spell . . . again. She shrugged herself out of his arms and stepped backward. Shaking a forefinger, she said, "Let us understand each other. You are leaving for some battle, I suspect. I will be going back to the Norselands. There is no life for us together. So, you will respect my wishes when I say, 'No touching.'"

"What about love?" He advanced on her.

She backed away. "Love has naught to do with it."

"Oh, I think it does."

"Stop it! Stop it right now!" She slapped at his hands, which attempted to touch her on first one spot, then another on her body. He was teasing, but she was not.

Before she could say "Stop it!" one more time, he lifted her over his shoulder, walked back and picked up the chocolate, and then went into the bathing chamber. She pounded his back the entire time and called him the vilest names she could think of.

He put her in the tub and stepped in after her, pressing

her against the tile wall to prevent her escape. Then, putting one foot on the side of the tub, he lifted the edge of his braies and pulled out a knife from its sheath on his calf. While she was gaping at the knife, he pressed it to the top of her busty-air and cut the knot of the laces.

"Noooooo!" she screeched as he pulled the laces out in one long strand. He then used the lace to tie her hands over her head to the showering hose. She had to stand on her tiptoes and clutch the pipe, lest she fall. Breathing in and out to calm herself down, she forced herself to stop struggling, realizing it would be useless to fight his greater strength. "You would take me against my will?"

"Never," he said, kissing her softly on her lips, even as she twisted her head, trying to evade his mouth. "I love you, and I'm about to show you how much."

She let loose with another stream of expletives.

"If you don't shut up, honey, I'm going to have to gag you." He stopped in the process of removing her shoes and tight braies. And he smiled . . . an evil grin. "Hmmmm. That gives me an idea."

He took off her braies, though not without difficulty and some expletives on his part. He left her with only the busty-air, which was gaping open, and the pant-hees. While she watched, warily, he stepped out of the tub, took off every item of his own clothing, then searched in the parchment bag she'd brought from the shopping mall. Inside, he found a pair of knee-high sheer hose, which was worn under braies or long gunnas.

With one of them, he did in fact gag her mouth. She continued to hurl nasty names at him, but they were muffled now. Then he used the other stocking to blindfold her.

She whimpered, frightened now.

"Don't be scared, sweetie. It's just a game. A game, I promise, you are going to like."

Hnefatafl is a game. Dicing is a game. This . . . is . . .

not . . . a . . . ooooooh! She felt cool air on her skin as he peeled the busty-air off of her.

There was silence then. What was he doing?

"I'm just looking at you, Hilda. You are so beautiful."

I am not beautiful, you fool.

"I know you think you're not, but you are, believe me. I want to imprint this image in my head for when you're no longer here, or when I'm no longer here. Well, enough looking. Sorry to take these off, but I don't want to get them dirty. I don't suppose they're edible . . . No, I see they're not."

Edible pant-hees? He really is daft.

She heard water running then.

"I'm warming the chocolate in hot water," he told her. "Don't want to jolt you with a cold paintbrush."

She sensed when he stood before her again. "Ready?"

She shook her head.

He paid no heed.

Then began the most horrible wonderful torture she could have ever imagined. He painted her breasts, taking special care to flick the bristles back and forth over her nipples, which were no doubt standing out like traitorous pebbles. He painted a line from her breasts over her belly, into her navel, and down to her nether hair. Then he painted from the inside of one ankle up her calf and knee and thigh. Then repeated the process. The whole time, all she heard was his heavy breathing.

"Now, what have I missed? Ah, yes, here."

Before she could imagine what he would do next, he inserted the brush between her legs and ran it along the channel. She could swear he was kneeling now. Yes, he was, she realized with a gasp as he parted her female folds with one hand and brushed that special nub of ecstasy that he had shown her before. He repeated the process in that place over and over till her belly tightened, her legs went rigid, and she bucked against the brush's handle till the tautness exploded within her in ever increasing and then decreasing spirals of pleasure. He had to hear her keening behind the gag as well as witness her coming apart, up close as he was.

"I hope that was as good for you as it was for me, babe," he murmured in a raw voice.

Outraged, she flailed from side to side as best she could without the use of her arms. "Let me go!" she screamed behind the gag. Even though the words were indecipherable, he had to know what she was saying.

"No, sweetheart, we are not going to stop. We've barely begun. Time for dessert."

He licked and licked and sucked the chocolate off of her then, making appreciative noises, holding her in place when she squirmed away. By the time he had consumed all of her, except for her female place, he said, "Now, my dear, for the best part. I am going to eat you."

What in bloody hell have you been doing so far, if not eating me?

She soon found out.

Kneeling down, he put her legs over his shoulders so she had no support other than clinging with her hands to the pipe, and then he proceeded to minister to her there. For a long, long time. She lost count of the number of times he made her come to climax. She lost count of who she was and where she was and how much she had resisted him doing this to her. When he finally released her legs and entered her, she participated fully and willingly in the rhythm of lovemaking.

And he was the one who cried out his pleasure in the end.

Chapter 21

When tables get turned . . .

Torolf turned on the shower, holding a limp Hilda in his arms. As the hot water hit them, he released her restraint and the gag. She immediately came to life, kicking and screaming.

He held her tightly in his arms for a long time, till the water turned lukewarm and all the fight seeped out of her. Then he gently washed her body and shampooed her hair.

"We'll talk later," he told her, gently putting her in his bed. "I need to go find Spike."

She said nothing, just stared up at him accusingly with those big blue eyes of hers. When he attempted to kiss her, she turned her face to the side.

So that's the way we're playing it. Forget how much fun you had. Pretend you didn't like it. "I'll be right back."

Before he put on his clothes and left the room, she was sound asleep. And he'd forgotten to tell her that he loved her. *Big mistake, that. Well, I'll make it up later.*

He found Spike and Serenity at the fire hall, paying the caterers and the band. Everyone else had left.

"Hey, Max, thanks for the cigars. Serenity is even gonna let me smoke one in bed tonight."

"Hah! Dream on, mister. You be sleepin' alone, if you do."

"Okay, sweetie," he said quickly and winked at Torolf. The gag gift that Serenity had given him was two X-rated movies, which she'd promised to watch with him as a birthday present. *Biker Babes* and *Hot Rods*. Spike said he wasn't giving *that* up for a friggin' cigar.

As Serenity went off to talk to the cleaning crew, Spike took the last two glasses of beer from the keg and walked over to a table, motioning for Torolf to sit down. "What's up, son?"

"It's Hilda. I can't explain all the details, but there's a danger. I need to find two bodyguards. Reliable men who can be with her at all times till I get back."

Spike raised his eyebrows. "And Hilda agrees with this?"

"Not exactly, but it's got to be done. There's this organization in D.C., the National Center for Alien Research, that thinks she's an alien. They intend to abduct her and take her to some lab for study."

"You mean dissection and stuff like that."

Torolf nodded.

"Holy crap! Why would they think she's an alien? . . . Oh, never mind. Yeah, I can make a few phone calls when I get home. When do you need them?"

"Tomorrow night. I've gotta be back on the base by six a.m. Monday, and I'll be gone at least two weeks. I wouldn't ask this of you if it weren't important. Focus is critical on a live op, and I can't focus if I'm worried about her."

"Don't worry. I'll take care of it."

"I'll give you a picture of the guy in question before I leave."

"Gotcha." Spike emptied his glass and set it down. "Care for the girl, do ya?"

He nodded.

"Love?"

He nodded.

"And her . . . does she love you?"

He pictured how angry she was when he'd left and hesitated. But then he said, "Yes."

"Are we talkin' wedding bells here, my boy?"

"No. It's too complicated to explain now, but Hilda will be leaving here in a few weeks."

"Don't tell me she's already married."

"No, it's not that."

"Well, hell, boy, go after her then. Make her stay."

Torolf didn't know about that, but he thought about it as he made his way back to the trailer. So much had happened to him in the course of this day. So many discoveries about his feelings and hers, as well.

Do I want her to stay? If she stays, it will mean commitment . . . probably marriage. Oh, boy! Maybe this is just lust overload. Maybe it will pass.

When he got back to the trailer and locked the door, he turned the lights out and made his way to his bedroom, where Hilda was still sleeping soundly. He took off his clothes and crawled in beside her. For a second, he thought about waking her for another bout of lovemaking. His you know what was certainly willing. But he decided to let her rest.

In the middle of the night, he dreamed he was in the middle of the desert, and it had begun to rain. One drop at a time. But then he realized the drops were only hitting one part of his body . . . his cock. His eyes shot open to see Hilda standing at the side of the bed, wearing a sheer red-and-black negligee, with her holding a tipped spoon of chocolate dripping onto him.

He grinned. "So, you plannin' on lickin' that off, sweetheart?"

"Actually, no, *sweetling*," she cooed.

The coo should have been a clue. That and the wild hair she hadn't bothered to brush. He must not have gotten all the hair spray out.

"You can do it yourself." With that, she left him to his own devices and locked herself in the bathroom.

"If I could, I would," he yelled after her.

He thought he heard laughter behind the closed door.

What a waste of a sheer negligee! What a waste of a chocolate cock!

In the end, he had to wash himself off in the kitchen sink. Not the way he had planned for this evening to end.

Don't you dare die, you lout, you! . . .

By the next evening, Hilda was so angry she could barely speak. And she was so frightened for Torolf that she could barely speak.

There were two burly men sitting on the solar couch . . . both of them biker friends of Spike's. They had weapons on the table and spyglasses on the windowsills. New locks had been put on the trailer door and windows.

All to forestall an attack by a man who thought she was an ale-yen. Now, Steinolf, him she could see making all these precautions for. But that paltry little sign-tiss. Hah! She could no doubt handle him herself.

Not that Torolf paid any attention to her protests.

Now he and his fellow SEALs were outside, dressed alike in what they called camouflage uniforms, heavy boots and on their *sherts* metal badges, which they called Budweisers. He looked serious and formidable and not at all the cheery fellow she had come to expect.

While the other SEALs waved to her and piled into a

large horseless carriage called an ess-you-vee, Torolf came over and pulled her to the side of the trailer.

"You will not leave this trailer until I get back. I mean it, Hilda. If there's anything you need, Ralph or Pete will get it for you. And your friends can visit you here."

"I cannot believe that you think I will obey your orders."

"You have no choice. I'll be back as soon as I can."

"Do not bother."

"You don't mean that, honey. Listen, I know you're mad about the gag and the blindfold. Okay, you're really mad, but I thought you would like it."

I did like it. That's the problem.

"Are you going to give me a kiss good-bye?"

She stood silent.

Hurt filled his eyes, but he straightened and said, "I love you, Hildy. No matter what happens, I love you."

A tiny cry escaped her, and she hurled herself at him. "Be safe," she whispered. "Be safe." And she kissed and kissed and kissed him till he moaned and the SEALs in the ess-you-vee hooted at him. Then she bit his bottom lip and pushed him away.

'Twas always good to get the last word in, so to speak, even if Torolf was laughing as he left her with a linen cloth pressed to his bleeding lip.

Heigh-ho, heigh-ho, it's off to work we go . . .

Torolf and his teammates arrived back at the base before dawn, were soon dressed for work—shorts, T-shirts, and boondocker boots—and made their way down to the grinder, where the other twenty or so members of their platoon were already doing warm-up exercises.

They were in prowl and growl mode now, moving toward a combat duty. Torolf was worried about Hilda, but he couldn't take that worry with him into the field. So all he would allow himself to think about was the mission, the mission, the mission.

First, they did a ten-mile run along the surf, watching with amusement as they passed a BUD/S class doing sugar cookies in the sand. Like SEALs everywhere, they ran, and ran, and ran. But in this case, the new guys were required to occasionally interrupt their runs with a dip in the surf and then a roll in the sand before resuming their runs. Rash city.

Next up was a couple of O-course rotations. Even being away only two weeks, they soon realized how out of shape they were, relatively speaking. The Slide for Life. The Wall. The cargo net. Hand walking on parallel bars. All of them seemed a little harder.

Once they were sufficiently covered with sweat and panting for breath, they went into the special ops building where they would get their first predeployment workup for this mission. Grabbing bottles of cold water from an ice-filled cooler, they all sat down.

Their commanding officer, Captain Gilman, took the podium at the front of the room. Getting right to the point, he said, "We leave for Tikrit on Friday. If all goes well, DEROS should be the following Friday." Then he pulled down a street map of the Iraqi city, pointing out the safe house they needed to take down.

"Our intel says Abu Saddami is hiding there. Check your folder for background on this tango. He's been around in al-Qaeda and other terrorist circles for a good ten years, used to be a cohort of bin Laden."

"Dead or alive?" Sly called out.

"Frankly, son," the gray-haired ex-SEAL said, "I don't give a flying fuck. This tango is so bad he doesn't deserve to live."

"Is he the guy who gassed that Sunni mosque?" Torolf asked.

The captain nodded. "We figure he has at least five

hundred kills under his belt, half of them civvies. He even strapped a suicide bomb on his wife." The captain grinned. "But then, he had two other wives just waiting in the background."

"Betcha it was the old homely one he sent out there, not the new, younger, hottie brides." This was Pretty Boy speaking.

They all laughed then.

"This afternoon and for the next three days, we'll work on urban mobility scenarios using a Hummer."

Pretty Boy raised his hand.

"Yes, Lieutenant Floyd, you will be the driver. And Petty Officer Dawson, you'll be the backup driver. Think you boys can handle a Hummer in those narrow streets under fire?"

"Yes, Captain, sir," both men answered smartly. Pretty Boy could barely hold back his grin of pleasure. Driving a vehicle in a hostile situation wasn't for everyone, but Pretty Boy loved the danger and showing off his driving talents.

"CQD must be employed in this situation. We have no idea if there will be friendlies in the building. Once you secure the tango, put a tight package on him while you leave the building till he's in the exit vehicle.

"Ten of you will go in the building, two men stay in the vehicle, and ten sharpshooters will protect the perimeter. You never know who'll pop up in some of these neighborhoods. We had a suicide bomber jump out of a trash can in Tikrit last week."

"And if there are more tangos than Saddami?"

"Take them all . . . every freakin' one of the bastards . . . even if we have to send in backup transport. There'll be helos in the vicinity, if needed."

They all nodded, understanding the vehemence of his words. Since 9/11, terrorism had become a global problem, and the viciousness of some of the assaults was beyond comprehension. As a result, the role of SEALs had changed dramatically, both in number and in skills. There were at least two squadrons and twelve regular platoons forward deployed at all times. No rest for the weary. Almost every SEAL harbored a hatred for terrorists . . . the worst kind of tangos.

"Okay, every daylight hour for the next four days will be spent in PT, O-course, CQD, and MOUT. We've got to practice over and over military operations in urban settings. Go to the chow hall now, and then we'll do hooded box drills or paint bullets, all afternoon." Hooded box drills were role-playing exercises simulating upcoming missions. "After that, more PT, chow down again, then come back here for some videos of the area."

"Should we bring popcorn?" one SEAL joked.

"Or crawfish poppers?" Cage added.

The captain relaxed his stern demeanor and smiled. "As long as you don't bring girlfriends. No necking in the back."

"Necking?" Pretty Boy hooted. "That is so sixties. I'm thinkin' more like f—"

"That'll be enough, Lieutenant," the captain said.

Torolf and his teammates had just left the chow hall and were heading toward the building where box drills were being set up. Thoughts of Hilda were occupying his mind when he literally ran into Ragnor, who had just arrived on the base.

"Where the hell have you been?" his brother asked, pulling him into a big bear hug.

"Would you believe eleventh-century Norselands?"

"Holy Thor! You did it?"

"Yep. Cage, JAM, Geek, and Pretty Boy went with me."

"Do you make mock of me, Brother?" Torolf had been in this country and time period for more than fifteen years, but Ragnor had only arrived five years ago; so his language still reeked of another culture.

"Nope."

"And Steinolf?"

"Gone, gone, gone."

"You ever were a slyboots. Didst occur to you even once to call me or our father to tell us this good news?"

"I've been busy." *I couldn't tell you without telling you about Hilda, and what a can of worms that would open!*

"A woman? You've been with some woman." His brother, sharp as a KA-BAR knife, guessed immediately. *So much for hiding Hilda.*

Torolf's face heated, confirming Ragnor's suspicion.

"I should beat your ass to the ground for putting us through this agony of waiting."

"Like you could!"

Ragnor was the first to relax his foul mood. "So, tell me true. Who's the new wench in your life?"

Torolf hesitated, then a slow grin crept over his lips.

"What does that smirk mean? What secret do you harbor?"

"Brunhilda Berdottir."

"*What* did you say? You cannot mean *that* Brunhilda Berdottir."

"The one and only."

Ragnor's left eyebrow raised a fraction, a trick he had mastered long ago. "Son of a troll! Are you in love with a woman who lives a thousand years ago?"

"I am crazy nuts about her. And she's here . . . by accident." Torolf's mouth turned up in what was probably a loopy grin, and he could not care less.

"How . . . when . . . I do not understand. Where is she now?"

"Hog Heaven. Don't ask. It's a long story, and you are not to tell anyone else. She's in hiding. I'll explain later."

Torolf turned and walked away from his incredulous brother. He couldn't wait to implement his plan for talking

Hilda into staying, because it hot-damn sure was going to involve seduction . . . his favorite thing.

You could say Hog Heaven became Hog Haven . . .

One day in this metal prison, and Hilda was ready to pull her hair out.

Her jailers were personable enough fellows—one a former policing man and the other a painter of buildings—but they took their job too seriously. Not only did they refuse to let her leave the trail-her, but they stood outside her sleeping chamber or the bathing chamber when she was inside those rooms.

There was one good thing about these men. When Jolene arrived on her doorstep that afternoon with a bloody nose, a black-and-blue chin, and bruises on her upper arms, Pete took her chin in his big hand and declared, "This was caused by a closed fist. Who did this to you?" Pete called his friends at the policing station, and they took Earl to a jail. An order was filed stating that Earl could not come anywhere near Jolene, and assault charges were filed. A hearing would be held next week.

In the meantime, Jolene was staying with Hilda for fear Earl would come after her. Which he no doubt would have done if her jailers were not standing watch.

The incidents had been so upsetting to Hilda and Jolene that both of them had ended up hurling the contents of their stomachs into the privy. And that's when Serenity had arrived. She had left her husband—for the time being—following a horrendous argument about see-gars.

The three of them sat at the scullery table, dining on the provender Torolf had purchased for the duration. Serenity and Jolene ate heartily of pasta, which resembled white worms with blood on top . . . a dish that Ralph had prepared for them, saying he loved to cook. Hilda sipped at tea—a delicious beverage she had discovered here—sweetened with white sugar, an absolute luxury in her time. And toast. Her stomach still felt unsettled because of the earlier melee but also at the sight of the edible worms and blood.

"I know it's probably just the menopause," Serenity said. "I tend to overreact to the least thing. But Spike insisted on smoking those blasted cigars around me. And you know how the curtains and bedding soak up that smell. Well, I had enough when—"

"What is menopause?" Hilda asked.

"That's a stage in a woman's life when her periods stop and she is unable, usually, to bear children anymore. Not that I've ever been able to bear children, but—"

"Me, neither," Hilda said, squeezing Serenity's hand in shared sympathy. "I was barren through three marriages."

Serenity returned the hand squeeze.

"What is a period?"

Serenity and Jolene both laughed, becoming accustomed to Hilda's constant questions.

"A woman's monthly flow," Serenity explained.

"Ah, the bloody flux." Hilda munched on a piece of toast, while Serenity and Jolene talked about birth control and how Jolene had secretly taken pills to prevent having children with Earl. Hilda's mind tuned out their conversation as a niggling thought pricked her brain, something prompted by the previous conversation. "Oh, my gods!"

Serenity and Jolene stopped talking and looked at her.

"I have not had a flux for many sennights, since before Torolf and his SEALs came to The Sanctuary. It must be the stress of all that has happened to me, though my time has always been so exact in the past."

"Or you could be pregnant," Jolene offered, unsure whether to smile or frown at the possibility, not knowing what Hilda's reaction would be to that suggestion.

Outrage, disbelief, exhilaration. That's what her reaction

was. " 'Tis impossible. Torolf always used a cone-dumb."

Serenity and Jolene smiled, probably because she had mispronounced a word, as she was wont to do.

"Condoms aren't infallible, Hilda. That's why I take the pill, as well."

"No, it cannot be. I am barren."

"Well, there's one sure way of finding out."

Hilda tilted her head in question.

"A pregnancy test. I'll go to the drugstore," Serenity said.

An hour later, Hilda stood in her bathing chamber with two women looking at an ominous color on a piss stick. She was pregnant.

The other women were laughing and congratulating her, and Hilda *was* happy. In truth, the sorrow of her life had been her inability to bear children, though she had never seen that lack till now. But this complicated matters so much.

Will I give birth in this country or the past? Would my unborn child be harmed traveling back in time? Will I be able to time-travel back myself, let alone with a child? And what if I go back now, and I am not pregnant in that time period? Will this be my last chance to breed? She put a hand over her flat stomach as if to protect the tiny being there.

"Max will be so happy," Serenity said.

"Will he?" Hilda wondered. "I won't tell him yet. I want to find the right time."

Both women nodded.

Is Torolf the type of man who could plant his seed in a woman, then leave the child of his loins forever? Hilda knew the answer to that question. He would take control of decisions, like he had taken control of her fate here by ordering guards till he returned.

So, when Torolf called Ralph on his black box that night, and Ralph handed the box to her, pressing it to her ear, she said nothing about the pregnancy. Besides, she knew he was going on a dangerous mission. He needed to focus his attention solely in that direction. Knowing of her pregnancy might be a distraction.

"How are you, sweetheart?"

"Just bloody wonderful. Where are you?" She still could not grasp the concept of his voice being in the box.

"At the base. I hear you had a little trouble there today."

"What? My jailers reported to you already? Didst they tell you how many times I pissed today, too?"

He laughed. "Don't be so stubborn, honey. And don't take your frustrations out on those guys. They're just doing their job. I'll be back soon. Then you can berate me all you want."

"Well, Jolene and Serenity are staying here with me now, and I will hear no objections from you."

"Doesn't bother me, if Ralph and Pete can handle all of you." He chuckled then. "You're setting up another sanctuary there, aren't you?"

That thought had not occurred to her, but she liked the idea. "Did you know people can have fat sucked out of their bodies in this country? And did you know that women can make their breasts get bigger? What a country this is, where people can shrink and enlarge body parts."

"Hilda, you are not getting a boob job."

More orders!

"What other new things are you learning?" he asked.

"Why did you not tell me I have a space between my front teeth? All these years, even when I had a polished brass mirror, I never noticed. But Lizzy told me of a mouth dock-whore who can fix them with caps."

"I like your teeth and your smile. Don't change them."

"You are just saying that."

"No, I'm not. Is that all that's new there?" he asked then.

She put the box away from her ear and studied it. Could he guess her secrets now? "That is all you need to know."

"Uh-oh!"

Uh-oh is right, you randy rabbit. Getting me with child.

"I need to go now. Ralph wants me to model my busty-air for him," she lied.

"You better be kidding."

"Dost think so?"

"We have lots of things to discuss when I get back, Hildy."

More than you know.

"So, hold on."

"Have I any choice?"

He chuckled, then seemed to hesitate. "I love you."

Hilda put a hand to her mouth as tears welled in her eyes. She wanted to spill everything to him then, tell him she was with child, that she was scared and confused and wished he were there to help her make a decision. In the end, though, all she said was, "I love you, too."

Pink Panther he was not . . .

Dick Phillips sat in a tree on the outskirts of Hog Heaven, his binoculars trained on the trailer where his alien stayed.

Two gorillas guarded his target, along with two other women. Were they aliens, too? The guards would have to make a mistake sometime. In the meantime, he'd called for backup, figuring he should take all three women in for testing . . . just in case.

He had a blind set up in this tree, like hunters used. On it he had his video and still cameras, both with telephoto lenses, a gun, a small cooler with food, a notebook, a tape recorder, and the high-power telescope.

His two-week leave would end soon, but no way was he going to give up this project. If the hospital wouldn't grant him an extension, he would quit. He could always get another job, but he might not ever have another chance to catch an alien.

This was the most exciting adventure of Dick's life. He was taking notes for a potential book. He already knew what suit he would wear on *Larry King*. Women would be impressed by all this work he was doing.

He smiled, thinking about all the good things in his future.

Then it began to rain.

When a trailer becomes a sardine can . . .

Torolf called her late on Thor's day . . . the first he'd been able to get to a talking box in days. He would be leaving early tomorrow . . . Frigg's day, and he would not be back till next Frigg's day. Or later. If ever.

She put a hand to her heart as she listened to his precious voice. Would it be the last time? She choked back her tears, not wanting his last word from her to be a negative one.

"Hey, sweetie," he said.

"Hey, sweetling," she said back.

"Ralph says it's getting a little crowded there."

"Not too crowded. I share a bed with Jolene, and Lizzy has the other bedchamber with Serenity." Lizzy was in the midst of a one-week break from her teaching job, and she had just left her live-in lover, who had been cheating on her. Hilda had not even known that Lizzy had a live-in lover. "I want to go outside, Torolf. Tell your guards to take us to the shopping mall, or the food mart. Somewhere. Anywhere."

"No, we can't risk it. I've had further intel, and that guy Phillips has been seen in the area. Buying electronic equipment. Food at a local convenience store. He's around there, honey, and you've got to stay put."

"I will," Hilda said, but just for Torolf's peace of mind. "Pete has developed an affection for Lizzy," she told him then.

"Oh, yeah? How affectionate?"

"Just smitten at this point. By the by, did I tell you that Tissie is coming to visit for a few days?"

"Hilda! It's only a trailer. There's not enough room for all those people . . . and bodyguards, too."

"We get by."

"Ralph says you've been sick."

"Naaay, I have not. Just a reaction to his worm and blood dish, which he insists on serving every blessed day."

He laughed. "It's spaghetti, hon, not worms. Try it."

"I would rather eat . . . worms."

He laughed. "Gotta go. I love you."

"I love you, too."

"See you when I see you, babe." Under his breath, before he ended their conversation, she thought she heard him add, "Pray for me."

Chapter 22

When Daddy goes marching off to war, hoo-yah, hoo-yah! . . .

"Go, go, go!" the commander's voice sounded in all their earphones.

Like clockwork, a Black Hawk flew overhead in the predawn light, and immediately a dozen SEALs, including Cage, fast-roped down to form the perimeter around this operation. Torolf was in the backseat of the Hummer, which started barreling down the residential Tikrit street, swerving here and there to avoid parked cars. There were no pedestrians this early. Sly was on one side of him and JAM on the other. Pretty Boy and Dawson sandwiched Geek in the front seat. They were all geared up and fully loaded, adrenaline pumping through their veins like junkies on a coke high. Coming to a screeching halt in front of the designated safe house, the doors flew open and he yelled, "Kill zone! Haul ass!" They all jumped out, rifles in position, and rushed forward.

"Open! Open!" JAM shouted in Arabic to the door.

They heard a rustle inside the house, but when the door didn't open, JAM stepped back, and Sly and Geek used a battering ram and their boots to knock the door in. Each of them headed in a different direction, as planned.

In the kitchen, he found a woman with a child in front of her. Both were dressed in Arab attire, which was suspicious for this time of the morning. There was a time when a soldier would have lowered his rifle for women and children. Not anymore. Too many women, and even kids, carried bombs these days.

"In here. In here," he ordered with his minimal Arab skills, motioning them to enter a small pantry. When they hesitated, even though they had to understand him, he shoved them in and did a quick full-body search, then gagged and restrained them. He shut the door on them and put a chair under the handle. It would hold for now.

When he left the kitchen, rifle raised, he saw JAM steering a gentleman in Arab headgear toward the living room wall. The unhappy gent was hurling an unending stream of Arab at him.

"Saddami?" he inquired.

"Nope," JAM said, motioning upward even as he quickly put handcuffs and a gag on the tango, then led him outdoors.

Dawson came from another room, rifle pressed into the back of a young woman whose dark eyes spelled hatred. She wore an Arab-style pantsuit—he forgot the name for it—and a *hijab*, one of those scarves that cover the hair and tied under the chin, hanging down to a long vee in the back. She spat out in clumsy English, "Evil American pigs! May Allah strike you dead!" She, too, got a gag and walking orders to the Humvee.

Then he and Pretty Boy raced up the stairs two at a time to aid Geek, who was about to break down a locked door. They used hand signals, not wanting to speak for fear they would reveal their positions to the tangos, who would then be able to blast some ammo through the wood barrier.

Geek broke the door down with a swift kick of his boot, then ducked, just missing the bullets from an MP5 submachine gun. He and Pretty Boy were crouched on either side of the door. Peering in carefully, Pretty Boy made further signals to him, and all three of them charged in, rifles blazing. Within seconds, Saddami lay on the floor, oozing blood from three different wounds: the forehead, the throat, and the belly. All around him were laptops, filing cabinets, and videotapes. Pay dirt!

Pretty Boy, being the communications expert, was already on his Motorola telling CENTCOM that they would need another Black Hawk to pick up the SEALs. Pretty Boy and Dawson could take care of transporting the perps.

They signaled for help to carry out all the evidence and soon had everything packed in the Humvee, along with the two captives, which immediately took off, gunfire hitting the heavy vehicles from some nearby houses.

"Disengage. I repeat, disengage," they all heard in their headsets.

Quickly, he, Geek, and JAM fast-roped up to a second Black Hawk, and just in time, too, because some tangos were rushing down the street, screaming epithets, guns firings. The SEALs could have taken a stand, but when the enemy was in your sights, you were in theirs. Always good to play it safe when the stakes were this high.

As the two Black Hawks flew away from the scene, and hopefully Pretty Boy and Dawson made it back to camp, no one spoke. They were breathing heavily, hearts racing, knowing they had escaped the reaper one more time. The pucker factor was high going in; coming out, it was pure adrenaline. Finally, still jacked up, they grinned at each other and shouted, "Hoo-yah!"

The entire operation had taken twenty-seven minutes.

One tango dead, two tangos in captivity, documents that could draw more rats out of their holes, and no good guys down. All in a day's work . . . a good day's work.

Only then did Torolf allow himself to think of Hilda.

No one was keeping Cinderella away from THIS ball . . .

Torolf had been back in Ah-mare-eek-ah for two whole days, and he had not come to her. To say that Hilda was seething would be like saying gammelost was a mite unpleasant.

Oh, he had called her often, but he kept making excuses about why he could not come yet. First, it was something called a debriefing. Then his team was required to go to a head doctor. Then there had been a press conference.

Well, Hilda had had more than enough. Especially since she had just asked him casually, on the talking box, "What do you think about having children?"

A deadly silence had followed her question, and then he had asked, "Why?"

"Oh, do not go getting your bowels in an uproar. I only ask because of a conversation I had today with Serenity. She was talking about her men-oh-pause and her regrets over never having had children. She wanted to know if I, being barren and all, shared her regrets."

"Ah, honey."

She did not feel any guilt over the lie because the lout making those cooing sounds of sympathy should be here.

"I was not seeking sympathy. I merely asked if you regret never having children."

"Regret? I'm too young for regrets in that regard, but as to kids . . . Holy hell, do you have any idea what it was like to grow up in a family with twelve brothers and sisters? It was always chaos. And, I don't mean to be gross, but I can still recognize the smell of baby shit and baby vomit from twenty paces. So, don't feel bad about not being able to have kids, Hilda. I wouldn't miss them a bit."

Hilda's heart dropped at that news. *He does not want children. Oh, gods, what do I do now?* "What time will you be here this afternoon?" It was barely past the breaking fast time.

"Uh, actually, there's a problem, honey."

Another problem. I am beginning to think he is avoiding me.

"I have to go to a ball this evening, and after that I *should* be free. The order came from the top. No ducking out. It's only one more commitment I have to get out of the way."

The lout is going to a ball and he is overdefensive. *Hmmmm.* Putting her hand over the talking box, she asked Ralph, who was eating worms and blood *again*, "What is a ball?"

Ralph shrugged. "A toy that bounces up and down." Ralph was getting accustomed to her incessant questions.

"You are going to a bouncing toy?" she asked Torolf.

He laughed. "Not that kind of ball. This is a fancy dance, a reception kind of thing."

Hilda did not say anything, but her fury began to rise. He could not come here because he was going to dance? With whom? Other men? Nay, he would not do that. She would bet her busty-air that there would be women there.

Without another word, she pressed the Off button on the talking box. She refused to come out of the bathing chamber every time the talking box rang and Ralph banged on the door. "Tell the lout to go . . . dance."

Torolf gave up finally, and for some reason the silence was even harder to bear than the image of him holding another woman in that form of foresport . . . dancing.

Jolene, who had been taking a nap, rapped on the door finally. Hilda went into the bedchamber with her and

Lizzy, who had just come back from the food mart. Serenity had returned to Spike after she'd deemed him suitably punished. Hilda explained why she was so upset with Torolf.

"I think I know what ball Torolf is going to," Lizzy said. She went out to the solar and came back with a large packet of parchments, called the El Lay Times. She opened the parchments to a page that showed a picture of two men, with haircuts similar to Torolf's, wearing fancy uniforms, different than the ones she's seen on the SEALs. There were also women in lewd gunnas that left the shoulders and half their breasts bare.

Lizzy grinned at her.

"What?" she and Jolene both said. Jolene was a much happier person since she had gone to court this week and got her husband put in prison. A law person was working on a divorce for her. Plus, Geek had been calling her on his talking box.

"I know what this ball is for. It's a reception at the Hotel del Coronado for the U.S. and state commissioners of education, along with a lot of education big shots. Although the event is touted as a recognition by the military of all that schools do in recording military history, they probably want an in for recruiters to go into their schools."

Hilda didn't understand half of what Lizzy had said. "Why does that make you grin so?"

"Because, honey, I can get us into the ball. My best friend was named teacher of the year, and she has extra tickets."

"But how would we get out of here, and where would I get the proper clothing?"

"You take care of getting us out of here, without the gorillas finding out. I'll get us some clothes. Look, it's only noon. We have plenty of time, even if we leave here by four p.m. Meet me behind Serenity's trailer at four, okay?"

Hilda nodded, a mite worried over how they could accomplish this feat and, yea, she worried over what Torolf's reaction would be to her showing up uninvited. Hah! He deserved a surprise . . . or two. The lout!

At four, Hilda went out to the solar and picked out various foods and beverages and carried them into the bedchamber.

"What are you doing?" Pete was the inside guard now, and Ralph was outside.

"Jolene and I are going to eat in my bedchamber, then watch some tea-vee and go to bed. Torolf should be here tomorrow." She batted her eyelashes at him with innocence, a trick Tissie had taught her.

Pete nodded. "And if Torolf calls for you again?"

"Tell him I am getting my beauty rest . . . for him." More eyelash-batting.

Hilda made Jolene go to the bathing chamber to relieve herself. She would not be able to leave the bedchamber till morn, if all went as planned. Then she locked the door from the inside, went over and unlocked the window. She waited till Ralph passed by on his periodic strolls around the trailer, shimmied herself out, and watched as Jolene relocked the window.

In a low crouch, hiding behind the various other trailhers as she ran, Hilda arrived at Serenity's trail-her where Lizzy was waiting for her in a black horseless carriage. Her friend, Sarah, the teacher of the year, was in the backseat . . . both her and Lizzy grinning at her ingenuity in escaping her "prison."

"We'll change in a motel room I arranged near San Diego," Sarah told them.

"I brought you the hottest gown, Hilda." Lizzy practically jumped up and down on the leather seats. "My sister, an actress, wore it to the Academy Awards one year."

And all Hilda could think to say was, "Torolf is going to be so surprised."

Dick was trying his damnedest to be a dick . . . a private dick . . .

Meanwhile, Dick Phillips saw the alien—the first one that had been in the hospital—crawl out of the trailer window. He rushed to gather up his equipment and put it in his trunk.

The black Toyota Avalon was already out on Route 10 by the time he caught up. He pulled out his cell phone once he had the vehicle firmly in his sights, two car lengths ahead.

"Phillips here," he told his boss, Mr. Atkins. "I've got the target in front of me . . . away from the goons at the trailer park. She's with two other women . . . not sure who they are."

"I'll alert Dorney and Olsen. They'll meet you once your target stops. Don't do anything until they arrive." Dick could hear the excitement in Mr. Atkins's voice.

"Roger that," he said, having heard that expression in a spy movie one time.

"Good work so far, Dick."

He beamed with pride as he followed his prey.

The prince and his froggie pals headed off to the ball . . .

Torolf and six other single guys on his team approached the Hotel del Coronado grimly.

None of them enjoyed decking themselves out in ice cream man duds—better known as dress whites—and parading themselves around like meat on display. SEALs had come a long way from the days when they were mere frogmen in the Navy. A lot more was required of them now, besides fighting the good fight, like showing up for dipwad events like this one, where they would be required to dance with unattached females from ten to seventy, often stammering teenaged daughters of important people.

"Maybe there'll be some hot teachers here," Cage said hopefully, glancing up at the banner, which read, National Organization for Better Education, NOBO.

"I never had a hot teacher the whole sixteen years I was in school," Pretty Boy pointed out.

"These are more likely education bigwigs, the movers and shakers in making policy," Geek explained. When they all frowned at him, he added, "There might be a few teachers."

"If we have dry chicken again, I'm gonna puke," JAM said.

"Hey, the Del serves primo food," Torolf told JAM, who had never attended an event here before, somehow having been off base every time one came up.

And, really, the Del *was* a neat place. Sitting right on the ocean, it was a huge white building, complete with cupolas, dormer windows, a red tile roof, and a lot of history. It was here that Edward, Prince of Wales, supposedly met the infamous Wallis Simpson, then abdicated the throne. The Marilyn Monroe movie, *Some Like It Hot*, was filmed here. And it was considered the Western White House by some presidents, like Ronald Reagan. The food was usually good, too, though a bit fancy for Torolf's tastes. "I hope they don't serve that avocado soup again, the one with bits of caviar floating on top." Colorful food items like that were a killer for white-suited gentlemen, like themselves, to handle.

"*Mon Dieu*, more old fart dance music!" Cage complained as they entered the ballroom.

"Not a good-looking woman in sight," Pretty Boy observed.

"Oh, great! I don't see one black person here. I hate it when I'm the token homeboy." This was Sly, who was African American.

"I'm sticking around here for two hours. Then I'm outta here," Torolf declared, sticking a finger under his tight collar.

"Hilda expectin' you?" Cage asked.

"Hilda has been expecting me for two days."

"Pissed, is she?"

"Royally. But I have a little gift for her that I hope will cheer her up." The worried expression on his face must have alerted Cage.

"A ring! You bought Hilda an engagement ring!" he guessed, and all the guys stopped and stared at him, big ol' grins on their faces.

I should have known. Cage might be my best friend, but he's got the biggest mouth this side of the Mason-Dixon Line.

"When's the wedding, *cher*? Can I be best man?"

Of course, you can be my best man . . . if there is a wedding.

"I get dibs on plannin' the bachelor party."

Oh, no! The last time Pretty Boy planned a bachelor party, there were lap dancers and cops involved.

"I hope you have the ceremony at your dad's vineyard. The one we went to there was so cool."

Yeah, that was cool. Ragnor and Alison. And, oh, shit, Dad is gonna kill me if I tell everyone else before him, and then Madrene will be ordering me around, telling me every-thing I should do, and Kirstin will be weeping because I'm getting married before her. It will be a god-awful mess.
"Really, guys, you're jumping the gun here. Hey, I haven't even asked her yet. She might say no. In fact, she might very well say no."

On and on his buddies went, ignoring his disclaimer,

razzing him, but he didn't care. He loved her, she loved him, they were going to be together, somehow.

I hope.

After the buffet dinner, some agonizing speeches, and the start of the dancing, Torolf glanced at his watch. *A half hour to go.* To while the time away, he asked Mary Jane Potter, the eighteen-year-old daughter of a state board of education member, to dance. She was cute and bubbly and not Hilda.

Was Cinderella this nervous before the ball? . . .

Hilda, Lizzy, and Sarah were walking up the steps of the Hotel del Coronado, and she was shaking in her three-inch high-heeled shoes.

"Mayhap this was not such a good idea," she said, gazing with awe at the massive white building with its red roof. " 'Tis a castle. Even the Saxons do not have such splendor."

Lizzy and Sarah laughed at her, already getting accustomed to her strange ways.

It had taken more than two hours to prepare themselves in the lodging place. They all looked wonderful, and Hilda felt like a veritable princess. A princess in a wanton red gunna. The gown was "strapless." That meant it bared the shoulders and arms. Who would have thought that her meager breasts could hold anything up? But it had a built-in device that not only held the gown up, but her breasts as well. The gown hugged her slender form down to the ankles, though it had a slit all the way up to the thigh, which exposed her leg in sheer hose. And, on her feet were the red high-heeled shoes, which she had protested heartily, being overtall already, but they assured her the shoes made her look statuesque, though why anyone would want to resemble a statue, she had no idea. Her hair was big and curly, as it had been at Spike's birthday feast, and her lips were painted bright red to match her gown.

They entered a huge hall where music was playing and people were dancing . . . a hundred or more, and all of them dressed in colorful gowns, some more scandalous than hers. Many of the men were dressed in white raiment. She could not wait to tell her women back at The Sanctuary about warriors in white. That thought made her gladsome and sad at the same time. *Will I be going back?*

Lizzy and Sarah took glasses of clear wine from a tray carried about the room by a man dressed all in black. No doubt another kind of uniform. She declined, just wanting to find Torolf. She walked among the dancers, being careful not to bump into any of them. Was that Ragnor Magnusson over there, dancing with a beautiful woman, also dressed in the white uniform? If it was, his jaw was hanging open with disbelief, gawking at her as if she were a ghost. Moving on, she saw Cage, dancing with an elderly lady with gray hair. He jolted back with surprise, then waved, pointing to his left.

And then she saw Torolf. And the lout was engaging in foresport—that slow dancing men in this country employed—with another woman. She was young and not nearly as tall as Hilda, with shiny black hair and honey-colored skin. She was lissome in all the ways that Hilda was not. And he was holding her close, laughing at a mirthsome thing she said to him.

A buzzing began in Hilda's ears as she stood stock-still, staring. The lout. The cruel, cruel lout. How could he do this to her? She waited, uncaring of the spectacle she was making, for the instant when he would see her.

And then he did.

Shock caused him to stop dancing and stare, eyes wide. *You should be shocked, you slimy maggot.*

He looked at her, then he looked at the woman still in his arms, then he looked back at her, as if in apology.

That was answer enough for her.

When clueless men ask, "What? What have I done?" . . .

Torolf was stunned speechless. Like a slow-motion slide show, he registered that:

- Hilda was here.

- Hilda looked screw-me-silly sexy in a strapless red gown with red screw-me-silly lipstick.

- Hilda's eyes looked happy, then so sad.

- Hilda thought he was with another woman.

- Hilda was gone.

I'll show you, bozo . . .

Hilda spun on her heel and walked proudly across the wide expanse of the dance floor till she got to the doors. Along the way, she ignored Cage's plea to stop and talk to him. To Lizzy, she said, "I'll meet you in the car. Do not leave on my account. Enjoy yourselves."

Once out the door, she began to run, which was difficult with the high-heeled shoes. So she stopped and took them off. Then she ran, tears streaming down her face.

I did not tell him of the baby. I will not now.

He is with another woman, even as he claims to love me. Why am I surprised? He is a man, like any other.

What a fool I have been! Never again!

When she reached the vehicle, she discovered something unfortunate. It was locked.

With a sob, she sank down to the ground, leaning against the cool metal. That is when a man with red hair walked up to her and asked, "Mzzz Berdottir? You don't know me, but I've been looking for you."

I'm sick of this frickin' hide-and-seek game . . .

Protocol was everything in the Navy. As quickly as he could, he apologized to the young lady he was dancing with whose name he could not remember. Then Cage, bless him, came over and asked her to dance.

Seeing his commander on the other side of the room, he walked up to him and stood stiff as a board until the captain recognized him. "Request permission to leave, sir."

The captain arched a bushy gray eyebrow at him.

"Emergency, sir."

The old guy must have noticed the tension in his body and said, "Excused, Lieutenant."

As quickly as he could manage, he was out the door. What a fool he was to think Hilda would have been just standing out here, waiting for him to get his shit together and invite her back inside to the ball.

For fifteen minutes, he searched the area. Then, for another fifteen minutes his buddies searched with him. The only sign of her was the red shoes on the hotel steps. Next, they found Lizzy and Sarah, who told him that Hilda said she was going to wait for them in the car. So they hiked over to the parking lot. No Hilda.

Where could she have gone?

It was silly, he would find her . . . eventually, somehow . . . but still this felt, ominously, like an ending. *Oh, my God! What if this is the way she's being sent back? No. Hilda is just being Hilda. Stubborn.*

"Look, guys, thanks for all your help, but I refuse to chase all over kingdom come to find her. She'll show up when she's ready. In the meantime, I'm going back to Hog Heaven. I think that's where she's gone."

She was in an alien place . . .

Hilda awakened groggily, not knowing where she was.

As she slowly emerged from her fogginess, she heard male voices in an adjoining room. Glancing down, she saw that she was lying on a bed, naked. *What happened to my red gown?* And she was tied to the bed . . . arms, waist, and legs. *I am captive. Ooooh, if the lout is trying more of his sex games with me, I will kill him.*

Suddenly, she recalled the last time she had seen the lout. *The lying, unfaithful son of a troll.* She was a strong woman. She had to be to have survived Steinolf. She would be again.

"Help!" she screamed.

Three men came running into the room.

So, it was not the lout.

"Do . . . you . . . speak . . . English?" the one man asked, the one who had accosted her beside Lizzy's car.

What a dolt! "Yes . . . I . . . speak . . . English. Dost . . . speak . . . Norse?" she said in the same slow manner he had addressed her. Hilda should be embarrassed by her nudity, but she had more important concerns than her modesty, like where she was and how she was going to get away.

"Mzzz Berdottir. My name is Dick Phillips, and these are my . . . uh, associates, John Dorney and Greg Olsen. Just relax. Do you want something to drink?"

"Nay, I do not want a drink. I want you to untie me this minute." *Dick? That is the name that men here give their manparts. Oh, good gods! The fool has taken the name of his manpart. 'Twould be like calling oneself Cock or Breast. The vanity of some men!*

"I can't untie you . . . not till my boss gets here." He tried to pat her on her shoulder, but she shrugged away as best she could. "Did you say Norse? Do they speak Norse on your planet?"

She rolled her eyes. "So, you are the demented person who has been following me. You think I come from another planet?"

"Yes." He nodded his head vigorously and smiled as if she had given him a compliment.

"Well, I do not. So, release me."

"I can't."

"You will be sorry if you do not. I have many friends in the military of your country. They will come after me." *I hope.*

"We know about those SEALs. Well, we'll just stay in hiding here till the boss arrives. Then we'll be off to the lab. They'll never find you once we get there. I don't even know where it is."

"She has awfully small tits," one of the men remarked to Dick. "Do ya think all the women on her planet have small tits?"

"No, every woman in my land does not have small breasts, but we do have powers . . : witchly powers that can shrivel manparts."

The eyes of all three men went wide, and then they glanced down at their private parts.

"Do ya think she's telling the truth?" one of them asked.

"Hell if I know, but I'm not takin' any chances," the other replied.

Both stepped back several paces.

"I also can give you warts all over your bodies, and webs betwixt your fingers and toes, not to mention turning all your teeth to rot." She figured she'd best stop there. She did not want to go too far in pushing the bounds of credulity.

The three men glanced at each other with question and concern. Then one of them said, "I'm outta here."

"Me, too," the other said, leaving only the Dick person.

"Why do you comb your hair that way?" she asked him

as he wrung his hands, no doubt wondering if he should stay out of the range of her eyes.

Dick's ruddy face went ruddier. "What way?"

"As if you are trying to hide the bald top. Really, it just calls attention to it."

"Are men bald on your planet? Do they know how to re-grow hair there?"

"Aaarrgh! I am not an ale-yen. By the by, what did you give me to make me fall into such a deep sleep? It better not be anything that would harm my baby."

"Oh, no!" Dick's shoulders drooped. "You're pregnant. Who's the father? Alien or earthling? Oh, this complicates things. We wanted to impregnate you ourselves."

Hilda did not understand what he meant, except something about him wanting to impregnate her. What an odious man! She would die rather than have him enter her body.

Dick's black box rang, and he picked it up. "Yeah, I have her right here. Uh-huh. John and Greg left, but it's okay. The target is restrained. And talking. Isn't this exciting? She can talk. I wonder what other things she can do. No, no, I won't do any testing on her till you get here tomorrow." After Dick completed his conversation, he looked at her and said, "Mr. Atkins has been delayed."

"How long?"

"Twenty-four hours. Don't worry, I'm going to give you a little more of this chloroform to settle you down."

"Nooooooooo," she screeched, her voice becoming increasingly fainter as the deep sleep overcame her again.

Torolf, where are you? Come for me.

Chapter 23

Give me a clue . . .

Torolf was so blistering, hair-pulling angry, he could barely speak.

Cage tried to talk to him. "Settle down. We'll find her. It's only been eight hours."

"Eight hours! She could be dead in eight hours."

"Be negative, why don't you?"

"Stop trying to be a freakin' Norman Vincent Peale."

"Stop being an asshole."

He stopped his pacing in the narrow confines of the trailer and looked at his good friend. There were probably tears in his eyes. "I'm sorry."

"Apology accepted. You owe Ralph and Pete apologies, too."

He nodded. He'd fired the two bodyguards the minute he'd gotten back for letting Hilda escape.

"Hilda is going to peel your skin off for blaming them."

Please, God, let her come back and peel my skin off.

The rest of the guys were back in Coronado searching for any traces of Hilda. The police and FBI had been called in, and due to some SEAL connection, they'd been willing to forgo the usual waiting time before calling it a kidnapping. Authorities were already over at the National Center for Alien Research, trying to confiscate files that might give them leads. The chairman was missing. Torolf didn't want to think about what his absence meant. Hilda's face was plastered on California TV stations, although it was the middle of the night, and who the hell was seeing it? Nobody, that's who.

Serenity came stomping into the trailer then, without knocking. She had a bathrobe on and fuzzy slippers. Her hair looked like it had been combed with a mixer.

"For land's sake, what're you doin', boy? Go find her."

"I'm trying."

"Doesn't look to me like you're tryin'. There's no need for you to sit here twiddlin' your thumbs. Go back to where she was taken. I'll keep a watch here in case she shows up."

"Thanks." He and Cage looked at each other and nodded. They both still wore their dress whites, now filthy whites. He checked his cell phone for the millionth time. Nothing. "Why do you think she was taken . . . that she didn't just take off?"

"'Cause the girl loves you, that's why. Even if you are a dumb schmuck. She wouldn't go away like this, not in her condition. She woulda made plans, careful plans, and she woulda told you first."

Torolf was only half listening as he gathered some gear together, but one word struck him. "What condition?"

Serenity gazed at him critically, as if unsure about answering him. Then, she revealed, "Hilda is pregnant."

Torolf's stomach dropped down to his feet, and the

blood drained from his head. He felt faint. "Pregnant? That's impossible. I used protection."

"That's what she said. And I'll tell you the same thing I tol' her. No, I didn't say that accidents happen, if that's what you think. I told her miracles happen."

Torolf put a hand over his mouth to stifle a moan.

This FUBAR just got worse and worse.

They were halfway back to Coronado, with the sun just coming up, when Serenity called him.

"Is she there?" he asked quickly.

"No."

Bile rose in his throat.

"Lizzy called me and said something that might be helpful. She said that they got a room at the Days Inn last night, about an hour away from Coronado. And, if this screwball has been following Hilda, maybe he got a room there, too."

"It would be stupid of him if he did. To take her to the same hotel where Hilda and her friends registered?"

"How smart could anyone be that believes in aliens?" Cage interjected.

"You've got a point there."

For the first time in the last eleven hours, Torolf was hopeful. He called Slick and the other guys. They were all equidistant from the hotel and should get there in an hour. "Drive faster," he told Cage.

"I'm already going eighty."

"Go ninety."

Please, God, let her be there. Let her be safe. Let her be willing to listen to me. Let her forgive me. And let her still love me.

He could swear he heard a voice in his head say, *Not asking for much, are you, buddy?* Probably his conscience.

Prince Not-So-Charming, better known as Prince Lout, to the rescue . . .

Hilda was kicking and biting and digging in her heels the best she could to prevent these two demented men, Dick and his boss, a Mr. Atkins, from taking her to some lab. She was not such a lackwit that she did not now understand what dissection meant, even if they did couch it in terms like "research."

She would have been screaming, too, but they had stuffed a cloth in her mouth before releasing her restraints. Although her hands were free, the gag was tied so tightly in back, she was unable to remove it . . . yet. They had thought that, between the two of them, they could get her dress back on and escort her to their vehicle without drawing too much attention.

"Maybe you should chloroform her again," Mr. Atkins said.

"Why me? She bit me last time I tried." The heel of his right hand was indeed bleeding.

"She kicked me in the nuts."

"How about we both jump her at once."

"Maybe. I could shoot you, Ms. Berdottir," Mr. Atkins warned, raising a piss-toll.

While the two of them were arguing, Hilda eyed the bathing chamber door. If she could run in there, perhaps she would be able to lock herself in.

"Don't even think it," Mr. Atkins said, clearly becoming angry. "I'll shoot you in the damn leg, if I have to."

"Okay, on the count of three," Dick declared. "One, two—"

Just then, there was a loud banging against the door, followed by some curses. Mr. Atkins, recognizing potential danger, ran across the room and pressed the piss-toll to her head. She'd been too surprised by the noise to defend herself, but she was able to yank off her gag. This time when the loud banging came, the door fell in, followed by Torolf and a dozen other people, some of whom she had never seen before. All of them had weapons raised, pointing at Dick and Mr. Atkins.

"Let her go, you sonofabitch." It was Torolf, in a crouch, with both hands on a pistol aimed at Mr. Atkins's heart. At the same time, he looked at her, noting her nude body, and asked in a choked voice, "Are you all right?"

"I'm fine. Mother of Thor! Where have you been? What took you so long? Didst stop to have cunning-tingles with your female friend afore coming to get me?"

Torolf grinned. So did some of the men behind him, despite the dangerous situation.

She turned her head slightly to address Mr. Atkins. "If you kill the lout, I will have to kill you with my bare hands."

Mr. Atkins was disconcerted for just that one second, which gave Torolf and the others the opportunity to shoot the weapons out of his and Dick's hands. Both of the miscreants fell to the floor, severely injured but not dead. At first, there was just chaos. Screaming, yelling, police sirens, and blood seeping from both bodies onto the light carpet.

Torolf wrapped a linen sheet over her shoulders and led her into the bathroom. "Stay here for a sec till we wrap this up."

"Orders again?" she complained, sitting down on the closed privy seat.

He turned and came back to her, lifting her up to stand on her tiptoes. Then nose to nose, he said in a raw voice, "Don't ever scare me like that again." And he kissed her long and hard, then shoved her back down to a sitting position. "Do not move."

She stuck her tongue out at the closed bathing chamber door. The lout! He still had not learned that he was in no position to give her orders.

There were noises and voices for a very long time, so Hilda decided to take a shower. The scurvy feel of Dick and Mr. Atkins's hands on her body lingered. She was still angry with Torolf, and she had good cause. It was his fault she had time-traveled. Then, he had nigh locked her in a metal prison. And the final indignity, finding him holding another woman.

But in the midst of the anger, she tried to be fair. He had rid the Norselands of Steinolf. He had taught her about love, the body kind and the heart kind. And he had given her a babe, although he did not know that yet.

She turned off the water and stepped out of the shower, drying herself. Staring in the mirror, she finger-combed her hair, then wrapped one of the big towels around herself.

Who was this person she saw in the mirror? Brunhilda Berdottir, eleventh-century Viking woman? Or Hilda Berdottir, twenty-first-century Viking woman? She did not know, but there were some things she did know. She would not screech and rail at the lout. Nor would she jump right back into his bed and his life again. Leastways, not yet. In many ways, she had been forced on him with the time travel, just as he had been forced on her. Mayhap, he would prefer freedom. Mayhap, she would prefer freedom. They both needed time alone to think, and in her case, to plan.

When Torolf opened the door, she said, "Take me home."

"Which home?" he asked, clearly concerned.

"*My* home," she said, and would not waver from the pain she saw in his eyes.

And then the home troops came marching in . . .

Hilda had kicked him out of the trailer at Hog Heaven, deeming it *her* home for the time being. That was a week ago . . . or, more precisely, seven days, four hours, and thirty minutes ago.

Enough! How much space does one woman need?

She was driving him crazy, not even allowing him to explain completely or apologize or freakin' seduce her. And, most important, she never bothered to mention that she was pregnant.

He knocked on the door of the trailer, glancing around, then doing a double take. There were quite a few vehicles here.

Oh, shit! There was a van with a Blue Dragon Vineyard logo on it, and those two vehicles there, he could swear they belonged to Cage and Pretty Boy. Yep, they had base passes on the windows.

He banged on the door harder this time. Torolf almost fell in when the door opened suddenly. Standing there, big as you please, was his father, who at fifty and more than fifteen years in this country, still wore Viking attire and long, light-brown hair down to his shoulders, with war braids on the sides. Torolf was tall; his father was taller and more husky. "It's about time you got your arse in gear," his father whispered. "I am sore tired of praising your dubious charms to the maid. Methinks she is no longer listening."

"Who asked you to come here?" Torolf hissed.

"Dost think I would allow one of my countrymen to be here and not make an acquaintance? Then, when I got here, I realized the dilemma you two are in, and I tried—"

"What are you two whispering about out there?"

He cringed. His brother Ragnor! "What is *he* doing here?"

"He came with me and Angela."

Torolf swore under his breath.

"I heard that." His father grinned and slapped him on the back, hard.

Stepping into the small living room, he saw crowded

onto every sitting surface available his father's wife Angela, Ragnor, Cage, Pretty Boy, and in the middle of them all, a distressed-looking Hilda. She had to be overwhelmed by this crew.

"What are you guys doing here?" he asked his buddies.

"We're your point men, doing some groundwork for you," Pretty Boy replied, and Cage added, "Geek and JAM were going to be tail, but the XO caught them sneaking off the base and assigned them to do a ten-mile run with some of the training class."

"I saw you at the base this morning, you never mentioned coming here."

A toilet flushed in the bathroom behind him, followed by the sound of running water. He turned. Oh, this was the worst thing of all. There stood his sister Madrene—a very pregnant Madrene—and she had fire in her eyes.

She backed him up against the door and pointed a finger in his chest. "You are the most lackbrained idiot in the world."

"But—"

"How could you treat a highborn Norse lady so badly?"

"But—"

"And not bring her to us immediately?"

"But—"

"And then place her in such danger?"

"But—"

Her stern face softened as she added, "But you rid the world of Steinolf?"

He nodded.

She wrapped her arms around him, pressing her big belly against him, and hugged hard. Into his ear, she said, "Good choice in a life mate, Brother." With those words of encouragement, she shoved away from him and huffed and puffed herself into sitting down in a big stuffed chair.

"Get out of here. All of you," he ordered. Hilda looked

relieved at his words, which prompted him to repeat himself. "I mean it. Go away. We can handle this ourselves."

"Doan look like yer doin' a good job so far," Cage murmured.

"I gave him a book to read, but he threw it at me," Pretty Boy said.

"What book?" Cage asked.

"*How to Win Women and Get Laid at the Same Time.*"

"Can I borrow it?" Cage put an arm over Pretty Boy's shoulder as they went out. "Not that I doan know everythin' there is ta know 'bout wooin' the ladies."

"Woo this!"

Torolf shook his head at the hopelessness of trying to get his friends to behave. His father and Ragnor both had to lift Madrene from her chair. Torolf nodded to a smiling Angela as she passed by after giving Hilda a hug and inviting her to Blue Dragon. Ragnor was about to follow after their father when he hesitated. "I could give you tips on—"

"Out!"

"Tell her you love her," was Madrene's whispered advice as she belly-butted him in passing by. "And buy more body paint."

"I'll try," he whispered back.

Soon they were alone, and Hilda looked as miserable as he felt. She wore jeans and a T-shirt. Her hair hung in a single braid down her back. No makeup. In other words, so beautiful he wanted to take her into his arms and never let her go.

But he didn't. Instead, he sat down on a chair next to the sofa where she was perched, tense with apprehension.

Okay, he was here. How to start? "I'm sorry."

She gave him a wary look. "For what?"

"Everything, but mostly because you misunderstood my dancing with that girl."

"You were engaging in foresport, and don't you deny it."

"I was not. I was merely dancing with her, as directed

by my commander. I also danced with his wife, who weighs about two hundred pounds. Do you think I was hitting on her, too?"

"You didn't come after me."

"I did, but I had to be excused first."

"Please. If you wanted something badly enough, you would not wait for permission."

"You're right. I should have come after you right away, but I didn't know you would really run away . . . or that you would be taken. My God, Hilda, I thought I would die when I couldn't find you." He reached for her hand, but she pulled it away. *I'm losing here. I'm losing big-time.*

"Why did you not come this past sennight?"

"Huh? You told me to stay away."

"And this time you chose to heed my words?"

Is she saying she told me not to come, but she really wanted me to come? I will NEVER figure out women.

With a deep inhale, then an exhale, he dropped down to one knee in front of her and handed her the small velvet jewelry box.

He'd surprised her, and she stared at the box as if it might have something nasty inside that would jump out at her.

"It's an engagement ring."

"What's an engagement ring?"

"It's when a man asks a woman to marry him, and she accepts. The ring is a symbol of that promise."

"A betrothal ring." She opened the box and gasped. " 'Tis beautiful."

"Hilda, will you marry me?"

She stared at him, and she stared at the ring. "I do not know."

She didn't say no. Hallelujah! He took both of her hands in his, ignoring her attempt to pull away. "Forget all this other crap. Apologies. Misunderstandings. The bottom line, I love you, and I want to spend the rest of my life with you."

"Where?"

Now we get down to the nitty-gritty. "A life *here*. I'm not going back again." In the silence was the unspoken admission, *Not even for you.* "Will you stay with me?" He thought about mentioning the baby, but he didn't want that to be her reason for staying or to think it was his reason for proposing.

"I have a life there. The Sanctuary. My women."

"You can help women here, if you want." Torolf's emotions were banging off the wall, waiting. "There's only one thing important here. Do you still love me?"

"You are such a clodpole. Women do not fall in and out of love like that."

He blinked several times. *She loves me.* "Well, hell's bells, Hildy, why didn't you say so?" He shoved the ring on her finger, then picked her up and carried her down the hall to his bedroom. At first she was stunned. Then she began to squirm. "Nay! Unhand me! Put me down! I did not agree to anything."

He tossed her on the bed, then crawled over her so that she would not be able to get up. "I love you." He tried to kiss her, but she turned her head.

A crushing weight came down over him. It shouldn't be so hard.

She put a hand up to his face. "I have been so angry, but alas and alack, it appears as if we are stuck with each other."

"Oh, Hildy." That's all he could say as tears welled in her eyes, probably a reflection of his own eyes. He already had her naked and was shrugging out of his jeans when he remembered something. "I bought you a present," he said.

Rushing up and outside, wearing only a pair of unbuttoned jeans, he got the package and came back inside. She was sitting on the side of the bed, naked, with her arms uplifted, undoing her braid. He stood in the doorway for just a moment, wanting to imprint this image on his brain.

He finished undressing and sat down beside her, handing her the gift-wrapped package.

"You bought me a present? Besides the ring?"

It was strawberry body paint.

"Why strawberry?"

"I thought you might have a *craving*."

It took several seconds for her to realize that he knew she was pregnant. Taking his hand, she placed it over her flat stomach and laughed. "The only craving I have is for you."

Strawberry Shortcake never tasted so good . . .

Afterward, they were both sated and lying in each other's arms, as well as in a pool of sticky strawberry goop.

"'Tis odd, but I have a craving for so many different flavors these days," she remarked idly, trailing a finger over his nipple, which caused another body part to react.

"Not to worry, sweetling. They have dozens of flavors, enough to satisfy all your cravings. Peppermint, peach, apple, coconut . . ." He smiled, and she kissed him.

He smiled again when she whispered against his smiling mouth, "Dearling, my favorite flavor is . . . you."

With sheer joy, he burst out laughing and told her, "There's an old saying that the best lover is a man who can make his woman smile in bed, but I think they got it wrong, Hilda. It should be: The best lover is a woman who can make her man smile in bed."

They both smiled then.

A lot.

And for many years to come.

Epilogue

Christmastime at Blue Dragon Vineyard was a marvel to behold in any circumstance, but this time it was spectacular.

Tiny white dancing lights were wrapped around the rare, speckled oak trees that lined the drive up to the big Victorian house. Red poinsettias were showcased in terra-cotta pots every ten feet or so on the low stone walls that bracketed the road. Blinking white lights, pine and holly garlands, and hundreds of huge red poinsettias decorated the wraparound porch. Lights also sparkled on the willow trees and all the grapevines. The inside of the huge house was equally festive.

It was going to be the first Yule wedding at Blue Dragon, and everyone was there. Except Hilda.

Where are you, baby? Don't chicken out now.

Torolf, in full dress uniform, stood alone on the porch, having shooed everyone else inside, forcibly. But it was past five p.m. The guests were here, both inside the house and in the lighted tents spread about the lawns . . . two hundred in all. But he had not seen Hilda for the past seven days, not even spoken to her on the telephone, thanks to his interfering family, who claimed it was bad luck.

Come on, Hilda. We can do this.

Everyone had thought she would ask Spike to give her away. He was there, of course, with Serenity and the others from Hog Heaven. But for some reason, which Torolf did not want to examine too closely, she chose Slick. Cage would be his best man, and fat-as-a-boat and shrewish-as-ever Madrene, Hilda's matron of honor. Seven other SEALs would form a sword honor guard, matched up with Lizzy, Linda, Jolene, his sisters Kirstin, Dagny, and Lida, and his stepcousins Suzy and Beth. In other words, a mob.

In the distance, a limousine could be seen approaching.

Thank you, God.

His heart started racing. He'd thought he was ready for this, but he was not. His collar felt suddenly tighter. His breath came out in pants. He heard voices behind him and raised a halting hand. He wanted no one here for this initial meeting but him and Hilda.

Once the vehicle stopped, the chauffeur got out and opened the back door. Slick, also in his dress whites, got out first and winked at him. Then he reached out a hand for Madrene.

"Oh, my God!" He put a hand to his mouth to stifle a cry.

It was Hilda, but a Hilda like he'd never seen before.

The chauffeur drove off, and Slick made himself scarce. It was only him and Hilda.

He went down the steps to her.

Maggie, his Uncle Rolf's wife, had lent Hilda her Norse wedding attire for tonight, but this was the first he'd seen it. The undergown was made of a gauzy white linen, ankle-length in front but trailing the ground in back. The wrists and circular neckline and hem were embroidered with intertwining roses in green and gold against a red background. The red silk overgown was open-sided in the Viking style with matching bands of embroidery, the colors reversed. Rose brooches held the shoulder straps together, and a gold-linked belt circled her waist. Her silver hair lay loose about her shoulders, a circlet of roses on her head. There was never a Viking queen who looked better than his bride-to-be.

"I was afraid you wouldn't come," he said.

"I feared you would not be here."

They both smiled at each other.

He took her hands.

"You look pretty," she said, preempting him.

He laughed. "And you look spectacular."

For a long moment, they just stared at each other in wonder, that they were finally going to do this thing.

"Hilda, before we go inside, let's exchange our own vows here. Alone."

She nodded.

"Hilda, will you be my life mate, in good times and bad? Walk at my side and bear my children? Love me forever?"

"I will. And, you, Torolf, will you be my life mate, in good times and bad? Treat me as a partner and not a servant? Value my opinions? Restrain your bossy nature—that is a new word I have learned—bossy? Make love to me whenever I want? Build me a home big enough to build a women's sanctuary? Give me children? Love me forever?"

His eyebrows arched at some of her demands, but in the end, he said, "I will. But can I amend my vows?"

Now her eyebrows arched.

"Will you let me paint your body whenever I want? Will you paint my body in return? Will you let me show you women's second favorite sexual position? Will you be my sex slave? Can I be your sex slave?"

She laughed and threw herself at him. He caught her in

his arms and twirled her about in a circle, kissing her bare neck. "I love you, Hilda."

"I love you, Torolf."

"Now can we get this marriage over with so we can start the honeymoon?"

"Spoken like a true Viking."

Some people say that Torolf Magnusson created a new Viking spot that night, not to be confused with the modern G-spot or the Viking S-spot. The trick was that it could only be found with the tongue . . . and chocolate.

And some people also say that Hilda Magnusson gave her new husband a special present that night. It had been purchased at The Horny Toad, and it was made of gold and . . . well, that is another story.

Reader Letter

Dear Reader:

Many of you have asked for Torolf's story. What do you think? Did I do him justice? Was Hilda a good enough match for this rogue?

I often say that you've got to love a Viking, and to me it was especially true in this book. The biased cleric historians of that time painted a tainted picture of the Vikings as rapers and pillagers, but mostly they were adventurers and settlers, leaving an overpopulated homeland with little tillable soil. Sure, there were some bad ones . . . just as there were bad Saxons or bad Scots of that time. The world will always have its Hitlers, Saddam Husseins, and Steinolfs.

You have to admire this hearty race of Viking men that was bred in the hard and frosty climates of the north among wild mountains and fjords. They had to develop strong bodies, sea talents, and independence to survive.

Aside from their good looks, these Northmen had law

codes that were the beginning of our modern judicial system. Their sagas were equal to the best of literature. And their sense of humor was evident in any writings of that time.

Old Norse is not the same as Norwegian. In fact, it is closer to modern Icelandic. During the tenth and eleventh centuries the Vikings speaking Old Norse were able to understand the Saxon English because of the similarities, and vice versa. In fact, many English words were derived from the Old Norse, like Woden's Day, Wednesday; and Thor's Day, Thursday.

I have an even greater reason for admiring these long-ago men of the north. Hard to believe, but I am a direct descendant of Hrolf, or Rollo, the first duke of Norsemandy . . . a Viking, for sure. I had been doing genealogy research years ago when that fact came up. It was only natural then that, when I turned from newspaper writing to novel writing, my first book and twelve subsequent books should be about Vikings.

That quote in this book about a soldier making love with his boots on came from an actual historical account.

And there is, indeed, an anonymous Hebrew proverb, "If a rogue kisses you, count your teeth."

Next up will be Pretty Boy and Britta's story in *Down and Dirty*. After that, what would you like to see? How about the dark and brooding Thorfinn? Do you wonder what happened to that lost baby of his? Could it somehow be found here in the future? And Cage probably should get his comeuppance someday, don't you think?

On the other hand, would you rather see a continuation of my other Viking series, straight historicals? Like Jamie the Scots boy from *The Blue Viking*, all grown up and rogue to the bone? Or James of Hawks Lair, the sad Saxon son of Eadyth, the beekeeper in *The Tarnished Lady*? How about Alrek, the clumsy Viking from *My Fair Viking*? And Tyra's sisters certainly deserve a book someday.

Your opinions are always valued, and your continued support is appreciated so much. Come to my website for something free and to sign up for my mailing list.

Sandra Hill
website: www.sandrahill.net
e-mail: shill733@aol.com

Glossary—SEALs

BUD/S. Basic Underwater Demolition/SEAL Training.

Budweiser. The trident pin worn by Navy SEALs.

cammied up. Face and bare skin surfaces blackened to blend in with the environment.

civvies. Civilians.

Coronado (California). The West Coast site of the U.S. Naval Amphibious Base and the Naval Special Forces Center, where BUD/S are trained. The other SEAL training center is located in Little Creek, Virginia. Coronado is also home to the famous Hotel del Coronado.

CQD. Close Quarters Defense, a system developed by Duane Dieter; an important evolution in SEAL training today.

DEROS. Date of expected return from overseas.

down range. Engaged in a live op; in harm's way.

friendlies. Nonenemy; indigenous people in a combat arena.

Gig Squad. A punishment inflicted during BUD/S where a SEAL trainee is forced to spend hours, after the evening meal and a long day of training, outside the officers headquarters, doing many strenuous exercises, including the infamous duck squat.

Hooded Box Drills. Duane Dieter, owner of a CQD school in Maryland, worked with SEALs for many years and developed this role-playing exercise in which a box is marked off—a space delineated by tape on a map or floor (in this case of *Rough and Ready*, the floor plan of the safe house they would be invading). A curtain is dropped to cover the SEALs' view of the box. When the curtain is lifted, they are forced to react on the spot to the new situation laid out . . . sometimes with lethal force, sometimes with nonlethal force.

NSW. Naval Special Warfare.

OUTCONUS. Outside of the Continental U.S.

SEAL. Acronym for Sea, Air and Land, est. 1962.

sims. Short for simunitions, paint bullets that emulate live ammunition, down to short-range ballistics and cyclic rates of fire.

Smee. Subject matter expert.

SOCOM. U.S. Special Operations Command.

SOF. Special Operations Forces.

tango. Terrorist or bad guy.

tight package. Military men surround the person they are protecting or bringing to justice.

UA. Unauthorized Absence, modern version of AWOL.

WARCOM. Warfare Command, as in Naval Special Warfare Command.

XO. Commanding officer.

Glossary—Vikings

Althing. An assembly of free people that makes laws and settles disputes. It is like a Thing but much larger, involving delegates from various parts of a country, not just a single region.

Birka. Market town where Sweden is now located.

Blood Eagle. A gruesome method of killing sometimes employed by Vikings whereby the ribs are slashed down the middle in back and the lungs pulled outside the body, like wings.

braies. Long, slim pants worn by men, usually tied at the waist; also called breeches.

break the raven's fast. To die.

drukkinn. Drunk.

gan dag. Good day.

ga ntt. Good night.

gunna. Long-sleeved, ankle-length gown, often worn by women under a tunic or surcoat or long, open-sided apron.

halberd. A combination spear and battle-axe on a stout pole.

Hedeby. Market town where Germany is now located.

Hesirs. Viking soldiers.

hird. Troop, war band.

Hordaland. Norway.

jarl. High-ranking Norseman, similar to an English earl or a wealthy landowner; could also be a chieftain or minor king.

karl. One rank below a jarl.

Jorvik. Viking-age York in Britain.

Jutland. Denmark.

motte. Steep-sided, flat-topped mound or hill.

nithing. One of the greatest Norse insults, indicating a man was less than nothing.

Norsemandy. Vikings ruled what would later be called Normandy. To them, it was Norsemandy.

odal right. Law of heredity.

sagas. Oral history of the Norse people, passed on from ancient history onward.

scramasaxes. Long-bladed, single-edged knives.

sennight. One week.

skalds. Poets or storytellers who composed and told the sagas, which were the only means of recording ancient Norse history, since there was almost no written word then.

straw death. To die in bed (mattresses stuffed with straw), rather than in battle, which was more desirable.

swale. A low-lying, often wet stretch of land.

sward. Large grassy area.

Thing. An assembly of free men called together to discuss problems and settle disputes; forerunner of the English judicial system; like district courts of today.

thrall. Slave.

vapnatak. Weapon clatter, the noise of banging on shields with weapons during a thing; a way of indicating a vote.

wergild. Compensation to be paid for killing a man.

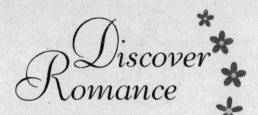